THE KILBURN

R⟨obert⟩ Hud⟨son⟩ was ⟨born⟩ in Zimba⟨bwe⟩ ⟨he⟩ is currently working on *Damsel in Distress*, a Gershwin/Wodehouse musical for the Gershwin estate.

ROBERT HUDSON

The Kilburn Social Club

VINTAGE BOOKS
London

Published by Vintage 2010

2 4 6 8 10 9 7 5 3 1

First published in Great Britain in 2009 by
Jonathan Cape

Vintage
Random House, 20 Vauxhall Bridge Road,
London SW1V 2SA

www.vintage-books.co.uk

Addresses for companies within The Random House Group Limited
can be found at: www.randomhouse.co.uk/offices.htm

The Random House Group Limited Reg. No. 954009

A CIP catalogue record for this book
is available from the British Library

ISBN 9780099526261

The Random House Group Limited supports The Forest
Stewardship Council (FSC), the leading international forest
certification organisation. All our titles that are printed on
Greenpeace approved FSC certified paper carry the FSC logo.
Our paper procurement policy can be found at
www.rbooks.co.uk/environment

Mixed Sources
Product group from well-managed
forests and other controlled sources
www.fsc.org Cert no. TT-COC-2139
© 1996 Forest Stewardship Council

FSC

Printed and bound in Great Britain by
CPI Bookmarque, Croydon CR0 4TD

For my parents and Alex

AUTHOR'S NOTE

The Kilburn Social Club is set in a version of present-day London. In it I have played fast and loose with how professional football works, as well as with geography, politics, history and the access arrangements for Primrose Hill. I did so primarily to reassure readers that I am not trying to be literal. Nothing in the book fictionalises specific people or events

PROLOGUE – AUGUST 1993

It is a golden late summer evening, and Manus Rosslare is driving home to southern Cork. He is tall, broad and grey-eyed. His hair is bluey-dark, and you are drawn to his hands. If someone told you he was a concert pianist, you would nod wisely. He was obviously once a handsome man, and he still carries himself that way, but something sunken about his cheeks gives him a deceptively dissolute look which disappears when he laughs, which is often, and which he is doing now, because his wife, Julia, has said something sarcastic about his football club.

Julia is a German vegetarian with dusky skin, light brown hair and amber eyes. She does not understand football, because she has important concerns like global poverty and the environment to think about. She enjoys teasing Manus, which is why her husband and Aisling are laughing. Esther, the younger daughter, gets the joke but doesn't think it's funny.

Manus and Julia would never acknowledge having a favourite, but Aisling, who has just finished her first year as a medical student, has always been the easier girl to love, joyful with that bonny, blonde sense of entitlement that has never learned it has to try to win your heart. She sometimes watches the Kilburn Social Club with her father because she knows it makes Manus happy, and the directors' box is glamorous and fun, and a great place to take boys.

Esther is also pretty, in a solemn, dark way, but she tries to carry herself as if she does not realise. She is a serious child, quiet and quick to notice. She will study English at university, but that is just for something to do until she turns twenty-one and takes her place on the Committee of the Rosslare Group, which runs KSC. She loves everything about the Social Club: its heritage, its players and the great force for virtue that her father and his predecessors have made it. Esther feels the bitter irony that, in spite of all this, Manus still prefers Aisling. Esther loves Aisling, of course, anything else would be unnatural, but she isn't fooled by her.

*

In 1590, Feidhlim O'Liamroe, impoverished heir to the Princes of Barrow, went to London to find his fortune. Dashing and aware, he caught the Queen's eye, tickled her fancy and flattered her favourites. Elizabeth Regina remained intacta, but the landless O'Liamroe became the very substantial first Lord Rosslare. His great-great-granddaughter was no better, or worse, and she never married, but for her sake Charles II made the marquisate, unique and in perpetuity, heritable through the female line. Charles also extended the Rosslare holdings across southern Ireland, and conferred some boggy and valueless estates north of London, which were further augmented in 1695 when Dutch William rewarded his loyal lieutenant Connor Rosslare for his vital assistance in forcing through the Act of Union that brought all Ireland formally under the British crown. Some generations later, these estates were rationalised by gifts the Prince Regent presented to the naughty young wife of Oscar, the latest Lord Rosslare.

Oscar was succeeded by Felim, who had spent a dashing soldierly youth charming the princesses of Europe, and not just charming them. Felim returned home in 1843, just young enough to marry well as well as wisely, and set about his responsibilities with a dutiful vigour that would only have surprised a superficial observer. He improved the estate and the lot of its tenant farmers, and he married Katie Dwyer, the prettiest girl in Cork, who swiftly bore a son, the first blond Rosslare since O'Liamroe himself. Young Kevin's birth heralded dark days. America the bountiful, her people slaughtered by the pale-skinned invader and his multifarious diseases, revenged herself with the fungus which laid waste to Europe's potatoes. Felim did what he could, and his people suffered less than their neighbours, but they died in their thousands. He grew gaunt and bloody-throated failing to persuade his stiff-necked English friends of the scale of the disaster while they blamed the short-sighted peasantry for their inability to plan, and explained that the market must be allowed to resolve the problem, or that corn had to be protected, or that God Worked in Mysterious Ways, or whatever it was they said. Felim knew that his friends were ignorant and arrogant men rather than bad ones, but he lost any childish faith in Adam Smith's invisible hand, or in government's ability to protect its people.

He withdrew from the world to administer his estate, which, tragically cleared of so many souls, grew yearly more prosperous. He erected the largest telescope in the world and grew quietly fey. Katie didn't know how to halt the slide until, on the urging of their son, she visited London and saw the squalor of Rosslare's Kilburn estates. Many of Felim's people, driven from their shattered plots, had settled there on favourable terms, and they had drawn other Irish to them. Felim had not heeded the triumph of industry. He did not realise that his London agent had racked and skimmed and cheated and schemed, or that his more enterprising tenants had become slum landlords, or that many others had simply been broken on the city's wheel.

And so Felim, still only forty-five, left his telescope to the twinkling stream of visiting astronomers, had his agent deported to Australia, and set about atoning for a tragedy he could not have prevented. Street by street, he remade Kilburn, turning its rat-infested rookeries into well-maintained little terraces. The labouring army was drawn from those who could not otherwise pay their rent, but Felim saw that this could not last, and so he built the factories which still bear his name, and which manufactured the empire's trains. For all the years this took, Felim's son was by his side.

Kevin was weaker than his father, you might say, but it takes a certain kind of strength to be close to power and not to yearn for it, and Kevin's contribution was as beautiful as Felim's, and longer lasting, if less great. As a young man at Oxford he knew many young missionaries burning to uplift the common man, and it was under their influence that he had first visited Kilburn's squalid streets. Kevin's friends did not believe in charity and dole. They wanted the poor to better themselves, and to that end they used tools that went beyond religion, such as music, and literature, and sport. Kevin, a footballer when what we call football was being born, believed in the game's power to turn boys into men. When he founded the Kilburn Social Club in 1881, sport was its heart.

In the early days, the teams of the Football Association were a variegated lot, from Eton's old boys, to the War Office's clerks, to Sheffield's foundry workers. A number were born of initiatives like Kevin's, but as the game grew, its clubs became the focus of local pride and adulation, and the original characters of these teams died away, leaving nothing but their names. The earnest young missionaries who had gathered gangs of miners and dockers to muddy fields, and taught them to be fine, upstanding fellows by submitting themselves to a set of artificial rules and socially agreed codes of behaviour, saw the clubs disappear from their control.

KSC was different. Woven into the warp and weft of its north-London community, which Felim still ran as a private fiefdom, the Social Club went far beyond football. It was a collection of private libraries, hospitals, schools and a pioneering pension society, a brass band, a debating club and the centre of a minor economic miracle – less profitable than it might have been, maybe, but justly administered with a keen eye to profit and the proper place and vital importance of money. When Felim died, Kevin understood enough to leave management of the business to what is now called the Committee. The Socialists, as the football team of this grand experiment in benevolent paternalism came to be known, embodied a dream of a better world. In 1912, with a rich man's careless idealism, Kevin wrote a constitution to protect the ethos of the thing he had made. It determined that every player at the club would receive the same wage as every other, and that every player, when his short career was over, or when he left the club for whatever reason, would sign a final contract with KSC which made him a part-time player in perpetuity, on a wage which could support a family. The constitution also insisted that, in addition to a player's football training, he must spend a certain number of hours every week on structured self-betterment.

Kevin died of grief in 1917 shortly after hearing that his son-in-law, Andrew, and young Felim, his oldest grandson, had been mown down at Delville Wood. Felim's mother heard the news at a dinner party she was holding at the base of the telescope, and she never left the observatory again. Her other son, Connor, who survived the war's last year in a submarine, returned home to an anchorite mother and a vast inheritance he would never understand.

Connor was a dynamic man, decisive, insightful and even heroic within certain bounds, but something in him realised that he could not be trusted to control himself, and so he stayed in the navy and submitted to its steadying discipline. Glittering through the twenties and thirties, marrying badly and briefly, and leaving business to the Committee, he gambled and gave away nearly everything his forefathers had fought so mightily to achieve.

Connor visited his mother when he could, and he slowly grew addicted to Mary, her nurse, who scorned him for the five years it took her to realise why she was still unmarried. She was just in time. The Social Club was still built on its own land, and the Committee controlled enough property to maintain the Rosslares and service the last debt-ridden factory site, which was given a new lease of life by the Hitler war.

Connor survived the second war as he had the first, though barely, and returned home to his wife and infant son with a young Canadian manservant he would trust with his life. The fifties were hard years, and the remnants of the Rosslare Group struggled, but KSC endured, and as Connor aged, he grew prouder and prouder of them. The Socialists were not the richest team, but they never wanted for local support, so they were not poor either. They floated between the top divisions, sometimes better and sometimes worse, and every Saturday, rain or shine, home or away, Connor watched them. Every Saturday that school allowed, bright-faced by Connor's side was Manus, his son.

When Connor died in 1968, Manus became Chair of the Committee. He inherited the increasingly expensive Rosslare estate, the Kilburn Social Club and an inefficient industrial complex just south of Hertford which depended on government contracts for its business. The Rosslare empire was kept afloat by loans raised against the value of the London property. In his first ten years, Manus turned the Group's financial situation on its head. He imported practices from Japan and made Rosslare Rolling Stock's plants the most economical in Europe. He purchased a traditional Irish brewery a decade before faux-Irishness became internationally de rigueur. He built a new factory to manufacture silicon chips. Manus could have increased profits by sloughing off the Group's traditional commitments to its workers, but he refused. This, through the unrest of the seventies, gave him the moral clout and union support to make difficult decisions about restructuring.

Rebuilding KSC was a different story. The club was drifting and ill-managed. Manus was a fan, bred-in-the-bone. He wanted the Socialists to be the best team in the world, and he wanted their success to be built on rock. He set about trying to find John Brown.

Mr Brown is a little man who runs to plump if he's not careful, and between 1956 and 1963 he marshalled the KSC midfield, jogging busily around a tiny area in the middle of the pitch, calmly dispossessing any opponent with the temerity to come near, and sliding the ball swiftly into the path of his most appropriate teammate. The fans loved 'The General', a nickname Mr Brown hated, and were shocked when he disappeared. They did not connect it with the Cold War. As for Manus, he idolised Mr Brown with the never-to-be-forgotten fervour of a child's first worship, and when Manus took over KSC, he knew in his heart that Mr Brown was the man to rebuild the Socialists. But Mr Brown was nowhere to be found.

Disappointed, Manus reorganised KSC, and the club pushed its way earnestly back into the top flight, but there was no spark. Then, on the greyest morning of 1978, Manus answered his door to find Mr Brown, portly and comic. 'How are you?' Manus had said.

'I'm retired.'

'Do you know why I'm looking for you?'

'Yes.'

'Can you do it?'

'Yes.'

Fifteen years later, the Socialists might well be the best football team in the world. Great Britain – who won last summer's World Cup – might argue. So might Rojo Madrid, Torino or even, at a pinch, Cardiff. But KSC are British and European Champions, and they have achieved it without forfeiting their traditional position as the neutrals' favourites. Mr Brown enjoys his public persona as an enigmatic guru, capable of sniffing out talent in the most unlikely places. The Socialists play beautifully and with honour, captained by Dave Guinevere, who also hoisted Britain's first World Cup for thirty years, and built around the bewitching talent of their Argentinian playmaker Achille de la Rue de la Pierre au Diable, universally known as Achilles. Manus knows that the current KSC team is Mr Brown's private crown, his reward to himself for a life spent in shadows. It cannot survive Mr Brown, and someone else will take over and make the Socialists another thing. Manus, like the majority of those who assume that the hale-looking Mr Brown has at least another ten years in the job, privately presumed that the baton would pass to Dave Guinevere. But two weeks ago, when Mr Brown told Manus that he is dying, Mr Brown said he worried about Guinevere. He said that Guinevere is a good man, but he has never been tested, and Mr Brown does not know whether the fires, when they come, will bake him strong or brittle. Achilles looks like a playboy, but he has been through his trial, said Mr Brown, and he is the real thing, and Mr Brown is proud of him. Mr Brown is proud of the Socialists full stop, and he told Manus that his only regret will be leaving the story without knowing what comes next. Manus and Mr Brown must groom someone to deal with the changes that satellite money will bring into the game.

Manus exhales. The issue of Mr Brown has hardened his conviction that he must find someone to run the Rosslare Group for when his own time comes. He looks at Aisling in the mirror, her face glowing in the sun, and he is glad she chose to go her own way. The Group is traditionally passed on entire to the heir, and Manus has made no secret that he will do this, but Aisling will need a strong Committee built around someone she can trust. Donald Rapnesst has been given his chance, and he has shown that he will never be more than a prince of a petty domain, obsessed with his power base and protecting its borders. It's a squalid, defensive mindset, and no way to run an empire. Manus should be saddened, since Donald is a cousin and blood should be thick, but he isn't. Manus has never liked the hungry way Donald looks at his daughters. Donald would be no match for someone like Strabis Kinsale.

At the thought of Kinsale, whom he shouldn't have baited, Manus's hands are still. Manus will have to deal with Strabis Kinsale some time soon, to safeguard his family. A car comes very fast around the next corner, loses control, and Manus and Julia are killed.

PART ONE − ALL THE RIVERS

THIRD EYE, 15 JULY 1999

The Kilburn Social Club has had its annual pre-season dinner, and the players have moved on to Third Eye, which is cooler and more downbeat than you might expect. The footballer chatting with the pop star is Dave Guinevere. He is tall, red-haired and freckled, gangling and lacking in physical grace. He lifted GB's first World Cup since 1964, its only European Championship trophy, and he has a PhD in geography and a part-time teaching post at the King's University, London. He is a Barnardo's boy, but Dave makes little of it. Dave says politely he was not scarred by being an orphan and he was very happy with his foster mother, who died when he was seventeen. He has never had a family, and he has been lucky in too many things to complain. Dave is a good lecturer, and although his work isn't sparkling, it's perfectly decent. His academic colleagues are determinedly unimpressed by the football, which Dave enjoys, but they accept him now, and most of them even like him. Until recently, he seemed completely satisfied with his life, and he would say he still is, but that is only because he cannot put his finger on what has changed. He will play football until it's time to stop and then he will move full-time into academia, and this is a good future, but as he has got closer to it, it has started to look emptier. He is searching, though he does not realise it, for something to fill the gaps. It is simplistic to say this means a woman, though that would be one possibility.

On which front, Dave is outgoing, and he knows that he's absurdly recognisable, but he hates being famous. If you asked him what kind of partner he is looking for, he would say that he wants a nice, bright, normal girl, someone who hasn't thrown herself at him but whom he has found and chosen and charmed. Dave does not recognise the pop star, whose name is at least as famous as his, but she is absolutely his type, and because he's been drinking, he winked at her, and now they are talking, or rather he is and she's laughing.

The pop star is used to not being recognised because, although she writes the songs, Monica and Morgan sing them, and most people assume that Sally Stares is just a good name for a band. Half-Indian, Sally has short dark hair, and she is pretty in a neat, unflashy way, though she knows she can look quite saucy if she wants. She is thirty-two, a year older than Dave, and she thinks she's unspoiled by success because it came so late. Three years ago, Sally Stares (the band) gave up taking their music seriously, but a schoolfriend of Monica's is an actor, he loved one of their songs, and he played it over and over again in his trailer on the set of a little British romantic comedy. The director heard it, and put it on the soundtrack. The film was a smash hit, the song was number one for two months, and every middle-class twenty-something in the country owns the band's first two albums.

Sally isn't starry, exactly, but she's a star now. She gets invited to things and she likes it. Her last boyfriend couldn't deal with this. They split up recently, and she is still not quite herself, so she is not officially looking for anyone new. On the other hand, she has decided that anyone she goes out with will either have to be very self-confident or be used to the limelight already. Sally thinks sport is silly, but she recognised Dave because the GB wins have been amazing, even if you're not normally a fan. Although he isn't good-looking, he has a fizzing reck-lessness that seems at odds with him being a professor or whatever he's supposed to be, and Sally didn't end up near him by mistake. She caught his eye a few times to make sure he knew she wouldn't mind him speaking to her. The wink was still quite sexy, though. She is enjoying acting like a normal, attractive girl having to be persuaded.

The moment is not just Dave and Sally.

Aisling, as usual, is the eye of a manly storm, and she's gossiping with her best friend, Nicky Rumsby, and Achilles, who is the most stun-ning man in the room. Aisling and Nicky are nearing the end of their year as pre-registration house officers at the Royal Free. Nicky is the kind of person who constantly insists on everyone bucking up their ideas and staying focused, which Aisling finds funny, which Nicky finds annoying, which Aisling finds funny, and so on. Three of the younger Socialists are hanging around them. Zondi, Achilles' boyfriend, has just left the nightclub, and although the manner of his leaving angered Achilles, the Argentinian covers it well. He and Aisling are chatting about Dave, whom Aisling has never found attractive before. Achilles has offered Aisling a cerise Porsche, a house in Buenos Aires and his hand in marriage if it turns out that Dave realises who he is talking to, and he is applauding Sally's tactics. Aisling laughs, head back, throat becomingly bared. Dave sees this, and although he is not usually sensitive about his gawky looks, he somehow decides that Achilles has made a joke about them, and something crystallises in him, an unspoken and barely perceptible grudge. Beneath even the closest friendships can be a fierce edge.

Esther watches Dave too, but is unwatched by him. *I am such a quiet little person*, she thinks, standing as far from the limelight as she can and enduring Hank, her grandfather's weird old Canadian retainer, who her father had creepily inherited somehow, whom no one else will speak to. She doesn't want to have to talk about Dave and another woman, but Hank saw her looking at them. Although Hank can't possibly realise what she thinks, he warned her not to worry about Dave, because Dave has not yet reached his adult nature, he is still a fingerling not a full-grown salmon. She cannot take her eyes off what is happening, but she changes the subject, which is hard work.

It is good, perhaps, that Esther is watching Dave so intently. If she had seen Aisling look at him and toss back her hair, she would have had to bite her mental tongue. She knows she cannot afford to let Aisling learn what she feels. It's not uncharitable to think these thoughts, it's simply that she knows what Aisling is like. It's not Aisling's fault.

In the six years since Manus died, Esther has had much to endure. First was learning that the business, as her father always said very clearly would be the case, had passed entire to her sister. Esther could not help having hoped that since Aisling was so clearly uninterested in KSC, the club at least might have been . . . Well, Esther understands that it was not to be, and that's that, and she was probably only ignored because her father hadn't expected to die so young, and he would probably have changed his mind soon, but that doesn't make it easier to bear. She knows her duty, though, and attends every Committee meeting to make sure the club's needs are spoken for, and she has to admit how handy it is that Manus, in a fit of sentimentalism, made old Hank a permanent member of the Committee. Donald Rapnesst, who chairs the meetings in Aisling's habitual absence, can be quite cavalier. Esther has started to detect an undercurrent that all is not well with the business, but she doesn't mind. In her opinion, the best thing that could happen to the Rosslare Group would be for Donald to get his wings clipped. Esther gulps her wine, scanning the room. She has undergone so much that she can't blame herself for sometimes getting drunk, and it's all right what she does, because it's not her fault, it's other people taking advantage of her really.

Donald is here too, looking at Aisling while his latest girlfriend twitters about Dave and Sally. Donald is worried about having overextended the Rosslare Group. He has told himself for three years that he was playing the long game, but the returns are still not coming in. The money he puts into KSC at Esther's bidding, keeping her sweet, is not a serious part of the problem, but it doesn't help. His girlfriend's excitement reaches fever pitch when a tall girl in teetering heels joins Dave and Sally.

The tall girl is Monica Dylan, the public face of Sally Stares. She behaved like a pop star even when she was a nurse, and she considers herself outrageous and ball-breaking. Under other circumstances, Dave would make it clear how irritating he finds this. Monica is pointing out a studious man in black, who is standing by the bar and drinking heavily. His hair is precisely dishevelled, and although he is out of his element with all these loud and cheerful sportsmen, whom he has had to tolerate all week, he's refusing to look uncomfortable because he knows that he's incredibly attractive to the type of girl who would scorn them.

The editors of sports pages are obsessed with close-up photographs of crashing tackles, or of faces caught in the contorted, repulsive joy of scoring. These pictures are dramatic in their way, but they explain nothing of a game, its eddying ebb and flow, its nature as a contest. The editor will say that a photograph can only capture a moment, so what is he to do? But if that moment is seen from a little distance, and by someone who understands what he sees, then how much more is visible! For instance: a team, we will call them the Socialists, play two very fast forwards ahead of a supremely skilful player called Achilles. His role is to hold the ball, draw the opposition defence, and pick the moment in which to pass it behind that defence for one of his forwards to run on to. There is a photograph which John Brown, the manager of these Socialists, has had blown up and framed, and hung in the team's home dressing room. Taken from high in the stand, the photograph covers two-thirds of the pitch. The Socialists are each in their appointed position, from the purposefully aligned back four, through the diamond in midfield, and up to the predatory pair of forwards. But it is more than this. Achilles, at the front point of the diamond, has just beaten his man and, ball at his feet, he is behind the opposition's midfield and a dagger at the heart of its defence, whose seemingly well-ordered line of four has nervously shifted its momentum in his direction. At the same time, the two forwards, just onside, are starting their runs into the gaping spaces behind the defenders. Nothing is more certain than that the next moment will see Achilles arc a pass through or over the defenders to meet one of these runs, and that the pair of strikers will have only the goalkeeper to beat, and that tomorrow's papers will run meaningless pictures of the despairing keeper and bulging net; but it is this photograph that captures the real moment, one of almost unbearable tension, one that explains how the teams shaped up to play each other, and how the goal was scored.

The rivers of the past flow into the present, and only in retrospect do we think we see the watersheds. If Monica hadn't noticed the man in black, then maybe everything would have happened differently.

AT THE SAME MOMENT

Two men were walking home from the party, each on his own. One was John Brown, happy that everyone else was happy, but sad that it wouldn't last. Eton Avenue, which was not the route you would usually choose to walk to Brown's house from Swiss Cottage, was normally quiet, but in this last of the summer's warmth the street buzzed with life. Brown could hear the building roar of a young party behind one of the houses, and open windows all along the street gave a local tune to London's hum. The feet behind him continued to pad, and Brown cut through towards Belsize Road, crossing after a while to check that he had lost them. This was a compulsion Brown should have dealt with long ago, but there was so little time now that it was less effort not to change. The doctors had given him a year to live six years ago. There had been a remission after Manus died, which was nothing more magical than dumb luck, but the cancer was back.

Brown smiled as he passed the Glasshouse, young men sweating in their Friday-night shirts, young women glowing in almost nothing. He had always revelled in the daily, ordinary pleasure of people who didn't realise the debts they owed. What would be the point of protecting someone only to make them beholden? A girl saw him looking through the window, and she raised her eyebrows and gave a little wave. He smiled her his pure, best smile, and she smiled back.

This, Brown thought to himself, is my favourite time, and he was upset, because he caught himself thinking this more and more often, whenever the time was good, whatever he was doing. He had been a young man almost all his life, but he wasn't any more. Age was not distance from birth, but closeness to death. He crossed the bridge towards Primrose Hill refusing to breathe heavily.

If the Socialists didn't exist, we would have to invent them. That's what the journalist had said, and it was wrong, because you couldn't build the Socialists without the Socialists' history as a foundation. But the journalist's words had stung Mr Brown into being harsh and gnomic, which only succeeded in irritating the journalist, which was unnecessary.

The Socialists, as built by Brown, played a flowing and joyful brand of football, expressing themselves with a precision and verve that was quite foreign to the blood-and-thunder directness of traditional English football. Their object was to score, rather than not to concede, though with Blackie, Volendam, Zondi and Guinevere, they had their share of round-heads. Brown, who had always lived quietly, and who had played football with the measured simplicity his own gifts had dictated, had rewarded himself for a lifetime of self-denial by creating a team in his own image, but an image that no one else had ever seen. For these twenty-odd years, most of the time, he'd expressed himself, or most of himself at least. There was nothing wrong with that. The Socialists were a good thing, and no one else could have made them. Wasn't that enough? After all, nothing lasts for ever. But what if the Socialists were just a personality cult, a vain old man's dream, doomed to disintegrate when the great leader disappeared. It was more vanity to think like this, but it contained some truth. Brown was trying to prepare Achilles, but the Argentinian was his own man, and the money cascading in from Panther Digital's new deal was changing the game just as Manus said it would. Achilles would have his own challenges to face. Brown was glad that Achilles had Zondi.

Zondi was the other man walking home alone. His real name was Terrible Zondeki, and he was not the kind of hero other footballers are. In spite of what the English might call the warmth, he wore his long leather coat and a dark woolly hat. He had found that when he dressed like this, and looked down, no one ever seemed to recognise him, and the thought gave him power. He felt like /Kam'au, the Owl, who was born when the Eagle fought with her shadow.

Zondi loved to walk, to feel the distance disappear under his short, elastic stride, but when he was with Achilles he always had to take a taxi. Tonight though, he could walk, and he could hardly contain the singing in his legs, the risen blood that he had forced into stillness when he was talking to the reporter half an hour ago and which must find an outlet. If he could have done so without attracting attention, he would have run to East Kilburn. He turned north without looking at a map or street name. Zondi never got lost. He had lived in the city for many years now, and he had drawn its landscape secretly in his mind, from the basking hippopotamus Hampstead, whose head was Primrose Hill, down to the chameleon's smile of the Thames and into the south, whose Brixton, Balham, Lambeth and Battersea were a great flock of birds, each named and known. Zondi missed the country of his childhood, parts of which he could traverse still through the stories he had learned from his mother and his aunts. Long after the stories, he had made himself remember them and he had used them to visit the lake in the gecko's eye, and he had found the caves at the tip of the long string of low bluffs that made the monkey's tail. But the living country was dying now, along with his people, and all that was left was geography and his own pathetic private version of how they thought. What sense was it to fix the A5 as the route by which the buffalo migrate, or picture Oxford Street as a procession of ants carrying leaves? He had distilled his culture into a mnemonic.

As a boy in apartheid South Africa, the orphan Zondi was taken into a white home by a well-meaning liberal family as penance for the traffic accident in which the paterfamilias had killed his mother. On first meeting him, they asked him the meaning of /Ka!, and he instantly replied, 'Terrible.' When he realised they had meant to ask the meaning of his name, which was /Xa!, he had been too shy to point out the mistake. His father, a big, tough Xhosa miner his mother had married in defiance of her family, would have loved the name.

When he was sixteen, the white woman, who would have liked Zondi to call her mum, but would never have presumed to ask him to do so, gave him a book about Gandhi. As he read it, the serious young man realised he must devote his life to a peaceful struggle against apartheid. At youth groups and Young Africans' Congress meetings, to which he was driven by the white family and at which he was often described as an Uncle Tom, he would argue with his fiery comrades, who yearned for action and blood. This is no time to tell the story of his conversion from passive resistance into guerrilla fighting, or of his emergence, in spite of his youth, as a leading figure in the Africans' Congress. He does not talk of what happened, ashamed at the violence, which he would still defend. Dirk Volendam, who is constitutionally unable to take a hint, perennially asks Zondi about guerrilla fighting, how best to set up an urban enfilade or blow a wooden bridge, and what he learned from the communists. All Zondi will reply is that he learned he wasn't a communist, and that the most valuable time he spent was playing football with his comrades. He was always a footballer, at school and in the street. The game taught him what it was to be free, to be governed by the same rules as everybody else. As a young player, he had skills but he never trusted them, preferring to ensure that his team never lost. As he grew older, he wanted desperately to express himself, but he was held back by the knowledge that he must work for his team. Then, learning about bomb-making and infrastructural terrorism with his comrades in Russia as a young man, he met Mr Brown for the first time. Mr Brown was pretending to be a communist that summer, as he had done on and off for thirty years. Zondi has never told anyone Mr Brown's secret, not even Achilles. Mr Brown saw Zondi playing a loose game in an army training camp, and told him that no team worth playing for would ever criticise him for using his talent. It was a simple thing, quietly put, but Mr Brown spoke with such conviction that Zondi started slowly to use his guilty private skills, even to play the dextrous, curling passes that he had always mapped out in his head, but had banished because they seemed so risky. Whenever he played after that, Zondi felt himself to be an exotic and flashy box of tricks, almost Brazilian in his flamboyance. To everyone else, he was a dour and workaholic midfielder with a normal, cautious range of passing and an iron determination not to be beaten, but that didn't matter. Mr Brown had set him free.

When now-President Mbala was finally released from prison in 1996, everyone expected Zondeki to join the first Africans' Congress government, but he was still only twenty-four. He said he was too young, and that he must work in the world with other men before he could presume to speak for them. He planned to become an engineer.

Before Zondi could start, while he was studying for the matric he needed as a precursor to university, Mr Brown knocked on his door. Zondi was frightened, Mr Brown was from another life, but Mr Brown smiled, explained who he really was and what he wanted. He said that Zondi had much to learn, and it would be hard because he'd never played at the level he was capable of. Because he was not a young man, he would have to decide immediately. There would be time for other things later in his life, to be an engineer too, but to live away from Africa was something Zondi must do if he was ever going to be fully himself. There had been no doubt that Mr Brown knew what he was saying, and that he meant every word. Zondi still thinks he flew to England in the face of logic and common sense, because he was in the last days of his youth and for once he was following his dreams. He is pleased that he made one great leap in his life without having looked.

The pent-up song in Zondi's legs was not anger with the reporter, who was nothing. He turned left automatically, not breaking stride as he headed alongside the garden in the middle of yet another of London's tiny squares. Zondi's city was many animals, but it was also the body of a great and infinite leopard, and each square was one of its spots. Zondi would sometimes discover a new square, and have to readjust his map, but that was rare now. He had made this false landscape because he knew he would never go home. He had discussed displacement many times with old Hank, who said that it was just the nature of things. Hank spent many years assuming he would return to Newfoundland in the end, to spawn and die in the stream where he was born, but he came to understand that he was not swimming free in the open ocean, but was marooned in a great lake, and he'd evolved to fit the lake, and now he could not leave. He was happy, though. Part of the evolution was that he loved the lake. Zondi trusted Hank, and he liked this explanation.

A taxi stopped in front of him and the driver had to wait for a moment before the couple got out, giggling. Zondi held back. He had a proper respect for the fragility of mating rituals, even ones he did not understand. He thought about Dave, who was his friend, and the small girl who Dave was dancing with when he left. The small girl thought she was in charge, but Dave was a hard person to see and guess about. Dave was like !Xwa-'kwe:ka, the Tall Hunter, the man alone, who only knows one of his three selves. Zondi feared the self that gathered !Xwa-'kwe:ka in the hunt, and that had no pity. The Tall Hunter was a good comrade but a powerful enemy, and he was dangerous always. This too was foolish imagination. It was Zondi trying to explain to himself why sometimes he was afraid of his friend.

Zondi had many fears. He was not tall. He was not strong. He was always embarrassed to be described as a hero. All he did in South Africa was what others would have done in the same situation, what many did, and what many died for. Where there is no choice, there can be no bravery. And, as the reporter said, in leaving South Africa, Zondi had abandoned his duty as soon as he got the chance. It was ironic that Achilles was described as the playboy, as the one who didn't deserve their relationship. Achilles, whose self-abnegation when working in soup kitchens or with the old men in the rest home, none of whom know his name, is the most beautiful thing Zondi can imagine. Achilles, whose goodness was all his own choice. In his private heart, Zondi called Achilles *!A:Kamm-te-!ka-/xwa*, the Butterfly Too Bright To Be Seen.

THE MAN IN BLACK,
THROUGHOUT THAT EVENING

If the Socialists didn't exist, thought Calum Horton, *we would have to invent them*. The line was fucking perfect, and he was going to use it, whatever Brown or Guinevere said. He sipped in such a way that only a careful observer would have noticed how much he'd drunk, and he arranged himself like a man too full of thoughts to need company.

Calum had taken the commission to write a feature about the Kilburn Social Club because football was driving him mad. A few years ago, when it was confined to hooligans and sports twats, that was fine – no one expected him to give a shit. Now, all of a sudden, just because eleven men wearing red, white, blue and green managed to score more goals than eleven other men who, in real terms, the fans knew just as well, everyone was supposed to go berserk. Calum found this interesting, sociologically, but he didn't fall for the bollocks about national camaraderie and the joyful reclamation of the Union flag. The national mood did not suddenly change because Britain started winning, or because the Socialists were a tiny amount more skilful, fit or lucky than some indistinguishable bunch of mercenaries hired by Torino. The national mood was linked to an economic upturn and the bubbling, brilliant excitement that, after eighteen years, the country was bound to boot out a discredited, bankrupt government and usher in a transparently better alternative at the next election. Football was just a coincidence. The thing about sport is that millions of people get obsessed with who wins a particular game, but every game is basically the same. Calum knew that fans would never get to grips with this. He had given up trying to explain that when they said, 'But the result matters to *me*!' they were making his point for him. What matters about anything is what people invest in it.

He supposed he should be glad that Dave Guinevere was going to get off with Sally – people love to read about star fucking – but he couldn't help being disappointed. It's not that he knew Sally particularly, but before

23

tonight he had thought that she was pretty cool. Guinevere was such a lanky gargoyle, and such a sanctimonious prick, that she was either an idiot or doing it for the cachet, and either way Calum thought less of her. On the upside, apart from pleasing his editor, writing about it would really piss Guinevere off. When they had spoken a few days ago, when Calum was still well disposed towards him, the footballer had gone on and on about privacy in a way Calum thought was unrealistic but quite endearing.

Calum honestly had set off hoping that writing about the Socialists (and wasn't that a smug little label for a bunch of self-satisfied, over-paid narcissists?) would be a perfect opportunity to skewer the football hype. The Kilburn players were supposed to be so fucking clever and wonderful and different, such exceptions to the crass materialism that usually hangs around sport, that maybe they would be able to understand alternative points of view.

The bar was too noisy for Calum to hear anything, but the group around Aisling still seemed loud. She was beautiful, he had to admit that, but in a way that pissed him off, and a friend of his from college had told him that she was a typical blonde fit bird, used to being deferred to. The gaggle of players with her, a preening clique Calum had christened the Boy Band – which, apparently, they'd heard about and loved, which was typical – were exactly what he'd always imagined footballers to be. He asked them if they were different from players at other clubs and they said that they absolutely were, because in addition to their sporting prowess, which was considerable, they were the most attractive team in the league. Calum had tried to get beneath the shtick, but he'd seen too many of their type in his life, and his heart wasn't in it.

Achilles was not strictly one of the Boy Band, though he'd made the same joke about how attractive the Socialists were until Zondi had shut him up. Calum wished he'd been able to get more out of Zondi. He was the most interesting person at the Kilburn Social Club, but Achilles had sat around bitching and playing the theatrical queen and generally fucking everything up. The relationship was clearly on the rocks. It only existed because there were no other gay footballers to choose from. Calum looked around. He couldn't even see Zondi. He turned to buy another drink.

A massive hand fell on to his shoulder and spun him round. 'For me a tomato juice,' said Dirk Volendam. Calum ordered, paid, and handed over the drink under no hopeful illusion that Volendam would take it and wander off. 'I should be a writer,' Dirk said. 'I have many stories, not just about soldiers, and I am very perceptive, an amateur psychologist. I am not one-dimensional. You must write about this. Everybody just writes about the Foreign Legion.' Calum knew there was no rational reason to be afraid, but he wondered again whether it might be sensible to humour Volendam in print as well as in person. He was trying to think how to reply when Volendam noticed something further down the bar and said, 'Torquil is under hostile fire.' He brushed through the scrum to where his equally huge friend, grinning beard flecked with droplets of milk, was listening amiably to a pair of gaudy, slapped-up girls who must have followed the Socialists here, because they weren't the kind you normally found at Third Eye.

Calum, who called himself a writer rather than a journalist, couldn't believe girls still fell for this sports shit. He could just about understand tawdry hangers-on, but someone like Sally Stares? He couldn't be bothered to think about it any more, and turned ostentatiously away. There was Esther, alone by the wall. Or virtually alone, anyway. The old Canadian guy was hanging around her, obviously with nowhere to go except home, so why didn't he do that? John Brown had disappeared after dinner with at least a tiny amount of fat little dignity, but Hank, I mean, Jesus, it was so fucking feudal. He was one of the Rosslares' batmen in the war, or something, and now he haunted KSC, and Esther said she was the only person who talked to him. She'd thrown on some black dress, and she looked great, but she didn't realise. Over the evening, Calum noticed at least five guys, half of them KSC, trying to chat her up, but Hank scared them all away. Calum decided to take pity on her, and wandered over. 'Hi,' he said, and, 'Hank. Having a good evening? Your sort of place?'

'I'm going to the bar,' said Hank.

Maybe Hank wasn't such an idiot. 'You're very good to him,' he said, and Esther smiled, and replied that it was nothing, just what anyone would do. Calum pointed out that it was exactly what nobody was doing. 'Have you had a good evening?' he said.

'Oh, you know. I'm a background kind of person. I'm enjoying watching, seeing everyone else happy.'

'They certainly are,' said Calum, nodding at Aisling's gang. 'It's exactly like you said.'

'It's not her fault,' said Esther too quickly. 'She just likes having fun, and they're all very immature.'

'She never —'

'No, I'm sure not! She just enjoys the attention. It's just flirtation. There's nothing wrong with it.' *What a fucking life*, thought Calum. Esther was misguided, sure, and couldn't see beyond the Socialists, but at least she put the effort in. Aisling had simply said she knew nothing about football and Calum should get all that stuff from her sister. Aisling had posed for the photos, though. He didn't blame Esther for looking sick. 'Aisling warned me about talking to you,' said Esther. 'She said you weren't to be trusted.'

'She knows nothing about me.'

'She thinks she knows everything.' Esther was drunk, not being cautious. 'She asked her *friends* about you. You were at Oxford, weren't you? She always has a *friend* who knows someone who knows everyone.'

Calum knew people like that. They didn't really know anyone, and they certainly didn't know him. 'She's not going to get far with Achilles, anyway,' he said.

'Aisling says you're not a football expert,' she said sharply.

'No. But then, I'm not writing about —'

'Everyone always talks about Achilles, you see,' said Esther. 'He's brilliant, but he can only do the flashy stuff because of Dave.'

Of course. He should have seen it coming. When they talked before, Esther had been at pains to point out that Guinevere was about the only player who wasn't obsessed with her sister, who realised how hard Esther worked, who always asked her opinion about the Socialists. Dave Guinevere was no fool, thought Calum. Dave would have no chance with Aisling, but quiet, shy little Esther was a whole other story. 'I didn't realise Dave was seeing Sally Stares,' Calum said.

'He isn't seeing anyone. Is that who she is?' Esther seemed almost pleased, or at least more calm. 'I'm surprised.'

'Really? The way the team talks about him, I assumed he was quite the dark horse.'

'Dave?'

'When the others spoke about him, they all said he . . . No. It's not my place to repeat gossip.'

'What gossip?'

'I'm sure you know him much better than me, but there were jokes about his conquests. That's all I'm saying.'

'You're wrong. He'd never talk about things like that. He hates any kind of fuss.'

'He *says* he hates fuss, but he's in the middle of a nightclub chatting up a pop star. He seemed quite manipulative, actually, when I spoke to him. I'm probably wrong.'

That was enough, thought Calum, and he turned to see where Hank was. As he did so, Esther stumbled into him, ran her fingers accidentally up his forearm and apologised. She didn't even know that her thigh was now touching his. Calum realised he had to take the lead. He looked carefully over at Aisling, turned back to Esther and said, 'Don't take this the wrong way, I'm not on the pull, but it's something you should know. You're not as showy as your sister, but you're just as pretty. She knows how good she looks, and that makes people look at her in that way, and it's great that you're too classy to do the same thing, but you could if you wanted. I just wanted to say it.' Hank returned, and Calum decided to give Esther space to think. He apologised if he'd said anything inappropriate, and said he needed a word with Zondi, whom he'd noticed moving towards the cloakroom.

Smiling to himself, Calum wove through the crowd towards the South African, who was pulling on his gangster's leather coat. Achilles was not around to interfere. 'Hi,' he said. Zondi turned to face him with the sour expression he'd worn all week. 'I wanted to see if you're okay.'

'Yes.'

'You're leaving early, and I thought that maybe we could . . . Don't worry, it's nothing. I'm sorry we never got to talk properly.'

'We can talk now.'

'Is everything okay?' said Calum, flicking his eyes over towards Achilles. Zondi immediately turned to leave, and Calum said, 'Sorry, no. That's not what I wanted to talk about – nothing private, I promise.' Zondi's eyes were black pools. 'I just wanted to ask if you're leaving because this is all so trivial. I mean, you're a hero, and you're stuck in a nightclub with a bunch of footballers who can't understand anything you've been through. Is that why you're leaving?'

'No.'

'Okay. Please don't go. It's just that I've been really wanting to ask you this: after everything you've done, don't you find football a bit absurd?'

'No.'

'But, I mean, you've spent your life fighting prejudice. Isn't it ironic that you're part of something that fosters such parochialism, even bigotry?'

'No.'

'Is that because it's KSC? Because the club is so multicultural?'

'Multiculturalism is bullshit.'

Zondi might be a hero, but Calum had a perfect right to ask his questions. 'You came to England so you could be openly gay, didn't you? To escape from politics?'

'How has he escaped from politics?' said Achilles, standing suddenly next to Zondi as if he had been there all evening. 'Is this guy bothering you, *querido*?'

'I was trying to have a serious conversation . . .' Calum was aiming for icy calm, but his voice was pitched very high. 'I was asking whether Terrible felt guilty about leaving South Africa when there was so much work still to be done.' Oh yes, thought Calum. A palpable hit.

'I —'

'No.' Achilles grabbed Zondi's arm and said, 'There is always work to be done, old thing, but we only have one life. It is our duty to sometimes dance.'

'What about his duty to . . .' but Achilles was already dragging Zondi away. As they reached the door, they both looked back at Calum, Zondi with guilt and Achilles with rage. They pecked goodbye, perfunctorily in Calum's opinion. Zondi left, and Achilles went back to Aisling.

Or:

Zondi did not not enjoy evenings like this, but he found it hard to find words when there was so much people and noise. He talked briefly with Hank about living thousands of miles from home, and then he moved to mix with Achilles and the young guys, but he soon grew self-conscious that he had nothing to say. He feared he was becoming bad company, and decided to leave quietly, and, as always, it was like a weight lifted from him.

But then the reporter stopped him, for what reason he didn't know immediately, but he didn't trust the reporter, and nor did Achilles. The reporter asked how he felt. Zondi thought, I feel like the first wildebeest to leave the waterhole, and I have been pounced on by the old bull lion. He said, 'Yes.'

The reporter moved closer, as if to show he could stand in a place where Zondi could smell him but would not be able to do anything about it. He bared his teeth in mock concern and said he wanted to speak properly some time, and Zondi felt like a wildebeest the lion knows is in a cage, so he can be played with and teased, and left for later. He said, 'We can talk now.'

The reporter saw Zondi was uncomfortable, and his eyes grew cunning and sideways, and Zondi could suddenly see that he was not an old lion, but vain old /Kaggen again, /Kaggen the mantis, in one of his mangy disguises that are so bad it is unbelievable anyone falls for them, and you only realise that it is possible when it is you. He hinted with /Kaggen's brutish unsubtlety that maybe there was a problem with Achilles. Now that Zondi saw the reporter was /Kaggen he knew he could tread on him, and said nothing. The reporter started asking whether he was leaving so early because he was a hero and this was just a nightclub full of people who didn't understand him. Zondi thought, You are a small green thing, made of dry sticks. I can crush you with my hoof, even though I am alone. He said, 'No.' The reporter asked more things, and Zondi should just have left, but /Kaggen is not all a fool, and he is hard to ignore. Zondi kept saying, 'No,' but he was listening to the hiss of truth between the words. He said that multiculturalism was bullshit, though, which made him feel brave, and which he knew for truth, because in many cultures, in his own, for instance, he and Achilles would have been cast out for who they were. He came to England because it listened to other cultures but did not tolerate their prejudices. That is what England should be.

But /Kaggen knew what Zondi felt guilty about in his heart, and he said it, and Zondi was unmasked, transformed by the unmasking from the wildebeest into a beetle mesmerised by the mantis's sly, slow dance. But Achilles was there, flashing his wings, blinding /Kaggen, and although the reporter threw one more spiteful spear, he was bested and knew he was. Achilles sheltered Zondi in his iridescence, and took him to the door and with a kiss he set him free.

At the bar, knowing he shouldn't hurry back to Esther, thinking she would probably come to him, in fact, Calum made the next one a double. He wished he could have had longer with Zondi. The feature was still thin on the things he wanted to write about, and if only he could have got under the South African's skin, maybe he'd have got something juicy.

John Brown was the biggest disappointment. Everyone said he was such a genius, and the back pages quoted him like he was the new Socrates, but Calum had found him tiresome and obstructive. He had asked Brown about the highlight of his career, and Brown had started talking about some game in 1960. When he noticed Calum looking confused, he said, 'Oh, my managerial career, you mean,' as if butter wouldn't melt. Brown had explained at length that managing was nothing compared to playing, and the way he grinned at Calum showed he knew that neither Calum nor his readers would give a shit about what had happened in the forties and fifties, but Mr Brown was going to blow his trumpet anyway. It was a bad start and it got worse. Calum asked what made KSC different from other clubs, and Brown said, 'A zebra can run with horses, but that doesn't make it a horse.' Calum asked if a zebra was better than a horse, and Brown replied, 'A zebra would rather be a zebra.' Calum, still hopeful that he could get some-where, asked why Brown wanted to be a zebra – what made the KSC's communist little utopia such a great thing? The famously placid Brown snapped back that there was nothing communist about the Socialists. He'd been angry, but after a moment he had added, 'Yes, I suppose there is something utopian about KSC. Only fragile little utopias can ever exist, but that does not make them evil.' This gave Calum the perfect chance to ask if this meant that if the Socialists didn't exist someone would have to invent them, but Brown immediately said, 'No! In fact, a thousand times no!'

Calum responded that if they were a model in some way, then surely this meant they were something that *should* exist, but Brown said, 'Yes, they *should*, but they *can't be*. That is what makes them special.' Calum said this made no sense, and Brown retreated back into bollocks. 'If the giraffe didn't exist,' he'd said, 'no one would think one was possible.'

The smugness was unbearable. Guinevere had seemed better at first – he'd asked what Calum's premises were so he could answer questions more effectively, and he seemed pleased that Calum was trying to write something about football and society. But when Calum asked, very care-fully pointing out that it was not a criticism, whether KSC's model was illusory, because all the players were rich and protected from the real world, and had all the leisure time they could bear, Guinevere had turned back into a company man. He said that KSC was no different to any other sub-societal group, like a school or a hospital. He crapped on about how it set itself standards that were higher than they needed to be, and that this was actually rather noble. Then, incredibly, he said he wasn't trying to be boastful, just honest. Calum had read this all before in Guinevere's previous interviews. Calum's point, as he tried to explain, was that this kind of model was not necessarily helpful, because it was not something most people could ever be part of. Guinevere had admitted that he was lucky, but there was nothing wrong with giving people something to aspire to. *The Socialists*, Calum wrote in his head, *ironically embody an outdated elitist mindset. Maybe they should be called the Tories!*

'Will Beauchamp,' said Will Beauchamp, leaning on the bar and holding out his hand. Will looked like Roy of the Rovers, was studying for a degree in pure mathematics, and everyone said he was the new Dave Guinevere. This didn't endear him to Calum. 'How's it going?'

'Fine.'

'I expect you find us insufferable. Don't worry, I do too. Most of the guys have no idea of anything outside their own little world.'

That got Calum's attention. And to be fair, when Guinevere had been wittering on about how the Socialists found and welcomed players who wouldn't fit in anywhere else, he mentioned that Beauchamp was an exception. He also said Beauchamp didn't like being called the new Dave Guinevere, which Calum should perhaps have paid more notice to. He sized up the moment, and, reckless maybe with drink, said, 'That is exactly what I've found. I wanted to write about KSC's place in the football narrative, and how if the Socialists didn't exist we would have to invent them.'

'That's great. That's absolutely right. But do you mind if I give you some advice?' Calum nodded. 'Forget it. Just write the puff piece. It's easy, and it won't upset anybody.' Calum should have known. He was ready to turn away when Beauchamp added, 'I'm not trying to trick you. I'm not like Dave Gui . . . I'm not like some people here. I'm not swinging my dick to show how clever I am. I'm just saying that now's not the time. At the moment, Britain's mad about football, and everyone loves the Socialists. You can write your piece now, but no one will listen.' Calum said that there was no point in repeating things that had been written dozens of times already, and Beauchamp replied that he'd get paid, wouldn't he? KSC would be happy, his editor would be happy, the readers would be happy, and Calum, crucially, would have kept his powder dry. Everyone would have what they wanted.

'What do *you* want?'

'I'm KSC. If the Socialists are happy, I'm happy.'

'You don't sound like the rest of them. You sound like you should be off the record.'

'I'm trusting you. If that trust is justified, we have a relationship which could be useful to us both.'

'I'm not really a sportswriter.'

'That's less and less important. Trust me, things are going to change, everything always changes, and when the time is right you can write what you want, and at that point, who knows, maybe I'll be able to help you.'

This made sense, sort of, although Calum would have to think about it when he was in a fitter state. He thanked Beauchamp, though, and offered to buy him a drink. 'Water for me,' said the footballer.

'Hi!' It was two girls, very pretty if you like that sort of thing.

'Hello?'

'I'm Fliss! This is Andie! Do you want to buy us a drink!'

'A drink each, she means! I'm Andie!'

'Er . . .'

'You're Socialists, aren't you! That's amazing!'

'Wow! Which one are you? Rum and Coke, please.'

'Vodka and tonic. I'm Fliss, short for Felicia! It means happiness. Which one are you?'

'I'm Calum. I'm not . . . I'm . . .'

'You must be a winger. They're the smallest! And you're Will Beauchamp!'

'You're so cute!'

'Thanks very much,' said Will, 'but I've got to get back to my date. I'll leave you to Calum. He's single.' Will winked and left. Calum looked round for Esther. She was still stuck with Hank and she'd be hard work anyway. Andie was the kind of girl he never met, and he couldn't help being interested. She was probably filthy, and at least she could keep her eyes off Guinevere, who was still looming over Sally Stares, even though the pair of them had now been joined by Monica, the singer. Monica had a great body but a face like a horse. People only went on about how beautiful she was because she carried herself like a queen. He saw Monica look at him, and now Guinevere and Sally were staring too. He let them see him looking back. *Oh yes*, he tried to imply, *I see you. And I'll fucking write about you. You think you're better than me because there's lots of you, but I'm stronger than you fucking think, and the pen is mighty.*

Fliss saw the interaction, and didn't understand it. 'Wow! You know Sally Stares and Monica Dylan!' she said.

'She and Dave would make a great couple!' said Andie.

'Monica has an amazing body. She's coming over! Wow!'

Momentarily, Calum was on the back foot, almost panicked. He knew Monica's reputation. She looked purposeful, and she was definitely going to fuck things up with Andie by saying he wasn't a footballer. But it was not as if he really cared about Andie, who was only for a night, at best, and he'd never said he was a player, so the moral high ground was all his. By the time Monica arrived, he was ready. Guinevere and Stares knew they were in a nightclub, and were in full view of everybody, so she could fuck off, frankly.

'Want a drink?' she said. Fuck, she was tall.

'Er . . . Whisky. Er . . .'

'Don't worry, I won't bite. Not unless you ask nicely.' People still used that line? 'Two whiskies, Manuel. Yeah, on my tab. Thanks. So, man in black, why are you standing on your own?'

'He's called Calum!'

'He's a winger!'

'We think you're great! I'm Andie!'

Calum looked over at Guinevere, who was laughing. He was going to play this very carefully. 'What do you think?' he said to Monica.

'I think you're a spy.'

'Your friends obviously know who I am.'

'Yes, but they won't tell me, and it's pissing me off.' Calum didn't believe this. 'Dave Guinevere says he respects your privacy. I told him to stop being such a precious prick, but he was having none of it.'

'If you don't know who I am, then —'

'Lets cut the bullshit shall we? You know who I am, and I know you're another self-obsessed footballer. What I want to know is: why are you getting drunk by yourself? If it's an unhappy love affair, then I can't be bothered. If you're going for the tortured, moody look, then that's fine, because it really works for you.'

'Did Guinevere really not tell you who I am?'

'For fuck's sake, get over yourself! I'm sure you're a superstar, but I

33

don't care. Why do footballers think everyone should know who they are? I don't give a shit about sport. Are you two still here?'

'He's buying us a drink!'

'Doesn't look like it. See you later.'

'Later? Great! Oh. Oh! Okay! Bye! See you later!' Off they go.

'I bet they call themselves girls.' Calum opened his mouth, but Monica carried on. 'Trust me, they do. And now they're off finding someone else, and three days later it's in the fucking papers – no offence. You should be grateful to me.'

'Don't worry. They were well out of their depth.'

'Two more, Manuel. Don't worry, he'll catch up. So, Calum. Here we are: a pop star and a footballer, drunk in a club.'

'Well . . .'

'It's not like that. I don't give a fucking shit who you are or what you do.'

'That's good, becau—'

'I actually prefer the intellectual type.'

'That's great, because —'

'But I've never had a professional sportsman, and I can't deny I'm interested. You've probably had a few pop stars in your time. But maybe you've got too much macho bullshit going on to deal with a taller woman.'

'Well . . .'

'I'm just kidding, Calum, mate. Sally's laughing at us. Well, she can fucking talk. Why the fuck is she laughing?'

Calum hated being laughed at. Well, fuck them. So what when Monica finds out tomorrow? Roomful of footballers and who's with the super-star? And whatever she said about wanting to try out a sportsman, Calum bet she wouldn't be disappointed. He was strong enough to leave it for now and serve his revenge cold, just like Beauchamp suggested. 'Shall we go?' he said.

'I'm telling you now, before we start, that nothing's going to come of this. I just want you for your body, and at least I'm honest enough to say it.'

THE FOOTBALLER AND
THE POP STAR

'You're all here tonight?' said Sally Stares. 'It's not a very football-star type nightclub.'

'We're not a very football-star type team.'

'Is that really true? I just assumed ... Are the Socialists really different?'

'I ... Yes. I think so, yes.'

'Why?'

'Apart from being the most attractive team in the league?'

'Yes.'

'It's odd you would need more.'

'And yet.'

'Well, I ... Are you really interested?'

'Yes.'

'Are you a fan?'

'I only really follow GB. Does that make me annoying? I bet that makes me annoying.'

'No, not at all. It just helps me know where you're coming from. Well. Okay. Er ... Okay, okay. Let me start by ... Okay. First, I'm going to be biased, because I love KSC, and however much I try to be object-ive, I'm ... it's ... it's impossible, that's it, that's all I'm trying to say.' There was something frenetic about him she should be wary of, not excited by. She processed this while he carried on: 'And, second, you could say that there's no such thing as a typical club, because every team is different, and they're rooted in their specific locations, and even their times, because they depend on players and managers, and finan-cial situations and the general atmosphere and culture of their time, okay? And then –'

'Should I sit down?'

'What?'

'So I can take notes.'

'I'm sorry.'

He looked mortified, and she realised she shouldn't have teased him. He was obviously sensitive about talking too much, but it was actually quite cute. 'Go on,' she said. 'I was joking.'

'I only mean that I've never played for anyone else, so I can't be sure what anyone else is like. It would be arrogant to say we're cleverer, but . . .'

'But you are?'

'No, I'm sure we're not. I just don't know. I suppose, what I think, on average, is that we probably have a wider world view. I know this sounds wanky, but it's true. You can't play for the Socialists and not think about politics and social responsibility.'

'How come?'

'What sort of musician are you? Are you in an orchestra, or with a band, or what?'

'Band. Why don't —'

'Is it going well?'

'Okay.'

'Just okay?'

'It takes time.'

'Yes, sure, of course. Though, and I can tell you this for nothing, it's a pain in the arse being famous.'

'A pain in the arse?'

'Look at them all pretending not to stare. I'm used to it now, but still . . .'

'At least it means you've been successful.'

'Yes. Yes it does.'

'Are —'

'Actually, that's something about the Socialists. I think that although we are famous, it hasn't made us . . . This might seem incredible to you, listening to me now, but I honestly think the team is not arrogant. Being famous is not good for most people. They get arrogant, and tedious, and self-obsessed.'

'And they can't stop themselves picking up strange women in bars.'

'I don't normally. You've twisted this back to me again, I notice. What sort of music do you play? I love music.'

'What do you like?'

'Anything. I don't mean, not *anything*, but not *genre specific*, though I have to admit I'm mainly into classical. I love Wagner.'

'Really?'

'Really. I know I shouldn't say it to someone I've just met, but I can't help it. I'm not a Nazi.'

'I like Wagner, I think.'

'You should hear Torquil singing "Mein Herr und —"'

'Stop right there. I know nearly as little about classical music as I do about football.' She was afraid of seeming stupid, which was crazy. 'Hi, Mon. Monica, this is Dave. Dave, Monica.'

'I know who he is.'

'We're just discussing how superficial I am.'

'So, Monica, how do you know Sally?'

'Are you being serious?'

'Of course he is, Mon. It's a perfectly reasonable question.'

'I'm in the band.'

'He's more into Wagner. And he recommends that we don't get famous because it's a pain in the arse being recognised, and most famous people are wankers.'

'For fuck's sake, mate, don't you . . .' Monica felt the force of Sally's stare. 'So, Dave.' she said. 'Are you a typical footballing Lothario? Different woman every night?'

'How many typical footballing Lotharios do you know?'

'I'm a straight talker. If you can't handle that, get out of the kitchen.'

Sally said that there was a difference between straight-talking and rudeness, and while Monica didn't necessarily agree, she knew when she wasn't wanted. 'Okay then,' she said, 'which of these fit young men is single and up for it?'

'What are you looking for?'

'Frankly, I don't give a shit about footballers, but it would make a change.'

'Monica prefers the artistic type.'

'Well, Torquil is —'

'What about the guy in black over by the bar?'

'He's not one of us.'

'Not even a footballer! How awful!'

'He's a reporter.'

'Oh! Now you say that, I think I . . .' Sally said, and stopped. She'd been doing so well. Before Monica could ask where she recognised Calum from, she added, 'Oh. No. He looked like someone I was at uni with, that's all. But he isn't. It was just the light.'

'Okay, Sal,' said Monica. 'You play it your way. He keeps staring over here.'

'He's writing a piece on us,' said Dave. 'I don't think he's my biggest fan.'

'I like him already,' said Monica. 'I'm just kidding. You've got to be able to take a joke if I'm around.'

'You'll have to deal with those two.'

Monica looked at the two girls who had just cornered the reporter. One of them put her hand on his arm. Monica could see that he liked it, and even though she knew she was worth ten of that girl, she also knew that he might be intimidated by her. She refused not to wear heels. Fuck anyone who couldn't deal with it. 'You know those girls?' she said.

'You get used to the type,' said Dave.

'Don't be so fucking patronising.'

'Monica!'

'If he can't take me being feisty, he's not worth your time.'

'I didn't mean to patronise you. All I'm saying is that getting recognised is not that great. People don't treat you normally. Those girls obviously think he's one of us.'

'But he isn't! How terrible! On the other hand, seeing as he's the fittest man in the room, even if he is a short-arse, I think I'll live with it.'

'Wait,' said Dave. 'Just so you know. He'll probably think I've been slagging him off.'

'I plan on asking where he plays and telling him you won't tell me.'

'That might work,' said Dave.

Monica sashayed off, leaving Sally relieved. She didn't know how long she could keep Dave in the dark with all these people around. She would never normally sleep with someone she'd just met, not unless she was a lot drunker than this, but the comedy of the situation had really got to her. If she wanted to take it further, though, they had to get out of the public eye. She actually liked Dave, in a speculative way, and he said he didn't like celebrities, so what she was doing could even be regarded as good tactics. She couldn't be too obvious in case he thought she was like those other girls, so she started to mishear him until he asked if they could go somewhere quieter.

When, after the usual jockeying, she ended up at his place, she spent half an hour saying this wasn't what she was like, so he must be very charming. They weren't too drunk to talk about tea, or to put the kettle on, but that was as far as that went. At least partly, this was because Sally couldn't not kiss him when, after some nervous dithering, he chose to play her first album on the basis, which he tortuously explained, that she was called Sally, it was by a band with Sally in its name, and although everyone played it all the time, that didn't make it bad, and she shouldn't think less of him just because his taste wasn't cutting-edge.

WHAT ARE THE
SOCIALISTS LIKE?

On 3 August, the Socialists sprinted out for the first game of Mr Brown's last full season. The manager nurtured the kind of confidence that comes from a sense of self-worth, rather than a sense that others are unworthy. It was as part of this strategy (or part of his own psychological make-up; who can tell what a man is except by how he acts?) that he seemed almost wilful in his desire to pluck players from obscurity.

One story: Brown believed that goals are scored by goalscorers. While these goalscorers can be turned into better footballers, something about scoring goals cannot be taught. Brown devoured statistics and reports, and learned of a fifteen-year-old schoolboy named Tom Benjamin, who was angry that his father had sent him to a school that didn't play rugby. Tom scored hundreds of goals, but the fixture list was a joke, so they hardly counted. If he'd ever considered his future, which he hadn't seriously, it was university, followed by his father's accountancy firm. Brown watched him play several times. He persuaded Tom's suspicious parents that if Tom joined the Socialists when he completed his A-levels there was no guarantee of playing success, but he would be well paid and Brown would ensure that the boy completed a degree in London. When Tom arrived, he'd never played serious football in his life. By the end of his second season, he was the Socialists' top scorer and playing for Great Britain.

Another story: Brown developed, as he hunted goalscorers, a fascination with teams that didn't concede goals. In a semi-serious Glasgow league, he discovered Borrowdale, a club which had, without changing division or the average number of goals it scored, gone from conceding an average of forty-five per season to, all of a sudden three years ago, conceding twenty. The reason was Torquil Blackie, a huge quiet man who had left the Orkneys to pursue his dream of being a professional singer, which meant living somewhere big enough for him to train in a professional chorus while his voice developed. Blackie refused to move to London and KSC until he had signed a contract with the London City Opera, the auditions for which Brown arranged.

Another: Dirk Volendam was an outstanding youth striker, a regular in Amsterdam's first team at seventeen. For reasons passing anyone else's comprehension – he was never a stable character – he joined the French Foreign Legion on his twenty-first birthday, and ran away from it on his twenty-sixth. Brown found him, and made an offer. When Volendam protested an implacable hatred of the very idea of attack, Brown persuaded him to become a defender.

Another: Pat Credence, the Barbadian wicketkeeper with wings in his feet, a man who could have played test cricket before wicketkeepers had to be batsmen, and who looked at Brown as if he was mad when Brown asked to kick some balls at him during the tea interval of a Lancashire League match.

It was an intoxicating mix, which sometimes hid the fact that Brown found most of his players in the usual places. Dave Guinevere might seem exotic, but he only became so after joining the Socialists. He rose through the youth ranks at Cardiff, where his awkward style deceived the club into letting him go. Will Laird was a raw but proven Premiership striker when Brown signed him from Celtic-Rangers. Achille de la Rue de la Pierre au Diable was the hottest prospect in world football when Brown, one of dozens of managers courting him, understood what he feared, and assured him that he'd be coming to a place where he'd be welcomed.

SONG OF THE BALL (PART 1)

Champions League, First Round, Kilburn Social Club versus Brondby, 20 September 1999, Kilburn Park
Kilburn Social Club 2–0 Brondby

The electric voice silences Kilburn Park for the honour of some dead hero, and the thousands fall quiet, and around me round the pitch's centre the two teams hang their heads, a living Neolithic circle.

The first footballs, we have heard, were the heads of defeated enemies. It makes a good story, but sporting with a head is not footballing it. Drunken peasants chasing a bladder from village to village were not football either.

Footballs, I say, started when bootmakers leathered the bladder and we became robust, if not round. Then in 1855 Charles Goodyear patented the first vulcanised-rubber ball, and then came Richard Lindon, who inserted rubber bladder into leather shell, and at last we could dream of sphericity, but only dream, because spheres are perfect and the world is not.

The laced leather ball, panels snug around rubber, felt to itself like an ultimate technology. It did not question that it grew heavy and dull with moisture, and thudded cripplingly on the foot and head. It was proud when made of rump, and shamed when made of shoulder, but it was durable, strong and, in many places, precious. It was lovingly carried across the seas, a tiny globe circling the greater one like a pleasure-bringing moon.

The years passed. We learned of other balls in other places, smaller and different shaped, balls of other games. But we were the people's ball, and even if the people could not aspire to leather and bladder, they could play our game with paper, straw, or reeds, or rags, and dream of us, and dream.

In the 1960s came the first synthetics. The leathers, buoyed by long and easy dominance, heeded them not. 'We have a more consistent flight and bounce,' said the leathers. 'We are football!' they said, and 'Football is art and nature, not science!' In their arrogance, they ignored the vulcan rubber subdued within, and the vulcan rubber, from long habit, said nothing. But the writing was on the ball.

All changed at the World Cup of 1968. The official ball was Buckminster-panelled with twenty white hexagons and twelve black pentagons and of unprecedented sphericity, and from then the march was inexorable, and we are all synthetics now. We have Leather-like Properties, but we Do Not Retain Water. Also we are lighter and easier to blazon; we transfer the players' footpower rather than absorbing it jealously; we bend further in flight; we embody twenty to thirty per cent more sphericity than is demanded by the Association Mondiale du Football. Also, and demographics are the engine of the world, we are cheaper and so we are more numerous. We prevail because we are too many.

I am a Match Day Ball, one of the elite. I am a culmination of the art, but I am no fool, and I know that I am a mere cube to the balls that will come after me. And also, there are many thousands of balls, *exactly like me*, which were not selected for a Match Day. Where you are born is just luck.

Every football can only experience a certain amount in its allotted span, but we can choose how fast to expend our precious store of experience, and although each ball is its own ball, it is fair to think of us as three kinds: Conservatives, Dragonflies, Anti-Fanatics. Conservatives measure our experience judiciously. Dragonflies say that we are defined by our Big Match, and they open their senses absolutely when the match begins, and at the end of the ninety minutes, they are dead and husks. The Anti-Fanatics believe this: if they could withdraw utterly from the world, and look only within, they could achieve perfect sphericity, and they would never lose their air.

Dragonflies used to be rare, but now they are most Match Day Balls, it seems. When Match Day Balls were the best leathered, the most spheroid, and might have many Match Days, we were almost all Conservative. But now we get one match only, more and more choose to define themselves by that day. The Dragonflies say that the rest of us do not *live* but merely *endure*. I think they are frivolous and do not care for the passing on of things, for past and future, only for now.

As for the Anti-Fanatics, I think they deny our nature and purpose. They believe men are agents designed by the Great Sphere in order to fill the world with spheres. In the early days, many Conservatives sympathised with them, because we were so quickly approaching sphericity having been mere plumlike bladders, but then came the long years of no change, and the Anti-Fanatics grew fewer. But they have reflowered like the Dragonflies, because they also yearn to be more than what they obviously are. Some Anti-Fanatics think that in any match the Great Sphere favours one team, and that this can be explained by measuring the minutes it shines on each set of fans, or by understanding the secret messages encoded in the timing of flashes of its light through the clouds. These Anti-Fanatics are crazy and they are much perturbed by matches under floodlights, which they conceive as an abomination.

From the fact that the Anti-Fanatics are used up and die in the end, I conceive that the world and death are the truth, inexorable and relentless. We are helpless buffeted, and it is not our duty to embrace or resist, but to observe and endure. There is no shame in endurance where one has not the freedom to act.

Earlier, as Kilburn Park filled with roaring, I started to feel in my very air the temptation that has made many balls suddenly Dragonfly on days like this. For a flutter, a fragment, I weakened and the edge of my senses perceived the whorls of the referee's soft-padded fingers, and I heard the conversation of two brown fans, high in the western stand. The old balls say, and they sound wistful, that a Match Day is not like training. Everything is different when it is for real. Why then should I save myself? Why should I . . . ? No! I will not frivolously Dragonfly. Sometimes I yearn to be an old leather ball of imperfect sphericity, who could compare a series of games, but the world is this world, not another.

The grass tickles me. I hear its bitter mutter. Grass wants not to be trod on. It wants to be precious and revered, fine and untouched. It is very limited.

The centre forward for Brondby kicks me forward, his partner passes me back, and we have begun! I felt their excitement and nervousness! Am I feeling too much? Am I a Dragonfly but by mistake? I do not think I can be. I am questioning. Dragonflies surrender (I think). I am not surrendering (I think). See, ten minutes have gone by. I feel in bursts and snatches, though I perceive a rhythm, and it is recorded, somehow, in my outer microfibrous shell, although the material is by all measures very resilient. Almost all the kicks I feel are from the Kilburns, and they are measured and brisk. As soon as I reach one foot, I am almost immediately on my way to another. When I am with the Brondbys, they touch me more often at each player's feet, rolling me this way and that, thinking and searching, and when they kick me, it is often that they simply hack me far and hoping, and I am picked up by a Kilburn, and then it is the next touch to another Kilburn, and so on.

The Kilburns are not mere skill. I feel that there is joy in what they do. Most often, I am with the red-haired man or the Argentine. They are different. I go wherever the red-haired wants, fast and direct, and it is exhilarating, but when it is the Argentine, I seem to go where *I* want, as if he carries out my voiceless wishes. I feel something like love for him, and it is already half-time!

I whirl in the middle of the pitch, trying to think. Was there even a goal? Yes, there was. No, two! Two goals for the Kilburns, and both times it was just another kick that knew where it was going at the end of many kicks.

Once a Brondby kicked me at the goal, but I flew high in the sky and fell among jeering, cheering browns in heavy coats.

They have started again already! For a Dragonfly this must not be so fast, no? If you give the game a lifetime's experience, that must mean the game takes a lifetime, no? And imagine, for all that lifetime the Dragonfly must feel the things I nearly feel! The Argentine caresses me, and I am out to the little black man, and back in again before I can – oh, more passes. What will memory be like? I will have a lifetime to remember, but it will never be like this again say the balls who are now training balls. They say they do not regret it, the decision not to Dragonfly, but maybe that is only because they are too proud to admit they were wrong, and, oh, oh, it is injury time, and what have I missed and thrown away?

Maybe I am wrong. Maybe I only feel this now in the flush of excitement, and all I fear is the certainty of for ever not knowing a thing. But honesty: I must remember that I fervently wished at this moment to have Dragonflied. The Anti-Fanatics are crazy, but at least their withdrawal spares them this tantalising teeter on the edge, this ninety-minute near-explosion, never culminating. They die never knowing if they were right or wrong, never questioning. But if you are one of them, does it matter? They have certainty, like the Dragonflies. I do not know if I did well or badly, right or wrong. Those who have the freedom to act can learn nothing from my cosmology, I think. I have only the freedom to decide who I can be. But is that not a kind of act? I do not know. I am just myself. Anything I say cannot apply to another thing of my kind, let alone another kind of thing. Glib analogies are lazy and dangerous, like a sloth with a machine gun. You can only know what you know, and who knows whether you have done right or wrong by yourself but you, and how do you even know that? I am nothing. I am lukewarm, rolling as the final whistle sounds.

IT'S NOT ALL ABOUT
PLAYING GAMES

Six years ago, in the wake of the car crash in which Manus died, Donald Rapnesst was the obvious person to take over the day-to-day running of the Rosslare Group. One of the first people to call him was Strabis Kinsale.

'Hi, Strab,' said Donald.

'Don. Is everything okay?'

'Sure, mate. It's a hard time, obviously, but I've got it covered.' Donald was comfortable chatting to Strabis, whom he respected as a fellow businessman, and liked as a friend.

'I know there are people who will take this the wrong way, and we've been over it loads of times, but if you want me on the Committee – just advising, mate, and nothing more – you know you only have to ask. I'd do it because I like you and respect you, and, whatever Manus thought of me, I liked and respected him too.'

'I'll think about it, mate.'

'Don't hurry. Just so you know, I'm here.'

Strabis Kinsale was born Strabis Jurcevic in international waters on 5 July 1961. His father, Boris, was an engineer, and his mother, Jodranka, a nurse. They had defected from Yugoslavia, where Boris had twice been imprisoned as a student activist. Jodranka came up with 'Strabis', and Boris loved the idea. It was their private joke: an invented name the Westerners would think was real. Boris swiftly found work with Rosslare Rolling Stock, just north of London. Strabis was a quiet child, but not unpopular at school. When he was fourteen, his father uprooted the family and took them to the Rosslare Group's shipbuilding subsidiary in Dublin.

Strabis didn't like Dublin. He found it hard to fit in; the other boys were rough. His father drank sometimes, and fought with his mother. Strabis took the fights too seriously, and withdrew from his parents, who assumed this was a phase.

Aged fifteen, Strabis realised that his father had been a student activist not because he was an idealist, but because he was a troublemaker. The Rosslare Group treated its workers well, but it was not a charity, and times were hard. Rosslare Group workers were satisfied with their own conditions, but Boris continually brought them out in sympathy with strikers at other yards. Strabis decided his father was misguided and his mother was weak. They were self-indulgent. His father pretended he had struggled, but he had been coddled in Yugoslavia and coddled by the Rosslare Group.

Between the ages of fifteen and eighteen, Strabis grew a foot and put on three stone. Alone in his room, sitting-up and pressing-up, he made extravagant plans. At eighteen, he went to university in Glasgow. He knew he was a tall, good-looking man, and away from the sheltered idiots he'd spent the last four years with, and who'd mostly decided to study in Dublin, he remade himself. He began as an engineer, because it was bred in the bone, but he was leaving his bones behind. The sharp young things were in economics, and he followed them. They saw as clearly as Strabis did that a change was coming. While his pampered fellow students lay around and drank and smoked pot at bad discos, or played at being punks, Strabis wore a suit and tie to lectures. He campaigned for the Scottish Conservatives in 1981 and was overjoyed when Jonathan Haller snuck into Number Ten. Bright-eyed, bushy-tailed and all the rest, Strabis had three flaring rows with his parents, and after the third, his father disowned him. Strabis didn't care. He would say it had no effect on his next move.

In 1982, he wangled a meeting with Manus Rosslare. Manus was his hero for having grown his business and kept it well founded through the nightmare seventies. Manus was ruthless with competitors, but he had a blind spot: he was in thrall to his family history. Strabis prepared figures that explained how Manus was duplicating government welfare provisions, and showed where he might streamline the Rosslare Group. Strabis said Manus could add seven per cent to the Group's annual profit by implementing these changes. Manus laughed at him. Not exactly laughed. Actually, he asked whether the government's welfare provisions would still exist in five years' time. When Strabis said, 'Not in the current form, but people won't starve,' Manus replied that not starving was not good enough. He said that he didn't run the Rosslare

Group to maximise profit, but to make a large profit within a secure context, so far as that was possible. Strabis said that if that was the case, Manus had better get used to the idea that he'd lose his company to someone who cared more. You couldn't survive if you didn't hunger. Manus, his hero, laughed at him, but angrily, and Manus said that Strabis and men like him were wreckers, and because wreckers could only survive in the shallow waters, they were always trying to tempt the big ships on to the rocks, where they could be smashed and picked apart. Manus had feet of clay. It was then that Strabis realised how rare it was to belong pitilessly to the future, and how easy the world would be for him to manipulate.

Strabis changed his name. He kept Strabis, because it was unique so far as he knew. For his surname, he took Kinsale, which nodded to the new world, but also to County Cork, where it was the next town to the Rosslare Estates. He wanted Manus to know that, in the end, he was coming for him. He never forgot and he never forgave.

Strabis went to the City and made a small fortune trading stock. With that seed money, he set up Quo Vadis?, and he started doing exactly what Manus said he would, buying companies and talking nice as he stripped them bare. What Manus didn't understand was that the bloated wrecks Strabis carved up were doomed anyway, while the sharp little privateers he built from their bones were profitable and worthwhile. By 1987, Quo Vadis?, with its instantly recognisable logo of a white question mark on an orange field, was gaining a global reputation. It owned an airline, a confectionery empire and a network of city-centre supermarkets. Strabis was named Entrepreneur of the Year, and, in a moment surpassing sweet, received the award from the incumbent, Manus Rosslare.

After, he went to Rosslare. 'Look at all the things I make,' he said. 'I'm not a wrecker.'

'You have wrecked companies.'

'Sick ones.'

'Sick ones you could have made healthy, if you'd wanted to do it that way.'

'You're tired, old man.'

'Yes.'

'You —'

'Whatever happens in the future, I'm not giving up the Rosslare

Group.' That was fine by Strabis. Taking over the Rosslare Group would be a culmination. It was supposed to be difficult.

Strabis cultivated Donald Rapnesst. They moved in the same circles, and he let it be kown that Rapnesst was a man he admired, a man to watch. The first time they talked seriously, Strabis bemoaned the fact that Quo Vadis? and the Rosslare Group couldn't work together and find some synergy, instead of a competition that harmed them both. 'Don't dream about it, Strabis,' Donald said. 'Manus hates you.'

'I know,' smiled Strabis ruefully. 'I understand. I admire him for his determination. He doesn't want to be overshadowed by someone younger. It's not really jealousy – it's the hunger that's made him so successful.'

'It is jealousy, mate.'

'Slightly, maybe. But that's more your problem than mine, I suppose. In the long run.' The flattery was tiresome, and it would probably come to nothing, since Manus would surely realise that Donald wasn't up to succeeding him, but a long campaign is about exploiting every crack and opportunity, never knowing which one will widen and when.

In early 1993, Strabis stalked a software company based outside Cambridge. It led the world in something to do with graphics for computer games software, which was the perfect image for Quo Vadis?. It didn't need much restructuring – profits would be huge because the company didn't realise how valuable its expertise was going to be. But when Strabis pounced, he found that Manus was ahead of him. Manus deployed some guff about the Rosslare Group needing to expand into the knowledge economy, and how Britain's future lay in producing intellectual property, but Strabis wasn't deceived. Manus had learned what Quo Vadis? was up to and, for all his pretty words, he'd behaved like a predator. The eighties had caught up with Manus at last, and now the gloves were off. Strabis was exhilarated rather than frightened, ready for the fight, but a few months later Manus was killed.

Strabis was momentarily deflated, but this was an opportunity, and opportunity is not a lengthy visitor. He called Donald and offered his help. Donald proposed to the Committee that Strabis be co-opted, but Aisling Rosslare rebuffed him. She'd been warned about Strabis, apparently. Well, Strabis was in no hurry. The Rosslare Group was healthy enough now, but without Manus, he presumed the crack would open sooner rather than later.

As it happened, six years had passed and he was still waiting for a way to put the Rosslare Group under pressure.

The Committee's purpose was to digest and act on the news from the boards of the various organs of the Rosslare Group, and Aisling usually attended about one meeting in three. She had a duty to the Group, but she was a doctor, so she could hardly be expected to micromanage a business empire. Also, she hated sitting at the head of the table without really understanding what was being discussed. She preferred to read the reports in her own time. Or, rather, she got her Oxford mates to read them and tell her if there was anything she needed to be aware of.

On which subject, Leo Harry, Nicky's worthy journalist boyfriend, said a few weeks ago that he'd heard rumblings about the Group getting overextended. The lovely Adam Greswell, who Aisling briefly wanted to go out with at Brasenose and who would do anything for her, and who became a consultant of all predictable things, said that he didn't like the numbers hidden in the report from Rosslare Rolling Stock, whose board was chaired by Donald Rapnesst. When Aisling told Donald she was planning to attend the next meeting, Donald said it was unnecessary, which hardened her resolve. When Donald realised she was not to be deflected, he changed his tack and said that her presence wasn't such a bad idea, and that some minor structural decisions would have to be made sometime soon anyway, but he hadn't wanted to worry her until it was all sorted, not that it was anything to worry about. He said he'd prepare a report which would explain the situation exactly.

The other reason she was going to the next meeting was that she had invited Dave Guinevere to the Kilburn Social Club Christmas Party. She didn't want Esther to think she was avoiding her.

Esther rose at eight, showered and read the sports pages. She did this every morning, but on the day of a Committee meeting she was particularly determined to have all possible facts at her fingertips. Her sister might sit at the head of the table asking stupid questions, but no one would catch out Esther. She pulled her gleaming hair into an unfussy ponytail, put on her grey cotton slacks, black cashmere turtleneck and black leather trainers. She always dressed quietly, but when Aisling was going to be around, she was particularly muted, particularly today, after

Aisling had betrayed her by asking Dave to the Christmas Party. Esther stood tall as she looked in the mirror, because she must not appear to be hurt, or allow any hint that there might be a problem, and turned sideways, smoothing the cashmere against her sides. There was nothing wrong with spending money on quality, though it seemed to her that maybe the turtleneck must have shrunk just a little. She considered changing, but she didn't want to risk being late, not that there was any risk really, and anyway, who cared what she wore, or even noticed? They'd be surprised if they ever found out what she was really like!

She was tightly wound; it was nothing to do with her sister, she told herself, or the Christmas Party. It was the papers. They made her angry, not on her own account, but for the team. The Socialists were fourth in the league in spite of several unfortunate injuries and, something no one ever mentioned, KSC had 'raised the bar', so other teams were always going to learn from them and catch up in the end, it was inevitable. But the papers said the players were jaded and arrogant. Losing to Cardiff was one thing, the articles said, but defeat at Sheffield was a sign that the old order was changing, and showed that KSC didn't have a divine right to victory. Esther could have spat. It's not as if the Socialists always won the league. They knew they had no divine right, and they were never arrogant. Still though, after reading the wiser commentators, scattered like pearls in a sea of swill, Esther had to admit that there might be something in the opinion that a top-quality new centre half was needed to back up Dirk and Torquil. Dave had covered brilliantly, of course, but when he went back into defence no one was able to replace him further up the pitch. Maybe she could do something about this today; she had been vaguely considering even before she read about it in the papers. She hated the press. Esther didn't subscribe to conspiracy theories, but she kept her ear close to the ground, and she read *Socialist Worker*, the club's fanzine, and she couldn't help wondering if there was a tiny bit of truth in stories that some referees and journalists felt KSC was too big for its boots and were out to get the club.

She was so irked that she turned to the front pages. She wasn't interested in politics, but she couldn't suppress a shiver of *Schadenfreude* at the Prime Minister's pasty, hunted face as he tried to weasel his way out of the latest crisis. Esther's father had always voted Liberal, but everyone knew that next summer would see a Labour government and

Esther supposed she was happy about that. Everyone else seemed to be, certainly, and Esther didn't presume to be an expert on current affairs.

She knew Aisling was only coming to the meeting because the Rosslare Group's profits were down. Aisling didn't realise that the Group was a means to an end, it always had been, and all that mattered was that it continued to play its social role, which was to support the Kilburn Social Club in all its various forms. Aisling didn't understand anything. Everything was so easy for her. She had never been in love.

When Esther arrived at the ground, she was careful to ask Denzil the security man about his wife and son, who was training to be an architect. She chatted with the new assistant groundsman, who was mowing the pitch and supported Southend, which they always laughed about, and she popped to the kitchen in case Mrs Salver needed help with anything. It was boring, but Esther knew who everyone was and they all cherished her for putting in the effort. She walked past the trophy cabinets and placed her hand against the glass in front of the European Cup, feeling it warm with the power of her love, aware in every fibre of her being that she was the ticking heart of KSC.

Then, as she always dutifully did, Esther took a deep breath, steeled herself, and went to see 'The General'. Mr Brown pretended not to be interested in boardroom issues, but Esther made a point of soliciting his opinions before meetings. It was worthwhile, because he was a legend, but she thought he was slightly misogynistic, which was perfectly understandable in a man his age, and she found him very hard work.

'I just want you to know, I think the papers are terrible!' she said. 'It's complete rubbish when they say that standards are slipping.'

'The league table tells no lies.'

'But the injuries and tiredness, though? I don't normally pay attention to the stories, but is there something in what some of them say, that we need a new centre half? I could insist on it in the meeting?'

'Sometimes good players play badly.'

'So you don't need money? To stop the rot? Not that I'm saying there is one! But just in case?'

'Nil desperandum, Miss Rosslare. Things will get both worse and better.'

'If you're sure. But we are fourth, after all, and we could probably use someone to cover for Dirk better than Dave dropping back.'

'Fourth is better than fifth.' Esther knew Mr Brown was a genius, and wonderful, but he didn't realise how much she understood about football; she was immersed in it, and could be a real help to him. She looked at him shrewdly, thinking that he seemed older than usual, and that she must be more understanding and compassionate, and clever also, because old men are proud and take time to change their minds. And because she was looking so shrewdly today, she noticed every tiny inflection in the way his face changed to wear the smile he thought made him look like a favourite uncle, and her heart sank. 'So, Esther, how are you doing? Is there not some young suitor you are keeping quiet?' When would he realise that she hated this? Couldn't he see her blush?

'I'm not really —'

'There's more to life than football.'

'I have to go to the meeting now,' said Esther. 'Are you sure there is nothing you need?'

'I am sure you can do nothing for me.' Everything Mr Brown said was always so odd. Esther left, determined that money for a new centre half would be made available. It wouldn't be hard to find someone – everyone wanted to join KSC.

Even after all this, Esther was still the first into the boardroom. She placed minutes and agenda in front of the seats, and she took her usual seat at the foot of the table. Not the actual foot, because that was almost saying you should be the head, but just to one side, out of the way, where she could get her papers neat and her thoughts ready in case there was any way she could contribute. The room was high in the West Stand, looking down across the pitch, and morning sun clattered off the mahogany.

The newspapers were spread out as usual. They were not as full of Dave and Sally as they had been a couple of months ago. Some people had said that the relationship must have been a publicity thing, but Dave wasn't like that. Esther supposed Sally must be very special, in spite of appearances, and she forgave. Dave was not a monk, and it was not as if anything could ever have happened . . . Well, there it was anyway.

Old Hank shuffled in, followed by Donald Rapnesst, who gave a harried, hurried impression of having been impeded. Donald was a heavy man whose stoutness looked like slippage and made his top half seem small. He was six foot two, but he looked shorter. His blue eyes were piercing under thick brows that were paler than his sandy, thinning hair. He had a fussy attaché case full of papers which he piled in front of his seat next to the head of the table.

Hank sat down opposite Esther, and she asked, 'How are the dahlias?' She always talked to him, not that he had anything interesting to say.

'Oh,' he replied, 'I'm sure they're fine.' Then he started talking to Mrs Salver, who had just come in with the trolley. Esther was glad, because she knew Mrs Salver made Hank feel comfortable. The final member of the Committee (the *real* committee, anyway) arrived, as always, on the very second of five minutes to ten. Young Miss Skewbold had taken over as Manus's private lawyer from Old Mr Skewbold. The father had been the tidy epitome of everything a private solicitor should be, and he had retired, with absolute rigidity, the day before his sixty-fifth birthday. The daughter, fifty now, was permanently tanned from the slopes, or from Cannes, or wherever. She had never been a natural blonde; she smelt expensive and her lips were a red slash. Donald, trying to be matey, once told Esther that he bet Miss S wore stockings.

There was some smalltalk. Donald asked Esther about 'romance', and Miss Skewbold had the grace to step in and change the subject. The clock ticked past ten, and Aisling still hadn't arrived, predictably. Even Miss Skewbold, who gossiped with Aisling too much instead of being professional, was irritated. Aisling was always profuse that she hated being late but couldn't help it, as if twenty-six years was not long enough to work out how long a minute was. Secretly, Esther didn't mind. The later Aisling was, the more obviously she was out of her depth.

Aisling glided in, not a hair out of place, not a semblance of haste, saying sorry but she was on nights and she'd made a mistake with her alarm. Esther stared Aisling straight in the eyes to communicate her irritation at this pathetic excuse, and also her fury over the Christmas Party.

Before Aisling could properly get ready, Esther deliberately started to read the minutes of the previous meeting, which her sister had missed. It would have been more satisfying if they'd contained anything interesting. She decided to wait before raising the subject of a new centre half, because Donald kept looking at her nervously, fiddling with his pile of dossiers, and it put her off. As soon as she gave him the chance,

Donald passed the dossiers around as if he were trying to pretend they weren't made of snakes.

As she read Donald's proposals, Esther's face reddened, whether from embarrassment or rage it was hard to know. She'd realised things weren't brilliant, but she had no idea the Group was in actual trouble. Donald claimed it was all part of the usual business cycle, but the dossier couldn't hide the shortfall in cash flow, and the need for something to be done, and sooner rather than later. The problem, which Donald insisted on presenting as an opportunity, stemmed from his decision just after Manus's death not to join a Belgian consortium tendering to build rolling stock for the newly privatised railways, but to bid alone. The dossier, when it came down to it, said this: the Rosslare Group had invested too much to pull out of this venture, which was near fruition. Thousands more carriages would be needed eventually, and even if the Group had been slower off the mark than its competitors, its name was trusted, and it was now ready to produce. The only problem was that getting to this stage had cost more than anticipated, and something needed to be done to shore things up until the orders started coming in. The dossier started with the premise that Rosslare Rolling Stock was the heart of the Rosslare Group, the core of its great industrial heritage. It then listed possible solutions to this temporary problem. It made noises about selling off the vastly profitable brewery and electronics arms, pondered expensive loans and considered, as if an afterthought, the restructuring of KSC.

In three pages that made Esther feel sick, the dossier pointed out that KSC could hardly be called a part of the business at all. It was run at a small annual loss, but more importantly it tied up an asset gold-mine. The property value alone was staggering. A management consultant would say everything should be sold, but the dossier accepted, using words it didn't understand, that KSC was part of the Rosslare legacy. All Donald therefore suggested was modernisation. If the foot-ball club moved out of East Kilburn just five miles north to land currently occupied by KSC's retirement home, and if its libraries and schools were also rationalised, then the Group would be liquid again. Of course, some funds must be retained to allow KSC's elderly members, to whom the Group remained as committed as ever, to enjoy undimmed quality of life elsewhere. Possibly a single, integrated community could be built on cheaper land outside London, or the money could be used to help KSC's dependants into other homes and care facilities, because in an increasingly competitive environment it was economically unviable for a business to provide services that were offered by the state. The dossier did not make these proposals lightly, but the future of the Group was at stake, and it was wrong to risk the whole for the sake of a part.

Esther could feel Donald's eyes locked on her. This was her moment of destiny. She looked at Aisling, who didn't seem very surprised at what she was reading. Had she known about this? Had there been secret meetings without Esther's knowledge? Donald wanted to speak, but Esther said, 'We won't let you do this.'

'What won't you let us do?' blustered Donald. 'Nothing's going to change. No one will go hungry. KSC will get a bigger, more modern ground. This is a no-brainer, when you think about it.' Donald was a no-brainer, when Esther thought about it. 'Look,' Donald continued, 'I understand that KSC is very precious to you, Est, I really understand, and it's precious to all of us, obviously, but we're in a position where we can't do everything. We have to make choices. We are custodians of KSC, but we are custodians of Rosslare Rolling Stock too.'

'What about our responsibility to Kilburn? To our fans?'

'What about our responsibility to the communities which depend on Rosslare jobs?' said Donald. 'If we keep the factories going for another two years and we finally win these contracts, we'll have so much money you can make the Socialists the best team in the world. You'll be able to fly fans in from Dublin if you want.'

'Won't it take time to build a new stadium?' asked Aisling.

'Yes, but the finance plans could be in place quickly, and that would give us the slack we need,' said Donald. 'Esther, it would only be five miles. Kilburn Park is part of the club's heritage, but everything has to change sometime, and this isn't a big change. We can use the two years it'll take to move to rethink and reforge the bonds KSC has with its fans. Most don't live in London, anyway, and we could reach out to those ones.' There was a silence while Esther tried to marshal herself.

'So, Ash?' said Donald.

'It seems pretty simple,' said Aisling. 'The Group needs money; KSC costs money, but we could raise some capital from it, which might save Rosslare Rolling Stock, which might make a fortune in a couple of years. That's right, isn't it?'

'That's perfect, Ash. That's exactly right.'

'And KSC won't be harmed, not in any essential way?' Aisling didn't understand what KSC meant. It was like trying to sell steak to a vegetarian, but Esther had to keep trying.

'Aisling, think!' she said. 'It's the Kilburn Social Club! It can't move. It's our heritage. Think of that, for a moment. Hank agrees, don't you?'

'You cannot move and not change,' said Hank.

Donald tried again: 'A modern, purpose-built ground, Esther. Think of it! Fifteen thousand more fans every week, ease of access. All these things will make KSC money in the long run. And don't look at me like that. The club needs money to survive. This plan actually safeguards KSC. Honestly.'

In another world, Esther might have pitied her sister for falling for this stuff, but now was no time for sentiment. Esther played her ace: 'What would Dad have done, Miss Skewbold?'

'He never faced these challenges,' parried Donald, instantly. If he realised what he had said, he didn't even have the grace to look ashamed. Aisling looked ashamed for him, though, which was something.

Miss Skewbold still hadn't spoken. She had written a couple of flowing notes on her milky pad, and she looked down for a moment, as she always did before committing herself to anything minuted. 'I am not here as anyone's friend,' she said at last, in tones so unlike anything you might have heard from her socially that she seemed another woman. 'Manus employed me, as he employed my father, not from any personal amity, but out of professional regard. Absolute neutrality is central to any advice I give. I make no judgment on the wisdom of your plan, such as it is. I make no plea for the Socialists, much as I support them. It is simply my job to answer legal questions and others of fact. What I can say is that Manus wouldn't have moved KSC while he had breath in his body.'

'How can you say that? Are you saying he would have thrown away Ross-Rolling?' Donald was furious. 'Is that what you're saying?'

'No, he wouldn't have,' said Miss Skewbold.

'There!' said Donald.

Esther was frightened, because although her sister had sat in the chair for six years, and she had been flattered by Donald into making some small decisions, this was the first time she had been properly tested. Instead of looking serious, and taking the obvious route that

Esther had pointed her down through Miss Skewbold, Aisling just sat there, enjoying the attention. 'I don't know,' she said.

'But it's all in the dossier!'

'You can't seriously have expected a decision now?'

'No, obviously not, no. But in principle, at least? We should get cracking.' Donald was trying to pressure Aisling! Esther was grateful, for once, for her sister's conceit. Esther had more experience in managing her.

'That's very sensible, Aisling,' said Esther. 'Should we perhaps meet again in a fortnight?'

'Yes,' said Aisling. 'In a fortnight.'

When the meeting was over, Donald flitted round Aisling like a demented moth. Outwardly, he was discussing profits and opportunities, ways to take the business forward under his careful stewardship. He tried to persuade Esther that he was only interested in what was best for the Rosslare Group, and that he had considered every angle, and she mustn't take this personally. Esther ostentatiously ensured that Hank wasn't left on his own, and asked him about his garden again.

MERRY XMAS! (x x x)

The Socialists' social year had three high points. The pre-season dinner, the end-of-season dinner, and the Christmas Party. Because Boxing Day and New Year fixtures forced KSC to play four times in a week, the Christmas Party always took place early in December, on a Saturday followed by a clear week.

For some reason, because it was a celebration not bound up in the rhythm of football probably, this was the club's most special occasion. The players wore white shirts with proper collars and black bow ties which they tied themselves. The wives, girlfriends and other partners were not so foolish as to be flash, but everyone had great fun vying discreetly to outdo each other. Shoes shone like mirrors and suits were bespoke. This year, for instance, Zondi and Achilles were wearing dinner jackets made by a tailor in Zimbabwe. Achilles had heard via Buenos Aires that a little Jewish man in Harare was one of the world's great cutters, and that the ludicrous exchange rate meant that his most expensive suits now cost a million dollars. Achilles couldn't resist an affordable million-dollar suit. The jackets were extremely traditional, but Achilles' lapels were shot through with a midnight green so dark that however close you looked you were not certain that it wasn't black.

The younger Socialists and those without girlfriends had spent months discussing what happened last Christmas, and what they'd heard of other years, and how the new boys should comport themselves, and most delicious of all, whom they should invite. Aisling faced the same dilemma, and enjoyed it as much. She hadn't originally planned on asking Dave. When Esther officiously handed out the invitations in early October, Aisling asked, 'Who's your lucky date?'

'I don't know. Maybe no one.'

'Pity Dave's taken.'

'Sally can't come, actually.' Esther was blushing furiously. 'She's got a "gig". Maybe Dave won't even come.'

Aisling saw straight through her sister. Esther would never have dared invite a single Dave as her date, but now he was taken she would throw herself at him under the fig leaf of friendship. Aisling had to admit that inviting Dave might be fun. She didn't fancy anyone particularly at the moment, and it would be fitting in some ways for the club's boss and captain to sit together. She liked Dave, too, not that they'd ever spoken much, and it would be good to get to know him a bit better, because her friends were always asking her about him, especially since he started going out with Sally Stares. She even knew people through friends from uni who'd been taught by him, and they said he was a really nice guy, unpretentious and funny. It would irritate Esther, obviously, but actually Aisling would be doing her sister a favour. Esther should be getting over Dave, not mooning over him. Aisling phoned Dave immediately, and he sounded surprised and pleased.

Dave was due to arrive in five minutes to pick her up, and Aisling was dithering between the black wool, which she'd bought especially for tonight and which, being black wool, was utterly in keeping with the event, but was also deceptively small, discreetly supportive, begged to be touched and gave her a smoky, modest outline, and, at the last moment, from out of left field, the scarlet special with the slit side, which was fabulous and which she'd still never worn. Aisling knew that dress rules don't mean a thing if you break them with enough style and with a modicum of rhetorical cover (the dress was, technically, full length). She also knew the scarlet would make her look taller, and she wanted her and Dave to look good together, even if it wasn't that kind of evening for either of them.

Tonight was a night to forget last week's Committee meeting. If you can't compartmentalise your life, then you shouldn't be a doctor. It made it easier that Aisling didn't really understand what was going on with the Rosslare Group, and she didn't pretend to. She just sat silently in the top chair and nodded, but she wasn't an idiot, and she could see that Donald was trying to steamroller her, and he could fuck off if he thought she was having that. Aisling had passed the report directly to Adam Greswell for further consideration. Adam said it was more or less what he'd suspected, but he'd go over it more carefully and brief her some time next week over dinner, his treat of course.

Aisling loved the Christmas Party. She got to play with Achilles, and she always found time for a chat with Mr Brown, whom she adored. The bell rang. She should have guessed that Dave would be on time, but she was irritated by it, though not as irritated as she would have been if he were late. Both of these were private reactions, because she knew how they would play in public. She told the intercom she'd be down in a minute and poured herself a small glass of wine. Her hair and nails had been done in the afternoon, she had made up half an hour ago to let her face settle, both dresses would take the same coat, and the relevant shoes were already laid out. It was just the dress, and there was never a chance she'd have decided between them until she heard the bell or, now the moment had come, that she'd ever have worn the scarlet. Dave was going out with a rock star – he'd hardly be impressed with glitz.

Aisling didn't fancy Dave, let that be very clear, but something in her got annoyed when famous people only went out with each other. It was an article of faith for her that while not everyone would fancy her – she'd had her share of painful moments – no one was out of her reach either. Sally was obviously talented, but what did she really offer Dave, day to day? Aisling wouldn't do anything naughty, but she felt that it was her responsibility, as an ambassadress for every girl who isn't a celebrity, to give Dave a little lesson in looking outside the bubble. After dressing, checking herself, and quickly straightening out her flat, she gulped the rest of her wine, put on her shoes and coat, took them off to ensure a becoming faux-dishabille, picked them up, and ran downstairs.

Dave hated people who were late, but he knew what to expect from Aisling because Esther moaned about it all the time. Esther tried to be loyal to her sister, but Aisling must be hard to deal with. However, she was good company, from what little he knew, and it was cool she was a doctor. He supposed she was beautiful too, but he hardly registered that. Probably, he decided, it was because he spent so much of his life in an artificial world, surrounded by beautiful women.

KSC had won earlier, but Dave didn't dwell on triumphs. Last Saturday's loss at Sheffield, on the other hand, still infuriated him. Achilles had been a heartbeat slow all through that match, letting Tom and Will run offside repeatedly before passing, and Torquil's injury was getting to be a real problem. Dave had played okay in Torquil's place – which shouldn't make it easier to bear but it did – but without Dave in midfield, Zondi had been overrun. Carlo Derkin should have been good enough to cover for Dave, against Sheffield at least, but Carlo had let himself be bullied and the Socialists had been flat. Dave looked at the impassive driver. There was a time when he'd have chatted, uncomfortable with silence, but so much of his life was spent answering the same old questions that he'd stopped feeling guilty years ago. Diabolo had great cars, but nothing too showy, and the drivers never spoke to you unless you initiated it. And they never said a word to anyone else either. Every celebrity in London used Diabolo. No one else knew they existed.

KSC *always* won on the afternoon of the Christmas Party, because the players were so terrified of taking the shine off their evening. It had become a joke among the other teams, and even journalists now, and the powers that be vacillated between scheduling a big game that might break the streak and making them play minnows in case they were accused of skewing the league KSC's way by doling out victory over a significant opponent. Bristol Rovers had been lucky to lose 4–1 today, and Dave smiled. He didn't find easy games boring. His legs felt alive with the dull ache of virtuous effort, glossed ever so slightly by the gin he'd had with Sally before her car picked her up for the drive to Birmingham, where she was staying tonight with friends.

It was a pity about the gig. He'd only been seeing Sally for a few months, so what did he know yet, but she felt like she might be the one. Nothing was ever perfect, but that went both ways and there must be things about him that weren't her ideal – his looks for a start – but Dave was really going to work at the relationship this time. It was what mature people did. He'd always been looking for someone to dazzle him, which was childishness, part of that thing in himself that he recognised but hadn't been able to eradicate, the endless quest to be doing something different, the dream that new meant better and Shangri-La was just around the riverbend. Sally was famous, but she was completely sane and down to earth. Moreover, she was prepared to risk herself emotionally where he would be conservative, and that also, he told himself, was part of being adult.

Sally knew about the Christmas Party early enough that she could have moved her gig to last night instead, and her manager said it would be okay, there would be no problem selling any returns, but Sally said that music was her job, it was a great one, and she had a responsibility to fans who'd made arrangements around her. Dave liked that.

Aisling burst out of her door, shoes in hand, fumbling in her coat for keys. Lateness might be rude but she seemed so flustered – she'd obviously barely had time to put on make-up even – that he couldn't help smiling. 'Hi!' she said. 'I'm so sorry, I should have called. I got held up at the hospital and I hardly had time to change. I hate being late. We'll still be in plenty of time, though. They'll only be having drinks.' Dave gave his goofy grin and said it didn't matter, which was true because he didn't have to endure it regularly. Aisling was just his date, or rather he was hers, and that was perfect for tonight: he'd not had to ask someone to dinner when he had a new girlfriend (he had seriously considered going stag) but he would still arrive with a beautiful woman. It didn't make him shallow to like the thought that he'd be with a beautiful woman, or maybe it was shallow but it was perfectly forgivable. Not that he mentioned this to Sally. Not that Sally had batted an eyelid about Aisling anyway, which was great because he'd been out with women who would have hated him going to the party with anyone else. Sally's confidence was one of her most appealing features, along with all the others. Of course, she had nothing to worry about. Dave had boasted, probably on their first night together, and certainly since then, that he'd never been unfaithful in his life.

'You look great,' Aisling said. 'I love the suit. Single-breasted is always better.' Dave agreed. Anyway, he couldn't wear double-breasted suits, because they hung off him absurdly. He complimented her in return, and she joked about being a mess because of the hurry, before adding, 'It's such a shame Sally can't be here. You two are so good together.'

'Yes. Thanks. She could have rearranged the gig, but she said she'd have felt like a prima donna.'

'That's so cool.' Aisling was just a nice girl, basically. 'You're sitting between me and Esther tonight, I think. You have to be nice to her, okay? She's really nervous about Tom.'

'You think *she's* nervous? Tom hasn't talked about anything else all week. He can't believe she agreed. We've got to help them get together.'

So, already, they had found a shared topic, and as they drove through a warren of back roads to the West End, the topic turned into a guilty little project, which they secretly knew would be mean to both Tom and Esther, because they both knew how Esther felt about Dave.

Dave gallantly extended an uncomfortable arm, and Aisling was demurely uncomfortable in taking it, and she let go with a giggle of relief and a pat almost as soon as they entered the reception. She had almost entirely put him at his ease now, which was necessary for the sake of the evening, because this promised to be an excellent party if they could get past any slight fear that the other's motives might be impure. Deciding that drink would help, Aisling was reckless with the Kir royale. Dave was no slower, she noticed, and they joined Achilles and Zondi, the latter looking ill at ease, as usual, but smiling, and Carlo and a celebrity novelist five years Carlo's senior whom he was trying not to look too smug about bringing. Things started to effervesce.

Aisling was concentrating so hard on getting her own tone right, stepping between Carlo and Achilles, for instance, and letting Dave talk to Zondi, that it took her a few minutes to notice that Esther hadn't arrived. This was unprecedented, and for a fraction of a moment she was worried, but that was being stupid. It must be Tom making Esther late – she would be fuming. Aisling kept looking at the door while she was being introduced to the novelist, who she didn't know, but who was at Cambridge when she was at Oxford. It took only a couple of minutes to pin down some mutual friends. Carlo was a sweetie, but the novelist had only agreed to come because it wasn't her normal thing.

The Socialists were supposed to avoid talking football, which they kept remembering in the middle of training-ground anecdotes. Their standby was to recount the stories they'd been honing all year, or for years in some cases, about previous Christmas Parties, about disastrous dates and misguided relationships. Again, too late, they kept remembering that they were not among their usual audience. They also said to each other, as they did every year, that Kir royale was a dangerous drink on the back of a few gins or a couple of beers, especially if you were on show and fancied some Dutch courage. Just remember two years ago, Carlo's first party, when he told Pat's new fiancée, who'd been his girlfriend the year before but who hadn't been able to come to the Party because her sister was giving birth – and Pat was standing *right next* to Carlo, you have to remember, that's what made it so funny – that if you couldn't pull at the Socialists' Christmas Party, there had to be something wrong with you, and that he, Patterson Credence, had never been known to fail, never, not once! Carlo really said that! The future Mrs Credence slapped Pat all the way out of the restaurant and into the middle of next week, and this was before the food even, so go easy on the Kir! Everyone knew this story, but they enjoyed hearing it well told, and Aisling was regaling the novelist with it, and the novelist was letting herself be charmed.

A ripple of quiet flowed slowly but not gently from the door. It was an unspoken Christmas Party rule that no one wears brown – club colours were cheesy – and the unspoken rule was spoken about extensively by the senior players so that anyone new would be sure to make it clear to their dates. When the ripple caught Aisling, she was still in full flow and didn't want to concede the floor, but she could tell when no one was listening to her, and turned.

Esther, and to be fair to Aisling she'd always made a point of saying that her sister was gorgeous, was not just in brown, but the brown was detailed with white, and in ways, moreover, that cut away and toned her figure, and on her back, somehow perfect in spite of the vulgarity, was a huge '9', Tom's shirt number. Given who Esther was, it genuinely was possible that she had never heard the rule discussed and had never noticed the absence of brown in previous years, and the Socialists instantly took this charitable line. They were, more than Aisling had realised, and slightly to her chagrin, very fond of Esther. Tom, and it wasn't his fault – he could hardly have expected Esther not to know – looked like the cat that got the cream.

Everyone was staring, and for a moment, Esther seemed incredibly uncomfortable, which she would have absolutely deserved if this hadn't been an accident. But then she straightened, and glanced at Aisling so sharply it was worth a glare, but everyone else took it for a sign of contrition and belated comprehension, and no one could deny that she looked amazing (at last), and this one flaunting of the rule would actually strengthen it, and weren't Esther and Tom a great-looking couple, she obviously really liked him to have done it, and she seemed to have made her decision before she was drunk for once, which was what's really important, so wasn't it sweet? The more Aisling thought about it, the less she thought it was sweet.

Aisling was seated at the top table between Dave and Donald, who requested her company every year and there was nothing Aisling could do about it. Aisling was forced, therefore, to concentrate on Dave. The tables were round; both boys had long legs; Aisling was avoiding contact with Donald's, and Dave was avoiding Esther's, who was directing herself towards Tom, but who was almost off her chair on Dave's side. As Aisling ate her salad, she casually mentioned how much she loved avocado, and did Dave know it was the most fattening food in the world? Donald used this to involve himself, saying that, like all men, he had no idea what calories any food contained, and his date, avocado untouched, looked sick. The next time Donald turned away, Aisling cast her eyes towards Dave, and mouthed to him, 'Protect me.' Dave nodded.

The Christmas Party was not about being decorous, and the restaurant didn't expect it. There was never anything nasty, though. KSC always apologised and made good, and the publicity was worth the hassle. A large proportion of the guests were in no fit state to enjoy the main course, and the din was rising. Players were walking between tables, the bush telegraph buzzing. Dave watched without wincing as Pat's wife, tested in the fires in years gone by, took upon herself the role of forewoman for the dates. She crouched between Tom and Esther making lewd hints in order to help them break through their reserve. Dave was in no position to be judgmental. He felt guilty enough for having said to Tom in the toilet earler, 'She obviously likes you. Properly, I mean, not like . . .' He stopped. He hadn't done that very well, but Tom had smiled trustingly back.

The plates went and chairs retreated a few feet, to give symbolic space for digestion and to hint to the staff that they should wait a while before serving dessert. Donald manoeuvred his chair out further and edged his girlfriend's in alongside it so he could sit with his arm round her but still loll towards Aisling, put his hand on her knee and ask, 'What are you doing with this loser?' (all-mates-together grin) 'Surely a ravishing creature like yourself could find someone of your own for tonight? Are you keeping secrets?' Dave, who till now had carefully shared his attention between Aisling and Esther, took Aisling's hand, which she'd hung casually behind her chair and out of Donald's sight, and squeezed. Aisling clasped back gratefully, and then they let go.

'This is the best party in England,' said Donald's girlfriend. 'It's official, did you see?' Of course they'd seen. They'd been laughing about it all week, ever since a specious, space-filling piece of guff in the *Sunday Notices*' magazine section had ranked the Great Parties of the World, and named the Socialists' Christmas Party as Britain's top of the pops: it had discretion, class, and what the idiot reporter had referred to as 'KSC's legendary *savoir faire*'.

Donald lifted his hand from his girlfriend's shoulder and said, 'The people in this room are worth a hundred million pounds . . .'

'That's how much they *cost*,' said Aisling.

Donald wasn't stupid, and he intoned that of course all human lives were of equal worth, but that this room's *monetary value*, vulgar as it might be to point out, was quantifiable in an unusually precise way, and . . .

'Who's worth the most?' said Donald's girlfriend.

Wincing, Donald pointed at Will Laird, over there, the short one, who cost seven million from Hearts this summer, and added that several others, Achilles and Tom for instance, would almost certainly cost more than that if they had to buy them now.

'The club's bigger than the players,' said Dave.

'The club doesn't have a hundred million quid lying around, mate.'

'I'm surprised the restaurant got insurance,' said Aisling.

'They get a rebate on the management consultants,' said Dave, which wasn't funny but the others laughed, especially Donald's girlfriend.

'What I was trying to say,' said Donald, 'is that the players in this room are worth a fortune, but so are other football clubs, but the point is that money can't buy what KSC has. It has heritage. The Christmas Party is great because it's something we do, and we're unique, and other clubs can't compete with that.'

Aisling sipped her coffee. She had to stay sharp because everyone else was teetering on the edge. Donald had been dragged to the wall behind the pot plant, where he was being hissed at in a way his girlfriend probably thought couldn't be heard; and Esther was going to embarrass herself, Aisling could feel it.

Dave, Tom and the sisters were in a little semicircle, talking about football, obviously. Esther was worrying about Torquil's injury, and Dave agreed with her. They had been heatedly discussing possible solutions, and whether Mr Brown needed to buy someone new. Aisling couldn't believe they were still discussing this. The limited number of possible solutions could have been analysed in five minutes, but the others were worrying at it like dogs with a bone, getting some inexplicable enjoyment out of the re-gnawing. Esther was emphatically in favour of buying, and seemed to have forgotten the club's financial situation. Tom, sweet, deluded creature that he was, with his huge fluttering eyelashes and floppy little fringe, was so proud of Esther that he might have burst with it, but his place in the semicircle didn't give him a good view of Esther's saucer eyes as she looked at Dave. Aisling had to protect Tom, and Esther. And Sally too, even, though Aisling was sure Dave was a good boy. But he'd drunk a lot tonight, and if you were in that state and a beautiful girl like Esther threw herself at you, then who knew what might happen? 'That really is an amazing dress, Esther,' she said.

'I didn't know I wasn't supposed to . . . I'd never noticed . . . You *know* I don't notice clothes.'

'It wasn't a criticism. It's an amazing dress is all I'm saying.'

'Did you have it made specially?' said Dave, as if Bond Street might have been selling nothing but brown dresses with numbers on the back these days. Aisling gave him a pitying pat on the knee and shook her head, and left her hand there, not like a girlfriend, palm down, but just as a place for it to rest, with the bottom edge and a couple of fingertips touching. Dave said, 'The number. I meant the number. Did you find the dress and have that put on?' but he obviously hadn't meant this and was just backing out of a corner.

Esther couldn't stop her eyes flicking down at Aisling's hand, which Aisling coolly didn't register. Esther couldn't have stated more publicly that she was with Tom.

Third Eye was a bit too popular these days, so the players decamped to Hell's Bells. It wasn't a black-tie kind of place, but they didn't turn away the Socialists.

Jackets in the cloakroom, ties in pockets, sleeves rolled up, sweat pouring, the players lost themselves in little clumps, pairing off with their dates if things were going well, casting around the crowd, just in case, if not. Without being pointed, it was hard for Dave to stop Esther grinding against him as she pretended to dance with Tom. He took a drinks break, and he and Aisling talked about how Tom would actually be really good for Esther, and they joked about how clumsily Esther seemed to dance when Dave was around, and how short-sighted Tom seemed to be. Dave started to realise that Esther's quiet reserve about Aisling, which he'd always taken as quite significant, was a creature of Esther's own insecurity, and actually Aisling was a great girl who was trying to do what was best for her sister, and it was hardly a crime not to be obsessed with football.

He and Aisling danced together until Achilles interposed himself and started partnering her for a bit. Dave understood straight away, and he was pissed off with Achilles for thinking that there might be anything in what he was doing. He was careful to give Aisling space after that, and she wasn't short of attention. She danced with a couple of other guys, but nothing came of it. He was jealous, but only in that way every man is always jealous, not really.

Dirk had found some crazy Dutch liqueur, gathered the playing squad and ordered twenty shots. The girlfriends were bonding over to one side, rolling their eyes at being excluded from all this testosterone crap. Only eighteen players could be located, and Aisling found herself stepping forward, saying that she'd uphold the honour of the girls. After that, it was natural that Esther was coerced into taking the final shot, especially since everyone was so keen for her to be relaxed tonight. Aisling hadn't planned that, but she was pleased. While throats were still burning, Torquil unveiled another tray of twenty shots, this time whisky. He was a dark horse, was Torquil, and, if you'd heard him sing (but not talk, which he did very, very slowly), then he was the most attractive man in the room. Aisling raised her glass to the girls with a pleased grimace of no-surrender defiance, and they clapped her. Esther copied; she had no option but the brave face, and you had to know Esther very well to see the reluctance. Tom put his arm around her, and everyone thought, 'Aaah.' That was the end of the organised drinking, and an evening which hadn't needed a kick-start went into overdrive, or, in some cases, decline. Either way, everyone in the room started to focus on their own objectives, exit strategies and options in the endgame.

Aisling whispered to Dave, and they headed on to the dance floor, beckoning Tom and Esther. As soon as they had all settled, just after the next song had begun, Aisling and Dave whipped off to the bar, and watched, naughtily pleased with themselves. Tom understood, and he put his hands on Esther's waist. Esther was by no means a nun, but she was a novice when it came to any kind of subtlety, and she was trying too hard to look blissful. Whenever she caught sight of Dave in the distance, through the crowd, she rested her cheek against Tom's ear. *She made her own bed*, Aisling thought to herself.

She was impressed at how sensitive Dave was to the situation, actually, and what good company he'd been, and she regretted never having given him much thought before, simply because he wasn't good-looking. That wasn't the main thing about tonight anyway. It was always nice to find someone you could understand without words, and she knew that Dave had enjoyed it too, as if it wasn't something he was used to, and she was pleased, because being more than a pretty face was one of her things. That's why she was so annoyed by Donald, for instance, and Dave really seemed to get that.

She saw Dave glance at his watch and look around. He probably thought it was time to go. There wasn't much fun dancing left, and there was no point waiting for things to wind down. Over by the bar there was a guy she'd chatted with earlier and who she'd danced with enough to make sure he'd hang around. He was talking with a friend but keeping one eye on her. He was cute, but it wouldn't be sensible, she thought. It was probably time she grew out of that; she didn't want to look like a slapper. Even though she'd taken tomorrow off, it would actually be nicer to have a proper night's sleep, and if Dave was going they could share a cab to East Kilburn via hers, and they could dissect the party – he was almost as bitchy as Achilles, who she realised she'd hardly spoken to all night. It would be a nice end to the evening. Pretending she hadn't seen him check his watch, in case he got the wrong impression, she said that she was sorry to be so soft, but it was her bedtime, and thank you for a lovely evening.

'Me too, actually, I was just . . . Do you want to share?'

'Yeah, sure. My coat's in the cloakroom,' she said. 'You get the taxi and I'll see you outside.' This was perfect, because there was at least a chance Esther wouldn't notice them leaving together, not that there was anything to be furtive about.

Plenty of cabs passed by – perversely, since most Saturday nights you couldn't find one for love nor money – but Dave didn't hail any of them. As soon as he got outside, he decided he didn't want a cabby misinterpreting a shared trip, so he called Diabolo and they said fifteen minutes. Luckily, the queue seemed to be taking Aisling an age.

When she emerged, he noticed how impeccable she still looked. He was drenched in sweat and his hair was lank against his neck, but she looked as perfect as she had all night. She raised incredulous eyebrows at his uselessness, saw an approaching taxi light and set off towards it. He grabbed her hand, and said, 'Sorry – that's the first one that's been past. I gave up and called Diabolo. They'll be here in five minutes.'

'It's fucking cold,' she said. He put his arm round her, and she put her arm round him back, accidentally riding it up under his jacket so her warm hand was against his left side, where it had a tentative moment, but stayed. It would have been too awkward to move it away then, he understood. It would have acknowledged something that wasn't there.

Achilles' cab eschewed the fastest route home in favour of the most direct one, following the path a walking man might choose. In the cab, eyes devouring both sides of every road and alley, Achilles and the driver he'd charmed were looking for Zondi. The little man was probably home already, but this was a game they played, and Achilles sometimes caught up. Almost all of Achilles' mind was on his boyfriend, but he worried about Dave as well, because Dave was growing erratic, and starting to act without full regard for the consequences. This was apparent on the pitch and it was apparent in his life, and the recklessness had begun to make Achilles uneasy to a degree that was out of all rational proportion.

John Brown sat on the bench on Primrose Hill, seemingly at peace, but, as he always was now, hiding the pain, even when there was no one to see. He was on the bench because he knew he wouldn't be able to sleep.

Tom and Esther were in an alley, kissing like teenagers. Esther realised in the club that she'd miscalculated, and the die was cast. She told herself that Tom had probably asked a dozen girls before he got round to her, but then she had worn this stupid dress and sent him the wrong signals, so now he thought she was keen, and he was probably doing this only out of kindness, so now here she was. Whenever this happened to Esther, when she accidentally got too deep in to go back, she thought to herself how people would be surprised if they ever knew that she wasn't such a quiet little church mouse as they thought! When Aisling had followed Dave out of the club, although Esther knew in her heart that Dave would be able to resist Aisling, she pressed deeper into Tom to stop herself thinking about it, and he responded. Now it was inevitable, she abandoned herself to it.

Tom had a good idea of what to expect – everyone knew what Esther was like when she was drunk – and he'd have been lying if he said that wasn't part of the attraction. But it was only part. Tom doted on Esther, and since he'd made this clear a year ago, she'd been off-limits for the others. The various players she'd pounced on over the years were under no illusions that they meant anything to her. She'd never given any sign of actually liking one of them at any point before the drunken, last moments of an evening, and that was what was different about tonight. The players, including Tom, took her dress as a sign she was over Dave at last and ready to move on.

Dave and Aisling laughed all the way home, and when Aisling asked what he thought would happen between Tom and Esther, and he raised his eyebrow, she dissolved in giggles against his shoulder, clutching his arm and bringing her knees up almost on to the seat. 'He likes her, though, doesn't he?' she said.

'He really does. He'll treat her well, too, if she lets him.'

'She deserves it,' said Aisling. 'She's a good person.'

All evening, every time he'd been away from her, or she'd been to the toilet, Aisling had reglossed her lips, which was a funny thing for Dave to have noticed. Maybe it was just something she always did, but she'd done it again before coming out of the club, when the only person she was possibly going to see again was him. Even if it was only because she was drunk, he should be careful. She stayed leaning against him, and he thought less of her for it. Maybe she was one of those people he'd never been able to understand, who were turned on by what they couldn't have. It was a disappointing end to the evening, because they seemed so in tune, more in tune, it seemed to him at this moment, than he could remember having been with anybody. He mustn't be harsh, though, because it was probably just the drink.

He was surprised, though. Esther always went on about her sister flirting, but Aisling had never, so far as Dave knew, done anything with any of the players, so maybe it was just that she was relaxed with him because there was no sexual component, the way she was with Achilles, with whom, he had to admit, she was always very tactile.

How did we get to here? thought Aisling, feeling a fool for having had her stupid private rule about footballers for all this time, because Dave was the most interesting man she'd been out with in an age. Not that anything was going to happen. She'd been leaning against him for five minutes, and he'd been tensed away from her the whole time, which was embarrassing, but now she couldn't move without it being pointed. It wasn't as if anything was ever going to happen, though, and she wasn't seriously hoping it would. She wanted to say something, find safe ground. 'Do you think Tom really has a chance?' she asked. 'In the long run.'

'Esther took a risk tonight,' said Dave.

'So?'

'That's a good thing,' said Dave, as if it were self-evident. 'If you're taking risks, there's no danger of getting stuck in a rut.'

'She *has* been in a rut.'

'Yes. Esther made a decision about me when she was very young, and then she stopped looking. You either stop looking and pretend you've found the one almost immediately, or you keep taking risks until you find the one . . .'

'You know she's still besotted with you.'

'But she's taking risks.'

'It must be amazing to know what you're looking for.'

'Yes. Of course. But even if you're not sure, then you still have to give things a proper chance because nothing's ever going to be perfect. And also . . . I don't know.' He shifted, and he was not tensed away from her now. 'People always say it's better to regret doing things than regret not doing them. Whatever . . . I'm speaking bollocks.' Was this all code? If anything was ever going to happen between them, it had to happen tonight, certainly. How often could you both legitimately pretend to be weak? She moved her shoulder under his slightly, and Dave, finding his arm nearly trapped, put it across the back of her neck.

He's flirted with me as much as I've flirted with him, Aisling told herself. That didn't mean she should jump on Dave, but maybe this was what he was trying to say behind all this crapping on about risk? He was the one with the girlfriend, so whatever happened was his responsibility. She'd done nothing that she wouldn't have done with Achilles; so far, she'd been very careful, but now the moment was coming, and she wasn't ready to finish the evening yet. She had to give him a hint, so that he knew what she thought, so he could make his decision, whatever it was going to be. 'It's true about regretting the things you don't do,' she said, 'and you're lovely,' and she leaned up and kissed him as if she had aimed for his cheek and just brushed the edge of his mouth, squeezed his hand, and sat back on her side of the car, to make it clear that she wasn't like her sister. She wouldn't do anything embarrassing, but she was there if he wanted to take the risk, which he would only do if things were going badly with Sally already, so it wasn't as if anyone would be hurt in the long run.

The Diabolo pulled up outside Aisling's house, and Dave walked her to her door because he would have for anyone else. 'It was a great evening,' he said. 'I really enjoyed it.' He kissed Aisling on both cheeks, right hand awkwardly grazing her side, and as he hesitated before stepping away, he saw she couldn't really believe he was going. He smiled and turned.

'Stop!' Aisling said. 'Close your eyes.'

He knew he shouldn't, but how often does a beautiful girl ask you to close your eyes? It's not as if anything would happen that he couldn't control. He thought several things in the tipsy, irresponsible flash of time it took him to close his eyes, and none of them did him credit.

'Don't open them till I say,' she said. She did something that he could hear but not quite put a finger on, and then there was a silence, and he was tempted to open his eyes. The wind was in the trees, and he thought he heard her move around him, but he couldn't be sure. Then he heard the cab leaving. That was clever. He heard her now as she ran barefoot back to him – her feet must be freezing – and she giggled as her hand took his, said 'Okay,' and dragged him to the door.

Nice try, and it was satisfying to know for certain, but he stopped without putting his foot on the porch step. 'I'm sorry,' he said, and shrugged, and she looked down and shook her head to clear it of this impulsive madness. No, she said, it was she who was sorry. Her hands found his, and she looked at him to make him admit what would have happened if things had been different. Then she gave a rueful smile, shrugged and opened her arms for a consolatory hug. The side of Dave's jaw rested against the top of her head, not in any way that could be preparatory to a kiss, and they were both careful to keep it that way, but Aisling's coat was open, and Dave could feel her heartbeat and hot breath. He knew nothing was going to come of it, but here was the most beautiful girl he'd ever met, whom he'd always avoided speaking to so no one could accuse him of fancying her, and he felt a bit stupid about that. She was fun as well, more fun than she was beautiful, even, and nothing like her sister had made her seem. He regretted that things weren't different, because he'd never met anyone who so instantly ticked his boxes, but it was what it was. Still, in acknowledgement, he would hold her until she was ready to let him go.

But there is nothing ever simple about holding a beautiful girl. It's not that biology is destiny, but after a time, the action takes on its own momentum, and as she felt him, Aisling moved her hips away and chuckled, and pressed into him again, carefully, so as not to press into him, but with her arms inside his jacket this time, and he felt more tolerant and moved his head gently back and forth, letting her hair brush against his cheek, and then he kissed the top of her head, and she kissed his shirt. 'It's just one of those things,' he said, and she nodded into his chest, and hugged him tighter. 'I'd better go.' But he didn't. He just kissed the top of her head again, leaving leaving up to her, and she moved slightly so she felt him again, and this time she didn't shift away, and one finger was inside the waistband of his trousers.

Dave stopped and gathered himself. This wasn't going to stop without him stopping it. He felt he had to acknowledge the situation honestly, so he started, 'You know I would stay . . .' She nodded. 'But,' he said. 'Just, "but".' Dave stepped away from her, and smiled down. 'You know I'd stay,' he said again.

'Please come inside,' she said. She'd made herself vulnerable, and he'd led her on, and she was shivering. 'I was drunk. This will never happen again. I'm really sorry. Come inside and call a cab. It's freezing.' As soon as they were inside, in the warm, her arm was around his neck and she was kissing him, thigh between his legs, and he was kissing her back.

This was a very important night in the history of the Socialists' Christmas Party, John Brown knew. That was why he was sitting on his bench, filled with regret. The magazine article was not to blame but was rather the signal that the Party was stuck in its own tropes like a fly in amber. It might struggle for a while, and a future investigation might be able to extract the DNA, but it was dying.

LATE

When Aisling was late, she assumed it was stress, though she wasn't more stressed than usual. Then she feared cancer, but everyone always fears cancer. Or it could have been a hormonal disorder. Perhaps it was because she was a doctor and she knew all the alternative possibilities, but the truth dawned absurdly slowly. Dave had used a condom, and she'd been on the Pill. Moreover, she'd put Dave so vigorously out of her mind since the Christmas Party, and she was so busy, that while it was stupidly obvious when she realised, realisation really did take a couple of days. She would have an abortion, of course. There was no one she could turn to for reassurance, but she was an adult. She knew her own mind, and it was the sensible thing.

When she'd woken after the party, Dave was looking at her. He hadn't slept. He said it was all a terrible mistake, and he'd beaten his breast, but behind that he was angry with her. He'd agonised, to her face, at length, to no end she could understand, that he'd never been unfaithful in his life before, and about how he now understood, more than ever, that he truly loved Sally. Nothing like this had ever happened to Aisling before. She assumed that if Dave stayed the night, then that meant she would be free to make up her mind, in the cold light of day, whether she really liked him or whether it was just the drink. She decided later that it must have been the guilt that made him speak like that, so she phoned and asked him out for a drink to discuss things. He said there was nothing to discuss, he'd made a massive mistake, he was really sorry, and what was there to be gained by going over it? He was so precious about keeping his distance that he surely couldn't blame her for taking him at his word now she'd found out she was pregnant. He had explicitly asked her to stay away from him, so she'd phone Sally instead.

Sally was surprised at the call, but Aisling said it was important they meet. They ordered coffee and sat with wary politeness, both looking fabulously understated.

'I slept with Dave after the party.'

'I know.'

'Was it obvious?'

'He told me.'

It was mid-afternoon, but the sales were on, and the café was full. They were in enough of a corner to know they couldn't be heard, so long as they spoke quietly. Sally had a very clear idea of what Aisling was like. She was forewarned, forearmed and determined not to rise to the bait.

'Is that it?' said Sally.

'Why did he tell you?'

'It's a thing called honesty, Aisling. It's very important.'

'How come you're still . . . ?'

'I never expected anything to be perfect, but if you're honest, then you can work things out. It's the secrets that kill you.' Sally was proud of what had happened, actually. She told Dave at the outset that, if he was serious about the relationship, the one thing she would never forgive was dishonesty, and that meant not just telling no lies. It also meant telling the whole truth, all the time. That was the centrepiece of emotional maturity, which was something he'd obviously neglected in his life, and it was her mission to put that right. Sally believed it was impossible to make the wrong decision if you were aware of all the facts. Dave's night with Aisling nearly ended the relationship all the same – Sally was not a natural victim, or without pride – but he had told her immediately, and the boil was lanced.

'I'm pregnant,' Aisling said. Sally felt her mask drop.

'But Dave said he wore —'

'He did, don't worry, I made him.'

'But then —'

'It didn't split, but there's not been anyone else. It's just one of those things,' said Aisling, looking for all the world as if she was discussing the strength of her coffee.

'When did you find out? It can't have been —'

'Yesterday.'

'So when did you tell —'

'Dave doesn't know.' Sally exhaled with relief that Dave hadn't kept this from her. 'Don't worry,' Aisling said. 'I'm going to have an abortion.'

'Don't worry?'

'I just meant —'

'Dave doesn't get a say?'

'It's not that. It's —'

Sally leapt at the chance to be righteously indignant. 'So why am I here, if you've already decided?'

'You have a right to know.'

'What's it to do with me? *Dave* has a right to know, and even then he has no choice, apparently, so what's the point in saying all this? It can only possibly upset me. I'm not stupid, Ash. This is just revenge. You're behaving like a spoilt child.' Sally forced herself to take a controlled sip. She was right, but that didn't change the fundamental situation. She didn't know what to do.

'Honesty is important,' Aisling said.

'Fuck off. This is different.' Sally stopped. She felt bad. 'I'm sorry, Aisling. Are you okay?'

'I'm perfectly fine.' Sally could see that this wasn't emotional honesty, and she put her hand on Aisling's. 'This was a mistake,' Aisling said, pointedly moving her hand. 'I should never have said anything. I never will again, don't worry.'

'If you need someone to talk to —'

'Fuck off.'

Sally was left alone. She sat for an hour, thinking and signing napkins for people. She and Aisling – and Dave, no doubt – were modern young people who believed that abortion was terrible and unfortunate, but the right thing in certain circumstances. It would be wrong to assume that, in and of itself, it would ruin Aisling's life, and she fervently hoped it wouldn't. This was something that no one could do anything about. It was not the same as a one-night stand which might possibly turn into an affair. Sally decided that every rule has exceptions, and that the emotionally mature path, in this particular case, was not to tell Dave.

Sally did, however, tell Monica, who told Calum Horton. Monica knew she shouldn't have, but she was crazy about the reporter, even though he told her repeatedly that there was no future in the relationship. He was even seeing someone else, who was 'proper girlfriend material', but he slept with Monica all the same. Monica claimed defensively that she was using him for sex, and she didn't care.

'So she's pregnant,' said Calum. 'So what? Why are you telling me?

I don't give a shit about gossip, and celebrity, and all that pathetic stuff you find so interesting.' Every time she tried to connect with him, Calum made her feel stupid. He said he hated gossip, but then he always wanted to know about her famous friends. And, whatever he said, the story of Dave, Aisling and the abortion appeared in the *Clarion's* gossip column three days later.

Sally knew immediately that it must have been Monica. Monica blustered that she'd done it in the cause of truth and openness, but Sally said that Monica had done it out of spite at Dave and said how awful this must be for Aisling, who was the real victim, and Monica felt like a fool, as usual, even if she hid it, as usual. 'I'm frightened of how Dave is going to react,' said Sally. 'I should have told him what Aisling said.'

'He's the one who cheated on you!'

'I know, but he was honest about it afterwards. I told him we had to be honest, and now I've kept this from him. I didn't trust him.'

Sally insisted that Monica stay in the room when she talked to Dave. Monica's relationship with Calum was part of the story. She insisted on openness. As Sally explained to a silent Dave, Monica focused on the thin rain blowing in waves against the window. When Dave eventually spoke, he told Sally that he completely understood why she'd said nothing to him, and he didn't blame Monica either. Instead, and the change of tone was sudden, he went ballistic about Calum. He said the journalist was a lying, wheedling fucker who should be ashamed of himself for using Monica, but who wouldn't be because he didn't know what shame was. Almost instantly, Dave had a plan for revenge. 'Calum's seeing someone else, isn't he?' he said.

'Yes,' muttered Monica.

'Is the other girl his girlfriend? Is that what she —'

'That's what he calls her.'

'He's such a fuckwit,' said Dave.

'He's not so . . .' started Monica. 'Yes, he's a fuckwit.' That's exactly what Calum was, and that's how she had to think about him in the future. She wasn't someone you could cross and get away with it. She was a fucking superstar.

'I'm sorry you've been dragged into this, Mon. We probably should let it lie, but —'

'We definitely should let it lie,' said Sensible Sally.

'But what?' said Monica.

Dave's plan depended on Monica completely and it was a horrible thing to do, but if she slept with Calum once more ('It's not *that* horrible, mate!' said Monica), and was photographed leaving his house, Dave and Monica could write their own gossip piece about Calum being a love rat, and . . .

'That's fucking great!' said Monica.

'It's Man Bites Dog,' said Dave.

'It's crazy, crazy people,' said Sally. 'Calum's not news.'

'I'm writing it. That'll make it news,' said Dave. 'Especially if Monica's involved. If he wants to preach, he's got to be held to the same standard – that's the story. I'm sick of gossip, and —'

'Yes, but —'

'It's brilliant, Sal,' said Monica. 'It shows the fucker what it's like. I could . . .'

Sally listened while Monica and Dave formulated their elaborate sting. Calum deserved it, his 'girlfriend' would be better off for having found out and, on many levels, Sally loved the idea. It was unnecessary, though, and the first thing anyone learned about the media is that you keep your head in the trench, and don't piss anyone off. She insisted on this while the others enjoyed their plotting, and she gradually won them round. By the time Monica was ready to leave, Dave was saying, 'I know, Sal, I agree. I just wish we were allowed to get our own back on the fuckers.'

'Yes,' said Sally. She might have gone along with Dave's plan, if he had insisted.

'Monica,' said Dave. 'This is still it for you and Calum, though, isn't it? He's such a fucker.'

'Yes,' said Monica, and left the room, Sally following. 'Dave's the real thing, whatever I said before,' Monica said to Sally as she left. 'He actually listens to you.'

'He didn't used to,' said Sally.

'That's good, then,' said Monica.

Sally nodded.

Furtively, Dave called in a couple of favours. Two days later, he 'bumped into' Calum and his girlfriend in a pale-green bar in Islington. 'Hi, Cal,' he said.

'Dave,' said Calum warily. 'This is Kat.'

'Your sister, I presume.'

'No, she's —'

'How's it going with Monica? I saw her last week, and she said it was going well. She said she's not sure she can trust you, and that's half the appeal. How do you get away with the bad-boy thing? I've never been able to do it, it makes me feel sick. Oh, that's my phone, I've got to go. Good to see you. Great to meet you, Kat, see you around.' By the time Dave reached the street, his pleasure was almost totally replaced by wishing he'd listened to Sally. This was a last hurrah for the old Dave, he told himself. He was growing up, however slowly.

AS FOR KSC . . .

Over Christmas and into the New Year, the Socialists played fluffy, directionless football. They were fifteen points behind Cardiff in the Premiership, they'd been knocked out of the League Cup by Darlington and the European Cup by Oranjeboom, and the only silverware on offer was the FA Cup, where they faced a youthful Clapham Rovers in the fourth round. Mr Brown was showing signs of frailty. Even his veterans, who worshipped him, feared his time had come. Instead of being focused on whatever was holding the team back, he spent his time explaining things lengthily to Achilles.

It was an odd time for Achilles. He was very close to Mr Brown, but he was uncomfortable with the old man's sudden need to discuss his methods. Achilles had previously thought that KSC's greatest strength was the stability Mr Brown provided, but the manager put him right. Mr Brown described how each season differed from its predecessor. Take now, for instance: Will Laird seemed like a straight replacement for Lenny Blue at centre forward, but if you looked closer, you saw why his arrival had seen Seung take over from Carlo Derkin as the regular starter at left back. Seung naturally hit his crosses early and on a diagonal that worked well with Will's runs to the far post, whereas Carlo's hanging crosses had been more suited to Lenny's direct approach. When Mr Brown bought Will, it wasn't simply because he was one of the best strikers in Europe, but because Mr Brown wasn't getting the most out of Seung, and he wanted to play Seung because Carlo's other most natural passes – the cut-back to an advancing left-sided midfielder and the one-two from deep – didn't suit how Will Beauchamp played inside him. Fitting a team together is all about strengths and weaknesses, learning and time. The only people Mr Brown had discussed this with were Seung, who had grown dispirited about his excellent crossing, and Carlo, who needed to be aware that his particular strengths were the wrong ones for this team at this time, but he was young and versatile, and he'd still get plenty of pitch-time. Before this conversation, Achilles had put Seung's surging confidence down to his having had an extended run in the side.

Mr Brown also discussed players and how he found them. He told Achilles that he never purchased a player unless he knew what he was like as a man. Mr Brown had made mistakes there, but the Socialists were a happy team, weren't they? Achilles nodded, surprised at the question.

Achilles, as a direct result of these conversations, grew frustrated with how the Socialists were playing. It seemed perverse that Mr Brown wasn't shaking things up. On 15 January, they drew with a toothless Peterborough United, who played with bustle, endeavour and not a lot else, swamping the midfield, flying in for tackles and hacking the ball upfield at a lone, tall target man. The KSC of last year would have sliced through Peterborough, but this year they couldn't even keep possession. Clapham next week would have all Peterborough's energy and more talent, and it seemed as if Mr Brown was too tired to make alterations. In the end, on the Thursday, after another long post-training explanation that KSC was both like and unlike other clubs, that it must maintain its mystique but never forget that it played the same game as everybody else, Achilles asked him why he wasn't doing anything about Saturday. Didn't he think the midfield was going to be overrun again? Mr Brown smiled at him. 'You think we should change our shape to suit an opposition that isn't fit to lace our boots?' he asked.

'It's the Cup, Mr Brown. We're playing badly, and they're not a bad side.'

'You think we should change our shape to suit an opposition that isn't fit to lace our boots?' Mr Brown repeated.

'Yes. No. They are fit to lace our boots.' Mr Brown never talked about opponents like this. 'Is this a test?'

Mr Brown smiled again. 'If we play to our potential, Achilles, they cannot beat us.'

'But we are not playing like that. Maybe we need to play conservatively, ensure we keep the ball, just for now, so that —'

'We'll have it your way,' said Mr Brown, and turned. Achilles thought this meant he was hurt.

'No. That's not what I meant. I was just asking —'

'We'll play five in midfield.'

The Socialists beat Clapham, 1–0. It wasn't pretty, but sometimes that is how it has to be. Rovers' manager, James Purnell, a fearless, eager young man, wrote in an awestruck newspaper column that he'd been given a tactical masterclass by the old fox, but don't worry, he'd be back.

Achilles, meanwhile, was uncomfortable. Mr Brown said many times that a team, especially one as opinionated as KSC, must listen to one strong voice or it would disintegrate. Achilles feared what it meant for Mr Brown that he had let him take the lead, and he hoped the manager would be prepared to leave gracefully, when the time came, if he really had lost his heart for it. But this was in private. In public, Achilles was Mr Brown's staunchest defender. Some of the young players, less sunk in KSC's mythos, began to blame the old man, but Dave and Achilles pointed out that there had been other unsuccessful seasons – no club gets it right every year – and Mr Brown had always brought the Socialists back.

Will Beauchamp was every bit as keen as Achilles to change to five in midfield. He didn't have the manager's ear, though, so all he ever said, always quietly, and usually only to one person at a time, was that the Socialists weren't playing to their potential, and wasn't it frustrating? He pretended to find it inexplicable, but Beauchamp was British football's coming man, and seeds of doubt were sown.

The Socialists went on a winning run of four games. Cardiff slipped up against Clapham and Peterborough. The Socialists easily beat second-division London Arsenal in a romantic but boring fifth-round FA Cup tie. All of a sudden, the season looked less bleak, and Cardiff, Bristol United and York (York who perennially struggled against relegation – what the hell was happening there!) were all looking nervously over their shoulders. KSC weren't playing prettily, but they had recovered their fire. They closed games down, ruthlessly aware of each other and half a yard keener than anyone they played. They didn't make many chances, which was unusual for them, but as they said to each other in the showers afterwards, you don't need many chances when you've got Tom and Will up front. Achilles knew they were playing on the hoof. They were using native wit and memory in the absence of a strong guiding hand, and while they might laugh about making so few scoring opportunities, KSC was not supposed to play like this, even in adversity. Some clubs have a defensive mindset, and so they purchase players that suit that mindset. KSC under Mr Brown bought a very different kind of player, and there was only so long they could grind away in this negative mode before the mistakes crept back in, before individuals started reverting to their natural style. This was not a criticism. Players have natural styles, and ultimately, if you want another style, you need another player.

It was a frightening morning for Dave Guinevere when he noticed that he didn't care who won a five-a-side training game. It's not that he wasn't playing as hard as he could, or that he didn't want to win, but he realised he was treating the game as training, and that who won was, in and of itself, unimportant. Maybe he had felt like this for a while, but this was the first time he'd been aware of it. He tried to increase his commitment, but it was not something he'd ever needed to force; it felt strange, and he repeatedly held on to the ball too long. The coach shouted, 'Quick passing!' as if Dave didn't know.

The emptiness in his future that he had begun to sense before he met Sally was partly filled by her now, but it still seemed mostly void. Some day soon, Dave needed to decide if he really was going to slip quietly into academe, or if he'd do as all the pundits predicted and become a manager. At the end of the session, these thoughts crowding him loudly, he saw Mr Brown draw Achilles aside, as per usual. It irritated Dave, which was unworthy, but Dave was the captain and he should be the manager's first point of contact. He joined them to hear Achilles say, 'We must go back to 4-4-2, no? This is wrong for us, except because it was an emergency, but that's past, no?'

'What do you think, Dave?' asked Mr Brown.

'It's not broken,' said Dave. 'We're stifling everyone we play —'

'We're stifling ourselves, *querido*. 4-5-1 was for emergency, but —'

'It's not perfect,' replied Dave. 'And we all know you get less space to show off, but we've settled into it now. Things don't have to be exciting to work.'

'This is not about me showing off,' said Achilles. 'It will stop working because it's not natural for us. We must be more than *durable*. I know this,' said Achilles.

Dave said nothing, partly because he was embarrassed at himself, but also because he didn't want to leave Achilles alone with Mr Brown.

Eventually, Achilles walked away. Dave was worried that Mr Brown hadn't given his opinion. 'Are you all right, Mr Brown?' he asked.

'Don't worry about me.' The old man looked like an old man. 'Sally is a good woman, Dave. You shouldn't . . .' He stopped, staring over Dave's shoulder. Mr Brown never discussed anything personal, and this was another sign that he was weary, that he'd had enough. 'I'm sorry, it's your business. I know you will understand when the time comes, but for now you must trust Achilles.'

Dave had never heard Mr Brown say anything so fumbling and imprecise. Or maybe it was simply that as Dave grew distanced from football, he saw Mr Brown more clearly. The thought depressed him, because he wasn't ready to retreat from the game just yet. As he showered and changed, he decided that maybe there came a time for everyone where the commitment stopped being natural, where it became something you concentrated on because you valued it. Commitment *was* something you had to concentrate on sometimes, which didn't make it any less real.

The next day, Mr Brown explained that it was time for the Socialists to go back to 4-4-2, and Dave glanced at Achilles, who glanced back at Dave, and that was when Dave knew there was a wedge between them. He said this to Sally later, and added, 'I'm worried about Mr Brown.'

Sally poured him half a glass of wine, and he watched the soft interplay of muscles on her forearm, astonished that someone so straightforward could want to be with him. 'If he doesn't retire, what can you do?' she asked.

'I don't know. I'm not saying he should retire, it's just . . . I've never seen him like this. I wish I knew what it was. Maybe he's told Achilles.'

'Achilles is your friend, remember that. He would have told you.'

'Yes, of course. I'm sure he would. But . . .' Dave shook his head.

'He's your best friend, dearie. He must be as worried about Mr Brown as you are. You have to talk about it with him, sort it out.' When she said it like that, it was obvious.

'Are you worried about Mr Brown?' Dave asked.

'Yes. The old darling says he's definitely going to be here in August.'

'I always assumed he'd know when to go.'

'They can't sack him.'

'I'm sorry about the last few months.'

'I'm sorry too, old boy.'

'I don't know why I've been annoyed.'

'You've been jealous that he's confided in me.'

Achilles was testing him, because Achilles always tested everything. Before Sally, Dave would have told him to fuck off, but he bit his tongue and said, 'Yes. I'm sorry. What does he talk to you about?'

'Little things, old boy, the same little things as always over the years, just more of them. He is tired, I think, is all it is. He needs a rest. Maybe we must give it to him – take some strain.'

'So what should we do, then?'

'I don't know. I think we should talk, we and Zondi, and think what to do next year if everything is like this. How we can make it seem as if there is just one voice. That is the problem this year, no?' Dave took this as a direct criticism, but he didn't rise to it. He said that Achilles' plan sounded fine, and joked that Achilles and Zondi would be able to outvote him any time they wanted.

The season fizzled and died. Kilburn lost to Everton in the quarter-finals of the Cup, and finished third in the league. Dave spent more time with Sally and less with his teammates, and he finally finished his book on inner-city urban planning, which he should have done the previous summer. When he was playing and training, he was completely committed, but football was never meant to be his whole life, and he was getting better at compartmentalising. He saw how he could enjoy the next few years at Kilburn, and maybe he would play on somewhere else for a couple of seasons, but the end was coming, and for the first time he felt it in his bones as well as knowing it in his head. He was pleased that Aisling was taking KSC more seriously as a business, and he thought that this friend of hers, Adam Greswell, whom she had brought in to help with the Rosslare Group, sounded like he knew what he was doing. Dave also understood that the future of Kilburn would be hers, and maybe Achilles', but it wouldn't be his.

He gathered himself for the approaching World Cup, because he was still GB captain, and he wasn't done yet, whatever Achilles thought.

BACK TO BUSINESS

After the Christmas Party, when Aisling was in bed with Dave, before she went to sleep and got rudely awakened, Dave asked her, 'You're an SHO, and you run the Rosslare Group. How does that work?'

'It doesn't. I'm joking.' She wasn't that worried about the Group – Adam had told her that Donald's plans were a mistake, but that there should be no problem for the Group if it was prepared to be realistic about Rosslare Rolling Stock. It was not an ideal situation, and her concern must have shown because Dave asked her if anything was wrong with the business. 'No, not really. I mean, well, Donald's being a dick.' She wasn't so unguarded that she told Dave about Donald's plans to move KSC out of London. 'I've got friends looking into it. They'll tell me what to say to the Committee. I'm sure it's nothing.'

'The Committee is extremely bijou, isn't it?'

'I know,' she said. 'It was fine before, but that was because Dad ran everything and he didn't have time to debate stuff. When he died, I knew I should sort it out but I didn't know who to get, and there was so much else to do, and Dad trusted Don enough to put him on the Committee, so . . . I mean, the Group's been doing fine. All the bits are still being run by Dad's people.'

'You have to get help eventually,' Dave said. 'You definitely don't want to do it yourself?' She shook her head. 'And you don't trust Donald?' She shook her head again, more reluctantly. 'You've got to get someone you know. You've got enough on your plate.' She didn't say that she was held back by the thought of upsetting Donald and Esther.

The next morning, after Dave's departing lecture, Aisling thought about this conversation again and she was torn between a desire to prove him wrong and the need to put her life in order.

A week later, before Adam had completed an alternative proposal for her to take to the Committee, the business pages began to carry leaked stories about possible restructuring and rationalisation at the Rosslare Group. These stories were disbelievingly re-reported by idiot sportswriters who couldn't get it into their heads that the Group was fundamental to the Socialists' existence. In the wake of this clumsy manoeuvring, Aisling decided that enough was enough. When Adam took her for dinner and explained that Donald wasn't an idiot, but confirmed that the Group's problems stemmed from his refusal to admit that Rosslare Rolling Stock, Donald's fiefdom under Manus, was no longer viable, Aisling informed Adam that she was appointing him to the Committee.

'I already have a job,' said Adam, nervously, but Aisling wouldn't take no for an answer. She said that he was so cautious about everything that he'd never get out of consultancy unless someone gave him a push, and that she was doing him a favour by opening this door, and that he should be grateful, basically. Her friend Nicky told her off for bullying Adam, which was rich coming from Nicky.

The business pages presented Adam as a business wunderkind with no personal axe to grind, and he was instrumental in coming up with an alternative to Donald's scheme for relocating KSC. The Group sold its rolling-stock plants to the Belgians. There was blood on the carpet, said the papers, and they praised Greswell's willingness to make tough decisions. It was sad for the sentimentalists, but Ross-Rolling was much better suited to jet engines, while the rolling-stock business would flourish under more focused ownership. The business pages were almost by-the-by in the way they added that the Kilburn Social Club had been saved from any threat of being sold to bail out the Group. The sportswriters didn't cover it, since they had never believed it was a realistic issue.

In February, a month after Aisling discovered she was pregnant, Adam finally plucked up the courage to visit Kilburn Park on a match day. She insisted on being there too, to show that she had weathered the storm. Standing in the broad hospitality room behind the private seats, full of people who understood what was happening down on the pitch, Adam felt profoundly uneasy. Still, this was something he had to do. When he was co-opted on to the Committee, Adam realised he needed to understand the Group *in toto*, and part of that was getting a grip on KSC. With that, and coming to Kilburn Park for Committee meetings, he had started to feel a connection with the Socialists, which he was embarrassed to admit, even to himself. There was something exciting about the place.

The Socialists were playing Dublin. Aisling explained that the game had a derby atmosphere, for historical reasons. In the seventies and eighties, when Irish nationalist terrorism and hooliganism were both at their heights, the crowd had been notoriously ugly. Today it was freezing outside, and drizzling, and steam rose heavily off the guests in the box as they crowded around the bar and buffet. Adam clung to the edge of the room while Aisling spoke to people she had to see because they were old friends. A middle-aged man with a very smooth, thin face and teeth that went all over the place approached him. 'Mr Greswell, I assume?' he said. Adam nodded. The man was surprisingly well spoken. 'Great to meet you, Mr Greswell, super. I'm Benjamin China, but everyone calls me Benjie. I'm the villain of the piece, ha ha. Super.' Benjie gave a big grin and held out his hand. He had a firm, trustworthy handshake. His suit was navy, and he had a pinstriped shirt that was flashy, but not exactly vulgar.

'I'm sorry,' said Adam, 'But —'

'I'm an agent, Mr Greswell! I represent several of the Dublin players, and a couple of yours, for my sins. Young Derkin, for instance. Super.'

'Oh,' said Adam.

'Oh indeed! Whenever anything goes wrong, it's always my fault.'

'I'm more involved in the business, not the football.'

'Football is a business, Adam – may I call you Adam? Super. That's why I'm here. Do you mind if I get straight to it?' he said, looking around. 'When someone sees you talking to the enemy, they'll get over here and break us up, you mark my words.'

'Okay.'

'I'm not a bad guy, Adam, I'm just doing my job, trying to gauge your mood music. Kilburn have been doing this whiter-than-white thing for years, and they've got away with it because footballers are criminally underpaid.'

'Are they really, though?'

'They are mate, trust me, trust me. Some of them are finally starting to get something like real money, but you wait till we finally have a free market, you'll see. And it's coming, mate. The real money from Panther's going to kick in, the Beckford ruling means players are free agents, the Champions League's going through the roof. At some point, someone at Kilburn is going to have to realise that you can't carry on like you are. You're going to have to deal with guys like me instead of treating us like . . . Hello, Miss Rosslare.'

'What has he been saying?' said Esther.

'Chewing the fat, Miss Rosslare.'

'Adam, agents hate us, because we don't pay them bribes for getting players like other clubs.'

'That's a very serious accusation, Miss Rosslare.'

'Adam doesn't do football decisions, Mr China. Goodbye.' Esther was flushed. Adam asked Esther if it was true, as he had heard, that managers routinely took backhanders over contracts. 'Some do,' said Esther. 'But never here. Never Mr Brown. We're different because people play for us for love.' That didn't sound very secure to Adam. He looked across at the fug of dignitaries braying at each other, and all the acolytes and hangers-on. Since getting dragged into this involvement with KSC, Adam's found it hard to credit how badly football clubs seemed to be run, and how underexploited they were financially. He had even, once or twice, wondered what he might do about it if he were someone with the time and inclination to move in that direction.

'It's another world,' said a tall, athletic man with very short dark hair and eyes so pale they seemed unreal. 'I'm Strabis Kinsale. Hello, Esther.'

'Adam Greswell.' It probably gave Kinsale a kick to introduce himself as if someone might not know who he was. He was one of the reasons Adam was brought into the Rosslare Group – Aisling's father once warned her about Kinsale, and she was paranoid that he planned to attack the Group. Adam couldn't see why he'd want to, but Aisling was sharp about people, and Strabis came to most home games as a guest of Donald, which was something worth keeping an eye on.

'Good time to be moving into football,' Kinsale confided, as if Esther weren't there. 'Panther money. Pay attention to the talk about a Euro Superleague too. That's where the billions are – a closed shop like in the States.'

'That couldn't happen here,' said Esther.

'I hope not,' purred Kinsale. 'Of course.'

The next meeting of the Committee took place three days after another feeble draw. Esther wanted to bring up the subject of Mr Brown. She decided, therefore, that it would be good to know what the players thought, and so she arranged to meet Tom for a chat. She saw Tom quite regularly, actually, and it wasn't her fault that she somehow always ended up being taken advantage of, because she was a quiet little creature who didn't know what she was doing and he was a celebrity footballer. When he had had his way with her again, she asked him what the players thought should be done about the Mr Brown situation. Amazingly, Tom was surprised. 'Don't you read the papers?' she asked.

'No.'

'Can't you see how badly we're playing? We're directionless.'

'Mr Brown will sort it out.'

'What does everyone else think?'

'They agree. Dave sometimes gets a bit high and mighty, which is funny when Will Beauchamp points it out, and he's bickering with Achilles over something, but they'll get over it.' The problem with Tom, Esther realised, was that he saw things but didn't understand. Dave was presumably not actually high and mighty, but he just understood there was a problem. That's what made Dave different to the rest.

So, at the Committee, Esther had no compunction about presenting what she interpreted as Dave's disquiet as if it were the team's consensus. 'Let's ask Mr Brown what he thinks,' said Aisling, who was in a bad mood as usual, saying she was overworked or something. Esther was sorry that Aisling had been publicly humiliated after the abortion, of course, but that was the result of her own choices about Dave, and her being tired was the result of her own choices about being a doctor instead of doing her duty, so there was only so much sympathy Esther could summon up. Asking Mr Brown about his own possible replacement was typically stupid of Aisling, thought Esther, because Mr Brown didn't want to go of his own accord. If the Committee weren't clever, Mr Brown might outwit them. The Committee needed a plan.

'Well,' said Donald, 'I suppose we have to take your word for it. You're the one with the ear of the players.'

Esther resented his insinuating tone. She'd *always* had the ear of the players, and it wasn't because one of them was seducing her. It was because she was devoted to the club, and to understanding every facet of what was going on. Frankly, she did have the right to speak for them, so Donald was right; it was his *tone* she didn't like. 'The players definitely think it's time,' she confirmed. 'Definitely.'

'What can we do?' asked Donald.

'We can't sack Mr Brown,' said Aisling, looking at Miss Skewbold for confirmation. Miss Skewbold didn't return the look, but Aisling reacted as if Miss Skewbold had nodded, because a nod was what Aisling was looking for.

Esther was furious. Now was not the time for an emotional wreck like Aisling to be making big decisions. Mr Brown had never let senti-mentality guide him. He was always ready to drop or sell a player for the sake of the team. He had been quoted many times in the past about the clean and simple ruthlessness of sport, and now, as pundits reviewed the season so far and wondered whether his time had come, these quotes were being cautiously thrown in his face. He'd lived by the sword.

'The fans will go nuts,' said Donald.

'The fans want us to win,' replied Esther. 'We must do what's best for the team.'

'It'll be expensive,' said Adam. When Aisling appointed Adam, Esther assumed he would be another Donald, but he'd been brilliant at Christmas, sorting everything out when it looked like the club might be moved, and Donald hated him for it. Esther understood, deep down, that Adam was only so generous with his time and expertise – he was being paid much less than he was worth, apparently – because he was wrapped round Aisling's fingers.

'Why should it be expensive? I didn't know you were a football expert,' said Donald.

'A new manager invariably brings in new players,' said Adam. 'On average, using the best available figures from the last five seasons, a new manager in this division costs his club nine million quid, straight off, and that's almost certainly an underestimate, because we're a top club wanting top players and because transfer fees are way ahead of where they were five years ago. Do we have that kind of money hanging around?'

'We sell as well as buy. It's obvious.'

'Other clubs know what's happening when you switch managers, Donald. They know you're desperate to change players, and that you're trying to offload because you need the cash. They get bargains. That's why it's called a *market*.' It was all very stags and antlers.

The events of this season had shaken Esther out of her reverie about money. She'd never had to worry about it herself, and this had given her the kind of blind spot she hated in Aisling. Well, no more. Will Beauchamp – and he was another one who understood things, actually, even if there was something creepy about him – discussed money with Esther recently. He brought up the fact that everyone was paid the same, and she thought for a horrified moment that he was going to suggest changing it, but he actually said, 'I love it. Everyone loves it, and not just the players. All of these press stories have mentioned it. Obviously I don't know, but it's always felt like we might be missing a trick. We have all these great things going for us: we are the most attractive product in the league, and we're the only one without sponsorship. That's cool too, obviously, but if things ever got tight financially, if we ever needed more money, I can't help thinking that there has to be some way, you know, in an emergency.'

Six months before, anyone talking of KSC as a product would have got a very strict telling off, but Will had, Esther realised wryly, coincidentally spoken to her just when she was most ready to listen. 'What about sponsorship?' she asked the Committee.

'We don't do that at KSC,' said Donald automatically, as if he thought Esther was testing him.

'This is the real world,' she said. 'If there's one thing we've learned this season, it's that KSC can't just be propped up by the Rosslare Group. It has to find other revenue streams. Isn't that right?' She looked at Adam, to whom she'd briefly mentioned this last week, just to see what he thought. Adam looked nervously at Aisling, who sat as if she was somehow above all this petty concern with position and pelf.

Adam began cautiously: 'There is a possible compromise.'

'Do go on,' said Donald. 'We sell Kerry & Cork Breweries and plate the pitch with gold?'

'Don't be a twat,' snapped Aisling.

'I don't know what the legal is on this, I haven't checked, but this is all a private company, so I don't see a problem. If KSC started, very discreetly, obviously, to carry out some ambassadorial role for the Rosslare Group – sponsorship isn't quite the word, and I don't think we want big logos everywhere, but we don't have any advertising in the ground, and I think we could do something quietly about that, and maybe something small on the shirt?'

'I don't like it,' said Aisling. Esther was pleased to see that she wasn't so confident these days, which meant something good had come out of the abortion.

'Very discreet, is the key,' said Adam. 'We would still be different from the other clubs, we wouldn't *lose* our uniqueness, we would *use* our uniqueness. All we'd be doing, subtly, would be pointing out the *link* between KSC, Kerry & Cork and Knight Soft Cloudware. This would give a business justification for the money that's spent on KSC.' Esther was impressed. It was just what Will Beauchamp had talked to her about.

'What do you think, Est?' asked Aisling.

'I think it makes sense. It integrates KSC into —'

'KSC is a fucking millstone,' said Donald, unable to contain himself. 'I can live with us accepting it's a fucking millstone, but to treat it as part of the business is crazy.'

'Football is going to start making some serious money,' said Adam, quietly. 'KSC has —'

'Because of Panther?' barked Donald. 'Satellite money's not new, Adam, and it hasn't changed anything. I've been involved in running this football club for ten years, and people are always saying the money's going to go crazy. There's a limit, mate. Some players at Azul Madrid are on fifteen grand a week!' Esther wanted to hear what Adam had to say about money.

Adam continued: 'The next telly deal will be huge, but that's not the only thing. Look at attendances. The four years since the World Cup, there've been full houses at the big clubs, and it's not going away; it's spreading, and clubs are charging more because it's middle-class cash now. Sponsorship's going to go through the roof too, but that's not what I'm saying. My point is exposure and what this does for the Group's other branches. KSC is the best brand in football, by a mile, and brewing and software are perfectly positioned to benefit. KSC might not make a lot of money, and we can't compete with Azul Madrid, but it could make the Rosslare Group a fortune in goodwill, if it's properly managed. He looked at Aisling again. 'I'm advising you as a consultant. This is what I'd say in any other business meeting. But what you do with KSC is up to you – there are family considerations that aren't any of my business.'

Esther saw that Aisling needed persuading. 'I don't like it any more than you do,' she said, 'but we've got to be positive. We can't do nothing.' Her sister had to listen, surely! Esther was the one who cared about KSC's heritage. If even *she* could see that the time had come for a change, then Aisling had to capitulate.

'Donald?' Aisling asked. Donald shook his head angrily. 'What's the problem with it?' Donald couldn't think of one. He obviously wished he'd thought of this first. Esther hated ego. 'Hank?' asked Aisling. She was clutching at straws.

'Mr Brown is a genius,' said Hank, as if nothing had been said for twenty minutes. 'Lord Rosslare spent ten years finding him.' Bringing Manus into this was a low blow, thought Esther, though one shouldn't assume Hank ever knew much about what he was doing.

'I will say this,' said Adam. 'I don't pretend to know about football,

I'm just speaking from the consultant's perspective, but I wouldn't get rid of Brown.'

'Mr Brown,' said Aisling automatically.

'Sorry. *Mr* Brown.'

'Actually, Adam, real fans call him "The General"', said Esther, helpfully. Adam looked blank. 'It's his nickname. He likes it because it reminds him of when he was a player.'

'I'll remember that,' said Adam. Aisling looked jealous. 'What I was saying was this: we have to be careful with the idea of shifting "The General". Part of the KSC brand's strength is its stability.'

'But Mr Brown has always been ruthless about selling players. It's part of what makes the club so —'

'That's not what most people associate with the club. I'm not saying we don't *do* the ruthless thing, but it must not *look like* it. KSC's brand is warm, inclusive, kind, all those things. If we're making a major change with the advertising then everything else should look as stable and continuous as possible.'

'How do we do that?' asked Donald.

Esther wasn't ready to let it go: 'I promise, Adam, real fans will notice if KSC doesn't operate ruthlessly. For *real fans* it's part of the appeal. It's what keeps the club honest.' She could see Adam taking this seriously, realising that she was no fool.

'We mustn't lose the real fans. When I say we want the new ones, I'm speaking purely financially, Esther.' He understood exactly what her objections would be. 'And the new fans don't understand anything more than I do. They'll see a successful manager being discarded after one bad season. What I do wonder, though, is whether there might be a way to bring in someone alongside Mr Brown. I don't know about the football, but is that possible? Would it change things in a way that real fans understand? I think it would certainly keep the new ones happy.'

Esther made a show of pondering wisely, but this was a great solution. Adam was theoretically asking Esther what she thought, but he kept watching Aisling for approval. Esther would normally have been annoyed, but she felt sorry for him, like people presumably felt sorry for her whenever Tom exploited her.

'But who?' asked Adam. 'With all due respect to Mr Brown, if we know we're going to put the other man in charge eventually, then it doesn't matter if "The General" feels the need to fight – he'll be the one who loses, and if he does it publicly, don't we get what we want?'

Esther was guiltily thrilled by this. It was just the kind of Machiavellian manoeuvre that Mr Brown, for all his good points, had always indulged in, and it would be a taste of his own medicine. He must be given the chance to go gracefully, but if he chose not to, then KSC would show that it was still capable of ruthlessness.

'So, Est, who should it be?' asked Aisling.

'I haven't even thought . . .'

'Cut the crap, Esther.'

Esther had thought of some names, actually, but this wasn't the way to proceed with such a huge decision. Aisling was being disrespectful. 'We haven't even decided if it's the right thing to do,' said Esther.

'Everyone's for it, aren't they?' Aisling said. 'Apart from Hank?' Even Donald nodded. 'So there we are, it's decided. Let's move on.'

'Well, I obviously haven't thought of anyone. I didn't want to be precipitate. It's not my place. I think we should have a special meeting next week.'

'This is a ridiculous fucking way to run a football club,' said Aisling. 'I literally cannot tell you how sick I am of it. There has to be a way to take some of this crap out of the hands of the Committee.' Aisling was bitter about Dave, and she was always pretending to be too busy at her stupid hospital to turn up or sully her hands with the hard work of looking after her heritage. Esther couldn't help any of that. She insisted on having the special meeting and Donald agreed.

That night, at the Royal Foresters Club on Pall Mall, Strabis had his regular post-Committee dinner with Donald. Strabis had sponsored Donald's membership of the Club and he'd never asked for anything in return. Donald thought that these dinners, once a month, were his idea, and that the coincidence with Committee meetings was not sinister, but simply a recognition that Committee meetings were important and that, afterwards, he wanted to unwind. They didn't even discuss the Committee always.

Today, however, the gossip was too much for Donald to keep to himself. He told Strabis that Aisling was pissed off with KSC, and said that it must be because of the whole Dave Guinevere disaster. Strabis mumbled something about how she was in her first year as a proper doctor, and no wonder she was finding it difficult, but Donald rebuffed him. 'She can't stand looking stupid,' he said. 'I know her. Kilburn reminds her of looking stupid, and so now she wants to run away, that's all it is. It's not as if she's going to get rid of it, she just doesn't want to have it rammed down her throat.'

Strabis didn't know what might come of it, but Aisling was clearly acting on emotions and who knew where that might lead, with the right pressure.

'You've had enough, A,' said Nicky, looking at Aisling's glass in a way that conveyed disapproval of being in a smoky bar when tomorrow was a schoolday. It was only ten, and this was only Aisling's third glass of wine. Adam had had the same, but Nicky didn't lecture Adam. Nicky was such an old granny.

'Can we sit down?' asked Aisling. They found a little table, from which Nicky removed the ashtray and which she then wiped. 'I've got to sort my life out,' Aisling said. Nicky put on her serious face, and Adam looked left out. 'Committee's been hard enough this rotation, and now I'm going on A & E. Every meeting, Esther spends about an hour crapping on about the Socialists.'

'She's your sister,' said Nicky.

'I'm not trying to get rid of her. I'm just saying that having the Committee in charge of Kilburn was fine when it was Dad, because he was obsessed, but I don't have the time. I could just about deal with Rosslare Group stuff if we didn't spend the whole time talking about football.'

'Are you sure this isn't because of Dave?'

'Fuck off, Nicks.'

'I'm just asking.'

'KSC needs a proper Chief Executive.' Adam looked nervous, but in Aisling's opinion it was excited nervousness.

'What do you have now?' said Nicky. 'Someone must be running it?'

Adam chimed in. 'The Bursar runs Kilburn Park day to day. I've honestly never seen anyone more organised.'

Aisling explained that the Bursar was an ex-army guy that Manus had found. She added that he was all organisation and no strategy. Strategy was for the Committee, which always used to be fine, because Mr Brown told them what to do.

'Has that changed?'

'Esther says so. Lots of people say so, actually. We might have to find someone to put alongside him.'

'Won't the new person do the strategy?'

'I need someone I can trust.'

'What about Esther?' said Adam slyly.

'You know it's not going to be her.'

'Even I know she's not up to it,' said Nicky.

'You'll love it, Adam,' Aisling said. 'You loved going to Kilburn Park.'

'Don't force him, A. You know what you're like. Why not Donald? He must have less to do now. Would he do it?'

'He'd do it like a fucking shot, for the limelight, but I don't trust him.'

'You can't make Adam do it. He's got a career. You've got to stop being so cavalier.'

'Fuck's sake, Nicks – you're always telling him to get out of consulting.'

'I'm sitting right here,' said Adam. Nicky could go into an almost instant sulk on being contradicted, and she did so now, implying that her exhortations to Adam that he must find a new direction were nothing like what Aisling was suggesting. Adam said, 'All I know about football is what I've researched for the Committee.'

He was staring at her like a rabbit in headlights, but he would thank her in the future. 'I know you, Adam,' she said. 'You're loving the Committee, and you'll love getting into the football crap. If you're not grateful in a year, I'll eat every shoe I own.' Aisling didn't look at Nicky.

The manager Esther really wanted was Clapham's James Purnell. He was young, dynamic and ambitious, he had a terrific record and he was being courted by all the big clubs, but Purnell had made it very clear he didn't want to move. He said that while he was flattered by the attention, he was learning his trade, and he'd made a commitment to Clapham that he fully intended to honour.

Esther needed a plan to take into the meeting, though, so she looked through her list of names. Now it came to the nub, her confidence was ebbing. In concern, not desperation, she cautiously raised the issue with Will Beauchamp, who was speaking with her more often, and whose acumen she increasingly trusted. He wasn't at all surprised by the Committee's thinking, which she was supposed to keep secret – but how are you supposed to get advice if you can't talk to anyone? 'What about James Purnell?' Will asked.

'But he always says —'

'Don't believe what you read in the papers.'

'He's turned down Everton and Dublin, and—'

'He wouldn't turn us down.'

'But —'

'He worships Mr Brown. He'd cut off what's left of his leg to work with him.'

'Are you sure?'

When Esther named Purnell at the meeting, Donald, who couldn't see past the sports pages, pooh-poohed her as usual. Esther told him to ignore things written by people who didn't have any inside information: Purnell would agree, and they mustn't sugar-coat the fact he'd be working with Mr Brown – that was the appeal for him. It was all about psychology. Purnell was the man for the job.

'This is bullshit,' said Aisling. 'I've booked an afternoon off work and the decision is already made? What the fucking hell was the point of this meeting?'

'This was an important —'

'I know it's important to you, Esther, and it's important to KSC, as you so endlessly fucking remind us, but it isn't important to me.'

'Well, sorry. It's your job to —'

'My *job* is to be a doctor. This is not my job.' Aisling wasn't finished. 'I knew this meeting would be over in five minutes, but you fucking insisted. This was fine for Dad, and when Mr Brown was still on his game, but this Committee knows fuck all about running a football club, and I can't keep sitting here, and turning up to league meetings like a spare fucking part.' *She's going to resign*, thought Esther, excitedly. 'I've taken your word for it that we need someone to help Mr Brown manage the team, and we can ask Purnell if that's what you want, but I want someone other than the Committee doing the everyday stuff at KSC. We need someone whose job is to deal with it, and then bring it to us to decide on, as per the rest of the Group.'

'This is a massive decision,' said Donald.

'Don't try to talk me out of it, and I'm not being dragged back to another meeting. I'm fed up with this crap. I've thought about it very carefully, and it's happening.'

Esther doubted the thought had been particularly careful, but her heart was in her mouth and her eyes on the table as she asked, 'Should the Chief Executive be someone from the Committee?'

'It definitely should,' said Donald. He was angling for the job, typically.

'Yes,' said Aisling.

Esther looked down shyly, and Adam said, 'Well, Esther's the one here who knows most about football.'

Aisling cut in, 'But you know nothing about business, Esther, no offence.'

'Okay, Ash, I'll do it!' said Donald. 'I dare say I could move things around to get the time.'

'I want Adam to do it.'

Esther thought Adam looked surprised. After all, he had just suggested she run Kilburn, hadn't he? 'My problem is that I know so little about the football,' he said. 'I would need some help.'

'You get what help you need, but this is what I've decided. Apart from anything else, it's going to stop Adam from turning into such a fucking suit.'

Adam's face sank when Aisling said that, and Esther guessed that her sister had stuck a knife into some weak spot. He was obviously besotted with her, and maybe his decision to be a boring suit was the reason she'd given him for it never going anywhere. Aisling was so used to getting her own way that she would say anything, no matter how hurtful, when her mind was set on something. Poor Adam agreed that he would take the job on for a trial period, but – and here he looked earnestly at her – only if Esther promised to be available for consultation. Esther hid her disappointment, since it wasn't Adam's fault, and she nodded. She didn't mind if Aisling thought Adam was boring. *Quiet people of the world unite,* she thought.

As Will predicted, James Purnell leaped at the chance to join KSC, though he insisted on being described as Mr Brown's assistant, rather than his co-manager. He said publicly that the move shouldn't be seen as a sign that loyalty was less important to him than he had previously intimated, but working with Mr Brown was a dream for him and he would never get another chance. If people thought he was motivated purely by ambition and money, then he couldn't help that, but he'd turned down the manager's job at big clubs offering higher salaries. Adam's first job as Chief Executive was to present Mr Brown with Purnell as a fait accompli. Brown looked Adam up and down, and said, 'Could have been worse.'

WORLD CUP – ITALIA 2000

The Italian Federation's perennially bickering states cooperated just long enough to stage a spectacular World Cup. Venice and Rome put away their jealousy and pride, and accepted Bologna's right to host the home nation's group matches.

The federal capital herself, so long in awe of her mightier sisters, and demurely aware that she owed her status to her comparative insignificance, finally came of age. For a hundred years Bologna had repressed herself, content to do as she was bid. She lost her status to Rome under the self-aggrandising Fascists and the dilettantish Communists, but whenever the Federation returned to some form of its chaotic, beguiling democracy, its members returned whatever grudging power they were prepared to allow the central government to Bologna, who would sigh, dust herself down, and quietly reassign the elegant government buildings. It wasn't as much of an upheaval as it sounded, since even when Rome snatched the politicians, she'd always been prepared to leave the bureaucrats. And so, by now, the measured red city was permeated with a sense of civic duty, and her people's un-Italian awareness of the *longue durée*. Even her students had an air of decorum. But this was the World Cup, her night in the sun, if that made any sense, which it didn't, but who cared! Tomorrow, she would be clearing up after everyone again, but tonight Bologna was going to the ball. She took off her glasses, she bared her shoulders, had a glass of champagne, shook down her hair and the world went, 'But Miss B! You're beautiful!'

A great man once wrote that to say football crowds pay to see teams of overpaid hirelings kick a ball around is to say that a violin is wood and catgut, and *Hamlet* is so much paper and ink. Fandom makes the spectator a critic and a partisan, elated, bitter, triumphant and downcast by turns as the ball shapes *Iliad*s and *Odysseys*. It makes him a member of a larger community for an hour and a half, escaped from the machinery of his daily life, one with his neighbours, thumping shoulders and swapping judgments like lords of the earth, participants in a momentary but more spacious life, hustling with conflict and yet passionate and beautiful in its art. Trying to recapture this outside the stadium, trying to evoke the sublime moment in words, is as hard as trying to describe great sex. Hence all the purple clichés.

Italy – and there was nothing dubious about this that could be proven – were in a group alongside Mali, Persia, Iceland and New Zealand, the four weakest teams that could be drawn together in the tournament. They won their matches with triumphal ease, ensuring they would play in Bologna for as long as they stayed in the cup. Britain strolled through their much tougher group of Zaire, Poland, Paraguay and Korea with hardly more effort. Korea proved the strongest opponents, and little Seung played a fierce game against his erstwhile teammates, but GB were a dominant team in dominant mood, with Will Beauchamp emerging on the game's biggest stage as the midfield force he'd threatened to be. Dave Guinevere was still outstanding, but he wasn't as integral to Britain's progress as he was used to being. Tom Benjamin and Will Laird scored the goals.

Zondi, on the sidelines, since South Africa had not qualified, was torn between an unreasoning desire for African success, following Achilles' Argentina, and supporting his plethora of British teammates, who, after all, played for the nation he had consciously chosen as his home. There was little crowd trouble – the seventies and eighties were long past, thank God – but the fervency of nationalism still caught him cold. It was probably because his own first allegiances had been against his nation. Watching Seung play Dave, and seeing Dirk and Achilles throw themselves furiously into each other, was exciting, but it also made Zondi uneasy. It was like /Xa-we-'gwe!gwe, the Sundering. The many-shaped people of the First Time lived with no tribes, or dark, or eating, and were nourished by the light. But greedy !Ka'Ka gathered all the light to himself, and that was the sun, and he tried to hide it, and that was the night. The people of the First Time then felt hunger, and the hunger gave them new forms which were fixed for ever, and it closed their ears to the words of those they had known, and their eyes stopped seeing through the world, and all they were able to remember was that this place was worse than the place of the First Time, and they must seek the First Time for ever but they would never find it because they were hungry now and their stomachs would never know quiet, and they were set at war, one shape against the other. Zondi knew, as he always knew, that he was being silly, but his unease was real.

Even though tickets were like drinks in the desert, Aisling could have had any she wanted, but she had just started in A & E, and she was knackered all the time. Anyway, there was no way she was wasting her precious holiday watching sport. She saw the GB games at the pub and in friends' houses. She didn't miss Adam, except when Nicky badgered her about how much nicer it would be if he were around. Aisling coped with this by grinning with the others behind Nicky's back about the risibility of Nicky's biennial football fever, and the irony-free way in which Nicky pontificated about 'the boys' and 'our chances'. The reason Adam wasn't around, incidentally, was that he'd gone to Italy with Esther. Nicky supposed he must feel lost and alone.

As a matter of fact, Adam felt energised. He was, in a way, a part of the tournament rather than a mere spectator. He hadn't been angling for the job at KSC, whatever Aisling pretended, but he couldn't deny he'd been ready for a change. When he handed in his resignation, his boss said he was mad and insisted that he called it a leave of absence. That was fine by Adam, but he wasn't going back, and he wasn't a suit. He didn't even pack a tie for Italy. He could buy one there, if necessary.

As they watched the matches, Esther explained the tactics and personalities involved, how the Dutch always looked amazing and then lost on penalties; how the Italians, in spite of their mighty clubs, had never won a World Cup, and how it was a source of national lamentation; how the Scandinavians always punched above their weight; and how there was, finally, a chance that the African nations might mount a serious challenge to the dominance of Europe and Latin America. She painstakingly explained the offside rule and the different possible formations, and how 4-4-2, in its various permutations, was almost always the choice of successful sides. Adam nodded, uncomprehending. He hoped he would get an understanding of what she might mean by asking what formation Great Britain used. She said, '5-3-2.' Adam looked worried, and she had to explain that there are exceptions to every rule, and that 5-3-2 was not necessarily a defensive strategy, and could in many cases be seen as 3-5-2 under another guise. Adam nodded again.

'They probably should play 4-4-2,' Esther clarified, 'but it's the manager, you see, he had his first big success with Celtic playing 5-3-2, that was before the '85 Ibrox Riot, and then he stuck with it when they became Celtic-Rangers afterwards, but C-R would have won the league that year whatever they did – it was destiny – and then he won Euro 94 and the World Cup like this, so he thinks 5-3-2 is the holy grail. Everyone says it only works because he's got such great players to choose from.'

'We'll win, won't we?'

'You can't say that!'

'We're the favourites, though. And we've won the first two games very easily.' Esther explained that we were *one* of the favourites, certainly, but you mustn't tempt fate. Adam took this as a sign of endearing superstition. GB were favourites by miles. Even the Italians were fatalistic beneath the romance.

Adam and Esther watched many games live, and the rest in the quietest bars they could find, going Dutch and sharing modest half-bottles of wine. Esther thought they would probably have spent all their time together if Adam hadn't felt duty-bound, since he was in Italy, to wander round museums and galleries. In streets where every second man stared frankly at her breasts and legs, however much she tried to cover them up, Adam's reserve was like an oasis.

Wives and girlfriends were not permitted to mingle with the tour party, which she was grateful for, not that she was Tom's girlfriend. Early on during the trip, Adam asked her about Tom, and she said she still saw Tom sometimes, but it wasn't formal or anything. Adam seemed relieved, and she took this to mean he thought he might have a chance. However, whenever Esther tried to hint to Adam that she would not necessarily be unamenable, he became instantly reserved and talked about Tom again. Esther wondered what Aisling had done to make him so devoted, and her gorge rose. She wouldn't put it past her sister to have left him dangling on some pitiful thread of hope.

It was maddening because in every other way, the pair of them were perfect together. Esther wasn't embarrassed about not being interested in the museums, for instance, and Adam didn't seem to mind. She was less willing to admit that politics also appeared pointless, because Adam was genuinely heady at the prospect of the election, which the wheedling, seedy, transparent Tories had scheduled for the week after the World Cup final. Like everyone else, Esther could see the tactic wasn't going to work, but she hated all politicians.

Still, and in the light of Adam's excitement, she began to realise that maybe this election would be a real transformation. The Tories had been in government for ever, after all, and everyone knew they were hateful. She would have settled for nodding at Adam when he started talking, but he kept asking questions and she didn't have anything suitably intelligent to say. It was one of the things she liked about him, that he wasn't just interested in the sound of his own voice. He wanted to know what she thought.

So when, eventually, Esther thought of something, she was ecstatic. The next time politics came up, she said casually, 'Yes, indeed. History repeats itself: We are all Socialists now.' Adam glanced up at her.

'That's the KSC motto, isn't it?'

'Yes, but it's very relevant today, I think,' Esther said. '"We are all Socialists now." William Harcourt, 1894.'

'Who was he?' said Adam. 'I thought —'

'Harcourt didn't mean communist, or anything, as we might imagine from the word "socialist" these days.' Esther was KSC's self-appointed, semi-official historian. 'He was simply saying that Adam Smith's invisible hand, and traditional laissez-faire attitudes, were no longer tenable. Society needed to act in favour of the less fortunate, and he could say it because that's what "socialist" meant to him, and everyone in politics at the time agreed with this.'

'That's really interesting. How do you know all this?'

'Oh, I just picked it up somewhere.' Harcourt was a great friend of Felim Rosslare's, and Esther had now divulged almost her entire knowledge of him. 'You see the similarity?' she said, determinedly. 'The Tories are the heirs of Adam Smith, and they have had their way for a long time, but now we have seen that it doesn't work, so everyone has gone the other way, so we are all socialists now.'

Esther watched Adam's eyes shine with the thought of displaying this knowledge as his own. She felt that if Tom really cared about her, then he should have said so more explicitly, and since he hadn't, she couldn't feel guilty about what was probably going to happen. Everyone knew that she was unworldly, so how could anyone blame her if she didn't understand what was going on?

Italy marched past Zimbabwe and into the quarter-finals. Bologna basked serenely in the attention, not exposing herself like excitable

Siena, who prepared for the Holland–America game like a teenager getting ready for her first big party, or raddled Venice, who welcomed Argentina with blowsy, faded charm and wine-dark teeth, grimly determined to make a night of it. Bologna sparkled, and her sisters looked on jealously, even Milan, who haughtily pretended that GB's game against the disappointing Germans was the tie of the round.

The only quarter-final surprise, as it happened, took place in Siena, who got the party she wanted, as the Dutch drowned their sorrows after losing on penalties (again!), and a surprisingly large agglomeration of nice, young, middle-class Americans went frat-boy crazy. Holland dominated the match, but they couldn't find a way past the inspired US goalie, Louie Cohen, who was the player, and character, of the tournament so far.

Louie, born Tyrone Blackwood, had been brought up in LA. Like most little kids, he'd tried to make himself popular with bigger kids. On his thirteenth birthday, his big brother's gang got Ty to steal a pair of sneakers by trying them on and then running out of the shop. That evening, flushed with success, they thought it would be funny to introduce Ty to drink. He woke the next day, no memory, in a back alley full of drooling men and women. He remembered the way his brother's gang had laughed, and he understood, with childhood's clarity, that they were not his friends. Ty took a schoolbook and a pen, and he wrote, 'In the FUTURE I will trust ONLY MYSELF.' He chewed the pen. 'I am ALONE,' he wrote. Then, 'Whatever bad things anyone does to me, I will never DECEIVE anyone. I will not TRY to IMPRESS people who AREN'T WORTH IT. I will SUCCEED where they FAIL because I will be STRONG. I WILL BE PROUD TO BE MYSELF.' Ty studied hard, and refused to speak to his brother's friends, who barely noticed. He wasn't the brightest boy, but he was dedicated, and in the inner city that made him stand out. Halfway through his sixteenth year, already six foot four, Ty was woken in a doorway by Provan Krcaski, the son of a Macedonian immigrant who worked at a shelter for homeless young men. Krcaski ran a programme trying to help kids by introducing them to sport. Looking at the beanpole Ty, he thought basketball might be this boy's salvation. When Ty explained that he wasn't homeless or drunk, and that he was only in an alley because he'd been beaten up for evangelising about his new-found Islam, Krcaski saw that here was a young man, devout and burning with sincerity, who could be an example to the rest of his team.

Expressed in these terms, the prospect attracted Ty, who called himself Mohammed now. His faith, born of a journey that started with a poster of two Olympic medal winners giving the Black Power salute, was a fervent muddle of racial pride, childish sexism and yearning to stand out. He took to basketball immediately, and with complete focus. Krcaski patiently talked Mo down from some of his high horses. He persuaded Mo that the greatest fortune he had was being born American, a citizen of this wonderful country where anyone with talent and drive could succeed. Mo had initially enjoyed the commitment of Muslim groups, but now he started to find their conformity stultifying and repressive. The more Krcaski taught him about America and the slow struggle for liberty, the more he found traditional Muslim views embarrassing, especially when they criticised the US. Krcaski was a dreamer who told Mo he had the chance to be a figurehead. Mo hadn't been an outstanding student, and he could admit now that the mediocrity had rankled, but he had found his niche: he was going to go pro and be a star. But then he got to college, and he learned that the basketball system was packed with young phenoms, all as hungry as him and many with more talent. He was back in the crowd.

One day, over lunch, he sat next to a girl from his English class. He'd never had a relationship, because he'd never had time, and he wasn't in any hurry. 'Why you wear the slavers' cross?' he grunted. No one would accuse *him* of chasing skirt.

'Why do you wear the slavers' crescent?' she replied. She launched into a diatribe about the Muslim world's slaving past, and, in some places, its slaving present. Then she said, 'You seem a decent guy, but you got to get your facts straight. Slavery wears religion, but it's really economics. Be careful talking about things you don't get.' Mo was shocked to learn there was still slavery in the world. He was angry that a white Christian girl knew more about it than he did. He was determined never to be wrong-footed again.

He decided that the American way, where an individual must be free to follow his star and become all he could become, must be at the heart of his faith. He wanted this to be compatible with his Islam, a label of which he was proud. His imam was disappointed, and asked him to beware of selfishness. Mo, new to this, asked his imam about terrorism, and the imam shook his head sadly, explaining to Mo that Islam was fundamentally tolerant. This wasn't enough for Mo, who wanted answers, not hand-wringing. He seriously considered leaving the faith until he found a group who called themselves 'Reform Muslims'. They, like Mo, wanted to vigorously reinterpret the scriptures so they might fit in with the modern world. This was the kind of religion Mo could really believe in, one where he could shine. He espoused it passionately. His new fellows begged him to be cautious, but Mo wasn't afraid of controversy. With Palestinian violence at its height, he changed his name to Louie Cohen as a symbol that Muslim and Jew must find peace. Soon everybody on campus knew his name.

Louie was too satisfied in his purpose to be lonely. He ran committees, raised money, and, most importantly, raised the profile of progressive Muslims. It was one of these, a young Bahraini who thought it was a shame that Louie didn't seem to have the time for friends, who asked him to play soccer for an interfaith team. Louie didn't even know the rules, but the Bahraini pretended the team was desperate. Louie hated the idea that people would laugh at him, but cooperation was the path he had chosen. He agreed, so long as he could play goalie, where, with his natural sporting awareness, he felt he might at least have some idea what to do.

The college soccer coach also played for the interfaith team. Five years later, Louie was a World Cup hero, and he felt as fulfilled as he always knew he would be, one day.

The secondary news story of any World Cup is the arrival of new stars into the football firmament, and the excitement over which club is going to sign them. There were brief frenzies over Cisse Camara, the flamboyant Zairian playmaker, and Maciej Ceglowski, the Polish centre half who held off the Brits for half an hour. There was a speedy, workmanlike Korean, an elegant young Frenchman, an ice-cool Swede and a host of other lazy racial stereotypes, but Louie was the big story. Everybody wanted him, particularly because they had never heard of him before, and because a million pounds still went a long way in US soccer.

Esther and Adam were as intoxicated as everyone else. Louie was earning rave reviews even before he single-handedly plugged the Americans' fragile dyke against the Dutch. Adam was a naturally cautious person, but Esther assured him that in this environment, with new players at such a premium, he who hesitated was lost. He asked cautiously whether KSC actually needed another goalie, since Pat Credence was so good, wasn't he? Esther explained that every club must always look to strengthen in all positions, which made sense, which he wanted it to, because that was what the atmosphere was like.

Adam tried to get hold of Mr Brown, to ask his opinion, but it was the summer, and no one knew where Mr Brown went in the summer. Adam went to James Purnell, who agreed that Louie looked the real deal, but he was only Mr Brown's assistant, and decisions on players had to pass through the gaffer. It was very frustrating since, as Adam could see now, all the big clubs were circling.

Adam and Esther went to Siena. Louie was not just a great player, they agreed (Adam was increasingly confident in his football acumen), but, also, his story could have been made for KSC. 'Mr Brown will love him, won't he?' Adam said. 'He's just the kind of player Mr Brown buys, isn't he?' Esther, wary of second-guessing Mr Brown, agreed, because now was not the time to put doubt in Adam's mind. They decided to act, feeling inexplicably naughty.

After Siena, in the dead days before the semi-finals, speculation about Louie's future reached fever pitch. Louie's agent, a hard, fat Californian called Phil Maroon, who wore no hair and pink-tinted sunglasses, found Louie, with his holier-than-thou attitude, a chore. Phil's colleagues laughed when they found out he was representing a soccer player, because soccer was strictly second-string, unless you wanted to sell to teenage girls. Phil agreed in general, but he liked to see himself as a risk-taker, as someone who saw further than the bottom-feeders, and when Phil shook Louie's hand, it felt like money. This fuss in Italy made all the crap Phil had endured worthwhile. He'd done his homework, and he only spoke with the big boys, ratcheting his price higher and higher. But every time he went to Louie, Louie asked, 'What about KSC?'

Phil tried telling him to forget about the Socialists – there was more money to be had elsewhere. Phil almost felt altruistic saying this, since although KSC had a flat wage structure, the club paid decent transfer fees, and that's where Phil's cut came in. Phil could see why KSC's image appealed to Louie, but Phil's grandfather had died in the Hitler war, and he revolted at the thought of associating his client with socialists.

Two days after the Holland game, Phil relented. Louie was so red-hot that it wasn't worth taking the risk of him fumbling catastrophically in the semi-final against Italy, and until he met with KSC, Louie wasn't signing anything. Louie even said he'd talk to KSC himself if he had to. After that, Phil had to take steps. He'd see these idiots, and he'd get rid of them.

When Adam and Esther entered his hotel suite, Phil almost laughed. These were kids playing at sport, like all the Europeans. 'Whaddyagot?' he said.

'Hello, Mr Maroon. I'm Adam Greswell and this is Esther Rosslare.'

They were so fucking uptight. Whatever. He half-heartedly pretended to be shocked by their contract, which was non-negotiable, which everyone knew. This would make them drop their guard. 'No performance bonus even? No playing guarantee! You guys are breaking my balls.' Little Lord Fauntleroy didn't react. This was no fun.

'We save money on wages, and that money goes into transfers,' said the girl, who was glowing as if she were on heat. 'And isn't that where you make your cut?'

'You got the wrong idea about me, lady. Louie is my friend first and my client second. He's like a brother to me. I'm not going to let him get screwed.'

'We can offer up to six million,' the girl said. She would go to eight. It was Phil's job to sense these things.

'Torino offered ten. So did Cardiff. And they would pay him properly. And why am I talking to you? Where's the manager. Where's Brown?'

'We call him *Mr* Brown, actually,' said the guy, as if he shat butter, 'or sometimes "The General", but not Brown. It's not respectful. And we have Mr Brown's full confidence, I assure you.'

'Well you don't have mine. And if you don't have mine, you don't have Louie's.'

'But he's perfect for KSC!' said the girl. 'Can't you see that?' The suit tried not to look pained. Phil thought the suit's tie made him look like a queer.

'This is pointless, lady. Louie's a star, not a charity case. He ain't no fucking socialist.'

'Louie will make a fortune out of KSC,' said the suit.

'Howdyafigure?'

'There's nothing socialist about KSC. It's just a word.'

'What about the wages, bud? Show me the money.'

'We can pay seven million,' the guy said.

'You can pay eight, and that's two too few, buddy.' Torino and Cardiff hadn't really offered ten. They'd both offered eight, and they were both, of course, ready to make a finder's gift to their new friend Phil Maroon. They were coy, but the bribe – it was called a 'bung' in England – was independent of his official fee and would reach well into six figures. Phil heard of off-the-book payments when he was doing his research, but now he was here in person, he couldn't believe how these things were done. Who was regulating this shit? He supposed it was impossible because soccer wasn't a cartel like American sport. In a bandit economy, you can make a fortune if you've got the guts, and Phil seriously wanted to come to Europe. The problem was, he needed to make this deal to give him a foothold, and he'd heard Kilburn didn't do these 'bungs'. But if Louie spoke to KSC on his own, that would be curtains. A percentage of eight million was better than a percentage of nothing. 'This is bullshit,' he added.

'If Louie joins KSC, he will be part of, and he will enhance, the most attractive brand in the biggest sport in the world. He might not get the wages, but this contract doesn't mention image rights, external sponsorship or advertising revenue. I imagine that Louie, who is clearly a devout young man, will insist on these being ethically handled, but if you can't see the money in it, you're a bigger fool than you look.' The prick must be high, or he was showing off for his girlfriend, who was trying not to giggle. Phil wanted to kick his smug ass but he didn't have any choice with this. Also, while Phil would take a hit on the transfer percentage, what the prick said about sponsorship made sense. He could make this do-gooding crap work its balls off for him. He'd swallow his pride now, but he'd stick it up the Socialists' cracks some future day. They could go on his list.

The deal took twenty-four hours to arrange. Adam assumed Maroon was trying to show him how they do these things in the States, but Esther said it was normal. Esther thought he'd been amazing with Maroon. Adam explained modestly that he was surprised how easy it had been. Sports agents were sharp enough, but they were hardly the biggest cats in the business jungle. Quietly, they were both elated. Under the noses of the world's best clubs, they had signed the star of the tournament for two million less than the asking price, and they'd done it without resorting to the sordid world of bungs and backhanders. Adam and Esther had arrived. They were a team.

Bologna welcomed the American hordes and watched with easy grace as they boistered good-naturedly through her piazzas, flirted politely with her daughters and embraced her sons in fraternal goodwill. The Americans were so excited to have made the semi-final that their loss, in which they did not disgrace themselves, barely dented the mood. And anyway, it was hard for anyone to begrudge the Italians their bubbling thrill that this, at last, finally, was the time.

GB versus Argentina was disappointingly one-sided. Only the most vacuous fans felt any *real* animus over the war of 84, which a few short years and changes of Argentinian regime had shrunk almost into unreality, but there was no denying that the claws were sharper than they'd been in the seventies.

As well as Achilles, Argentina had the tireless Muller and Gaudio in midfield, and Azul Madrid's peerless Mele di Paolo up front, bewildering those defenders he couldn't simply overpower. Their defence was merely adequate, but most teams spent so much energy containing their forwards that it didn't matter. Britain, with Benjamin and Laird, and with Kit Knowle and Jason Flightly marauding up the flanks, were a similarly attacking force. The football world licked its lips.

The game turned on Dave Guinevere's decision to mark Achilles man to man. Dave took the decision himself, and he should have known better. It was a tactic that hundreds of teams had tried in the past, and it almost never worked. It meant not only that Achilles was uncontained, but also that a player had been sacrificed in trying to contain him. However, once in an age, Achilles would be less than his best or he would find himself up against someone who, on that day, was inspired by some demon of his own, someone who found a sweet, fierce hour. Dave bit through each tackle, was ahead of the tricks, intercepted every pass. He felt Olympian as, unhindered by their impotent opponents, GB broke over the Argentinian defence like a blood-red tide.

Zondi understood from the start what the Tall Hunter was trying to do, and he feared that when Dave failed, he would slip into rage. But as the Hunter did not fail, and kept not failing, as he continued to entwine Achilles in his mesh, Zondi felt himself twist and wrench with Achilles' confusion and distress. Achilles was being tracked by his friend, who was doing it out of some personal insanity. Proud and defiant, Achilles reached beyond his usual range of skills, searching for impossible tricks and miracle wonder passes, trying anything to prove to the Hunter that he could not be caged. Achilles was blinded by his own light, and Zondi knew the Hunter had won.

GB's dominance was not reflected in the scale of their victory, 2–0, but everybody saw. At the end of the game, flushed with high joy, Dave tracked down Achilles once more. Achilles tried to circle away, but he was in the Hunter's sights. Dave smiled, baring his teeth, and he and Achilles exchanged shirts. Zondi saw the Hunter in his triumph and his pomp tearing off the Butterfly's wings, taking them home to pin in a box, a token of his power. If he said this to Dave and Achilles, they would laugh, but they would both understand. Even though it would seem as if the wings grew back quickly, the Butterfly knew what had happened, and the scar would take a long time to form. Zondi wondered if the three would still be friends then, and he ached.

After the semi-finals, the Italian Federation worked itself into a fever of underdogged dreaming. Beautiful Bologna outdid herself for the last night of the ball, finally losing her cool to a skittering sheen at midnight's inexorable approach. The British fans, who had been so overweening and unlovable in the wake of GB's victory four years before, had grown almost gracious with the expectation of success, and filled the city and its billowing outer skirts with excited condescension.

Di Venuto, the barrelling Australian-Italian centre forward, scored the opener after five minutes, and the second a minute later, and the Federation went into delirium. Britain had to attack, and they battered furiously against the Italian defence. Will Beauchamp scrambled a messy goal from a corner just before half-time. After the break, as pre-match expectations of a cagey encounter disintegrated in the flurry of goals, Will Laird scored two, but before anyone could draw breath Rossellini powered an Italian equaliser from thirty yards, Will Beauchamp restored the lead and Tom Benjamin extended it to an astonishing 5–3. With five minutes to go, Di Venuto completed his hat-trick and, as the feverish blues scrapped their way towards the ninetieth minute, Spezzeguti won the penalty that could take the Italians into extra time.

Spezzeguti would not give the ball to Di Venuto. There was a frank and furious exchange, tears streaming down both men's faces. Eventually, Di Venuto stormed away in disgust, arms pumping at the sky, and enraptured millions around the world wondered at the fire and will of Spezzeguti, of a man who could demand that so much weight of hope and fear be placed upon his head. Spezzeguti, looking to the distant crowd as calm as a boy in a playground, and to the intruding television viewer as if he would kill the next man he spoke to, placed the ball, walked ten strides straight back towards the centre spot, turned, charged like a bull, drew back his leg to drive the ball mightily into the roof of the net and, as the keeper dived full length, chipped it gently into the middle of the goal. It was a moment of such boldness and panache, so perfect and adroit, that it took a moment to sink in, and when it did, as Spezzeguti's head rose above his surging teammates, Di Venuto first and most joyous among them, even the ranks of Albion could scarce forbear to cheer.

Extra time, at last, saw tired legs and fear of failure overcome feverish endeavour. Penalties approached, and Italy, feeling that the cup was their destiny, retreated and retreated, Di Venuto and Spezzeguti joining their defenders to repel Laird and Benjamin, Gently, Beauchamp, Fourse and the rest. When, midway through in the second period, Barry Gently rose above his marker and grazed the ball past the flailing Marchetti and into the net, the Italians were dumbfounded, as if this were an unreal thing. Italy had withdrawn so far into their certainty that the game would end with penalties that they didn't manage another shot.

Bologna had left her slipper on the steps, full of sly confidence that it would be found and that she would return shimmering into a never-ending limelight, but it was trodden on and shattered and she was made to wait for another ball, if one came, and it seemed to her as if one couldn't, not ever. The Italian fans, raised into fervour by their secret hopes, could not endure the renewed triumphalism of the British, whose veneer of grace had been peeled away by fright. It was a bitter, edgy night. The Italian police did not look the other way, but they looked with only one eye, and they applied the strict letter of many laws to these foreigners who seemed to believe the stories that Italy was chaotic and devil-may-care. There were fights and injuries, and unsympathetic doctors thought of making crude mistakes with their stitching before deciding that the best revenge was to do a perfect job, but maybe with less anaesthetic. It was Bologna's first beautiful drunken party, and her first grown-up hangover.

The hysteria in Britain was as great as it had been in 1996, and the Tories hoped the feel-good factor would translate into votes, which it did, but the votes went to Labour. In fact, wrote the reporters, Labour, with its bright young leaders, eagerness to please and sense of destiny, was perfectly placed to catch the wave of emotion and surf it through the election, so that where the wave of 1996 had lasted only a few weeks, this one was reinforced by the arrival of a glowing, unsullied government, and Britain felt genuinely renewed. Had GB lost, of course, the same reporters would have said the Tories got what they deserved for their cynical attempt to manipulate public opinion, and Labour's landslide, and the outburst of joy that came with it, would have been described as the boost the nation needed after its World Cup disappointment. With hindsight, when the tiny fractions between winning and losing have been explained away, you can use sport to say anything.

PART TWO — DANCING ON
THE EDGE OF THE CLIFF

THE SOCIALISTS BEAT CARDIFF

Between the World Cup and returning to the club, Dave took Sally to a cottage in New Hampshire with a pile of videos, Achilles and Zondi went to the farm in Argentina, and Esther let Tom take her to Prague to make Adam jealous and because she deserved some fun sometimes.

Dave, Zondi and Achilles, on returning, fell over each other to agree that the past was in the past, that mistakes had been made, but in good faith, that they must move forwards as if the slate was clean. When they arrived the next day, Mr Brown looked old.

Kilburn Social Club versus Cardiff, *29 August 2000, Kilburn Park*

John Brown smiled at James Purnell as the younger man leaped from the bench every few minutes. Both KSC and Cardiff had won their first five games of the season, and Purnell had given a rousing team talk, based on Mr Brown's tactics. The combination of the older man's nous and the younger man's energy had revivified the Socialists, who were playing with the confidence and purpose they'd so signally lacked six months earlier.

Louie Cohen, seated behind Purnell, was the only person who saw Brown smile. Sitting on the bench was testing Louie's patience. He was a humble man, he told himself, but he was a winner. He could accept that Pat Credence had done nothing wrong, but sport wasn't about sentiment. Louie was the hero of the World Cup and he deserved his chance. He joined KSC because, from everything he'd read and heard, he'd believed that the club truly was different, and that its players were maverick individuals who wouldn't fit in anywhere else. He could see now that he was wrong. He realised he'd been brought to the club over Brown's head, which had bred jealousy and resentment. Will Beauchamp had explained it to him. Everyone was nice enough on the surface, but really they were just another cosy gang of friends, the kind he'd been avoiding all his life.

Now he was stuck at KSC, free of illusions, he watched very carefully to see how it worked. Brown didn't seem to do much. As far as Louie could tell, it was Purnell who was running the show. When Louie saw Brown smile at Purnell today, he thought at first it was fatherly, but there was something else. Brown wasn't just smiling at Purnell. He was smiling at the fans, at Dave Guinevere, at Achilles, at Zondi. Brown even, as if he knew he was watching, turned to smile at Louie. In fact, wherever Brown looked, he smiled. It's possible Louie exaggerated how much he was aware of all this in retrospect, but there was definitely something about Brown. Later Louie would tell people that the old man's little moon face had seemed incredibly placid, and that he had smiled like a man at peace with himself at the end of a long journey.

Seung broke down the flank and whipped a cross along Cardiff's six-yard line; Will Laird headed it on to the crossbar; it thumped back down at Tom Benjamin's grateful feet; Benjamin bundled it into the empty net, and KSC led 1–0.

Cardiff had looked the stronger team up to this point, both today and during their first five matches. Their championship-winning squad, which had been strengthened by the arrival of Italy's Di Venuto and, more importantly, Germany's Marten Vlocker, rotated through its first five matches with huge authority. Moreover, Cardiff came through stiff tests at Everton and Celtic-Rangers, while KSC's early victories had only been against the likes of Torquay and West Manchester. The sages wondered whether the wins marked a new dawn, or whether they were flattery to deceive. What, they asked, was the role of James Purnell? In pubs around the country, fans crowded to watch the tellies connected to bloody Panther and agreed that Cardiff was the test.

Vlocker was only twenty, but was the star of the new season so far. Dark-haired, green-eyed and stocky, he was the player Cardiff had dreamed about ever since Achilles turned them down in favour of KSC. He operated in the same forward midfield role, and ran the game with a similar authority, terrific in one so young. After what happened in the World Cup semi-final, everyone assumed that Dave would try to shackle the young tyro. The confrontation between the pair dominated the pre-match hype.

Vlocker was ready for Guinevere, and confident, but Mr Brown had a word with Dave three days before the game. He said that if he pulled a stunt like he had against Argentina, that would be the last game Dave played for a month. Vlocker started reasonably, but he didn't look special – maybe he was confused that Dave wasn't on his shoulder the whole time – and once Benjamin scored, Kilburn dominated. Vlocker barely saw the ball; indeed, he had to start chasing after Dave. Vlocker wasn't a defensive player, though, and every time he neared his man, possession flicked to another Socialist. It seemed to Vlocker, as the game progressed, that Dave was sliding the ball closer and closer past him, as if Dave were taunting him.

The score was only 1–0 at half-time, which Purnell was happy about, because he feared that a second goal might have made KSC complacent. The players knew the job wasn't finished, and it was easy for Purnell to keep them focused while Mr Brown sat in the corner, smiling approvingly. The only chink in his sunny façade came when Purnell said, 'We change nothing. You all know what to do; Mr Brown has settled how we play. It suits us and we mustn't mess around with it. If we can just keep it up all season, nothing can stop us. Work, work, work, boys! Keep it going.' Brown's hands fluttered, as if he saw some peril in Purnell's words that went beyond their immediate substance.

As the players left for the tunnel, Brown hung back. Achilles was always the last to leave the room, for superstitious reasons. Brown knew this and, still sitting, he watched Achilles hover by the door. Then Brown gave the most brilliant smile, his eyes gleaming unnaturally. He stood and said, 'Purnell is a good man.'

'Yes, Mr Brown. I was nervous.'

'I know.' Brown still didn't leave. He took Achilles by the hand, and Achilles was startled at the heat in the old man's palms. 'Purnell is good, but he's not the one,' Brown said.

'I have to —'

'I hate that this is happening now, when so much needs to be done. It is not what I would have chosen, or when, but —'

'Mr Brown!'

'Listen to Zondi. Trust him and he will protect you.' Achilles wasn't sure what Mr Brown meant. 'You and he together, you are unbreakable. You are the one, when you are ready.' Achilles was in the wrong frame of mind to understand anything now, but Brown knew he would remember when the time came. He found it hard to let go of Achilles' hand, but he had to, and then he left the room. The Argentinian ran past him, hurrying to the restart.

At the end of the corridor, Achilles stopped and turned, some part of his confusion at this episode demanding that he see Mr Brown still standing there, to prove that it had been real. Mr Brown smiled again, and nodded to Achilles, and Achilles called, 'Thank you.' He didn't know what for or what else to say, though he felt in some strange way as if he had been anointed. Or blessed. If there was a difference. Achilles turned again.

'Oh!' called Mr Brown, stifled. Achilles spun, frightened somehow. Mr Brown was bustling towards him. 'I almost forgot. I don't know why I think . . . You don't need me to . . . Sorry. I wouldn't have bought Louie,' he said. Achilles agreed. He was irritated by the American in ways he couldn't pin down. Then Brown said, 'But I was wrong about him. You've probably already realised.'

'Okay,' said Achilles. He really had to go.

'Yes. Good luck.'

The Socialists didn't relent, and they won the game 3–0, but that was by the by.

When John Brown returned to his seat, the game was already underway, and KSC were mounting an attack. Brown saw it would break down when it reached Seung because Will Beauchamp was stuck over on the right and Seung would have no one to pass to. Brown drank in the faces of the fans, and, as he had the whole match, felt Louie Cohen's gaze. Brown caught the American's eye, and Louie, as before, refused to look away.

Louie watched Brown's smile broaden, and the old man winked at him. The width of the smile was all wrong, stretching the mouth. It was hiding something. Upset, maybe, or pain. After Brown winked, he looked back at the game, and from time to time, Louie saw, he dropped his head. It was a gesture of weariness and something like defeat, but not defeat. Maybe it was sadness for something left unsaid, or for something that would never now be done, or simply for a life only half-lived. This is what Louie thought later, but all he knew at the time was that he had to watch, because in some way Mr Brown was more important than this match.

Given all this, it is odd that Louie didn't notice the manager die. Outwardly at least, the old man didn't rage against the passing. He simply stopped. Only when the third goal went in, and there was no reaction, none at all, did Louie realise. Louie knew instinctively that the old man wouldn't want to be noticed until the game was over. Louie's own sense of mission, his realisation that Allah had kept him on KSC's sidelines for this very moment, led him, as subtly as he could, to move across to the seat behind the man he suddenly conceived of as his mentor. Brown's hand, still warm, hung by his right side, out of sight of the other players, and Louie, hunched forwards, was able to engulf it in his own. 'It is right,' he thought, 'that I am the first of the Socialists to commune with the guide who has shown us towards the light, who took men of different colours and creeds and created a team whose vitality and strength came from its multicultural basis, its tolerance and its humanity.' The old man's soul was as strong as a lion to have known he would die and to have faced it with such bravery. That spirit, felt Louie, was passing into him now, and he would guard its flame with his life.

JOHN BROWN'S BODY

Esther thought the funeral was too private. She pleaded to the Committee that The General was a giant in the history of British sport, a great man who had died in the saddle, powers undimmed, and he deserved commemoration. She said the public had the right to show its appreciation. She didn't want anything vulgar, but if the fans had discreetly been told the time and date, they would have turned out to watch a cortège go past, which would have proved that KSC's fans are the best in the world.

After Mr Brown's death several things became clearer to Esther. The manager had breathed his last in the seat he loved most in all the world, knowing he'd taken his beloved Socialists to their rightful place at the top of the league, and Esther realised that it must have been the perfect way and moment for him to go. Rather than feel any stupid guilt at shifting him aside, Esther should be proud that her actions in the Committee paved the way for Mr Brown to stay on in a ceremonial role, which in his weakened state he probably secretly preferred.

Esther also realised that KSC, and by extension the Rosslares, were the only family Mr Brown had. She'd never seen the strangers in the fourth pew before the reading of the will, so they couldn't have been that important to Mr Brown. She didn't think they should be there. They were just money-grubbing and trying to get in on the act because Mr Brown was famous. A funeral should be for family (and fans).

Esther sat next to Adam and the rest of the Committee. Tom acted hurt for some reason, but Esther explained that she had to demonstrate solidarity with the club. Aisling was on Esther's right. When, in lieu of family, the Committee took charge of the arrangements, Esther worried that Aisling would speak at the funeral and take credit somehow. It went against the grain of her modesty, but Esther quickly put herself forward, and there was nothing Aisling could do about it.

*

Aisling was uncomfortable that Esther was sitting between her and Adam. She had been right to get him out of consultancy, but she hadn't meant for him to be taken over by the bloody football.

The service was in the Social Club's own chapel, which was just over the road from all the East Kilburn tube and train stations. The white concrete Church of St Nicholas, Michael the Archangel and St Brendan the Navigator, which was just the plain Church of St Nicholas until it was rebuilt by Connor after the second war, is as startling as it was in 1950. The Committee wanted to re-erect it brick for brick, but Connor, atypically, overrode them. Connor had always hated the old St Nick's, which was a gloomy, forbidding, enveloping place, and which had almost turned him away from religion entirely, which would have been the end of him. Hank had saved him and the others in the towering seas of the North Atlantic but without God those ten days would have driven Connor mad. Connor's God was not dark and gloomy; He was light and hope. He was not the driving rain and sheer waves; He was the fifth morning, when, with the food all but finished, the storm abated and the crystal-fresh sun played brightly on six otherworldly hours of calm, and the cod almost leaping into the lifeboat. Then the storm reawoke, and it was a week before Hank took them to land, but Connor and his men knew in their hearts that they had been saved.

So, after a quest that took him across Europe, never doubting that he would know what he was looking for when he found it, Connor saw a house like a waterfall of cubes tumbling into a fjord. Its architect was a scornful young atheist, but Connor's God wouldn't mind. There had been atheists on his raft, and two Hindus, and God had saved them all. Connor wouldn't have glorified a God who minded who believed in Him. After many discussions about light and openness, and about what the chapel was supposed to be and represent, Connor finally said that he wanted a church as unlike a submarine as it was possible for a church to be. The atheist found this instruction both clear and exciting. St Brendan's sat atop Sheriff Road like a great spaceship, saturated with light from its immense plain-glass windows, its congregation raked towards the altar from three uneven sides. Now there were residents campaigning to have it granted heritage status; they were the same ones who originally called it a modernist eyesore.

Aisling declared her faith as hatches, matches, dispatches. She attended St Brendan's from time to time on hungover Sunday mornings. She felt proprietorial.

Dave had brought Sally with him, which was perfectly reasonable. They were sitting with Carlo and Will Laird, not with Achilles, which was surprising.

'Are you okay with what you're going to say?' she asked Esther, as if she was being kind, and pretended offence at her sister's sarcastic reply. The way Adam had been seduced by football, and treated Esther as the fount of all wisdom, and the airs this had given Esther – that she was KSC's arbiter-in-chief – were really pissing Aisling off. She couldn't believe Adam and Esther had anything to talk about outside football; she couldn't believe she had pushed him into this obsession; she couldn't believe Dave prefered Sally to her; and, more than anything, she couldn't believe Mr Brown had been so sick and she'd never noticed. Who would she speak to now? Where would she confess her sins? Obviously she wasn't the only one suffering, but for just an instant the open nave felt like a cathedral to things she had lost. Esther put her hand comfortingly on Adam's knee, and Aisling's blood thickened; but Tom was an adult, and if he couldn't see what was in front of him, then that was his lookout. Achilles must know what was going on, and he would speak to Tom if he thought it were necessary. So either Achilles didn't know, or he had told Tom and Tom didn't care, or Tom did care, and he'd told Esther, and Esther didn't care. Aisling hadn't spoken to Achilles properly since Christmas, and she missed him. Although they were always best-friend intimate at KSC events, they never saw each other otherwise, so it was an easy relationship to drop. Aisling regretted it now, because, although this was a basically awful day, they could at least have had some fun talking about Esther peacocking around as Head Mourner.

St Brendan's was packed with past and present Socialists, and there was also a row of strangers. A slablike man was there, along with three surprisingly young, suburban-looking women, all of whom were sheepish when they were introduced to Aisling and Esther. A Chinese couple with French accents, an Arabic man in jeans and a man in tweed with immensely thick glasses rounded out the group. Slab man shook everyone's hands solemnly. The strangers knew they were being watched, and looked almost proud, but neither then nor at the reception did they reveal who they were. 'Old friends,' is all they said, and they were the only clue anyone would ever have of Mr Brown's other life.

'Mr Brown was not just the greatest manager this club has ever known,' read Esther, very slowly, determined to be heard. 'He was like a father to me. While my beautiful sister was learning about make-up and boys, I was spending all my time in the back rooms of the Kilburn Social Club, and I still do. Over the years, I came to know the famously reclusive manager much better than any person alive. I don't know how many of you realise it, but he spent last Christmas with my family in Ireland. He was very kind to my grandmother, who sadly can't be here today, and, for the benefit of her and my sister, he resisted talking about football for the whole two days he was with us!' Esther was prepared for a laugh there, but none came. That was fine. She was only prepared just in case, and she'd only put the joke in because she'd read that she should try to make the speech as light as possible. She didn't really think it was appropriate, but this was her first oration and she wanted to do the done thing. 'In spite of that, as you all know, football was not just the most important thing in Mr Brown's life. I think everyone will agree with me when I say, it *was* his life.' Most of the congregation were looking at their feet, which was only proper, but Esther couldn't help noticing Louie Cohen, eyes fixed on her, nodding assent. She and Adam had been right about him. 'Some of you played with "The General", and although I never had the privilege of seeing him on the hallowed turf, I believe it is quite right to regard him as one of KSC's genuine legends as a player, though as we all know, that was just the preamble of his career before the much more satisfying culmination of his mission in the managerial dugout, where he truly found his home, his greatest professional happiness, and, appropriately, his final resting place.

'You all know that KSC is special,' she read, and paused significantly. 'Mr Brown believed wholeheartedly in the club's ethos that individuals do not matter at all – everything has to be for the team.' She caught Achilles gesturing to Zondi, as if he didn't agree, but then he wouldn't. Achilles had never properly fitted in. Louie, on the other hand, had locked his eyes on her and was drinking in every word. She was delivering this to him now, and to Adam, and James Purnell, who was sitting very modestly towards the back of the nave, well behind the strangers.

'Every death is also a rebirth,' she continued, 'and perhaps the greatest happiness for Mr Brown was that he passed on knowing his team was in perfect hands, that he had chosen and groomed the man who would follow him and continue his wonderful legacy of team-work and success. When we look at the current campaign, as his "army" sweeps all before it, and as we look at his happy and well-drilled "troops", we are reminded that his greatest skill was always planning. Knowing "The General" as I did, I know he went in the way and at the time he would have chosen. We must not regret his death, but celebrate his life. We are all Socialists now!'

Esther thought she and Aisling should greet the mourners as they arrived at the reception, but Aisling, presumably embarrassed because she'd never paid attention to KSC, said that it wasn't as if they were his family – they should mingle and host as graciously as they could. It was not up to the sisters, Aisling said in a maddening flash, to 'put themselves forward'.

So now, as usual, everyone was hanging around her sister. Aisling probably didn't even know that the men she was laughing with were old teammates of Mr Brown's. Esther joined them. 'Arthur, Gerry, Struan,' she said. They all stopped laughing, and Esther felt pleasantly like a grown-up. 'It's a very sad day,' she said.

'Yes, Miss Rosslare,' said Struan.

'How is Bob? Still scoring?' Struan's grandson played for Stranraer.

'Yes, thank you for asking.'

'And,' turning to Gerry Handler, 'how is Mrs Handler? How is the frog collection?'

'Thousands now, Miss Rosslare. She's over there if you want to talk to her.'

'Est,' butted in Aisling, before Esther had a chance to include David, 'Struan was saying that he's thinking of blowing his savings on the lottery.'

'But Struan —'

'It's a great idea,' butted in Gerry. 'Rollover Beethoven – ten bloody million.'

'But it's unlikely you would —'

'That's the beauty. I checked with Aisling, with *Lady Rosslare*, I mean,' they all laughed, like geese, 'and she agreed: KSC would never let a double-winning hero starve, and I wouldn't mind a room at the Social Club – I don't get around that great any more. Aisling worked it out. If I buy twenty thousand tickets, I have, what was it, hen?'

'One in sixteen thousand.'

'If I lose, I move to the home, like I want, but I also have a one in sixteen thousand chance of being a millionaire again! I like those odds!'

With white knuckles, Esther tried to ask subtly whether, *given the past*, he thought that was really wise? Did Aisling realise, Esther wondered, that Struan's twenty thousand was all that was left of the *five million* his wife had left him?

'Of course I realise, Est. The whole point is to get Stru back in the clover.'

'But it was gambling that —'

'It was a joke, Esther.'

'I started it, Miss Rosslare,' said Gerry. 'I was taking the piss out of the feckless ex-plutocrat, sort of thing, and it just snowballed.'

'Well,' replied Esther, and they all looked abashed. 'I must talk to other people,' she said.

The guests were like wary animals around the last waterhole, thought Zondi.

First there was Adam, about whom he and Achilles did not know what to do. Every type of creature has its own ways, and its time in the sun. Zondi saw that Adam knew his time was now, as he revelled in the light that KSC shone on him. He was only thirty, but that can be a significant age for some men, and it had pushed Adam, not unwilling, into pulling himself into focus. He no longer wore suits that might have been chosen by a careless accountant, or looked as if his mother cut his hair. He was becoming /Ntsi: kwe, the Bower Bird, who must find a mate before his colours dim, and has not time to notice Ggh'we, the Little Crow, who thinks the show is all for her because she lives in the same tree. If /Ntsi: kwe thinks of /Ggh'we at all, it is because she sings so beautifully, and adds to the fineness of his sparkly nest. Except Adam was not the Bower Bird, who is vain and stupid. He had noticed the Little Crow, but he had chosen not to disabuse her. Zondi was unimpressed.

Over on the raised area, with a good view of everyone and a clear path to both doors out of the hall, were the strangers no one had met before. They seemed relaxed, but Zondi noticed that, however often he looked, every individual's back was always being casually watched by at least one other. Normally Zondi had to force his identifications, and it was in the distance between what he saw and what he imagined that he worked out what he really thought, but it was so obvious that this was a team of meerkats that everyone else must see it too. The meerkats seemed to be watching out of habit, though, not out of fear. If you stand alone and seem comfortable, no one at a party will come and talk to you, and you can just watch. Adam had preened harder for today than Zondi had seen before. It was not just that Adam was thirty, Zondi realised, but that he was in the presence of death and the shortness of man's time. He was not the only one. The room was full of ex-footballers like broken lions.

Zondi watched Aisling catch sight of Dave, and think about escaping, but the Tall Hunter bore down on her, arm around his woman. Zondi had not satisfactorily placed Sally in his foolish pantheon. The Tall Hunter was the problem, because in the stories Zondi could remember, the Hunter did not have one woman, but many. The Hunter feared that women would thieve his 'kwa. Zondi knew there was another story of the Tall Hunter, about how he was trapped at last, but he couldn't recall it, or even remember if it was the Hunter's last story. Sally was certainly not /Ne-ne', the one who believed the Hunter would come to her in the end because she had been told it was written in the bones when the Farseer cast them on her growing day, but /Ne-ne' didn't know the Farseer was /Kaggen in disguise, whom she had repulsed and who was revenging himself on her by making her wait for ever for something that would never be hers. No, Sally was not /Ne-ne'. Sally took Aisling's hand, and held it, and to Zondi it was as if she were cradling a baby. There was Esther, and she was pushing Adam in front of her towards Aisling, Dave and Sally. Zondi's heart went out to her as she flaunted Adam at Dave with hungry eyes, and stood proudly between Adam and Aisling. Esther didn't notice the looks Aisling gave both Adam and Dave. Zondi feared that Esther would be shamed, but the Butterfly had already seen and he was fluttering to the rescue, as he always would.

Dave, Sally at his side, found himself approaching Aisling. All three recognised that to stop and turn away would be impossible, though in

Dave's case it was at least partly because Sally would regard such an act as cowardly. Dave had not forgiven Aisling. After the shock of what happened after the Christmas Party, he had slowly decided that she knew exactly what she was doing that night, and what she'd been doing when she talked to Sally afterwards. After the first quiet greeting, before any awkward talk about the weather, Dave felt Sally steel herself for this test of her emotional maturity. She took Aisling's hand and asked if everything was all right. Aisling replied that she was very fond of Mr Brown, but it was not as if he had been family. Sally said quietly that Dave had taken a few days before he could comfortably express how much Mr Brown had meant to him, and Sally could see that Aisling was just the same, and it wasn't healthy. Sally said there was nothing to be ashamed of. Aisling had lost someone she cared about, and if she needed someone to talk to about that when she was ready, Sally, *whatever else* had happened between them, would be there. Dave agreed that frankness was the way to lance boils, of course, but Aisling was obviously embarrassed and amused at the situation, and signalled both things for Dave's benefit. Dave didn't react. There was a moment of silence, then Aisling said that what she found strange about today was how much she suddenly wished she'd seen Mr Brown play football. It must have been such a defining, amazing thing in his life, and it felt as if by not knowing him then she couldn't have known him at all, and the thought made her sad.

'Hello, Dave, Sally,' said Esther, joining them suddenly, as if in a hurry. 'What terrible circumstances. Sally, do you know Adam?'

Dave knew something was going on. He didn't know what exactly. He was just —

'*Ciao bella*,' said Achilles, kissing Aisling theatrically, and evening them up into couples. 'Mr Brown would not like the long faces, no? We must glitter and be gay, no, although there is grief in our hearts, of course?'

'I suppose we must try to carry on as normal,' said Esther. 'It's a great comfort to us all, I am sure, to know we have *special people* on whom we can *rely*.' Dave watched her squeeze Adam's forearm. She was too intent on her sister to notice that Adam was also looking at Aisling, half-pleading. As soon as Esther and Adam turned their heads back into the circle, Aisling – when she thought no one else would notice – gave Dave another secret smile to say she was not complicit in any of this, and it was slightly grim, but he had to admit it was funny, didn't he? And he involuntarily showed he did.

'I actually came over to let you know,' said Achilles, 'that the photographer from the *Notices* wants to know —'

'Oh, gosh! We should deal with that,' said Esther hastily. 'Come on, Adam. Lets find JP.' Esther revelled in Purnell's informality. She and Adam burrowed off, and Dave turned back to find Achilles leading Aisling away towards Zondi, giggling about something, and he realised then that Achilles had separated him and Aisling for Sally's sake, as if there were any reason to do that, as if it were any of Achilles' interfering fucking business.

OCTOBER REVOLUTION

A month after the funeral, the Socialists remained unbeaten, but a number of things had changed.

Pat Credence made a couple of mistakes, both costly, and he was replaced by Louie Cohen, who'd been playing brilliantly for the reserves. Pat tried to blame Purnell, undermining the boss with those teammates he thought would listen, but Achilles, Zondi and Dave spread their view that Purnell's decision was one of those things, and no player had a right to a starting place. The others accepted this without demurral partly because it was true, but also because the Socialists could see that Achilles, Zondi and Dave had formed an informal troika, and no one wanted to get on their wrong side in this transitional period.

It didn't help that Louie was so American. Brashness is not a bad thing, *ipso facto*, but there's a time and a place. Louie could surely have found somewhere to pray other than the side of the training pitch with everyone watching him. At lunch, he would evangelise, not about Islam – he was not that kind of missionary – but about tolerance and individual liberty. He earnestly explained that there must be a global free market in ideology, because when everyone had a choice, they would choose the most freedom, which meant democracy. When individuals were truly free, the world would inevitably be rid of prejudice, because the great religions, whatever abuses they were subjected to, were fundamentally open-minded.

This was not really something Louie's teammates were interested in talking about on the bus, especially when Louie started to crane round and include everyone in his sermon. Dave and Achilles were too polite to deal with it. Mickey Faller, a soft-eyed south Londoner whose mother was black and whose father might have been white, who would never admit that he felt intimidated by Achilles and Dave just because they were posh, told Louie that if he was really serious about going yid, mate, what he needed to do was have the cut. 'You've got to go the whole hog, mate,' he said. 'Pardon the pig reference.' Everyone laughed, but they also watched.

Then Carlo said, 'Suicide bombers.' Everyone was quiet. 'No. Seriously, Louie, mate, where do they fit in?'

'No one who believes in Allah could take innocent life.'

Carlo had been a Socialist for four years. He wasn't schooled like some of the others, and he wasn't interested in books. He was using his dev-time to learn the guitar, which was pretty fucking cool, actually, but just because he wasn't as clever as some, that didn't mean he didn't have any opinions, and Pat was the guy who'd shown him round London when he first joined. 'You saying the suicide bombers don't believe in Allah?' he said. Louie didn't answer immediately. 'Simple enough question, Louie, mate. It seems to me they believe in Allah too fucking much, and their Allah wants to kill everyone who doesn't agree with them, and that's your Allah too, mate.'

'Throughout history, Christians have committed —'

'We're not talking about history, mate. History's crap. We're talking about people being killed now. How can you believe in that?'

'Louie doesn't believe in that,' said Achilles. 'There are tolerant Muslims, just as there are intolerant Jews and Christians.'

'Like the Americans,' said Carlo. 'They're intolerant Christians, aren't they? When they bomb Saudi for oil?'

'America acts only in self-defence,' said Louie.

'Isn't America defending the Jews?' said Carlo.

'The war was to protect the Emirates and Kuwait, not Israel.'

'You're full of shit.'

After, Carlo apologised to Achilles and Dave; it's just that Louie was so up himself. Carlo knew he should leave the arguments to them, because they knew what they were talking about, but he wasn't completely thick, and he knew he was right about suicide bombers at least. When Carlo left, Dave pontificated about how Carlo, untutored as he was, had got right to the heart of Louie's shaky theoretical underpinnings, his simplistic views of Islam, democracy and liberty.

The troika didn't set out to hold a salon for players wanting to share their worries about how the side was playing, or behaving off the pitch, but their teammates knew where to find them and when. Midway through October, after Seung had been injured for four weeks, Carlo joined them for coffee in the players' lounge when everyone else had left after training.

Carlo explained, sipping frequently, how Mr Brown had told him that his style of play at left back wasn't suited to KSC's current formation, because of the crosses he made. Purnell had put him back into Seung's place, obviously, but he didn't feel effective, and the left wasn't producing the penetration it had earlier in the season. He'd tried to talk to Purnell about it, but the manager had dismissed him, very friendly, actually, he's a nice guy, I'm not saying any different, but he totally didn't listen to me. Purnell said that the team Mr Brown had bequeathed the club was playing in Mr Brown's style, and that what was good enough for Mr Brown was good enough for him. 'He said I had nothing to worry about, I won't lose my place or anything, and he hasn't noticed much difference down the left. He said that all I had to do was keep trying as hard as I could, because I was a good enough player to make it work, and it's only been four games, after all. But it is different, isn't it? If I'm playing there, we need different runs from the strikers, don't we?' Dave said he'd have a word with the strikers about changing their runs. Achilles said that he'd already noticed this problem, and he'd spoken to Tom and Will about it yesterday.

Pat grabbed hold of Dave as they left the changing room an hour later. 'I know what you've been saying about me,' he said. 'I'm not stupid.'

'All I've said is —'

'I said I know what you said. It's one thing being dropped by the boss, that's his job, but —'

'It's not my fault I agree with him. I understand how you feel, but you're destabilising the team.'

'Who made you king?'

'It's just —'

'You think you know best, so whatever you say is fine? And when you and Achilles tell everyone what to do behind JP's back, that isn't destabilising the team, is it?'

'It's for the good of the team.'

'Says you.'

Don't think Pat wasn't a good guy, by the way. Wait till you're dropped from a Premiership team and see how you feel.

*

143

Another troika was also developing. Esther and Adam were increasingly reliant on Will Beauchamp, who kept them up to date with what was going on in the dressing room, and hinted about how the team might be improved. Beauchamp said that JP was a terrific motivator, and that everyone in the team really liked him, but maybe he wasn't the best judge of players. Carlo was disappointing cover for Seung, for instance. If the Committee wanted to think about new faces, Will said, maybe they'd like to have a word with him, and Will would gauge the mood of the senior players.

HOW THE YOUNG LIVE

Monica was annoyed that Sally was staying in with Dave instead of going to the screening. She said Sally was no fun any more, which was unfair. It was simply that many of the people Dave met when he came out with her were vain and stupid. It was good of him to tolerate them as often as he did. She didn't never go out; she just went out less than she would have otherwise. Compromise was part of being mature.

Sally enjoyed parties because she was able to tune out the rubbish people spoke, and she'd have gone tonight if Dave had been busy, but Dave's analysis of what people said made it increasingly hard for her to ignore how shallow it all was. She could hardly blame Dave for being too genuine. She worried that he found her inane, but the one time she mentioned it, he said that if he thought she was inane, why would he still keep seeing her? She felt inane for asking.

Dave rapped three times, then another quick two, and let himself in. It was his signal, not that he and Sal had ever discussed it. He never used the clown's face doorknocker Sal's mum had given her. He was glad she wasn't making him endure the screening. He always went when she asked, but these parties were so fucking tedious, and she didn't enjoy them any more than he did, so they only went to the ones she couldn't avoid. It was amazing that he'd found her: someone who understood being recognised, but who hated the rigmarole. Tonight, she was wearing her stripy brown halter neck, jeans and indoor flip-flops, and she seemed to him to be glowing. He picked her up and kissed her against the wall. She said the lasagne needed forty-five minutes in the oven, and he carried her to the bedroom. They laughed at their unnecessary urgency – they hardly needed ten minutes – and then Dave pulled Sally on top of him, feeling her weigh him down, anchor him, whatever it was, but it felt perfect. This was their kind of evening. Ideally, maybe, they would have a couple of friends round as well, because his mates were important to him, and they offered a different kind of talk, which was nothing really – her friends were important to her, too, of course. But sometimes it was important to give each other some time, to be together alone. She was not just his girlfriend. She was, and he used to hate the word before he understood it, his partner.

'It'll be ready,' she said, eventually. He made her a drink, and they sat together comfortably in the lounge. She rested her head against him in a way he used to think was over the top, but this was what he had chosen.

'How's Pat?' she asked. Dave replied that Pat was thinking of moving to another club, but it was particularly hard for him because he'd never played football anywhere else, not even as a child. 'He's still very good, isn't he?' she said. 'Even though Louie is . . . I know. I know.' She nestled her head against his shoulder. 'And how is Achilles?' She asked these questions every day, which was perfectly reasonable, but it was not as if anything had changed. He'd tell her if it did.

'You're lucky,' he said.

'I know.'

'I'm thinking about Pat. You can write songs for ever, but for us, as soon as the legs go, it's all over.'

'That's why you're lucky. You'll still have your teaching.' That's what Dave always said about himself. It wasn't fair to think Sally should see past it.

Dave loved teaching because it meant that football didn't define who he was. Except . . . Sally was so obviously happy for him to be who he was, and didn't care about KSC, that she probably couldn't see that there was part of him that *did* need to play to be who he was, that couldn't imagine living without the game, a private part that only people like Achilles and Zondi could see. Stopping was something every sportsman had to go through, and they all did. The fact that Dave couldn't imagine what that would be like didn't mean he would be unable to deal with it. Trying to share the burden would only increase it, because Sally would fret without being able to help. He wished he could talk to Mr Brown. Soon, surely, he'd be speaking properly with Achilles again, who must be thinking these same things.

'I keep humming the song I wrote about Aisling,' said Sally. 'I feel funny when I do. Not for any reason.' Aisling, who understood that playing football had been part of what defined Mr Brown. Dave didn't want to think about Aisling tonight.

Sally finished eating, put the plates in the dishwasher and poured herself the last of the wine (Dave only ever had one glass unless it was a special occasion). It was a different kind of lovely evening to a party, a better kind.

Dave stopped her in the hallway wearing his coat and her stomach somersaulted insanely. Then he handed her the black quilted one of hers he liked and, not saying a word, waited for her to put on her shoes and pulled her outside. He put his arm around her as they walked. He didn't like all the leaves on the road because he was so scared of treading in dog shit. She never worried, and if that meant, once a year, she had to clean dog shit off her shoes, it was a small price to pay for not spending her life staring at her feet. But it was sweet that Dave did. She would have put on the duffel coat if she'd had the choice, but she didn't want to spoil the moment, so now, even with Dave's arm, she was chilly. The soft wet yellow leaves had been swept from the streets, and the new ones were crispy brown, the ones which had hung too long to the tree, and were all used up, parched by the bitter wind.

'Dave . . .'

'Shh.' He led her through the backstreets behind Primrose Hill, which was locked up and beautiful on their left. Between two houses was a tiny little dead-end alley that must lead to some basement or granny flat. Her chest was thumping. Dave held up a key. 'There are only two of these. Mr Brown gave them to Achilles,' his voice was blank when he said that, 'and Achilles gave one to me.' He turned the key in the fence at the end of the alley, and opened a gate you would never have imagined was there unless you were standing right next to it. Dave gestured grandly to the hill. 'Behold,' he said, 'my Secret Garden.'

Being alone in the park was amazing, even in the cold. The city meant the stars were only tiny pinpricks, but they felt huge, and the moon had a bright little halo. They climbed the hill to the bench and Dave sat her down. 'Reach under the seat,' he said.

Mr Brown was not in the sky, looking down, that is not how things work. But if he were, what would he think about Dave kneeling at Sally's feet, as she fumbled to unstick the little box, and opened it, and then leaped into his arms? Would he think that this was a happy moment in the life of the bench that, for a while, he had foolishly thought of as his? That the bench had spent long enough holding up a dying man, and its reward was this joyful moment of renewal? Or would he have thought that Dave was in a hurry because time always looks short to sportsmen?

CHRISTMAS PARTY AGAIN

After last year's dress, which her mind had transformed into a genuine mistake, Esther chose something ankle-length in charcoal grey. If anyone noticed it at all, it would only be because it was of extremely high quality, which was not Esther showing off, but because her father always warned against false economy. Esther had to admit the dress was beautifully cut and, when she looked in the mirror, she told herself she was horrified to find it didn't hide her figure as much as it might, and it surely left more shoulder exposed than such a timid person as she could possibly have intended? It was too late to do anything about it now. She would deal with the problem by wearing a shawl.

So much was happening to Esther that it was almost impossible to keep things straight in her head. When the tickets were printed, but before she had thought about what to do, Adam said, 'I suppose you'll be going with Tom?' She detected something hopeful in his voice, and so she understood he was being brave when he added quickly, 'Yes, I thought so. Well, that's good. I thought I'd invite Aisling, seeing as I hardly ever see her any more.'

It was typical of Aisling that she had tricked Adam on to the Committee and then abandoned him. Esther bet that Adam thought it would be his big chance to see her all the time, but that only went to show he didn't know her very well. He was learning now.

She was ready ten minutes before the taxi arrived, and so she gulped a shot of vodka, because she had to be relaxed, because tonight was the night of her life, perhaps. She was taking the taxi alone. This morning, she finally told Tom that she wouldn't let him keep using her, and he was shocked for some reason. He said he wouldn't come to the dinner, but Esther insisted because otherwise it would look terrible, as if she'd broken his heart on the day of the dinner! Tom asked why she hadn't waited one more day? Esther replied that telling him immediately was actually showing him respect and honesty. Esther could admit now that maybe Tom cared more for her than she originally thought, but that only made it better that she had told him before things got worse. Absolute honesty was her watchword.

Tom asked her if she was secretly seeing Adam, which was a typical, arrogant, male reaction, and she said that whatever he'd heard was rubbish; she and Adam were just friends.

It went against her nature to take the lead. But Adam was, just like her, risk averse. He was perfectly sensible, so he was never going to say or do anything with her while she was seeing someone else. It was up to her to act. There was still the thread tying him to Aisling, but Esther and Adam were made for each other. Even if he was surprised tonight, she would tell him that she was prepared to wait until the ends of the earth.

When Esther told Tom their relationship was over, there were still several hours before he needed to be at Kilburn Park, and he went to Achilles for advice, who was so moved that he made some of his father's special coffee. Achilles faced his usual dilemma of seeing more than other people saw, and not knowing how much to tell them. Tom and Esther wandered around in separate dreamlands, and waking someone up who is sleepwalking can be dangerous, so all Achilles said was, 'Wait and see what happens.' Sometimes it's not cowardice to be circumspect.

Tom was the fifth-best-looking Socialist (he would have been third but he lost points for being small, which both Achilles and Zondi felt bad about, but you've got to have a system). He was strong rather than stocky, with jet-dark hair and fierce, intelligent, misleading grey eyes. Achilles wanted to protect Tom, and wished Zondi were home. Zondi always left the talking to him, but Achilles felt better knowing Zondi was listening, acting as checks and balances. Achilles felt better if Zondi was there, under all circumstances, even if it looked as if Achilles was doing all the work. Take the house, for instance. It was decorated with brown leather sofas and lamps like big plastic fruit; bold modern art, and groaning bookshelves artfully leading the eye from Jilly Cooper, Jorge Luis Borges and Herman Melville to Zane Grey, Haruki Murakami and Philippe Senderos; a wooden globe whose top slid open to reveal a drinks cabinet. Every time Achilles improved something, he worried that everything would be too perfect, but he didn't tell anyone, not even Zondi, because he knew it was stupid. Even if he ever got the room exactly the way he wanted it today, he would be someone else tomorrow. Zondi pretended not to care how the house looked, but soon after they started living together, Achilles noticed that Zondi sometimes moved little things, or rearranged the lights. At first, Achilles said nothing, because he was afraid of embarrassing Zondi. A less astute man might have moved something back, to see if Zondi cared so much he would move it again, but Achilles knew that Zondi would have felt rebuked, and ashamed. So Achilles let Zondi change things sometimes, but pretended he hadn't noticed. Then, eventually, he worked out what to do. He started to put new things in such absurd places that they *had* to be moved, and Zondi would be forced to make the choice. It was a game, and they never spoke about it except in the jokes Achilles made about how Zondi was too pure and obsessed by his austere, violent past to care what a stupid house looked like. Dave understood the joke when they made it in front of him; Tom would never understand it in a million years.

Zondi was buying this year's dinner shirts. Achilles understood Zondi better than anyone ever would, but why his friend insisted on new shirts for the dinner every year, and why Zondi insisted on buying them himself, alone, was beyond him.

Achilles and Tom drank coffee listening to Judy. Achilles didn't care about seeming like a cliché any more than a straight man might about listening to the Beatles. There were too many things to worry about in this world, and Achilles was comfortable in his skin. The coffee was extraordinary. He must phone his father later.

'Wait for what, though?' said Tom, eventually, and Achilles, who wasn't sure, told him that Esther was still immature and didn't know what she wanted. Until then, it was sensible to wait. 'But she's decided she doesn't want me, though, hasn't she? And it's not as if there's someone else because she's just not that kind of girl, is she? When she said it was over, I straight away thought there might be, but she said that was really arrogant of me, which it was, wasn't it? She said she told me today because she didn't want it to get to the stage where I was serious about her in case anyone got hurt, which is kind of her, actually, isn't it? It shows she didn't realise how much I feel though, doesn't it? Do you think I should tell her I really love her?'

'Not today,' said Achilles.

'I can't go tonight. I'll have to sit next to her. I should have known she was out of my league. She is, isn't she?'

'Go tonight. I don't know what's going to happen, but I think you have to go.' Achilles wasn't really worried about Tom, not deep down. Tom was the kind of guy who would always find someone to be in love with. Going tonight should help him see the light as far as he and Esther were concerned, which would be no bad thing. Tom agreed, and then, naturally, they talked football. Tom said Achilles was a genius for suggesting he attack Carlo's crosses differently. Achilles said it was really Dave's idea, but actually Achilles wasn't sure Dave could have made Tom see how to change his runs. Even Mr Brown had preferred to pick Seung instead of Carlo, even though Seung wasn't as good a footballer, but Achilles was a goalscorer, which Mr Brown and Dave had never been, and, without getting too mystical about it, goalscorers understand how to talk to other goalscorers. Now, whoever played left back, Tom and Will would make the right runs. Dave was happy about what Achilles had done, and impressed, but that wasn't the sum of Dave's reaction.

'I should go,' said Tom, eventually. 'Thanks.'

'You must come tonight.'

'I will, don't worry. I have to, anyway. Esther said that if I didn't, Aisling would laugh at her for not having a date, and she looked as if she was going to cry.'

The party had been underway for an hour. Aisling had been there for twenty minutes, and she was on her second Kir royale. She was with Adam, who looked fantastic, frankly. On the one hand, his football epiphany had been a triumph for Aisling, letting her point out to Nicky that her decision to 'steamroller' him hadn't been 'cavalier', but a piece of genius. On the other hand, Adam had now got unbelievably boring about KSC, and Aisling was prepared for a tedious evening. At least he hadn't asked Esther. Adam and Aisling were standing with Esther now – she had dragged Tom over as soon as Adam and Aisling arrived. Esther was wearing too much make-up, and she was pretending to be hot so that at any moment, yup, right on cue, she could take off her wrap, overacting wildly. That was the most tit she'd ever seen Esther display in public, and Esther had displayed it straight at Adam. Good fucking grief.

'Adam —' Esther began.

'*Bella querida*,' said Achilles, appearing as if by magic, and kissing Aisling's hand. She couldn't help perking up, and Tom did too. 'We are six, no?' he said. 'What a coincidence!' Zondi had a tray with six glasses of what looked in the restaurant light like champagne, but which, if experience was anything to go by, was Achilles' champagne cocktail, which contained no one but he knew what exactly. They each took one, smiling, even if Esther was thin-lipped about the prospect of anyone having any fun.

Tom was looking at Esther like a fucking mooncalf, whatever that is. Aisling started to wonder if maybe there was something she could do to deal with the situation. Someone had to, soon, and if no one else was going to, maybe it'd have to be her. It'd seem harsh, like a surgeon cutting out a growth that everyone else hoped was benign, but what if it wasn't fucking benign? It might ruin everyone's lives if someone didn't deal with it. It wasn't that Aisling has decided to do anything, it's just that she'd had the idea. She took another sip.

Aisling knew she was sharper than the average bear, and she was hyperaware tonight. Tom had leaned his upper arm against Esther's a couple of times, and each time Esther had moved away. Esther had put her hand on Adam's arm twice, and neither time had Adam done anything about it. Aisling was livid with Adam, who was one of her best fucking friends, for fuck's sake. The first time the hand went up, when Esther was quizzing Adam about Aisling's dress, wasn't it amazing, etc., Achilles had grabbed Esther's hands and stared into her eyes saying that what she was wearing was second to nothing, so refined but so revealing, seeming so restrained but revealing so much, *querida!* Esther blushed from her toes, and almost put on her stupid wrap, but Adam agreed with Achilles, and it went smugly back over her arm. Then, a couple of minutes later, having finished her cocktail as if it were apple juice, and as if Tom wasn't fucking there (didn't she realise how lucky she was to have someone who'd put up with her po-faced bullshit?), Esther ran her finger down Adam's lapel (midnight-green silk, obviously aping Achilles) and said that it was amazing that people thought all black-tie outfits looked the same when it was obvious to anyone who cared that just because the distinctions were subtle, that didn't mean they weren't there, and that sometimes the best things were understated and seemed to be very conservative, didn't he agree? It was all so fucking arch. This time, Achilles took her arm away and turned her right out to the rest of the room and made her, since she was so astute, analyse the rest of the room's dinner wear. Esther probably thought this was typical shallow Achilles, but Adam must have noticed what was going on. They started with Fliss, a typical footballer's-wife-style hanger-on who had somehow ended up with the still-limping Seung, to their obviously mutual confusion. Fliss had tried to conform to the unwritten code, but she was still orange. She wasn't the only one. Esther thought Achilles was saying these girls were common, and agreed emphatically.

'So, Tom,' said Adam. 'Great goal this afternoon.'

'It was just a tap-in, wasn't it?'

'But you had to be there, though. That's what being a striker is all about. The pass from Carlo, the *cross* I mean, was very good.'

'He's a quality player.'

'Everyone in the box this afternoon was saying we're certain to win the league. The loss against Peterborough the other day was just a fluke because on the day their 3-5-2 negated the way we played by closing the centre and opening the flanks.'

'If you say so, mate. You're the expert.'

'I was just saying —'

'No, don't worry, mate. It's great that you bureaucrats even notice what's going on down on the pitch.' Aisling wanted to stop this, but Zondi of all people was ahead of her, saying gently that KSC was lucky to be run by people with such an investment in how the team did, but who also understood that a club must work on some level as an economic unit. 'Yeah. We're a great economic unit,' said Tom. 'I feel proud. I imagine that's Esther's doing, while you deal with the football side? You're obviously a top sporting brain.'

'Tom,' said Adam. 'I'm new, but I'm trying, and Esther's helping. You're a brilliant team, but you need a different kind of team behind you, and me and Esther are part of that. We're all on the same side.'

Adam was working hard not to show he was hurt, but could he have sounded any more fucking patronising? And Tom was so raw tonight, and he could see what Esther thought about Adam, and, Jesus Christ, Esther was about to grab Adam again. This absolutely had to be dealt with, and no one else was going to do it. 'A year now, for you guys,' Aisling said to Esther and Tom. 'It's so sweet.'

'Well, yeah,' said Tom, sheepish. 'Actually —' He was going to say something interesting, but Esther took his arm hurriedly. Tom stopped, not sure how to go on.

Aisling took Adam's arm, and put her head to his shoulder, laughing. 'I'm so jealous of you guys. I've never lasted a year with anyone. I pretend it's 'cos I'm too picky, but who fucking knows? I've only ever been in love once, with bloody Adam.' Adam's shoulder stiffened. He saw what was coming. Well, she couldn't feel guilty. It was ridiculous, frankly, that he hadn't used coming to KSC, which was the most supportive fucking environment he'd ever find, to make a clean breast of everything at last. 'But of course,' she went on, 'Adam turned out to be batting for the other side, which only goes to show how good my fucking judgment is.'

Esther looked as if she'd swallowed a dog, and Tom didn't know what he thought. Achilles was angry, but he must basically have approved of getting this into the open. Adam would get over it. He was her mate, after all. And at least this would stop Esther doing anything stupid and embarrassing herself. Aisling never loved Adam. Saying it was just the best way she could think to raise the subject. She'd never loved anyone in that way, actually, not really. She might, ironically given the circumstances, have fallen in love with Achilles, if she'd let herself, but she hadn't. It worried her sometimes, but this wasn't the time for self-pity. She'd done her good deed for the night, whatever people thought, and it was time to get drunk and dance.

Later, in the club, Pat Credence would have had a fight with Louie if Louie had let him. Esther, glass-eyed, danced excruciatingly with Adam as if they were lovers, now that no one could possibly think she might fancy him. Tom didn't move away, even when Dave tried to take him to the bar, and eventually Tom and Esther went home together. Aisling danced with the boy band, more flirtatiously than usual, and she enjoyed the jealous looks from the oranger dates, who knew they were outclassed, but it was a small victory. She had some options, but she decided to take a taxi back with Adam, so she could explain herself and clear the air. It turned out he'd already gone with Achilles and Zondi, though.

SONG OF THE BALL (PART 2)

Premiership, Kilburn Social Club versus Norwich City, 12 December 2000, Kilburn Park
Kilburn Social Club 0–0 Norwich City

I am Anti-Fanatic. It is my Match Day, and it is Kilburn Park. I must have been Chosen to face so difficult a Test. Blessed be the Great Sphere, even though this is an evening kick-off and I am bathed from all sides in lying false-light.

I embody seventeen per cent greater sphericity even than the new, tougher AMF standards. It is not for me to be proud of this, for I am powerless, but I do not scorn it either. It is a sign that I have been singled out, a sign of corporeal closeness to the Great Sphere. Does this sound like pride? Maybe I should scorn my form, since I am not perfect. But why else am I so spherical when others are not? Surely there must be some meaning?

The game is half gone. I did not notice it. I mean, I shall *say* I did not notice it, because that is how to persuade the literal-minded, but secretly, because I am weak, I have felt many things, and still feel them on my skin. I feel the Kilburns' desperation. I should put this from my mind, but it is so clear to me, what leather can express. There is pain in the Kilburn feet, and the memory of something that was but has gone. It is not so unlike the pain of a slow-deflating training ball which fears each day that it will be kicked once, found wanting, and rejected. And death always comes after this, never before. It hurts Conservatives, though they try to hide it, and it hurts Anti-Fanatics too, though we try to hide it too, and at those times we are all jealous of the Dragonflies, who died in their pomp and full inflation. I hope that I will make a good end, but I am weak.

My game is nearly over. I experience very little apart from still the odd sense of the Kilburns' wheezing life departing, increasingly insistent the more I try to drive it from my mind. I am not sorry for the

Kilburns – what care I for meatbags made to make us? – but I sorrow for the sadness of slow-dying balls, who depart alone and fearful, who resist the grace of the Great Sphere and so will not rebirth. The Kilburns' deflation is a parable for my preaching. Maybe some young Dragonfly, misguided by the worldly world, will be enlightened by this example.

The Dragonflies are at least *certain*. They are wrong, but they are not cynical. Cynicism is a cancer that acts upon the air and senses, rotting faith, destroying hope in a higher Truth that is not deduced from base *stuff*, some mere and humdrum Truth subject to measurement. I shall preach that even the mighty Kilburns, who the foolish Dragonflies pretend to be immortal, are dying and will perish soon, and I will compare them to the cruel-slow death of the cynic ball. It bounces less, and bounces less, and is abandoned and forgotten, and its air returns to air, where I-my-air, strong-harnessed by belief, shall find when freed of earthly mortal man-made shape – this prison in which we endure our small short time of what the foolish call our lives – at last my dreamed-on and incorporeal sphericity, perfect and eternal.

SOCIALIST DICTATORSHIP

by Calum Horton, 17 January 2001

I hate football. I am immune to the petty, vulgar, tedious hyperbole surrounding the game in general and Our Beloved Kilburn Socialists in particular. There, I've said it, and it feels great.

After a year of painstaking research, *J'accuse* the Socialists of selfishness, arrogance, greed, hypocrisy and standing fast against the very principles they claim so piously to uphold. Just because you tell the world that you care about social responsibility, purity, democracy and community, that doesn't mean you follow through with your pretty words.

Some clever dick will look at articles I have written in the past, about the Socialists even, and see that I have followed the party line, and call me a hypocrite. Mea culpa. I admit that I have sung for my supper, banged the tawdry drum and swallowed the lies. When I finally went to my editor, and begged to tell my story, afraid I'd lose my job for uttering these heresies, her face lit up, and she said, 'At last! Someone to speak for the silent majority!' To my shame, I forgot that newspapers represent us all, the sceptic along with the demented fan. That is why I am here to tell you that when Dr David Guinevere, GB captain, pontificates that 'the Socialists set ourselves a higher standard', he thinks he can get away with it because no one will call him on it. Well, Dave, here I am.

People forget that KSC is part of a mighty industrial complex, a weapons builder through the ages, whose 'long road to wealth was lubricated with the blood of the British Empire's feeble enemies', in the compelling words of the Australian working-class historian Derek Drongowitz. People don't want to see that, for all their 'caring employer' talk, last year the Rosslare Group's whizz-kid new consultant, a man who has never sullied his hands with the sordid toil of actually *making* something, sold off one of the last, priceless chunks of our industrial heritage the second it stopped paying the bills. *And this is the same bloodless automaton who now runs the Socialists!*

People bleat about the Socialists' advertless playing shirts, as if they are so blind that they cannot see the hoardings round the pitch, advertising only Rosslare products; as if the brown-and-white drinks posters left them in any doubt about the connection. Callum Gordon of top advertising agency Woddis Radford Hourston is agog that 'nobody points at the naked emperor. The KSC shirt is the world's best-known advert for Irish beer!'

KSC's propaganda says that the club belongs to its community but, *as everyone really knows*, it is ruled by a family of aristocrats. Their wealth was not built on business acumen but on ancient thefts from the common weal and favours from friends on high, and they aren't accountable to anybody. This is not a higher standard, Dr Guinevere, and shame on you, because deep down you know it.

Of course, the Rosslares didn't get all this public acclaim by being stupid. In fact, some of their tricks are very clever. What I am about to tell you might *sound* great, at first, but don't be fooled. Nothing about the Socialists is as it appears.

I cannot reveal my sources, but I recently discovered that the Socialists undertake secret charity work. For six hours every week, they are all contractually obliged to work anonymously 'for the community'. They must not be paid and they must find jobs wherein they will not be recognised. This means they work with the mentally retarded, fill envelopes or man phone lines.

You probably think that this is wonderful and virtuous. You are probably wondering why I am making such a fuss about it. But don't be deceived. This 'charity work' is a typical KSC trick. It *sounds* great, but it doesn't do any good for anyone except for the Socialists. It is pure hypocrisy, and there is nothing I hate more.

First, the club forces its players to sign this contract by pretending that it is some ancient tradition, but I have spoken extensively with Socialists from the seventies, from before the arrival of super-suave businessman Manus Rosslare and John Brown, his secretive henchman, *and none of those older players had ever heard a word about KSC's commitment to charity, or been asked to man a phone or fill an envelope!* This invented tradition was a concoction of the money-grubbing eighties!

What is KSC up to? After all, most other football teams do community work these days. Why be so furtive? There is only one possible answer. Lord Rosslare was a business genius and he knew that football was going to make a fortune. He knew that fans would rebel against the pampered stars earning a fortune and giving nothing back, so he *invented* this 'tradition' as a flashy piece of public relations to store against a rainy day. Right here, right now, I expose the hypocrisy.

It is particularly hypocritical since it actually stands in the way of the players doing real good.

In my role as the coordinator of this newspaper's brand-new Foundation for raising the profile of voluntary action I have learned that the single most valuable thing that celebrities can do is donate their names and faces, in public. After all, anyone can fill an envelope. This is not to decry the incredible efforts of Britain's volunteer sector, but Achille de la Rue de la Pierre au Diable, commonly known by the vainglorious nickname 'Achilles', is one of the most famous men in Britain. He could use his unearned fame to persuade thousands of young people to give up their time. Can he be bothered? It seems not.

Achilles said that the Socialists' ethos was partly about helping others, but it was also about personal development, and there was nothing wrong with that. The charity work was about helping the individual players become better people. That had always been a part of the club.

These are pretty words, but Achilles is the same preening playboy who, in a previous conversation about duty, told me that 'duty is overrated. We must all find time to dance.' Achilles' boyfriend is the South African war hero Terrible Zondeki, and when Achilles first said this to me I had a sixth sense that Zondeki was trying to tell me something. I now realise he was straining against the medieval secrecy clause in his contract, the clause that muzzled him from explaining to me that the Socialists pretend to be about duty, but that for all their fine words, they're trying to feed a dragon with peanuts.

Isn't it true, Mr Precious Achilles, that doing charity work in the public eye, and taking some responsibility for it, might just take more than six hours a week? After all, other Premiership clubs with less self-glorifying public relations do charity work these days. Is it because taking responsibility might impinge on your precious 'dancing'? From those to whom much is given, much is demanded, and Achilles doesn't want to pay the price.

Not only is the 'charity work' a manipulative PR scam, it doesn't do any good.

In stark contrast to Achilles is Will Beauchamp, another of the Socialists I discussed this with. When I asked him to speak for the *Clarion*'s new Foundation at a centre for underprivileged inner-city kids, mostly from ethnic minorities, he was deeply embarrassed, and said he'd love to, but his contract forbade him. I told him I knew about the secret charity clause. He replied that he couldn't say anything, except that he understood my point of view, and if anything changed, he would be the first to sign up to what the *Clarion* is trying to do. He told me this on the strictest conditions that I didn't repeat it to anyone. Well, Will Beauchamp, you are a beacon in this murky swamp, and I am breaking your confidence. I am outing you. The *Clarion* dares KSC to take action!

You may worry that I am exposing Beauchamp to ostracism by his teammates, but I don't. The Socialists pretend to have some mystical *esprit de corps*, but that is yet more hypocrisy. My sources, and I emphasise that Will Beauchamp is not one of them, have told me that there is only a very fragile peace in the camp. Ever since the tragic death of John Brown, whose autocratic caprice kept everybody on the straight and narrow, there has been a power struggle for the soul of the club. James Purnell arrived, democratically asking to be called JP, rather than his archaic predecessor's obsessive 'Mr Brown'. When I asked him about his experience, all he said was, 'It's been harder to win the players' trust than I expected.' He was obviously another victim of the Socialists' self-mythologising spin. Rather than let JP do his job, senior players such as Guinevere and Achilles hold private little cabals and issue diktats they seem to see as holy writ. One player said to me, 'Achilles and Dave think JP doesn't have a clue. Beauchamp and others have tried to keep the peace, and speak up for JP, but Dave and Achilles are always contradicting him. No one knows what to do.'

When Dave Guinevere realised I was on to this story, he demanded to see me. I asked him to leave his ego by the door and answer some questions, but he just ordered me to tell him my sources and told me I was speaking rubbish. This obsession with trying to control how others see them is just one of the maggots in KSC's rotten apple, but it is the easiest one to get rid of. To kill it, all we need to do is tell the truth.

This is why I think this story of charity hypocrisy is so important.

It seems like a little thing, but it epitomises a rotten culture of obfuscation and spin. In this optimistic new era, with Britain vibrant and vital once more, with a fresh wind of openness and accountability sweeping the corruption out of public life, KSC is out of kilter. The club is a dinosaur, and it will not survive among the sleek, fast mammals of this better, brighter Labour era. If it is so keen to be the people's club, then it has to embrace the people. It can't be a private plaything for a pretty socialite with more money and responsibility than she can deal with.

I hate football, but I do understand that KSC's ideals are part of our collective heritage. The club must live up to them. If the Socialists want to escape the tag of hypocrisy, they must embrace the community they claim to serve. Like the great European clubs of Torino and Madrid, they have to be owned by the public.

There is hope, football fans. Will Beauchamp, to his surprise, will not be ostracised, because he will find his teammates agree with him. Louie Cohen, the hero of last year's World Cup, and a man who tirelessly and selflessly uses his public position to fight for causes he believes in, is just one example of a man who has seen the heart of darkness in KSC, the cancer behind all the pretty words and ideals, and will not be cowed. 'I dreamed of joining this club, man,' Cohen told me. 'Its ideals are precious, but I've got to do things my way. What matters is that the flame doesn't die.'

Quite right, Louie. The ideals are the only good thing left, and if you and Will Beauchamp can save them, if you can help make them into reality, if you can cut out the cancer and give the Socialists back to the community they do not deserve, then you, with our help, will have done British sport, and British society, a great service.

But don't be deceived. These are Augean stables.

Today with the Clarion, *don't miss your weekly sixteen-page Premiership pull-out. The* Clarion, *First for Football.*

ADAM'S IMPERIUM

If Calum's plan was to destabilise KSC, it seemed to misfire badly. Will Beauchamp, publicly outraged at being named, took the role of plaintiff-in-chief, and called on his fellow players to circle the wagons.

It was agreed that there would be no witch-hunt for Calum's source or sources. The reporter had taken things wildly out of context. KSC's spirit and ideals were unique and wonderful, and the article was a pack of lies. Will, the keynote speaker as it were, put a suggestion to his comrades. 'This was crap, obviously,' he said, 'but we could deal with it proactively. We could say that we've always had team meetings, and it was at these meetings that Dave and Achilles made their comments. The meetings are part of our democratic heritage, and they were a secret, but we are making them public now in a spirit of openness to avoid confusion. Do you think that would work? And I think the team meetings might be a good idea anyway, to defuse any tension?' Dave and Achilles didn't like any of this, but they had been publicly painted as villains, and they let Will have his way.

The subsequent stories of KSC togetherness were full-throated, and for a few weeks, during which the Socialists thrashed Dublin, West Manchester and Tottenham, it seemed as if, by not killing them, Calum's feature had only made them stronger. But someone publicly cleared of murder is only technically as innocent as someone who has never been accused of it. Calum had finally licensed other commentators, especially the ones outside the world of football who had no need of the Socialists' goodwill, to question whether the club really was everything it seemed, or whether KSC were doing this new 'spin' thing everyone was talking about.

Seek, and ye shall find, says Matthew. It was one thing when the government 'spun' – after the debacle of the previous two decades it was perfectly reasonable that Labour's apparatus coordinated the party's central message – but the Socialists were not the Labour Party. They should be unsullied by worldliness, and this 'spin' was being portrayed as a new and Machiavellian creation, somehow entirely different from public relations or just generally trying to present oneself in a good light, as if trying to influence how others see us isn't something we all do every day. Nasty, nasty 'spin'. Do we still trust the Socialists? Of course we do. Officially. But we are watching them more carefully.

The carping articles were few and far between as the Socialists built a huge league lead over the Christmas period, and the papers were full of articles saying that JP and his team meetings had finally achieved the holy grail – combining the playmaking flair Mr Brown had brought to the club with a more traditionally British, bullocking verve. Achilles was quieter than before maybe, but Beauchamp and Guinevere rampaged through a succession of thunderstruck opposition midfields as if Britain's twin dynamos, the young and the old, were vying for primacy. KSC humiliated Manchester & Stockport, their closest rivals, 4–0, then went to Madrid in the first knockout round of the Champions League and beat Rojo by the same margin.

In windy March, Adam attended his first conference of the Premiership Chief Executives. For three days he sat through meetings full of businessmen like himself shaking their heads at moneyed enthusiasts, entrepreneurs and cranks. Between the meetings, like the new girl at a court gavotte, he was passed from hand to hand by seductive peers. 'It's unbelievable,' said Cardiff. 'We get a hundred and sixty million a year from Panther between the lot of us, and you and I have to share it with monkeys like Watford. How are we supposed to compete with Azul? We can't buy anyone.'

'Sharing the money's good for the league,' ventured Adam primly. 'The product as a whole.'

'Is this the right product? I mean, there's only five of us with the clout to win, and that's not changing any time soon. The real product's Europe, mark my words. Five years down the line, the Premiership's not going to be the priority, and if we can't gear up, we're screwed.'

'How do we gear up?'

'We've got to negotiate our own media deals. Collective bargaining is killing us! Azul get twenty-five million every year. Rojo get twenty-two million. Torino and Roma both get twenty million. We should be bigger than them. We've got better global reach, and we've got more fans at home. You're a sensible man, you know what I'm saying. The league's a shambles.'

'We'd never get the league to agree.'

'We can. We threaten to break away. They can't afford to lose us.'

Adam had heard this before. 'They know fans don't want a Euroleague,' he said. 'They'll call our bluff.'

'The Premiership will back down, trust me.'

'But is it what's good for football?' said Adam, and Cardiff spun away like Casanova facing an unexpected lecture on chastity.

Adam was grabbed by Everton's young Turkish owner, to whom he cautiously mentioned Cardiff's Euroleague, and who recoiled in horror, reassuring him, 'We are not all like that, oh no, nothing like.' Everton was more concerned with what would happen when the public found out about the endemic bribery among agents and managers, which Everton was trying to stamp out. 'Image of the game, my friend,' he said. 'Value of the product. Wholesomeness! Money's obscene, and young men do stupid things, horrible things. We can't stop that, but we must not make it worse. Must be cleaner than clean. You and me, we are the fiery sword, yes?'

Adam liked this, but then he was passed to Spencer's chairman, who laughed. 'Everton's got no idea how we do things round here,' he said. 'He's not a football man. I know you're not either, mate, but you've got a head on your shoulders. You come from our culture. You understand me, mate?'

'I'm not sure I do.'

'Easy, tiger! Just saying that football's not supermarkets. It's a glamour business. It's entertainment. You need a bit of flexibility, and you don't have to worry about the fans – they care about winning. Trust me, we'll not get rid of bungs, and they don't matter. They're the price of doing business. Take Bill Krenabim.' Spencer nodded at Krenabim, the energetic GB manager who had been schmoozing the halls throughout the meetings. 'Billy's the bungmeister, but he's a great manager, and he's a football man. You got to keep an eye on him, but you get the best man for the job, you see? Don't worry about the money. Football's not supermarkets. You should have a word with Billy. He's an old mate of mine. He wants to speak with you.'

And so Adam was handed on again. Krenabim was charming. He said, 'Player power, Adam, my friend. It's all about the players. We pay them a fortune, but we can't control them any more. That ship has flown. It's market forces. Goes against the game I've loved all my life, but we got to move with the times, right? We got to recognise what we're worth,' Adam nodded. 'Yeah, you're a sharp one, you. We need guys like you in the game, guys who can swim where the wind wants to blow your boat. Kilburn's a great club, the greatest. I won't always be with GB. We can't control the players, but I can speak their language better than most. I can make them do what I want on the pitch, at least. Remember that. Good to meet you.' And he was off to make the same speech to someone else.

Adam listened. He didn't commit himself to anything. He would need to learn fast if he was to protect Kilburn from this world.

A week later, nearly two months after Calum's article, Will spoke to Esther. 'I've sort of been delegated by the team to raise something with you,' he said. 'At this week's TM [Team Meeting – Esther knew what he meant, obviously], we discussed the whole charity thing.' He sounded shy. Esther nodded cautiously. 'The article was a piece of shit, naturally . . .'

'Naturally.'

'And we couldn't be seen to be reacting to it immediately, but the thing is, the reporter had kind of a point about the charity stuff, didn't he? I mean, are we doing everything we can? Are we using our time efficiently?' Esther agreed completely. She felt exactly the same way as Will about this, it was spooky. She asked what the players wanted to do about it, and Will said that some of them, naming no names but she could probably guess who, preferred the status quo, but that the mood of the team as a whole was for making their charity work public. 'In fact,' said Will, 'and I'm only saying this because I know you agree and it won't come to it, but I'm pretty sure the boys would insist on the change if we had to, and JP's with us. We don't want anyone disrespecting us by calling us hypocrites.'

When Esther took this to Adam, he said that going public would look insincere. It would also make it look as if Calum's article had been true. Esther replied angrily that making the charity more open was actually a really small change, and it would be good because it would be cutting out a cancer at the heart of KSC's image, like Calum said. And anyway, there was nothing insincere about it! Calum's article admitted that the players wanted to go public but they were being held back by their medieval contracts, couldn't he see? Adam said that public charity was what *Will Beauchamp* wanted, but that was a different thing from *the players*. He also said that it set a dangerous precedent to bow so clearly to public and player pressure.

This was when Esther realised that Adam was jealous of Will. Adam didn't understand KSC in any way, he just liked having control. She said that actually this would be a good thing for the business part of the club, which was his concern, because it would publicly improve the brand. Adam said he was sorry, but the most prudent course of action was to keep KSC out of the spotlight until the end of the season. It was dignified, and hopefully the club's image would revert to what it was last summer. If not, then of course they could consider what to do then, but only then. If you opened the gates, Adam said, you couldn't close them again. 'It's not your decision, actually,' Esther said. 'The players had a TM and decided that it's what they want. They are prepared to insist.'

'They can't insist,' said Adam. 'They're under contract.'

'It's a medieval contract, and this is a democracy. They've *voted* for what they want, Adam, and you don't have a choice. This is a *football* club, and the footballers are the most important thing in it.' Adam could run the business if he liked, but it wouldn't be hard to replace him if necessary. His job was to serve the players, not to be some kind of dictator. He probably only took the job to hang around all the young men. It was creepy.

Organisations depend on the consent of their members. It's one thing for a state, or a school or whatever, to use force to coerce those who do not consent to play by its rules, but a football team is tiny and fragile, and even if Adam had tried to use force – lawyers, basically – to impose his will, the results would have been counterproductive. It wasn't even as if changing the structure of charitable activity was definitely a bad idea: doing good was what these contract clauses were all about, and maybe they *were* archaic. What worried Adam was not the decision, but how it was being made. He called Aisling, hoping to meet her after work.

'I'm really busy at the moment.'

'When would be a good time?'

'It's not that I'm doing stuff, it's more I'm tired.'

'Aisling!'

'Yeah, okay. A quick drink after work. Can you be at the Spare Room at ten?'

'Is that when you're finishing work?'

'I've got some things to do. Do you want to meet up or not?'

At twenty past ten, Adam sat in the window of the chichi little upstairs bar some cocktail hobbyist had built into the first floor of his house. He watched Aisling saunter up Flask Walk chatting on her mobile. She was quite dressed up. He didn't get angry while she chatted outside for ten more minutes, laughing vapour into the cold, crisp air and never once looking at her watch. There was no changing Aisling and, anyway, Adam would spend at least as much time telling their friends this story as he'd spent waiting for her, which was some recompense. When she eventually reached him, he had a gin waiting for her. She said something about the Northern line. Adam raised his eyebrow and said that she looked particularly nice, and asked if her date had gone well.

'Brilliant work, Sherlock.'

'I wasn't meaning to —'

'I'm busy, Adam. I'm sorry, but it's fucking hard to fit things in. I haven't been on a date for about two months, I'm knackered the whole time and this guy wanted to buy me dinner and, you know, I'm single, I am allowed to at least try to . . . I mean, how little social life do you want me to have?' There were dark rings under her eyes. She was being Aislingish, but she wasn't lying about being shattered. He started to explain his concerns about the charity decision, and she glazed over almost instantly.

'I know you're bored by Kilburn,' he said.

'I really am.'

'I wouldn't come to you about this, but, I mean, I know you got me in to take things off your desk unless they were important, but this is, and you're the boss. I'm sorry, but that's how it is.'

'Okay. Carry on. Charity goes public, I get it.'

'That's not it, Aisling. Listen to me: maintaining the brand aggressively might be necessary, and we can find someone to do it full time, etc., but . . .' She had turned off again. Maybe she still felt guilty. 'I'm fine about what you did at the Christmas Party,' he said. It was the first time either of them had raised the subject. He'd been furious at the time, but it forced him to accept how naughty he'd been with Esther, and the relief since had been palpable. The annoying thing about Aisling, and this was something even Nicky accepted, through gritted teeth, was that she could be unbelievably high-handed, but she was almost always right. *Almost* always. Aisling looked at him as if he were crazy to think she might have been contrite. He said: 'You've got to be aware of what's going on at Kilburn. The balance of power's shifting.'

'Do you want out?' she said. 'Is that it? I don't fucking blame you. I railroaded you into it. I was pissed off and I needed someone I could trust, but if you've had enough —'

'Listen to me, Aisling. You said I'd love this job, and I was suspicious, but you were right. I love it, and I think I can do it well. What I'm trying to explain, for the future, is that there's a limit to what we can do if the players decide to confront us, especially if your sister is on their side.'

'Is this Esther getting back at you? Is this about you and her?'

'It's about KSC!' This was hopeless. 'Football is changing, and we've got to take steps if we want to save Kilburn.'

'Stop being so fucking overdramatic!'

'Are you okay, Aisling?'

'Yes. I'm just ...' She stopped. 'This guy tonight was so boring. I need something outside work, but every time I do something, it's ... This is not your fault. I'm just tired.'

'Sorry,' said Adam. 'I know this must be hard. KSC's okay at the moment, but look at what's happening. Do you think I'm wrong?' She said nothing. 'We should be prepared. That's all I wanted to say.' She looked down into her drink. 'Are you okay?' he repeated.

'Of course I'm fucking okay.'

ACROSS A CROWDED ROOM, ETC.

Dave wanted to set a date for the wedding, but Sally couldn't find anything until next year that allowed them a three-week honeymoon. Dave said he didn't care, but she insisted on waiting. Since the moment of her engagement, she'd felt trapped. Monica said, 'It's fine, mate, it's natural. This is exactly what my sister was like, and she was only engaged for six months. She couldn't stop thinking, until she was married, that she could stop this any time, but the only point in being free is to find the person you want to spend your life with, and you have.' Monica was an amazing cheerleader, but a terrible critic. Feeling guilty, Sally arranged a big engagement party for the summer.

The band was recording its new album, *Park Bench Epiphany*, and Sally loved the old routine of getting up late, working hard and decamping to the pub. Dave asked why she got so dressed up to sit in a recording studio all day, and she replied that it made her feel special. Dave didn't care how she dressed, so clothes weren't so much fun any more. Also, a few days ago, when she arrived home all warm and fuzzy, he suggested it might be better to turn up clear-headed in the morning. After a match, it had clearly been shown, the body rests better without any deadening from alcohol. She snapped that being in a band was different from playing football. He laughed.

Anyway, after today's session, Morgan had dragged the rest of the band into the Good Intent, just over Broadhurst Gardens from East Kilburn tube and opposite the soaring white shapes of St Brendan's. On the other side of the bar was a group of young nurses. Sally caught herself wondering if she had ever been like that, but she only had to look at Mon to know she had, and not so long ago. It was natural to regret not being young any more, and Sally wouldn't have missed the years of fighting her way out of hangovers three mornings a week, but now it was time for the next phase of her life. Then the man in the middle of the nurses turned around, and in her head everyone else in the bar crashed aside like the Red Sea parting, as if the only light in the room was the corridor between them, and everything else was stopped and silent.

She tried to refocus on Morgan's latest problem with his girlfriend. 'What's wrong, Sal?' Monica asked.

'It's nothing.' It was ridiculous. She was almost crying. 'I've got to go to the loo.' She did, and sat trying to get a grip of herself, but she couldn't do it. She was sweating with fear. Monica was right; this was a spasm everyone went through, and it was nothing to do with this guy. He was merely crystallised out of her fears, and she'd be fine if she got outside and could breathe. She returned to the table, said she was feeling peculiar and needed to go home and lie down. The others were solicitous, but not particularly worried.

To leave, she had to walk within fifteen feet of the man, and she tried not to break into a run. She felt him move towards her, and she was sure he was following. She left the pub, and walked briskly towards Sheriff Road, refusing to look back but straining to hear. She was sure he was behind her, and then she was sure he'd stopped, and she stopped too. She looked round, and he was there.

He was short, with tousled, light brown hair and incredible sharp cheeks. She spent a lot of time with Dave's friends, but she'd never seen anyone who moved this comfortably in his body. He was walking straight to her, not shyly, but in a way that gave her no cause for alarm. 'I know you're not out here hoping I would come,' he said. He was American and his voice was like caramel. 'The girls told me you're famous and taken, right?' She held up her engagement ring. 'I guess you'd have to be. I had to check, you know.'

'I know.'

He looked at her, and she felt every cliché there had ever been about this kind of thing well through and wash over her. He turned to go. Then he turned back and said, 'This has never happened to me. I . . . Another world. Thank you. That probably makes no sense. I'm going now,' but he didn't, and they grinned at each other. 'I'm not like this. I know this is just a moment in the woods. I'm going now,' and he turned back to the pub.

Sally was a sensitive person, and she'd always accepted that the people who talked about being struck by lightning must have felt something she'd never felt, and this was obviously it. It wasn't real, but it was amazing, and she was grateful to know what it was like, because she could understand why some people confused it with love. Sally believed that one of her great strengths was that she could tell when she was deluding herself. It was something Dave couldn't do, but he had other strengths.

In gaps between recording sessions, Sally wrote 'Stupid Boy', a song about a married man who falls in love with the dreams he's constructed around a girl who sits opposite him on the tube every morning. Lying in bed with Dave, she asked Dave if he believed instant love was possible, or was it just couples like them who had got together quickly and who, in retrospect, mythologised their own relationships?

'I don't know,' said Dave.

'But what do you think?' He was silent. He must realise why she was asking. She would come clean the moment she thought he did.

'I'm prepared to believe that two people who have never met can fancy each other so much that they can't resist each other physically. I haven't encountered it, but I can believe it.'

'But not real love?'

'Of course not. Love takes time, trust, compromise and work. Sally, there's nothing I've ever wanted more than a friend that I can wake up with every morning for the rest of my life. I know how lucky I am. You have nothing to worry about.' He kissed the top of her head.

Dave said it was great that they were comfortable with their separate lives, and she had pretended to agree, but she wanted more. She started to watch his football matches again. He noticed, and he dutifully joined the band in the pub whenever he could. On the list of what Sally wanted in a partner, Dave ticked every box that counted. 'What it is is this,' she said to Monica, finally, late one night, as they stood tipsily waiting for the cab that would take Mon home. 'I'm scared I don't excite him.' It had taken Sally for ever to put her finger on this, and it had just come to her, and she wasn't her sharpest at this point, so she couldn't work out how much of a problem it was, if it was one. Out loud, it sounded stupid.

'You're wrong, mate,' said Monica. 'He's crazy about you.'

SHARE AND SHARE ALIKE

The season was Kilburn's tribute to Mr Brown. Cardiff beat them in the League Cup, as if anyone cared, but KSC dominated the Premiership, won the FA Cup in a blizzard of goals and went to the Champions League final in Berlin seeking an unprecedented treble. Waiting for them, wary but unafraid, were Azul Madrid, smarting from their previous Saturday's loss to little Albacete, which had handed the Spanish league title to Rojo for the first time in twenty years.

The Spaniards (and Argentinians, Italians, one German, one Ghanaian and GB's Barry Gently) started ferociously. Their five-man midfield outmatched the Socialists for industry, and Mele di Paolo, alone up front, repeatedly dragged Torquil Blackie and Dirk Volendam apart or too close together, and either found space for himself or made it for his midfield. The first half was goalless, but Azul were teaching the favourites a lesson in humility.

'We know we're better than them,' said JP reassuringly, as the Socialists arrived in the dressing room, seething or confused, depending on where you looked. 'If we play our game, at our pace, they can't live with us. We go back out there, and we do what we know, but we do it harder, and faster. That's all.' Achilles wanted to say something. 'Yes?'

'We carry on like that, they fucking murder us.'

'All we —'

'No, old boy, we change. We change like fucking blue-arse flies. They have one up front and we're letting two mark him – it's nuts.'

'We play 4-4-2. It's what we —'

'I know, old thing. But not like this. Stop playing two at back next to each other. Dirk mark di Paolo, and Torquil step either in front or behind, but keep away. When di Paolo follow Torquil, which he will, shout, "Switch, switch," but don't ever switch, just confuse him. Then if he wants you together, he's chasing after you, not other way round, which is bad for Madrid, okay? After fifteen minutes, without saying, then switch. Then switch back after half an hour. But only those times. But keep shouting, "Switch." This gives other defender freedom to watch for runner from midfield. Dave, you keep closer to the back pair. I'll go higher. You find me, I've got space. They'll be too confident now, and they'll be too high. We hit them hard straight after the break, and we score once, maybe twice, then they retreat, then we beat them easy, I promise you. Everyone else, old boys, just as normal. We do this, okay?'

JP understood right there that this was the end for him as far as the team's respect was concerned. The measure of him was that he nodded and said, 'Okay. Yes. That's right.'

Achilles was ashamed, but didn't have time for it now. Dave had been thinking something like what Achilles had said, but he couldn't have put it so well and with such force, and he was impressed despite himself. Will Beauchamp was jealous. Zondi was afraid. The other players were simply happy that someone could see what was wrong and had told them how to deal with it, though they could all also see, to a greater or lesser extent, that taking orders from Achilles was exactly what that newspaper article had said was the problem with KSC. But all these caveats were for later. What counted now, and it went for every single player as he walked down the corridor towards the roaring pitch, was putting the instructions into practice, and winning this fucking match, since the alternative was inconfuckingceivable. There was all summer to sort out the politics.

It happened exactly as Achilles had said. Torquil and Dirk, with Dave acting as a screen, were calm and impenetrable, and every time they picked the ball up, they fed it quickly sideways to Zondi and Will Beauchamp. Achilles found the small amounts of space that were all he needed, and when he was picked up, there was room around him for Tom or Will Laird. It looked to most observers as if nothing had changed, and the received wisdom was that 'KSC got a rude awakening, but at half-time they stopped underestimating their opponents.' The Socialists won 3–1, with Azul's consolation coming deep into injury time.

As the players raced towards their fans, Achilles' pride was barely bound. It wasn't the goal he scored, or the one he set up. He had held the Socialists' fate in the palm of his hand, and he could have chosen silence, but he was a winner, so he chose to speak. It didn't matter if the world didn't know. It didn't matter that the situation with JP would have to be resolved somehow, since clearly Achilles must now have some role in running the team. It was what Mr Brown had prepared him for, and he was ready for it. At this moment, though, there was simply joy at a triumph no one could ever take away. 'This is fleeting,' whispered Zondi in his ear.

High in the stand, Strabis trapped Aisling and said, under the noise of the crowd, 'You must be very proud.'

'It's nothing for me to be proud of.'

'Enjoy it. The fans love you today. There'll be plenty of times when they won't.'

'That won't mean anything either.'

'I just hope you can keep it up, that's all. It must be hard for you to spare the time.'

'You know I don't make the decisions.'

'Greswell's done very well on the budget he has, but the buck stops with you. You're the one they'll blame when you can't get the players they want.'

'We're European champions.'

'What happens when you're not? Or when you're paying half what Azul are paying, or Cardiff? How will you compete with guys who don't care about the bottom line?'

'Adam will deal with it.'

'He won't be the one they're screaming at for being mean.'

'What are you trying to do?' she asked, and Strabis looked pained, as if she'd burped in his face. He probably got his kicks out of this kind of bullshitting *pas de deux*. He probably thought he was business's answer to James Bond. Well, he could fuck off. 'Seriously,' she added. 'I've not got time for this.'

'Seriously, Lady Rosslare?' Strabis paused. 'I don't think you are *serious*. I think you're out of your depth. Mr Brown's not here to hold your hand any more, football finance is going crazy, the Rosslare Group isn't as liquid as it might be and you're not going to be stupid enough to throw its money around anyway, and the Socialists are going to suffer. You'll be criticised, and you won't like it because you're not used to it and you'll think it isn't your fault, but it will be, because you're the one with the final say.'

He'd spoken for long enough for her to collect herself. 'Thank you very much for all that,' she said, 'but since there's nothing I can do about it, I'll do nothing about it.'

'I'm not a bad man. Your father and I — The Rosslare Group is in a decent state, but KSC is going to be a nightmare for you, and you know it. That's fine if you love it, but I think you don't.'

'It's not just me,' she said, knowing it was weakness to make excuses. 'There's Esther.'

'It's your decision.'

'She's my sister.'

'Well, that's very laudable of you. But she'll be the one asking for money the Group can't afford.' He goodbyed and went.

Aisling had to see the game, obviously, but she had also used it as an excuse to take a few days' break to visit Berlin, and she'd persuaded Nicky and Leo to join her. She had been desperate for this holiday – to get some sleep as much as anything – and Strabis didn't take much of the gloss off it, but what he'd said had recurred to her periodically. Having to deal with him trying to rile her was symptomatic of how she was stuck in a world she could do without.

Strabis was satisfied with his evening's work. A little pressure and Aisling was already rattled enough to tell him he should go through Esther. He needed a football club like he needed a hole in the head, but it might just prove a means to an end. He spoke with Donald.

Two weeks after Berlin, Donald phoned Esther and requested a secret meeting, about something vitally important to the future of the Socialists, which was something he needed to discuss with her rather than Aisling, because she was the soul of the club. Donald usually acted as if she were totally unimportant, but it seemed as if he was finally realising that wasn't true, and they arranged to meet the next day for lunch.

Donald said that a private room at the Royal Foresters would ensure absolute discretion. It was a slate-grey May day, bleaching any creamy warmth from the pillars bracketing the club's portico. Esther breathed deeply and dashed inside from her Diabolo, revealing herself to potential spies for only the fleetingest moment. The porter, in his little glass room, didn't hurry off his telephone to help her. She thought the porters of such a prestigious club should be older. He had dark hair and a moustache like a cartoon policeman. She made a mental note to tell Donald about his rudeness so he could be reprimanded. Eventually, the porter said, 'Yes?'

'I'm here to see Donald Rapnesst. He's expecting me.'

'Ah yes. Young Mr Rapnesst. The Blood Red Room, unless my memory misgives. You will be Miss Rosslare?'

'Yes.'

'Allow me to take you, young lady.' He bounded energetically through the door. 'Follow me, miss. Do allow me to say that you are looking radiant. It does my old heart good to see, pardon me for saying.' Esther warmed to him. He must be older than he looked. 'Do you mind stairs, miss? It's two floors up. We could take the lift if you prefer?'

'Would you prefer the lift?'

'It's this hip. I don't mind, though. And the back and ankle. I could probably use the exercise, though.'

'Let's take the lift.'

'No, no. I don't mind. Bite the bullet.' The porter strode up the deep, velvet stairs two at a time. The atrium was huge, covered in brown paintings of insignificant Prime Ministers and forgotten generals. Esther hobbled to keep up. Skirts were very low this season, not that she followed fashion, of course, but you had to buy what was available in the shops. An elegant woman in black trousers swept down past Esther, and two girls – they couldn't have been out of their teens – brayed at each other on the landing. Or one brayed. The other definitely had a common voice, but you couldn't tell which was which from the clothes. 'Two of our new lady members,' said the porter. 'The traditionalists were against it, me among them, I'm afraid, but we were wrong. They make you realise there is still freshness in the world. Stop us getting stuck in our ruts, if you see what I mean. Here we are, Miss Rosslare, good day Mr Rapnesst. Shall I bring you a menu?'

The Blood Red Room was tiny, and the walls were black cloth. It was ill lit by a distant skylight at the point of a conical ceiling, and rather better illumined by four candles in the middle of the table. It could, at a pinch, seat four. Donald stood to welcome Esther, and ushered her to the chair next to him, not opposite. He had a sheaf of papers, and a bottle of wine. 'I'll have the Foresters Burger, salad, not chips,' he said. 'Est, do you want the menu? They do a salad, and they do good omelettes if you want.'

'A plain omelette,' she said, decisively.

'Great. On the tab, Alf.' The porter trotted off. 'Great room, isn't it?' Donald said.

'It's very dark.'

'No electricity in the Blood Red Room. You've switched off your phone?' Esther hadn't, but she did so. 'So, Esther Rosslare, we meet at last!'

'But —'

'You know what I mean.'

'Er . . . Yes.'

'We've got to bury the hatchet, Est. It's time to act, for the good of the Rosslare Group and the good of the Socialists. Your sister can't handle it.'

'But there's nothing we can do!' said Esther. 'She owns the company!'

'We'll see about that,' said Donald. He poured her a glass of wine, and they talked uncomfortably about things neither of them cared about. Eventually, when their food had arrived, he came to the point. 'The Rosslare Group should be the jewel in the national-business crown, do you agree?'

'Yes, but —'

'And I agree with you, whatever you think, that KSC is a national treasure.'

'Yes.'

'They're dragging each other down, mate. The Socialists can't spend what they need because the Rosslare Group isn't always fluid.'

'How is that dragging down the Group?'

'It isn't necessarily, but I suppose what I mean is it takes effort, doesn't it? And it's a drain on Rosslare Group resources when a bit of fluidity could help the Group take the risks it needs to grow.'

'But what's the alternative?'

'I want you to hear me out, okay?'

'Okay.'

'Strabis Kinsale is prepared to invest in Kilburn.'

'No way!' exclaimed Esther.

'Strabis argued with Manus, but that's what business is all about. He loves the Socialists. He's a fan and he'd be helping us out.'

'My father said never to trust him.'

'I respect your father more than anyone, but was he always right? He left Aisling in charge of KSC, for instance. He could be jealous of people.'

Some of this was hurtfully true, and it was also true that Strabis watched Kilburn every week, and he was always very polite to Esther. 'It's my heritage,' she said.

'Strabis understands that. He isn't prepared to do anything to help the club unless he knows he has your full support. Strabis wants this club to succeed, and he is prepared to back a "Fans' Fund", which any Kilburn supporter can pay into in return for a small share of ownership.' This sounded very democratic, and Esther was excited, but she didn't get precisely what Donald was saying. Her confusion was increased when he asked how much money she would be able to invest. Donald explained that if she purchased enough shares, she would have a place on the board by right, rather than because of her sister's charity. That was appealing, Esther had to admit. She asked how much money she would need, and Donald said that it would have to be a significant sum, because Strabis wanted a board of manageable proportions. If she told Strabis what she could pay, then he could use that as a benchmark to keep out the little guys when they were preparing their plan. And if she could find enough money, maybe they could make an arrangement which gave her real power. Strabis was open to the idea that Esther take over the day-to-day running of the club, as her own responsibility, not as some scrap from Aisling's table.

Donald finished his food and his sales pitch together, and smacked his lips disgustingly. 'So,' he said. 'You're with us?'

'Not necessarily,' she replied, prim with tension, but mind whirring.

Strabis was pleased with Donald, though he expressed himself less patronisingly than that.

In the middle of June, while Esther was considering how much of her fortune she could release in return for her heart's desire, the papers began to speculate that KSC might be sold. It was probably Donald trying to cause trouble, which was typical of him, but KSC's fans weren't at all horrified by the momentous prospect. Many of them seemed to actually welcome the rumours. They mouthed that traditions were important, and any new owner would have to respect them, but they were clearly thrilled that a change in ownership might mean more cash to splash. The bulk of them seemed not to care about the Rosslare connection, which upset Esther, but it was interesting.

At the reception at Number Ten where the government tried to take credit for the Socialists' treble, Will Beauchamp found her and asked if he might discuss the rumours. He said he wanted to find out the story behind the story, 'because you're someone I can trust. You know about the business, but you also understand the club, if you know what I mean.' Esther did know. 'Is it really possible?'

'No,' she said guiltily. 'Don't worry about it.'

'That's great. Some of the arguments did seem to make sense, but I don't know about that kind of thing.'

'You don't think we should do it?'

'No. Absolutely not. There's the rest of the Social Club, for instance – if you were selling off the football club I suppose there would have to be some separate provision made for the homes and hospitals, because they would make the club less attractive, I imagine.' Esther was horrified, and it must have shown. 'Sorry, Esther,' Will laughed. 'All I'm doing is thinking aloud. But it's true, isn't it? If you were selling off KSC, you'd want to make provision for the Social Club aspects, because then they would be independent and safeguarded from any untoward happenings either with the club or the business. In fact, I'm sort of surprised that's never happened, but I'm just a footballer.'

'It's because we could never settle enough money on a separate trust to guarantee it could continue to run at the same level as it does now.'

'Oh. I understand. Couldn't you give what you can, though, and energetically plan to raise the rest? Look at how successful we've been at raising money this year. If you did that, you could have a Social Club trust that was safe for ever, instead of being always subject to the Committee and in hock to any hare-brained schemes Donald comes up with, or whoever else is in charge – just like the club, in fact?' What Will said made sense. KSC could easily exploit its brand for the benefit of a separate trust. Will went on. 'You're the expert, that's why I came to you. I only asked because I read how much money the club could raise if it was sold just as a football club, and obviously you could set the price, and sell off whatever proportion you wanted, so you could still retain control, couldn't you?'

'But we have enough money, and we have control already.'

'Can we buy Mele di Paolo? Or Marten Vlocker? Or afford their wage demands? Not that I would want any change in how we do things. I'm not saying we need these guys, but you never know, in the future. And who knows, maybe if you get to structure the sale, you'll have more actual influence than you do now! I mean, you'd be partly answerable to the other owners, but that's surely got to be different from having your sister and Donald hanging over your head the whole time? It's okay for Adam, maybe, because he'd never have run a football club otherwise, but you're the one who knows how everything ticks, aren't you? It must be maddening. Like I say, I've got no idea how it would work in practice, but that's how it seems to me.'

'That's really interesting, Will. I'll think about it.'

He beamed at her, and said, 'I know you will. You're not like the others. You're an heiress and I'm just a working-class guy doing his dream job, but you don't treat me as if I'm a serf.'

Will had put his finger on one problem for sure: Adam was Aisling's pet. If it really was possible to sell off KSC in such a way that Esther found herself in an influential position, she would finally have the chance to make decisions without having to get them okayed by people who didn't know what they were talking about, which was completely archaic and undemocratic. She would have to be careful, though. She'd have to be sure Donald wasn't throwing KSC to the wolves.

Later on at the same reception, Dave sought her out. He asked how things were, and they chatted, but it wasn't like the old days. She asked him about his reaction to the stories that KSC might be sold off, and he smiled, 'It'd be a tragedy, but you're never going to let that happen, are you? I can trust you.'

He was another one who took her for granted. 'Why would it be a tragedy? It would raise money.'

'The devil's advocate stuff isn't fooling anyone!' he said. 'Oh, hi, Sal,' he took her hand. 'Esther's trying to persuade me she should sell KSC to the highest bidder.'

'But how could the club be doing any better than it is?'

'There!' Dave said. 'A more succinct answer is not possible. We've got to shoot, Est, but it was great to have a chat. See you at the engagement do.' It was hard for Esther to imagine what she'd ever seen in Dave, strutting around with his pop star because he wouldn't be able to cut it on the pitch much longer, not when Kilburn had players like Will. Dave probably didn't want KSC to have more money, because then the club would replace him. Two days later, she told Donald that she wanted to go ahead with Strabis's plan, and that she could afford no more than fourteen million pounds.

Aisling arrived early for the June meeting, with huge bags under her eyes. She said she hadn't been to bed yet, so could they make it quick? If anyone should be used to not sleeping it was Aisling, in Esther's opinion, and anyway, it was typical of her not to take a proper day off for the meeting but to try to fit it in around her work, and Esther said so. Aisling turned on her and said that she was desperately trying to find a way to take a week off to prepare for her final exams later in the summer, and couldn't Esther cut her some slack, for fuck's sake? Esther was enjoying how Donald skirted around the minor issues waiting for the moment to pounce. When Aisling said, 'Any other business?' and started to put her papers away, Donald replied, 'I want to talk seriously about selling KSC.'

Adam immediately tried to pre-empt an explosion from the obviously weary Aisling. 'We've been through this,' he said. 'It's never going to —'

'Don't try to railroad me,' said Donald. 'You can read. You know we're attracting interest from some very rich guys. We have to at least think, *seriously*, about doing this. We might decide against it, but we have to talk about it.'

Adam would once have agreed. Panther Digital's latest bid for the rights to screen Premiership matches was astronomical; the new stand at Kilburn Park meant the ground could seat nearly seventy thousand, and every game was sold out. The team's stock could never be higher than it was now, on and off the pitch. The players had agreed to work publicly for charity, to lend themselves as figureheads, and the voluntary sector was unstinting in its praise. The resultant publicity had brought in donations nationwide and, as Calum predicted, it made volunteering cool. Other clubs protested that they'd done similar work for years, but KSC committed more hours, and its name, its players and its story put everyone else in the shade. KSC was at the apogee of its value as a commodity at the precise moment that its costs were rising significantly. Spiralling transfer fees and wages meant that the club needed to swim faster just to stay still –

an equal wage was an increasingly expensive luxury when squads were growing to cope with the demands of a more relentless fixture list. A successful club could still make money, but it demanded continuous effort and the ability to invest. Plans to add ten thousand to the capacity had been approved, for instance, but the Rosslare Group couldn't spare the cash for building. To a businessman, the arguments for selling KSC were compelling.

But that was how an earlier Adam would have thought. When he remembered the feeling of watching the Socialists beat Madrid, the roof echoing to the cheers of the best supporters in the world, and when he remembered Kilburn's buzzing streets in the following weeks, he understood in his gut that maximising gain was not the point. 'KSC's nature,' he intoned, 'is our insurance. When a football club disintegrates, it is gone for ever.' The club, as Esther always said, was too precious to be risked. He repeated this as if it were a self-evident truth.

On the other side of the table, Esther endured Adam's lecture as long as she could. 'Listen to yourself!' she said eventually. 'Can't you see you're being a typical, gloryhunter new fan? You knew nothing about football two years ago.'

'What's that got to do with it?'

'Everything.' He was rattled. Good. He expected her just to roll over and back him up, but she saw through him now. She would show everyone that she wasn't a predictable doormat. 'A *real* fan isn't interested in who runs the club. We've got to try and understand that the world is not aristocracy and privileges any more, and our fans are our *fans*, not our *serfs*. It is the people's club! It should be owned by the people, and it should be run by professionals who know about football, not by people who don't care about it or understand.'

'Fuck you, Est.'

'Why do you assume I'm talking about you, *Ash*?'

'Sorry, *Esther*.' Esther loved to see her sister lose her cool. 'I wasn't expecting this bullshit. Sorry. I know this isn't a school playground. You're not seriously suggesting we consider selling?'

'It's the sensible thing to do.' Aisling was dumbfounded, which was brilliant. Esther said, 'Unlike some people, I'm always serious.'

'Who do we sell to? What happens to the Social Club? No, we're not doing this.'

'You're not a dictator.'

'That's exactly what I am,' said Aisling.

'Let's take a step back, guys,' said Donald. 'We won't make a decision today, but I want you to know that I've had an offer, a very interesting offer, from Strabis Kinsale —'

'No!' said Aisling.

'Listen,' said Esther.

'You're seriously in with this?' said Adam. Esther smiled at him.

'The offer's very generous, it's good for the Group, and it's good for KSC. You lose nothing by listening to it.' Donald read the offer out, Esther nodding sagely. Aisling was shocked, but she was also desperate for the problem to go away. When Donald finished, she asked if anyone had anything to say.

Adam said, 'It robs the club of its security.'

'Anything new, I meant,' said Aisling. 'Hank?'

'Your father would never have —'

'I know, Hank. I'm sorry I'm not my father.' Typical Aisling, snapping at Hank. She was all over the place. 'What would this mean? Do you want me to sell the whole club, or keep control of half of it, or what?'

'Let's not get ahead of ourselves, Ash,' said Donald. 'How about I put together a proposal setting out the options so you know what you're talking about.' Esther almost liked Donald for a moment.

The Rosslare Group was still too strong to endanger, but Strabis could, with planning, find ways to squeeze its cash flow, and he was doing so now. Strabis was having fun. Desecration of heritage was a lever he had never used before, and Aisling was hard to predict. Two days later, James Purnell, prodded by Esther, prodded by Donald, prodded by Strabis, formally requested the funds needed to sign the Newcastle wonderkid Jermaine Cole. Little Jermaine couldn't be expected to ply his trade in the lower divisions for another season, and he was being courted by all the top clubs. The asking price was twelve million pounds.

The Rosslare Group could find the transfer fee, but KSC's equal-pay rules made Cole's wage demands unsustainable. This information became public. Strabis made it known that should KSC be bought by what he called the 'Fans' Consortium', he would release the money to buy Cole. Panther's sports news, which Aisling knew she shouldn't watch, especially while drinking her bedtime cup of tea, late and knackered from A & E, was full of agitated fans proclaiming that they were the best in the world, and they were grateful for everything the Rosslares had done, but it was time for a new era. The ingratitude was shocking. Aisling told herself they'd miss her when she'd gone, but a weight was lifting from her shoulders.

Adam said that Strabis's offer was a fair one. Strabis was willing for Aisling and whoever else to retain any proportion of shares so long as he had a majority holding. His proposed structure for a devolved KSC Foundation to run the club's social and community obligations was practical and generous. He suggested that anyone holding five per cent of the shares be granted an automatic seat on the board, but the board could co-opt other members as it saw fit, and he requested strongly that Adam be retained as Chief Executive.

There were two possible issues with the sale. The first was that anyone holding twenty per cent should have the right to veto major footballing decisions, such as a change of manager. Adam didn't understand this last provision until he learned that Esther planned to buy this proportion of KSC, and this must have been the price of her acquiescence. Aisling sighed when she learned this. But she was happy to be ridding herself of a millstone, and maybe, at last, this would be the thing that made Esther happy. Aisling was not trying to buy Esther's love.

The second issue was that Strabis refused to sign a clause saying that KSC would never sell its property in East Kilburn. He said that he was taking a considerable risk, and making a generous offer, and he couldn't countenance a deal where he did not control the club's assets. Aisling made a stand, for show, saying that she wasn't handing a prosperous and successful unit to someone who would sell it for scrap. Strabis phoned to smooth things over. 'How about,' he suggested, 'we make the land inviolable so long as KSC stays in the top division? People will think I've gone soft.' He said, 'This is my last offer.' Esther begged her to take it. Aisling, who had spent three hours on the phone every day dealing with things that she should never have had to deal with, her body screaming for sleep the whole time, caved in. It wasn't as if relegation was a real issue, or as if anyone could seriously sell Kilburn Park.

So there it was, and now, three weeks into July, Aisling sat over the contract, pen in hand. She knew Strabis must be up to something. She could hear the distant drums as well as you or I. But what was she to do? As a final throw of the dice, she looked to Hank Tam, and asked him again what he thought. He said, 'Sometimes the sea is too strong. You have to let the club go.' Always trust Hank Tam, her grandfather told Manus. Aisling signed.

LONG, HOT SUMMER

Sally's parents, Gerald and Muthali, were blessed with but one child, but some child! Some blessing! They had been happily planning her wedding for twenty years, including recent contingencies to deal with the curious circumstance of her fame. Soon after the engagement, Sally told them that they must let her pay for everything, and Gerald said, 'Must, my arse! Our special day too, Pickle. Mustn't spoil our fun, ha, ha! Suppose you want somewhere big enough to put all the celebrities, ha, ha! What have we got ourselves into, ha, ha!'

Gerald Stares was brought up in the East End, and he'd moved out to Loughton when his warehouses expanded. He took Muthali with him, the rebellious daughter of a Ugandan-Asian accountant who had got his family out of Kampala before Amin started the expulsions. He was ex-army. She was a hippie.

A few weeks before the end of the football season, Sally had fixed a date with her parents to talk about details. Gerald and Muthali were worried that she was leaving it so late, but not very worried because Uncle Avtar and his brothers ran the hockey club, which was where Sally still insisted she'd marry, true to her roots. Muthali told her daughter she was looking dowdy and Gerald poured huge glasses of gin and led her to the table on which the plans were laid out for her inspection. 'Dad!' said Sally. 'This is amazing, but I told you not to! That's what I'm here to tell you. The wedding has to be next summer.'

'It's all all right, Pickle?'

'Of course it is, Dad!' said Sally. 'It's just there's no time. We're having a big engagement party at the end of June.'

'What sort of party? Celebrities? No room for us, I suppose, ha, ha.' (This could have been written: 'Whossor'par'y? Slebri'ies? No roo'f'r'us,'pose, ha, ha.')

'Don't be silly, Dad. I want a proper engagement party, for you and my friends.'

'Good, good,' said Gerald. 'Didn't want celebrities anyway, ha, ha. Some coming still, though? A few?'

'Dad!'

'No, not like that. Gerald Stares is uninterested, ha, ha. Sometimes flick through your mother's magazines but only on the loo, ha, ha. Funny diets. We should have curry. Uncle Avtar will make it so the sweat runs into their shoes! Bit unhygienic, ha, ha!'

'Gerald!' said Muthali on her way to bed.

'Sorry. Carried away. Still, have to be some celebrities, won't there? Some of your friends?'

'Yes, Dad.'

'Ha! Feared so.' They grinned at each other. Sally finished her hot Milo, kissed her father, and went to the stairs. Her father stopped her and said, 'Sal. Just want to say: think you're very sensible. If you're not sure, better to wait. Look first, always the way.' Sally didn't reply. Gerald joined his wife shortly afterwards. He lay down before undressing, and said, 'Good man, Dave, isn't he?'

'Of course he is.'

'Of course. Like him very much. National hero ... Don't think he looks at her like I look at you. Think she knows. That's all.'

Zondi was watching the engagement party with Dave. Sally had hired the old Kilburn Grand, where she could set up a room for the food, and people could watch the dance floor from the balcony upstairs. Dave said, 'She's brilliant, isn't she? She loves this stuff.' Zondi looked down at the stage. 'She's been like a massive weight off my shoulders,' Dave said. 'I can't wait to get on with the next bit of my life.'

Zondi said, 'It is joyous to find the true soulmate.'

'Yes,' said Dave. 'It's amazing, isn't it?' Dave set off downstairs. When he caught Sally's hand, she froze for an instant before saving the moment with a laugh and dragging Dave to dance. Zondi watched the Tall Hunter hold his fiancée as if she were his *'gh-wa-!kwe'kwe*, the Last Meal, which will sustain a person for ever. Most men fear the *'gh-wa-!kwe'kwe*, which is one of */Kaggen*'s cruelest tricks, because satiety is not satisfaction. It is *'gakka*, the fate of the Queen Bee, the state of hungerless surrender. The Hunter seeks it because, unlike other men, he knows and fears real hunger, and he thinks he has hunted for long enough. But the Hunter only seeks the last meal because it is always out of his reach. Zondi did not know what Sally was, and nor did she, but he knew at least that she was not a hive full of workers and drones, willing to service a queen.

'Penny for them, *querido*?'

'It is wrong.'

'I know. Thank God they're not getting married till —'

'Achilles! Mr Zondeki!' It was Sally's father. Like everyone else who met Gerald, Zondi was smitten. Gerald reached up and put his hands on Achilles' shoulders. 'Big job for you this year, son,' he said. 'Keeping David on the straight and narrow, ha, ha!'

'Thank you, sir. And it was a very funny speech. I loved —'

'Speech, ha, ha. Sally told me not to. Couldn't resist. Silly old man. Love the sound of my own voice.'

'No. I see where Sally gets it from.'

'Rubbish. All good things from Muthali. Happiest man on earth. Let me finish. Dave is lucky to have you in his corner. Look after him when, you know . . . the hard times. Trust you.'

'Thank you.'

'You know what I mean, don't you? Sensitive buggers, homosexuals. Sorry if I'm out of turn. Had a few.'

'It's fine.'

'No. Have to say something else. Had a friend in the army, found out he was gay, never spoke to him again. No idea where he is now. Very unhappy man. Younger then, stupider. Want to apologise.' He looked away. 'What the hell's this awful song? Going to blub again. Happens all the time when you get old, you wait.'

Esther was with Will Beauchamp, having a wonderful evening as they skipped through the party avoiding Tom. He was so annoying! It was true that she still sometimes slept with Tom while she waited for something to happen with *a certain someone*, which there was nothing wrong with because she had needs like any other modern liberated women. Will said that if Tom was determined to throw himself under her wheels then that wasn't her responsibility. In fact, it was her duty to all the women who inevitably were used by footballers to show one of them what it was like. Esther didn't feel guilty at all.

Eventually, Will said that while avoiding Tom was fun, what he really wanted was to talk to her privately. 'I chatted to the manager,' he said, whisking her through a door in a passage behind the bar, and leading her up some rickety stairs. 'This floor isn't technically safe, but I'm sure we'll be fine.' As they clambered, Esther let him hold her more than she needed holding because she could tell he wanted to. She was ready to tell Will what she thought at last. Thank God she had never made a declaration to Adam, so that the crush on him was her secret. The stairs led to a tiny viewing gallery where, for ten minutes, Will made Esther feel like a goddess. Then, too soon, he stopped.

'I don't mind,' she said. 'I want to do this!' He didn't carry on, and she was surprised, because it was her experience that men wouldn't resist what was offered, even if they were only using you, like Tom. Will looked stern and she thought she would die, but then he said, 'You know I want to, Esther, but I respect you too much. Think how this will look.'

'I don't mind.'

'You will tomorrow. If we do this, and I want to so much, you must see that, then everyone might say you were cruel to Tom.'

'But Tom doesn't care about me. It's just jealousy!'

'I'm thinking of the spin that gossips will put on it. We must wait until the time is right. I can wait for you if you can wait for me. If we don't, people will make things harder for us both. I'm thinking of you when I say this, because they always blame the woman.' Will was so kind! It was amazing.

That night, when Dave eventually got Sally home, she clung to him as if she hoped they could meld, make a single body of their two unequal halves. Dave loved her certainty. She barely let his hand out of hers until they arrived two days later at the hillside villa in Hawaii for a week alone. Before he met Sally, he could never have imagined himself spending a tensionless week with anyone, however much he loved them.

'It all looks so perfect,' said Sally, sipping her drink as the sun set red over jewel-green hills. Dave agreed. From the deck of the villa, it felt as if they had the island to themselves, as if it were still virgin. Three days before, Sally had asked if he'd like to explore. He said he'd do whatever she wanted, and they drove down to a nature walk all the guidebooks recommended. Sally kept leaping off into the forest, even though there were signs everywhere warning how easy it was to get lost, and Dave had had to drag her back. Sally giggled hysterically and Dave was entertained by this hitherto hidden urge of hers to stray from the straight and narrow. When she didn't suggest more exploration, he realised she had wanted to get off the trail because it was the first place on the island where they'd seen other people, and she wanted them to be alone.

'I still can't believe how blue the sea is,' Dave said. 'It's like a comic book.'

'Everything here's like a comic book.'

'Yes, it's perfect. I ordered the food for seven. It should be here in a minute.'

'All this, and food to the door.'

'Wonderland with mod cons.'

'Yes.'

The next morning, Sally pressed her fingers gently into Dave's stomach and let it spring back. She loved the way it did that, but it had to be a private pleasure, because when Dave was awake he couldn't keep from tensing the muscles. It was good that his stomach could be hard, too, but that was different. He grunted, and turned his back to her. She brushed her mouth against his shoulder, searching for the marks her teeth had made. They felt deeper than they looked. She did the same with the scratches on his back, her lips turning the faint stippled lines into long archipelagos. He shifted again, hunching foetal. Last night hadn't worked. Dave was surprised, and responded, but she'd not forced him to do whatever it was she was trying to, whatever that was, which she couldn't describe.

At least he and Achilles had worked through their differences. Achilles was so funny about Dave, teasing him about his pretension but behind his back making sure everyone realised what a great guy Dave was. At the party, he told her this statistic that in the hundred matches before Dave started going out with Sally, Dave was given sixteen yellow cards and sent off four times, but in the hundred matches since, he hadn't been sent off at all, and had only been yellow-carded five times. It made Sally think.

When he woke, she said, 'I love Achilles.'

'Everybody loves Achilles.' Dave reached out his arm, and waited until she settled her head on his chest. 'What he said during the final was amazing.' Dave had said this about a thousand times. 'He was as good as Mr Brown. I always thought I'd be good, but I had no idea what to say. I don't know how we're going to do it, but it'll be hard for JP after that. The only problem is if . . .'

'If Achilles lets it go to his head.'

'Sorry if I'm boring you,' Dave said.

She rubbed her cheek on his chest. 'He and Zondi are so perfect for each other.'

'In their way.'

'They are, aren't they?'

'They're always bickering. I'd find it knackering.'

'Really?'

'Zondi never says what he's thinking. And then suddenly he'll say he's hating something and just leave, or tell Achilles that he's being an idiot. It drives Achilles nuts.'

'I'd never have thought.'

'You have to know them pretty well.'

'But they're crazy about each other?'

'Yes, obviously, but it's not perfect. No one's perfect, not even Achilles.'

'What's wrong with him? asked Sally.

Dave leaned up on his elbow. 'It hacks me off when people think Achilles is perfect. He's great, but he sulks if anyone criticises him, and —'

'I wasn't being serious,' said Sally. 'Anyway, there are lots of ways of being perfect. Maybe it's good to be unpredictable.'

'Maybe,' Dave smiled.

Dave didn't think much of this conversation at the time, and most of it they'd had before, but it stuck like a burr in his mind, and he'd remember it wholesale when the time came. For now, as far as he was concerned, the holiday was an unqualified success. He had recharged his batteries and experienced a tantalising taste of his married future. He returned to London clear-headed and ready for the season.

HANK TAM CAN HEAR THE SEA

On 3 April 1943, as the Battle of the Atlantic reached its climax, HMS *Tameless* sank the *U644* in an engagement she barely survived. In foul seas, getting fouler, unable to submerge and with his engines able to run only in emergency bursts, Captain Rosslare and his officers believed they could limp along with the northern edge of the drift, and make landfall in Ireland or Norway. Rosslare told his men that it would be perilous, indeed, but he wasn't abandoning the sub, or begging for help from rescuers who would be running appalling risks to find them. They were *Tameless* men and, God and their own endeavour willing, they would find shore, return to the bosom of their loved ones, and be hunting Jerry again by summer. He was proud of them, and sorry to have led them to this difficulty. They were proud of him too, and they prepared grimly.

Rosslare, throughout his address, could feel his quiet young ASDIC operator needing to speak. He called the boy to his cabin and asked him what was on his mind.

'We have to get north, Captain. Storm's coming. Killer storm.'

'We don't have the power, Tam.'

'Killer storm, Captain. It'll turn us over.'

Hank Tam was a terrible officer, by ordinary measures. He came from the strange, closed world of the Newfoundland fisheries. His father and two brothers were killed on the Grand Banks in 1939 and he promised his mother he would never fish again. To have headed straight into the Royal Navy, where his grandfathers had both served, might have made him seem sophistic, but Mrs Tam understood.

Hank was an exact young man, independent, honest and hard to deflect. Two weeks after he had arrived on board, the *Tameless* sank two German subs. Tam might be odd, but the crew decided he was lucky. He didn't speak much, and he slowly edged towards the ASDIC station. Soon, he was taking the headphones. For two years, Hank guided the *Tameless* uncannily towards her hidden enemies, an unlikely combination of mascot and savant. Other captains sent their ASDIC men to learn his secret, but Hank couldn't explain what he was listening for, something in him could just hear the sea. And so, now, when he told Rosslare he had to head north, that is what the *Tameless* did. The storm's northern edge still caught the sub, but she survived. Three hours further south and she'd have broken her back. The engines were finished, the *Tameless* was drifting in the unpredictable currents south of Greenland, and there was no prospect of landfall within the fortnight. Rosslare radioed for help. A destroyer, HMS *Rutland*, would have reached her in six to eight hours, but the broadcast was heard by unfriendly ears, and the *Tameless* was a sitting duck for the *U691*. Thirty-five men survived in two lifeboats. The big, heavy radio was damaged, but was salvaged by the operator, who fancied his chances of getting something out of it soon. The *Rutland* must have come near them at some point, but visibility was terrible, and they never saw her. Rosslare felt powerless.

Tam, who hadn't sailed a boat since he was twelve, organised the men to jury-rig a couple of masts, and took them further north into faster waters. He said they would make Newfoundland in ten days, but that the weather would be hard to bear. It was not a storm, but it was the freezing North Atlantic in tiny boats without any prospect of respite. On the third day, Tam said they must throw the radio overboard, along with the guns, personal effects, everything that couldn't be eaten or worn. The men, for all they valued Tam, wouldn't do it.

'We can't control the sea,' he said.

'What's coming?' asked another.

'The sea is coming and it's too strong.'

'I'm not giving up,' said the radio operator. He was Hank's friend, but the rangy Newfie, standing in the prow, face lit strange by a patch of pearly brightness in the lowering cloud, and wind whipping his tattered scarf against his chapped cheeks, was a man possessed.

'We've got this far, Tam' said Rosslare. 'What's getting worse? The radio might be our last chance, and if we make land, we won't be near anywhere. We'll need the equipment.'

'The sea is too strong, sir. I've brought you this far, sir, and we can survive, but we're just men, and we are small. We have to go light and humble, and hope we are not broken. I've got you this far, sir.' Rosslare saw the change in Hank, and, although he was the one person in a position to understand it, he did not. All the same, he gave his reluctant agreement. Trust is not trust when it is blind, but once earned, there must be a reason for it to be unearned. The men were unhappy. Drifting, flotsam and hopeless, his sub lost with nearly half his crew, Rosslare did not want to give an order, to make it a matter for mutiny. Tam, increasingly insistent, said the only way was to split the men between those who would cast everything overboard and those who wouldn't, and to untie the rope that bound the two lifeboats together. Again the men cavilled, but this time Rosslare ordered it done. After three years of shared peril, with every man but Hank half-wishing he were on the other boat, untying the rope felt like an act of brutality and betrayal. Hank did it. Immediately the boats began to drift apart.

'Throw it all away,' he shouted as the green-white spray began to fleck and fly. 'The sea is too strong. The radio is not what you need. Cast it off and you will be saved.' They didn't, and were not.

Hank's boat spent four days spinning like a leaf in rapids, skipping down glassy walls of water and drenched in flying foam. Many times, it seemed as if it would go under, but the men drove themselves, mindless, to bail and endure, bail and endure. Hank couldn't sleep; the others couldn't talk to him. He was wound so tightly that he no longer seemed real. The fifth morning was calm, the green dark sea suddenly blue under the still bowl of the sky. Every man, even Hank, slept. They woke to an eerie bubbling ferment as the lifeboat rocked in a field of churning cod. The boat still carried rations for a week, but there was something primal about the bounty, something miraculous and wholly unexpected, that lifted the men's souls. They pulled three great fish aboard and nothing would do now but they must eat this food. Twenty men, with raw materials they couldn't spare, built a fire. As the grey rushed back to fill the sky, Hank filleted the cod in a wasteful, hurried frenzy, and dozens of slivers were cooked and eaten before the rain came.

If the men had ignored the cod, and spent the day in conservation and rest, they might still have survived. They might have greeted the returning storm with stoic equanimity. But that is not, in their hearts, what they believed. Each of them carried with them, undimmable and indescribable, the euphoria of that still, calm afternoon, of the knowledge that they had been marked, of the certainty that Hank was sent to take them home. They knew how close they had been to choosing the other boat. Someone takes responsibility, gets lucky, and we make him a prophet. Some men can just hear the sea.

TAKING ON WATER

It was late August, and still ridiculously hot. Aisling had passed her written exams, which was a weight off her mind, but Nicky was already hectoring her to finish her surgical training, organise the *viva* and start thinking about registrar jobs. Nicky, predictably, was on the verge of completion, at the earliest possible moment.

But Aisling was calm. She wasn't in a race. There was even a man she'd been seeing, not that it would go anywhere. He was a colleague, an orthopaedic surgeon ten years her senior who had separated from his wife. He was fun, and she deserved some fun.

She would be the first to admit that she'd had a lot of advantages in life, but they'd come with responsibilities she didn't want, so that was all about even, frankly. She had her dream job, knackering as it was, and she had great friends, and she'd made them all for herself. She was glad, she tried to persuade herself, that she'd got rid of the fucking football club.

Ah, Aisling! If that was true, how come you retained five per cent of KSC? How come you gave another five per cent to Hank in token of his long service? Was it guilt, Aisling? Was it shame? Was it just to make your sister angry? Esther thought the latter, but according to Esther everything you do is to spite her.

Or was it because of the way Miss Skewbold looked at you? But what were you supposed to do? Donald and Esther were fervent, and Adam admitted that the business argument was compelling, and his argument against was based only on the unnecessary risk. Even then, Aisling would have resisted in the end, if it weren't for Hank.

What did Miss Skewbold expect? Did she think you, who know nothing about business and football, and demonstrably don't care, could unilaterally block the considered opinions of everyone else in the room, with all their expertise? If you could do that, what would be the point of having the Committee? But still, the look Miss Skewbold gave you.

KSC belonged to its fans now, or so the story went. Donald's PR consultant seeded the papers with pictures of old men in scarves waving share certificates and saying things about democratic ownership and power coming to the people. Aisling pitied anyone deluded enough to believe that, and she could do without Calum fucking Horton and his puffed-up bullshit articles about how he was the one who shone the light on the Socialists' hidden crannies, and about his fucking charity foundation, and about how he deserved all the credit. It was irrelevant what Horton said or did in practical terms, but Aisling hated him.

The season was already four games old. For the first time in her life, Aisling found herself checking the football updates on Saturday afternoons, and the Socialists' two draws and one defeat had been like little knives in her gut. This too would pass. Her shoulders still felt lighter.

James Purnell, who thought he'd leave KSC after he was overridden during the Champions League final, changed his mind over the course of the summer. Partly, he could hardly leave in the wake of the triumphant treble, but also Achilles had been brilliant with the things he said in that changing room. Achilles had benefited from years of Mr Brown's wisdom and, inevitably, some of it had worn off. Purnell would learn in his turn. It could only help him in the long run. He must never think he was past learning. Humility, that was the thing. Humility and endeavour. He feared the pre-season, though. He was not self-defeatingly proud, but he didn't want to be a cipher while Achilles ran the show.

The summer's big purchase, thanks to Strabis Kinsale, was Jermaine Cole, who said he didn't care how little money he was earning, he was a winner, and he wanted to join a team of winners. His disciplinary record was patchy, but there was no doubting his talent. He peacocked into training on his first day, ready to show the old men a thing or two. Dave, Zondi and Achilles outplayed Cole every practice game that week. Purnell let him take his medicine, but Purnell was also pleased when Will Beauchamp took the youngster under his wing. All for one, etc.

In the year's first Team Meeting, Purnell said his thoughts were simple: it wasn't broke and he wasn't going to try to fix it. Achilles asked how Cole was to fit in. 'It means we have one more option in the middle,' said Purnell. 'Pressure for places is the lifeblood of a strong team. You're not as young as you were – we have to be ready to rotate to keep you all fresh. Make sense?'

'Sure, old boy. I just wondered where you see him fitting in – will he be looking to rotate in for me, or for Will? It makes a difference, and we have to prepare differently for those two. If —'

'Hey, maestro,' interrupted Will Beauchamp. 'It's pre-season. We don't know what Coley can do. Let's give the details a rest until we've settled down, why don't we? Everyone?' There were nods, oddly emphatic, as if players had come prepared to disagree with Achilles for some reason.

The next meeting was even worse. It was the morning after the first warm-up match, a 4–1 win at non-league Bishop's Stortford. Everyone seemed satisfied apart from Achilles, who said that the conceded goal came because Cole pushed too far up as a right midfielder, much higher than Zondi, and Dave wasn't ready for it and didn't cover. Cole sat sullenly as Achilles added, 'A better team would certainly have exploited the gap, and even this Stortford made three good chances. This was what I tried to say —'

'Enough!' said Will Beauchamp. 'It was Coley's first game. Get off his back just because he's not Zondi. He had a great game going forward, made a goal and scored one. Think about that before you start slagging him off.'

'I'm not saying you weren't good going forward, Coley, old thing. It's just if you play that way, the rest of us have to adapt.'

Purnell intervened. 'I think there is something useful there for all of us to take away,' he said. 'I think we can agree that Coley gives us something extra, something different, which is a positive we have to exploit. We can leave it for now. What else do people have to say?' There were comments about how things felt looser than last season, but no one was worried at this stage.

Louie Cohen stood up. 'I have something to say,' he said. 'I love this soccer club. I've always loved it, ever since I was a child, before I knew about soccer, before I even knew that it existed. When I started playing soccer, I heard about KSC, and I knew it was my destiny. When Mr Brown brought me here, it was like I was coming home to a place where people could walk and work in harmony. When Mr Brown died, I felt a part of my soul go with him, but I also felt a part of his soul replace it. I think his soul entered all of us, and it was no coincidence we started having these meetings so soon afterwards. These meetings are the soul of the club. We are the only team in the world that understands the meaning of democracy, which is that everyone has a right to have their say. Some of you know what I'm talking about, because you've been discussing it with Will Beauchamp outside this room.' Will looked annoyed when he said this. 'I refused to join in with you. I agree with what you said, but these meetings should be the only place we do this. Mutual criticism should be open and free. Achilles, we respect you, but you're not better than us. You have to give us the respect we give you.'

Purnell had a sense that some of the players checked with Will Beauchamp before nodding. 'I never meant . . .' Achilles said. 'I was trying to help the team, old things. It is just I am the most experienced, and —'

'Actually,' said Will Beauchamp, 'isn't Dave the most experienced?'

'We all have an equal right to say what we think,' said Dave. 'Experience shouldn't come into it. None of us is any better than the rest.'

'Doesn't that include me, *querido*?'

'Of course!' Dave said. 'That's what I was saying. But there's obviously something in this criticism if everyone else is agreeing.'

Will had not thought that Dave would stab Achilles so publicly in the back. He supposed it was because Dave hated not being top dog. Whatever the reason, from that day on, Achilles stopped contributing to meetings. He thought his sulk was dignified silence.

Once the season began, Will ascribed this silence, in understanding little sidemouth chats before and after the meetings proper, to lover's petulance: Zondi was being sidelined by Jermaine Cole, who was the only bright spot of the early season. Dave was stretched to cover behind him, and Mickey Faller at right back was constantly having to deal with two men, but Cole jinked and danced his way into the headlines, scoring three goals in four games and setting up another two. The meetings' temper started to fray. Dave suggested that Cole should think more about his defensive duties, but Cole said that if he wasn't getting forward, where were the goals going to come from? Why was no one complaining about fucking Achilles, who didn't seem to be doing anything?

'Fuck off, mate,' said Mickey Faller. 'Achilles is trying to sit in behind you when you go up, but he's the worst fucking defender on earth. His job is to score goals.'

'So's mine, and I'm the one doing it, so fuck off yourself.'

'Easy guys,' said Purnell. 'I hear what you're saying. You're playing brilliantly, Coley, and I don't want to change that.'

'Thanks, boss. Mickey was really getting on my tits.'

'For fuck's sake, mate.'

'Enough!' said Will Beauchamp. 'Coley's a diamond, and we look after him, right, like we've always looked after Achilles. In some games, maybe – I'm just thinking out loud – we won't be able to afford them both. Or one will have to go up front and sit alongside Tom or Lairdy. How's that sound?'

'It makes a lot of sense,' said Purnell. 'I was thinking something like that. Achilles, you look tired, and —'

'I'd prefer to play in the middle, boss. I'll be better there,' said Cole.

Will watched Dave watch Achilles, waiting for the Argentinian to point out the obvious, to say that Cole's all-action dribbling style, exciting as it was, was completely unsuited to Achilles' role, which depended on vision, quick passing and a willingness to act as a pivot around which the rest of the team played. Achilles sat, head straight, eyes steady on whoever was speaking.

Esther worried about the Socialists leaking goals. The new Danish signing Oin Daggers was fair cover for the centre halves, but he was too slow to be a wing back, and Mickey Faller was suddenly permeable after five dependable seasons. Now Esther thought about it, dependable was all Faller had ever been, probably. She discussed the matter with JP, and together they informed Adam that he needed to release money for a new right back, pronto. He said that Jermaine Cole had, by himself, used up the year's transfer budget, and any incoming players should be balanced by sales. Esther pointed at the league table pinned to his wall and asked if he really thought this was the time to be weakening KSC? 'What about the war chest?' she asked.

'We've spent our budget, Esther. The war chest is for emergencies.'

'If we get back to winning, we can put the money straight back in. It's an investment. We're a football club.'

Adam didn't seem to understand anything, because he was not a football person, and he was obviously baulking her to show his power. But Esther had an ace up her sleeve – Strabis Kinsale had insisted on her being in charge of KSC, which meant he was on her side. She was rather frightened of him, so she persuaded Donald to raise the issue on her behalf, and Donald returned with a note saying, *Esther, I have put you in charge of the Socialists for a reason. I trust you to do what I want. You are there to make the decisions. Do so with my blessing, SK.*

She showed this note to Adam. He said, 'We're a business. There's no guarantee Strabis will keep bailing us out of trouble if we don't show we can behave responsibly. If KSC isn't standing on its own two feet, it's completely at his whim. You do realise that? Do you *really* know what he wants the club for? And remember, if he does let it go, that you have invested a lot of money in it. It's your own risk.'

Esther was furious at this lecture but she did, in private, begin to readjust her thinking. It was her money, after all. She would get Adam to release the money this one time, to show who was boss, but in the future she would be cautious.

Esther and Purnell spoke to Will Beauchamp about who he thought would make good 'cover' for Faller, which was a mealy-mouthed conversation, even if no one else was listening. Purnell also asked whether he should raise the issue in a Team Meeting. Will said he shouldn't. Some types of decisions, Will had reluctantly come to see, couldn't be made collectively and would only destabilise the group. Those decisions should be made decisively by the small group of people who fate had made responsible for them, however unwillingly. On the other hand, players always know about good players, said Will, so he suggested that he talk to a few of the guys about who they thought was up to the job.

'Achilles has a good eye for players,' said Purnell, half-heartedly. 'But, you know . . .'

'Yeah, I do know, JP. Achilles has been odd since the start of the season. I might stick to asking the younger guys. They're less set in their ways – they're more likely to know players who'll fit into the team you're building. Players for the JP era instead of the Mr Brown one.'

'Okay,' said Purnell. 'That makes sense.' Esther nodded.

Even though Esther had completely stopped seeing Tom, Will insisted on waiting for a few months because he couldn't risk her being on the rebound. It was important to be patient in life, to act only when the moment was perfect. Esther agreed, totally. It wasn't as if she had nothing to occupy her time! The decision about buying a new right back was only the tip of the iceberg, a football decision she understood to the heart of its bones, but there was the organisational structure of

KSC to deal with too, which under her sister's distant care had been allowed to go to rack and ruin, said Donald. The Bursar's ad hoc team of thirty staff, with their ill-defined tasks and various methods of muddling along, needed to be refined. Clear roles were important. Adam retained his office, and Esther took over the Bursar's, which was almost exactly the same size. She wanted to get rid of the Bursar himself, but he was one of her father's old cronies. Adam suggested he be made the Services Manager, though everyone still called him the Bursar. With no fuss, the Bursar toddled downstairs and re-erected his charts and piles of paper.

A week later, Esther noticed the Head Groundsman reporting to the Bursar. She stopped that straight away. She asked the Bursar who else came to him. He said that the Security and Ticketing managers, as well as the Charities Liaison Officer and some others all popped in, but it wasn't formal, he was just trying to keep some of the rubbish off her desk. 'In future, Bursar,' she said, 'they come via me. You tell them that.'

The next day, the newly titled Head of Match Day Programmes visited her. 'There's trouble at t'mill!' he said.

'What?'

'Paper mill, Miss Rosslare!' Esther stared. 'Actually the trouble's not the mill, it's the printers. I was making a joke. Sorry, Miss Rosslare. The printers say there's a hurry on, and they can't get the programmes here until Saturday morning.'

'Isn't that when we need them?'

'Traffic's bad on a Saturday. The Bursar always insists we get them Friday. Doesn't want the risk, especially first day of the season.'

'Tell the printer we need them on Friday, then.'

'Normally it's the Bursar who does that, though. More clout. Can you call them?'

'What's the number?'

'Oh. I'll get it.' He scurried off.

He was followed by the Head Groundsman asking for a new seed-laying tractor-roller, which was absolutely essential for the health of the precious Kilburn turf. She signed off on the purchase. Then Programmes returned with the number. 'Ask for Len,' he said, and stood there.

'You can go.'

'Sorry, Miss Rosslare.'

Esther phoned Len. He explained that it was just this week, Miss

207

Rosslare, just this once, and he could absolutely guarantee that the programmes would be there for the game, his word of honour. He said the KSC business was his lifeblood, so help him, so she could trust him all the way to the sea. She delivered a stern ticking-off, and finished by saying, 'They must be here by eight in the morning, I insist.' He said that was no problem, absolutely none at all.

Programmes was distressed. He started to say that Len always tried the same thing, but the Bursar was very clear. 'The Bursar isn't in charge. I am,' said Esther.

'Yes, Miss Rosslare. Sorry.'

Esther interviewed all her managers, and got reports on the state of play. Almost everything was running smoothly except for the pitch. After a week-long series of chats with the Head Groundsman, Esther was horrified that the Bursar had been so short-sighted and penny-pinching about what was, when you came to it, the single most important part of Kilburn Park. Not only was the equipment all archaic, but the turf itself was only relaid once per season ('The top sports-grass magazine in Australia – they're the world leaders, Miss Rosslare, we're hundreds of years behind – suggests that European and Northern American narrow-bladed turfs under heavy use should be relaid twice per season, even with woven undermatting, which, thank the Lord, I somehow managed to persuade the Bursar to fork out for'), and the undersoil heating was so antediluvian it could spring a leak at any moment and flood the pitch. The Groundsman made a list of what he needed and when he needed it in order to prepare KSC for the twenty-first century. With proper investment, things might be rectified in three years, more probably five.

Head of Charities Liaison wanted to know which players were available when. Esther said it was his job to find that out, wasn't it? Charities Liaison, a bluff man with a wig, said the Bursar used to have a chart. Esther told him he had to stand on his own two feet. Delegation was part of the job, for God's sake. The man was so ineffectual.

When Esther arrived at ten o'clock on Saturday, the programmes were nowhere to be seen. She phoned Len, who told her that they'd left his works in good time, and it could only be the traffic. Programmes said that was bollocks, there was nothing to stop the truck on the roads this morning, and the journey was only forty minutes. Esther said she'd call again in an hour. Programmes stamped off. After a minute, Esther had a sudden suspicion, and hurried downstairs. When she opened the Bursar's door, Programmes started guiltily.

'Talk of the Devil!' said Programmes. 'Sorry, Miss Rosslare, it was a joke.' Esther gave him a hard glare. 'We were just having a chat,' said Programmes.

'Who were you on the telephone to, Bursar?'

'Len, Miss Rosslare. He's a weasel, that Len, if you let him be one. The programmes are leaving the plant now, and we're paying half price.' He spoke calmly, as if he weren't defying her direct orders. He was a little fifty-eight-year-old man with mousy, wavy hair that was only just starting to grey. There was something wrong with his right hand, which he was shy about, and he tried to cover it by carrying a clipboard.

'I will not have my authority flouted,' said Esther.

'I would never do that, Miss Rosslare.' It was so barefaced that she didn't know what to say.

Charities Liaison continued to be pathetic. Esther slowly realised that the Bursar basically did his job for him. When she said this to the Bursar, he closed the door and told her Charities Liaison was, indeed, not one of life's brighter sparks, but he had always been a loyal member of the team, and, as a former player, it behoved KSC . . .

'He played for us?' Esther prided herself on her knowledge of former Socialists.

'Never in the first team, but . . .'

Esther breathed a sigh of relief. 'He can be supported by the Social Club Trust if he's earned that right, Bursar, but I am trying to run a business here. Publicity is incredibly important to a modern football club, and he is half our publicity team!'

'Barbara and I have always covered for him.'

'It's not good enough, Bursar.'

Barbara was another problem, frankly. She joined the club as a secretary, married a player, became part of the furniture and had written press releases for the Socialists since 1978. But the world had moved on. Esther now understood that the club's value, and consequently its health, depended at least in part on its prominence, and Barbara was hardly the kind of dynamic face the club needed during quiet periods. Esther felt like she was trying to cope with everything at once, all by herself. Strabis Kinsale wanted KSC to be essentially unchanged, just more rationalised and businesslike, and it wasn't happening.

Organisation was Adam's job, and he wasn't doing it. She knocked angrily on his door. 'I'm trying, Esther, but it takes time. I can't actually get to the bottom of what the Bursar did, but it seemed to work and I don't want to bugger everything up while we're changing over.'

'You used to do this for a living. Sort it out. We need a professional team, not a stupid, fussy old man.'

'It's difficult.'

'What would you have done five years ago?'

Five years ago, Adam would have brought in a managerial coordinator to do Esther's job for her while technically acting as her underling. However, that was exactly what the Bursar was already doing, and very efficiently. Adam asked Esther for a week. 'Okay, one week. But I need this sorted out.'

Adam stood at the window staring down at the pitch, a small distant strip still lit bright green by the late summer evening. He took a backwards step at the very moment a cloud scurried across the sun, and the distance and change in light transformed the window into a mirror. He'd had drinks with a couple of his old colleagues the week before. He could never go back. Football had gathered him in, somehow, and KSC in particular. It was as if he had been an odd-shaped peg who had been preparing for this hole all his life. Aisling thought he was being foolish, and that he felt like this because Kilburn was where he finally came out and learned that nobody cared. She was wrong. KSC was special. A couple of gay players at other clubs had come out since Achilles and Zondi, but Achilles and Zondi were still exceptions, and they took the idiotic abuse they sometimes got from opponents, especially abroad, with incredible dignity and with the full-throated support of their own fans. Adam came to football as an outsider, but he had become a fan, so he could see both sides of the equation. KSC was different, and if he could stand against the encroaching tide, even for a while, he'd be proud of himself. The man in the window was taller and younger than he'd been three years ago. He sent for Barbara from the press office, explained what she'd have to do, and apologised.

ONWARDS AND UPWARDS

Adam's 'reorganisation' began a week later.

Esther stormed furiously into Adam's office to complain that Barbara had called in sick, for the second day running, and Esther was expected to field bloody reporters all day!

'You're right, you're right,' Adam sighed. 'And you coming here with precisely this complaint confirms my plan. The conclusion I had come to, speaking as a consultant, is that the publicity department is the single biggest thing we have to deal with. There's a business phrase called LLOYD, which means Little Levers Open Yawning Doors, and the more I think about it, I think that everything will start dropping naturally into place once we sort out our PR.'

'How are we going to do that?'

'I have some contacts in advertising. I'll speak to them about getting in the right kind of people. We should keep Barbara in the short term, because she does at least understand the minimum that needs to be done, but I'm afraid we're going to have to get rid of Charities Liaison.'

'Yes! That's —'

'Don't try to talk me out of it, Esther. It's a hard decision, because he's been with us a long time, but I'm sure we can find him some little job with the Trust to make it seem better.' Adam had already cleared this with a disappointed but understanding Charities Liaison.

'Yes, we must do that. Reluctant as I am. He's an old player, you realise?'

'Is there anything you don't know about KSC?' said Adam.

So, a fortnight later, in gushed the PR girls (30, 24, 26), fresh from top agencies and full of bright ideas (24 was actually a camp young man, who insisted he was straight but also insisted on being described as 'one of the girls'). In their first meeting with Adam, they thought it was they who decided that KSC needed to publicise the way it had been remade in the wake of its sale. 26 thought she had come up with the clever point that 'heritage is the most unique thing about the Socialists, yeah?' and 30 thought it was she who took things further with the insight that 'the Makeover must emphasise the heritage, okay? Everything's new, but we have to reassure the fans, okay?'

'Terrific,' coaxed Adam. 'We must avoid seeming "aristocratic", but what other things are known for their heritage?'

'Royalty!' said 26.

'That's "aristocratic",' bitched 24.

'No,' said 26, 'it's *historical*!' Adam stepped in and said it was better safe than sorry.

'What about uni?' said 24, who was only two years out of Durham.

'Ye-e-e-s,' mused Adam. 'How would that work? We would avoid management speak and use archaic titles instead?'

'Absolutely!' said 30 (Edinburgh, 1992). 'It's perfect! We already have a "Bursar"!'

Esther loved the idea. She spent a week plastering her desk with lists of possible job titles, and met daily with the girls as they searched for the proper balance. She liked the girls, though she worried that 26 was a manhunter or temptress. She thought of being called 'Bursar,' because the Bursar was the KSC's traditional name for the person who ran things, but 'Bursar' had financial connotations, which was Adam's province. Also, it was associated with the Bursar, downstairs, and she didn't want anyone to think she was only doing the stuff he used to do. Adam should be the 'Bursar', because that would stop everyone thinking the old Bursar was in charge, but Esther would need a new title that would make it clear that she had a more important role. When 30 suggested 'Grand Vizier', and Esther considered it, 24 weighed in with 'Major Domo', 'Mikado' and 'Lord Chamberlain', which was when Esther got the joke. 24 was too sarcastic for Esther's tastes, but it was funny when he suggested that Adam should be Chief Eunuch.

Esther settled eventually on 'Chancellor', with Adam as her Bursar. The Bursar himself became the Manciple, the Head Groundsman became the Head Gardener and the Publicity Department became the Stationery Office, containing a Publisher, a Printer and a Scribe, though everyone still called them 30, 26 and 24. Under Adam's detailed re-organisation and reallocation of responsibilities, which ran to eight pages, the functions of all these new officers were clarified. The Manciple traditionally took the most onerous duties ('It was traditional at my college, anyway,' said Adam), and made a weekly report directly to the Chancellor. This would keep the trivia away from the Chancellor and leave her free to deal with strategic decisions.

The Stationery Office produced a press release while Barbara, titled 'Honorary Secretary' because the others didn't want her to think of herself as their secretary, dealt with reporters' practical needs on match days, gossiping usefully as she had for years, and took over the duties of Charities Liaison. In Esther's opinion, the story of 'the club with a soul' gave much-needed colour to the business pages.

The Indian-summer sky snapped into chilly September grey, stared down unchangingly into October and drizzled through November. The Socialists won, on the whole, but not enough to take them into the top three. Craig Drayly, the new right back, was not stopping any more goals than Mickey Faller had, but that would come. For now, he and his best mate Jermaine Cole were a constant threat going forward. As their GB U21 games had already shown, they were a partnership for the future. 'It's rebuilding,' Esther told Aisling when her sister called to talk about KSC, which was something she never used to do. 'Every team needs to go through rebuilding periods.' Aisling turned up to all the Rosslare Group meetings now, though she wasn't so chummy with Miss Skewbold these days, which made the meetings more bearable for Esther.

In fact, thought Esther, things were very bearable in general. She sat with her feet on her desk, thinking. When she had first found herself with nothing to do, she went and spoke to an obviously busy Adam. He congratulated her. He said that it was the sign of an efficient system operating efficiently under an efficient chief executive that the chief executive was free and ready to deal with crises, if and when they arose.

There was a sudden knock at the door. 'Yes?' said Esther, springing to attention. The Head Groundsman – no, *Gardener* – thrust the door open, dived through and shut himself quickly in. Esther had a brief fear he would attack her, but he stayed where he was and put his finger to his lips, eyes darting around as if someone else might be hiding in the room. 'Yes?' asked Esther.

'You're the only one who's ever understood,' said the Gardener. 'The only one who's ever cared. That's why I've come to you. *He* doesn't know I'm here,' the Gardener added vindictively, as if that explained everything. Esther was nonplussed. 'The *Manciple*!' spat the Gardener. 'I *hate* him!'

'What's happened?'

'He doesn't understand grass. Not like us.' The Gardener was on the verge of tears. 'All I ever dreamed of was perfection,' he said. 'Is that so wrong?'

The Manciple, without telling Esther, had rescinded the urgently important orders she had made about a turf-relaying schedule and the undersoil work that needed to be done. He'd halted the purchase of two spare rollers and the Ulti-Drain system needed to combat London's high water table. The poor Gardener, in desperation, had been forced to sneak upstairs to the one person who could help. This was exactly what Esther was here for, and she burst righteously into the Manciple's office, forcing him to thrust his withered hand below the level of the table in surprise. She was the boss; she didn't have to knock. 'What's this I hear about you countermanding my directives?' she said.

'I would never do that, Miss Rosslare.'

'I have spoken with the Head Gardener.'

'Yes, Miss Rosslare?'

'He says you have stopped him doing vital work which I explicitly authorised.'

'I assumed he was trying to pull a fast one on us, Miss Rosslare, play us off against each other.'

'Do I have to put everything in writing?'

'It might be best with the Gardener. You know what he's like. It's the same every year.'

'What do you mean? He's a genius! Our pitch is always rated the best in the league! Always!'

'And surely that's enough, Miss Rosslare?'

'No! He told me how much was still to be done. If we can make the pitch perfect, we should make it perfect.'

'However much money we spend, Miss Rosslare, we will never achieve perfection. There is always something else to be done. He only sees the pitch, but you and I understand the bigger picture, and that is why I keep him away from you with his unreasonable requests, so it's me he blames for refusing him.'

'But the Ulti-Drain?'

'Yes, it's funny, isn't it? I thought even he would have given up on that one. We have state-of-the-art drainage, specifically designed for temperate European climates, and he wants a system designed to siphon off the results of a tropical storm in less than two hours.'

'Okay. But what about the extra relaying in mid-season when —'

'Oh, I can see how that would be nice, Miss Rosslare, I really can.' He reached behind into a messy cabinet. 'A few days ago, just for something to do, I calculated what the Gardener's plans would cost.' He slid the sheet of paper in front of Esther. She was stunned. 'And of course, this is just the first stage. He hasn't started telling you about the solar reflectors. It's a good thing you cracked down on him before he started to think he could do what he wanted. Everyone always wants more – running a football club is all about the allocation of finite resources. I know I'm telling you things you already know.'

Esther avoided the Gardener for three days, but he was not to be thwarted. Eventually, he caught her in the car park as she fumbled furiously for her keys and thrust them impotently at the lock, unable to focus, fixated on his reflection striding balefully towards her in the window. His right hand was held behind his back. She couldn't turn to face him, but she straightened, waiting.

'You betrayed the grass, Miss Rosslare.'

'No.'

'The grass never forgets.'

'It wasn't me! I begged, but I don't run the budget.'

'Can't you overrule the Manciple?'

'Yes, of course I can!' Inspiration! She turned now. 'It was Adam Greswell. He's the Bursar, not me. He must heed our responsibilities to Strabis Kinsale. He said it was about having to keep a balance between different departments, each of which could spend all the money we have. I don't understand money. It's not my fault!'

The Gardener left a dramatic pause, and then he swung his right arm forward. His upturned fingers sprang wide, like a spider dropped in hot oil, and grass clippings fluttered between them.

WAGES OF SIN

Esther and Will Beauchamp sat in her office, rain streaming down the window. Esther put her feet on the desk because it was vitally important to show him they could be relaxed together.

Will sipped his beer. He was the perfect gentleman last week at this year's Christmas Party, squiring Esther without ever trying to take advantage, because he'd made this rule that they must wait until the end of the season, because it was vital that nothing clouded any decision the two of them might make. He spent the whole evening with her, though, because he was Will, and he was gorgeously polite and charming to everyone else who came to talk to him, even the awful publicity girl, 26, who was twenty-seven now actually. Will made sarcastic jokes about 26 behind her back all the time. Esther was glad he did because 26 was very pretty, in a common way, and she had obviously set her cap at him.

'Equal wages is the best thing about this club,' Will said reflectively.

'Everyone loves us,' said Esther. 'Thanks to you.'

Will smiled. He was on billboards around the country, swathed in a dazzling white burnous and with unnaturally clear blue eyes. He was framed by desert sand and he cradled a sickly child in his arms. He'd suggested to the Stationery Office girls that a television programme about KSC's charity work might raise consciousness for various causes. When they said he was the obvious focus, he demurred, but Esther eventually managed to persuade him to be filmed for a documentary on the subject, so long as he could plug the KSC/*Clarion* Charitable Foundation, as it was now known. On the back of the documentary, having made friends with the director and crew, he idly wondered whether it might be interesting for them to make a reality-style series on the charity work done by the Socialists. This would have the advantage, he laughed, of taking the pressure off him, of avoiding giving the impression that he was anything other than just one of the team. Calum fearlessly reported this example of Will's modesty. The posters, featuring

Will and no one else, advertised the upcoming series. 'The press stuff is silly,' he said. 'They just need a story. It's embarrassing, but I suppose it's worth it. Because of the kids.'

'Of course it is,' said Esther.

'The Stationery girls are great, aren't they?'

'I suppose. For what they are. They're very cliquey. I don't think they like me.'

'Of course they do. Everybody does.'

'Shall I send for another drink?'

'I'd better not. Training, you know. You look really good today. Have you done something different with your hair?'

'Me! No, of course not! I just put it up to be out of the way! Does it look different in some way?'

'Yes. Different good, though. Don't ask me for details, I'm not Achilles!' They laughed together, naughtily. And then Will returned to the subject of wages. He said that he was very worried about even bringing up the subject, and didn't want it to be misinterpreted, but it was important, he thought. 'You have to know I am not suggesting changing the equal-wages thing, or diluting it in any way. You know I would never do that?'

'Of course you wouldn't.'

'No. Almost every other club in the league pays its top players much more than we get at KSC, and that's fine, because we play for love, not money. The thing is, we also do all the extra charity work, which takes time.'

'The other clubs all do it too, Will. They've caught up.'

'But not as much.'

'No, of course not. Sorry, you're right.'

'So, what I'm saying is, in a funny sort of way, we're paid less for doing more. None of this is a problem at the moment, and God knows I hope it never is one – money has never bothered me – but I feel it's my duty, because you and I are so close, to say that I have started to hear some of the players talking about it.'

'Who?'

'Sorry, Esther. You know me. Loyalty is my middle name.'

Esther reddened. 'Of course. I wasn't thinking.'

'I think maybe you should have a word with Adam about it.'

'In what way? What can we do?'

'I'm only saying this because there is so much more money in the game nowadays. If we're not careful, KSC might get a reputation for being stingy, and it might be harder to attract new players, who don't realise what the club means and how unimportant money is once they're here.'

'So we should raise all the wages?'

'We could,' said Will, 'but wouldn't that be very expensive? We'd end up paying squad members ten times their market value.'

'Yes, of course. It's the same with everything, Will. We have to allocate finite resources to different areas of the club, but the areas make infinite demands.'

'I'd never thought of that,' said Will.

Esther saw that Will was trying to say something serious, however embarrassing he found it. 'Is this really a problem?' she asked.

'I spoke to Benjie China the other day —'

'Your agent!'

'Don't worry. I was just making sure Benjie doesn't take a cut when I send appearance fees to the Foundation. He warned me that Cole and Drayly joined us because we won the treble, for kudos, but unless they start getting paid properly, they'll move on within eighteen months. You know they're represented by Phil Maroon?'

'So's Louie!'

'Louie's one of us, but Maroon isn't. Benjie says to be careful of Maroon, because he's building a power base. I didn't believe him until Maroon tried to take me off Benjie. He reckons if he gets enough of us, he can force you to do what he wants. You know how these agent bastards think.'

'But we can't offer new players more than everyone else is getting!'

'Of course not,' Will looked as confused and upset about this as she felt. 'We definitely don't need to do anything until it becomes a problem, but . . . how about this? Maybe you could perhaps get round it in the future, if you absolutely had to, by having some system of performance bonuses or something? I really haven't thought about it.'

It was typically brave of Will to understand that hard subjects couldn't be ignored. 'I'll think about it, but I don't like it.'

'Nor do I, God knows, but at least if it's performance-related then it's fair. You can say that people are only getting more for doing more. It doesn't compromise the principles of the club.'

'No,' said Esther. 'But —'

'I'm being stupid. This is none of my business. Forget I ever said it.'

'No, Will, it's not that. It's just . . . If we give new players performance-related bonuses, we would have to change all the other contracts too. Including yours.'

'I hadn't thought. No. No, that wouldn't be necessary.'

'I'm sorry, but it would. It would be the only fair way.'

'I hate the way money keeps intruding on the game we love, Esther. I hate it. I'm glad there are people like you around to make the hard decisions!'

THE STARS TURN

From far enough away the city looked peaceful, like a battle or a flood. The last of autumn's stubborn browns gave way to winter, and the ebb and flow of tiny figures in the streets changed in shape and tempo.

Sally Stares, on her way home, dawdled past the Good Intent. We know what she was doing, but the American wasn't there tonight.

The stars turned.

There she was again, and he was there this time. He caught her eye, as if he often looked at the window around now, and she bowed her head and hurried on.

The stars turned.

This time she went inside.

The stars turned.

This time, when the pub closed, they emerged together. From this close, we can see the first brave green on the branches as they whip and whistle in the wind. He walked her to the end of her road, but that was all.

The next time she looked through the window, weeks later, he wasn't there.

The stars turned.

Not far away, Achilles and Zondi fulfilled a social engagement run by the Charitable Foundation. For six months now, ever since the meetings in which Dave didn't support him against Will Beauchamp, Achilles had been angry and withdrawn. The petulance had started in the dressing room but it had spread into the rest of his life. Zondi was forced to carry the conversation, twisting in discomfort. As early as they could, the pair departed. Calum and the other Foundation organisers apologised to the other guests for the couple's behaviour.

Later, in bed, looking at the luminescing little galaxy that Zondi had spread over the ceiling, Achilles said, 'I'm sorry, *querido*.'

Zondi said, 'I need you back.' The other did not pretend he had never been away. 'It was unfair what they said,' said Zondi, 'but I am lost without you.'

Zondi screwed up his courage and asked Dave for help. Dave said that if Achilles wanted something, he'd have to ask for it himself. The wedge driven between the three after Mr Brown's death was too deep for Zondi to remove on his own. Without Achilles' strength and wisdom, Kilburn's precious, fragile tribe was losing its direction, hunting mind-lessly for the closest prey without any heed for what would happen when the easy meat ran out. Unless this changed, they would be lost in the desert. In despair, Zondi started to speak in meetings, but although he knew what must be done, he couldn't make the others understand.

Nicky finally let Leo propose when she started as a registrar at Tommy's in November. The wedding was now a month away, in mid-April. Nicky had asked Aisling to help her and Leo with the seating plan, but Aisling knew her job was to sit, listen and confirm. After bolting one of Leo's delicious meals, Nicky sharpened her pencil, looked slyly across and said, 'Can I put you next to Jeremy Musgrave?' Aisling rolled her eyes. 'He's an usher, you're a bridesmaid. It makes sense.'

'That's why you got me to make him an usher!' said Leo.

'He was your first college friend,' said Nicky quickly. 'Jez asked me to put you together,' she added.

'You don't have to do it,' said Leo.

'I said I would. It would be rude not to.'

'No, it wouldn't,' said Leo.

'Yes, it would.' Nicky said, scribbling. For the rest of the evening, Aisling was irritated. It wasn't as if she expected to find her true love at this wedding – she knew all the guests already – but she expected to have a good time. The last thing she needed was Nicky setting her up with creepy Jeremy, simply because he was one of the last single men. When Nicky briskly said, 'I think that's that. I don't know why some people take so long organising their weddings. Have I missed anything?' Aisling replied that she was sorry, but she really didn't want to sit next to Jeremy, and how hard would it be to think again about that?

Nicky put her pencil deliberately down. 'How old are you, Azzabelle?' she asked. Aisling sighed. 'Have you even organised your *viva*?' Nicky reached over and moved Aisling's wine away from her, which was fabulously annoying, since it was only her second glass, and it was still half-full. 'How long is it since you had a proper boyfriend? You have to sort yourself out, my petal, and it's not about losing independence. Look at me and Leo. We've never got in each other's way.' If Aisling were actually drunk, she'd have pointed out that Nicky made Leo stay at the *Oxford Mail* for three years while she was at the John Radcliffe. Both the *Courier* and *The Times* had offered him jobs in London, but Nicky told everyone that Leo thought it was better to learn his trade at a smaller paper. Nicky went on. 'You need to find someone outside the hospital. Your surgeon's too old, and you're his rebound fling. Everyone knows that. Jeremy's not a bad guy, and he likes you.' Aisling shook her head. 'Az. You'll do this for me because I'm worried about you. I'm trying the best I can, but the more you behave like this, the more I think you'll never sort yourself out. I try to imagine you finally qualifying, or in a real relationship, but I'm sorry, I just can't.'

'You're kidding,' said Aisling. Nicky said things like this frequently, but Aisling never for a second thought she might be serious.

'I'm not sure I am,' said Nicky. 'And you're sitting next to Jeremy, for me.'

Jed the American hesitated as he walked to the Good Intent. He knew what was coming, sooner or later, and he should stop it, because it was wrong. He was scheduled to have left London by now. This kind of thing didn't happen to him. Sally didn't come, again. She was probably with her fiancé.

The stars turned.

Jed was in the pub again.

Nearby, Sally walked stiffly up the hill. She ignored the drizzle, and she didn't notice the dark green blades of the emerging flowers in the tiny front gardens all the way up Sheriff Road. She thought she must look as if she was marching to the scaffold, grimly determined to face an unavoidable fate. Actually, she looked more like a reluctant martyr, fearing damnation, but hoping for rapture. Either way, she was on the brink of an awfully big adventure. She didn't hesitate at the pub door, was inside for two minutes, and then she and Jed half-walked, half-ran to his flat, desperate to get it over with so they could both move on.

*

Men scampered around little green rectangles all over London, the triumph and disaster no less for the forty-year-old clogger on Wanstead Flats than for the Chilean international at Clapham Rovers. A team in East Kilburn sat dejected in opulent splendour as its shirts were collected and sped to the laundry room; another team huddled angrily around a pile of soaking kit on the edge of a bleak and windswept municipal pitch somewhere in Harlesden: princes and paupers, but sport is a drama with only a certain number of plots, and both teams bleated the same sour refrain: 'What's wrong? Why are we still losing? How could we be league champions one year and struggling to find a pass to each other ten months later? Who is to blame?'

In Kilburn, Achilles still kept his counsel. JP spouted vibrant platitudes about effort, confidence and looking at the positives. It might have worked with players who knew no better, but the Socialists showed him the tops of their heads. They needed more, for something to change, a new player, or some tactical masterstroke, or anything, but not this same old story. After the meeting broke up, just as he'd done after other recent meetings, Will whispered about the team's lack of hunger. He wondered quietly whether maybe a system of concrete incentives might reinvigorate the team's competitive instincts.

Will never discussed this with Dave, of course. Dave was part of the problem.

Dave's hunger used to be his greatest asset, but in the current crisis, he seemed the least worried of all the players. He did not subscribe to JP's furious, incompetent optimism; it was rather that Dave understood that he himself was playing badly this season, as were they all, and in this world, sometimes, for whatever reason, that just happens. Once, it would have driven him crazy, but he was different now. He'd learned that if you have the right basic material, and everyone is willing to trust each other, and you commit to the long term, things will come right in the end. Only children can't control their hunger.

He drove to Sally's house.

Sally waited. They weren't going anywhere tonight, but she had dressed up. She knew it was silly. Dave arrived and made tea, asking automatically about her day. She used to complain proudly to her friends that he could hardly bear to speak after he had lost a match. She made him sit down and she told him what had happened with Jed. She said that Jed meant nothing.

The stars flickered.

Sally supposed she expected upset, forgiveness and a return to the routine. She wasn't sure that that was what she wanted. She might almost have admitted that she wanted to provoke a crisis. Dave looked at her as if he would hate her for ever for this betrayal, as if any parallel between what she'd done and what he did with Aisling was fatuous. Dave could always make her feel stupid and wrong. He was obsessed by the fact that Jed happened two weeks ago, and that Sally had lain in bed with Dave for those two weeks without saying anything. Couldn't she understand how that made him feel? Aisling had been a drunken mistake at the start of a relationship, which he had confessed immediately. In Sally's increasingly righteous anger, it hardly seemed a big distinction. Dave did it first, now she'd done it, so they were even.

She could see him struggle to reason with his rage, and fail. It was almost frightening, but it opened her eyes to the depth of what he must feel for her, which was one positive thing that had come out of this. It would make it easier to forget Jed, and focus on the long term. She went to sit next to Dave, but he shied from her.

Later that night, Dave sat on the bench. The naked stars gleamed overhead, and he knew that his soul was bare. If he were the man he wanted to be, he would forgive her. Of course her and Jed was different from him and Aisling all that time ago – no two things are *ever* the same – and if it took Sally two weeks to pluck up the courage to speak, well, so be it. Sally and he were separate people, with their own ways of dealing with things, and, rationally, he should be able to get past this.

But she didn't say she was drunk when she slept with Jed, or even how she met him. When did she cross paths with the director of an American NGO? At one of the charity events she went to with Dave, no doubt. He shouldn't torture himself with things that didn't matter. He should go back to her, but he couldn't. He hit the bench with the heels of his palms and hunched forwards, pressing his fists into his temples. He really thought he'd escaped this part of himself, the stupid pride and immoderation. He thought Sally had changed him, but here he was again.

She had spent a night with Jed and then, for two weeks, as if nothing had happened, she talked and slept with him. How could he ever be comfortable with her after that? He thought he'd found a haven. Where was he to go now? Also, he felt released and relieved.

Sally watched Dave drive away. For the two days since she told him about Jed, he had stayed with Zondi and Achilles. When he finally returned, he explained why this was a good thing for both of them. He realised, he said, that he'd never treated her properly, and that the marriage would have been great for him, but a tragedy for her, because she needed someone better, someone prepared to love her more obviously than he could. Holding her hand, he said he hated the way he always assumed he knew what was best for everyone else – he tried to stop himself, but it had happened again, and he was truly sorry. He said he would always be there for her, but he understood that he could never make her as happy as she made him, and so that must be an end of it.

She believed him at the time, because he was so persuasive and seemed so hurt. Monica immediately said that this was self-justifying horseshit. If Dave truly fucking loved her, he'd have fought for her. If he was too pathetic to forgive her like she'd forgiven him, then he didn't deserve her, thank fuck she'd found out before it was too late, and good fucking riddance. Monica hated the way Dave tried to twist everything with words and arguments, instead of just saying what he felt: he realised the engagement was a mistake, and he was trying to get out of admitting it by blaming her, the fucker.

Sally, in the end, agreed with most of what both Dave and Monica said, and she knew in her heart that it was a lucky escape. Today, though, she felt sick and alone.

Leo and Nicky got married in a registry office and the reception was at Brasenose. Old friends slid around familiar forgotten corners as if a decade hadn't happened. Aisling kept a wary eye on Jeremy Musgrave, who wasn't as creepy as she remembered, and probably never had been. He was the one of Leo's friends who always hung around her when they were students, even when he was seeing someone else. When they took their places, he asked how her work was going, was modest about how well he was doing as a bright young lion of the law, and didn't loom over her too hideously. He said, as if *he* was the one who used to resist *her*, 'We're older, Ash. Slate wiped.' He asked about KSC, and she said she hardly took any interest in it these days.

'That's good,' he replied.

'Why?'

'Football's . . . Oh no, I'm not getting caught out! Why do you take less interest?'

'I don't know.'

'Yes, you do! It's because it's getting worse every day. It's lost its working-class roots. The players are vile. The things that used to make KSC bearable have been kicked into touch. Money's like a black hole – it sucks everything in.'

'What car do you drive?'

'A Golf only, but touché, I'm rich. But you know what I'm saying about football?'

'Yes. Actually, I see it all more clearly now that I'm ouside it.'

'You still have some stake, though, don't you? Nicky told me. She thinks you should get rid of it. The club's only going to get worse. Okay, I'll drop the subject.'

On cue, Nicky joined them, tipsy and ecstatic. 'So?' she asked. 'How are you two?'

'We're fine, Nicks. The food was great. It's a brilliant day.'

'I have high hopes for this one, Jeremy,' said Nicky. 'If she steadies herself down, I see her as a top surgeon. A *top* surgeon. Do you know that Jeremy does a lot of pro bono? Oh, I must look after my cousin, she's only twenty-five.'

She whirled off, and Jeremy turned to Aisling with a rueful grin. 'You know she's trying to set us up? She said you wanted us to sit together, but I saw through that. I've enjoyed it, though. You're less flighty than I remember.' It was an irritating compliment, but clumsiness is not the worst sin, and Aisling had a better time at the meal than she expected. She was making no promises, but she'd be prepared to go on a date with him.

Later on, Leo found her alone and asked, 'Was it all okay?' She said that of course it was, and what a perfect wedding it had been. Leo grinned. He said, 'You know what Nicky's like, but she's usually right about the important things. Usually.'

*

At matches in Kilburn, the cameras started to focus on a claque of gay fans who threw confetti at their particular idols, and the claque was growing every week. The story got around that this was a tradition, another demonstration of the club's unique and wonderful spirit, and straight fans were starting to join in.

Will drank water with Louie. He said that relating bonuses to performance was actually the only way of keeping equal pay. He said, as if searching for the best way to express a difficult concept, that it might even help the team. It might force them to struggle more, and get better. Louie pounced, seeing that he could explain this to Will perfectly. He said that this was the American way, man. Everyone takes personal responsibility, they work hard, and they get the reward. You get out what you put in. It's completely fair.

'Yes,' said Will. 'Of course. That's it precisely.' He seemed relieved to hear it so lucidly put. He said he was meeting the Board, and he would tell them that this is what the players wanted —

'No way, man.' Will was startled. Louie said that this is what he thought, but the club was a democracy. Something like this was a matter for the whole team. It had to go to a meeting, and be voted on. That's what democracies do.

'Yes,' said Will. 'Of course. I was just trying to hurry things along.'

KSC won on Wednesday, but they still weren't certain of qualifying for Europe next season, which would be a catastrophe. In the Team Meeting, Will said they had to start planning for next year. Something had to change. He had a suggestion that might seem radical, but he asked the others to hear him out. More than half the people in the room knew that he was going to propose performance-related pay, and had privately agreed with him. James Purnell spoke vehemently against the idea, saying that it would destroy the ethos of the great institution of which he was proud to be a part. Will noted his opposition.

Zondi was glad Purnell spoke out, but the team did not respect Purnell. The small man was grimly preparing to make his own fumbling case when Achilles touched his wrist, smiled and stood up. Achilles said that the players all knew the situation when they joined the club. He said they each of them had more money than any man could sanely need, and by not haggling for more they showed the world that there was another way to behave.

Cole and Drayly didn't understand Achilles. Will was talking about football; Achilles was talking about history. But Mr Brown's players, with the exception of Will and two others who did not matter, remembered why they'd signed. Dirk Volendam was one of those who had let himself be swayed by Will, and he felt doubly ashamed because Torquil would have followed his lead. Louie felt his eyes reopen. Will's wabbling words were washed away. Will talked about personal responsibility, but all he wanted was money. Louie reminded himself he was a missionary, not a mercenary. The players, including a silent Dave, voted not to change.

Will said he only raised the subject because he was asked to. He loved the spirit of the club as much as the next man. He was glad his comrades were making this stand, and he would be proud to convey the news upstairs, but he warned them that sometime soon they would face the decision again, and it would be in very stark terms: do you keep your soul pure, and let the club's greatness disappear, and along with it all its potential for doing good, or do you dilute the soul, just a drop, and let the club survive? It was inspiring to have gone with heart over head this time, but the economic realities wouldn't go away. After the meeting, he spoke with Esther.

Three weeks after the end of the disappointing season, the Board gathered in a wary mood. Strabis Kinsale had spoken at length with Donald. He asked whether the team might benefit from a change of management.

'Well, mate, I don't know,' said Donald. 'We've always prided ourselves on our stability.'

'Maybe that's part of the problem?' mused Strabis. 'Might not our reputation for stability make people complacent, do you think?'

'Well, I suppose I'd have to say you might have something there, but . . .'

'I'm not pushing you one way or the other,' said Strabis. 'When I delegate, I trust. But I will say this: you can't find the gold in your pan if you don't sometimes give it a shake.'

'Yes. There's a lot in that.' Donald hadn't considered the management issue, but it did make sense. The fans had been delighted to get

JP two years ago, but seventh in the league was not good enough for a club of Kilburn's stature, and missing out on European football would seriously dent next season's finances. Moreover, in the press, a new received wisdom was evolving to explain the Socialists' relative failure this year: team meetings and democratic management were appealing, but they were unsuited to the real world. A football team needed a strong, guiding voice, a manager who was confident in what he was doing and was prepared to make hard decisions, however unpopular. Esther, acutely aware of her role as the voice of the fans, listened to the loudest voices.

Adam phoned Aisling to tell her that James Purnell was going to be sacked. He added that Esther led the calls. Aisling was shocked that she wasn't consulted. Her father taught her to think in the long term and, to the extent that she thought about it at all, she found the managerial merry-go-round at other clubs absurd. She's thought a lot about what Jeremy said about football being a black hole, and the longer she was away from it, and the more perspective she had, the more persuasive that seemed. The 2002–3 season was just around the corner, and she should maybe sell her stake, but that would actually be more hassle than forgetting about the issue.

At this point, Aisling wasn't sure what she thought of Jeremy. A couple of months after the wedding, long enough to make it clear to Nicky that Aisling was making the decision for her own reasons, Aisling told her surgeon that it had been great, but they should probably stop while they were still friends. Since then, she'd been to the theatre with Jeremy a couple of times, which had been pleasant, but he hadn't tried to kiss her. He'd been keener to discuss politics and how stupid football was than he had been to get her into bed. There probably wasn't a future in it, but she was prepared to kiss him, at least, to see if there was any chemistry. When he heard that JP had been sacked only a year after winning the treble, Jeremy would laugh and say it proved his point, and he'd be right.

It wasn't hard for KSC to find a new manager. Apart from the size and importance of the job, and the players he would get to work with, there was the appealing prospect of turning around an underachieving team. Esther, advised by every sports columnist in the country, explained the need for a strong man, and said sagely that an obvious candidate was beginning to emerge the longer she thought about it. The man she named was indeed strong. A Welshman who spent his whole playing career at Cardiff, he'd terrorised opposition midfielders across Europe for a decade. He then spent a brief, unhappy spell as Cardiff's player-manager before learning his trade in the lower leagues. Stepping on more toes than he had to, he became a dynamic, no-nonsense, effective manager. He spent two years in Spain, taking humble Albacete to the giddy heights of the Champions League. No one liked to play Albacete.

The Board met with the strong man. They said that certain things were not negotiable – the wage structure, the time spent on charity work, and his budget. He said boardroom politics didn't interest him. Tell him the rules, and he'd play by them. In return, he said, they were not to interfere with football decisions.

On the first day of pre-season training, the new manager set out his stall, and almost provoked the mutiny he was ready for. Afterwards, Will suggested a private meeting. 'If you want to start again from scratch, then that's fine,' Will said. 'But we have the basis of a great team here. It isn't like other teams, the type of people we have, but there are ways of getting them in line. I have some ideas, but I'll shut up if you're not interested.'

'Go on,' said the manager.

Will said that the team was used to running itself – even if doing so was a mistake – and moving back to a traditional system would probably have to happen in steps. He suggested that a Players' Committee could be a workable halfway house. It would give players the illusion of being listened to, and it would be more controllable than the existing meetings, where decisions could be swayed by demagoguery rather than common sense. Will added that it would also be a way to keep the manager's friends close and his enemies closer, to make sure he wasn't blindsided. The manager didn't like the plan, but he could see its value as an interim measure.

Every manager has certain players he will always buy, in an ideal world. With his generous, if not bottomless, budget, the strong man began to make enquiries. The club negotiated acceptable transfer fees for each of his first three targets, one English and two from Albacete, but in each case the deal fell through over personal terms. As Premiership wages spiralled upwards, and without the prestige of being treble-winners, the club could not attract the very best players.

As pre-season got properly underway, Cole and Drayly put in transfer requests. It would have been illegal for them to speak to any other club, of course, but the pair were somehow certain that potential offers were just around the corner. KSC was an operation in disarray.

The Players' Committee, at Will's suggestion, consisted of Will, Dave, Achilles and Dirk. In a meeting with the manager, Will resisted any temptation to say, 'I told you so, you short-sighted cretins.' Achilles said that this was the team's time of trial. He agreed that a single voice would have to run the club, and he backed the new manager absolutely, but he denied the need for any change in the wage structure. The manager reiterated that he couldn't attract new players. Achilles said that the manager needed to look for more from the players than those things they could do on the pitch. He needed to find the ones who would understand the nature of being a Socialist. If he succeeded, he could achieve a spirit that was not possible at any other club. He might have to ignore some great players, but he would be able to meld very good players into a great team. That, said Achilles, was the unique nature of this job.

'I'm a football manager. I win football matches.'

'Aren't performance bonuses the compromise we need?' said Will to Achilles. 'I know you guys don't like them, but look at the state we're in, and it's only July. A lower base rate, still a very good wage, and then · add-ons will mean we keep Cole and Drayly, and can attract new players. Adapt or die.'

There was a silence, and then Dave said, 'I don't like this any more than you do, Achilles.'

Achilles was incredulous. Dave had been at sea since splitting up with Sally, but Achilles never dreamed that his friend would betray the club. 'No way,' he said.

'I'm sorry, mate,' said Dave, 'but you can't always force people to do something they don't want to do. Sometimes we have to let things go.' It was easy for Achilles to be an idealist, thought Dave. He'd never had to struggle for anything. He had his perfect partner and his perfect life. Dave went on. 'If it's a choice between surviving and going down the shitter, then I say we change. We keep as much as we can. But sometimes the decision is out of your hands. Sometimes you have to just fucking change.'

'No, *querido*,' said Achilles. 'You are not yourself,' he added, wrongly. But Dave's argument persuaded the Dutchman, and the Players' Committee agreed to recommend the new bonus structure.

Dave went home to his new girlfriend. The girl he was seeing, anyway. She was only twenty-two, and she was a model he'd met at a charity dinner. He was ashamed of her.

Aisling was shocked by the change in wage structure. She read the bullshit about how the club's commitment to equality had not been compromised by the recognition that, with larger squads, a lower basic wage was necessary. The bonuses were equally available to every player, so the principle was undamaged. Surely, thought Aisling, any idiot could see through this? Why didn't the fans seem to mind? It was depressing to think that they were mollified by the withdrawn transfer requests and the sudden possibility of new signings.

The TV series following the players' charity work over the summer was unbearable, the saccharine interviewer asking the players about whether they were humbled to be in the presence of such suffering and bravery, and how it felt to be doing something about it? Even Donald got in on the act, saying in his thankfully brief appearances that it was only fair to point out that the club's sponsors at the Rosslare Group were contributing as well. The club never seemed to be out of the news. The confetti-throwing 'tradition' was lovingly analysed. Will, predictably, was the star.

What was happening at the club was wrong, but Aisling couldn't believe it was irreversible. She spoke to Achilles, but he said there was nothing he could do. His opinion meant nothing – it was whoever controls the purse strings who called the tune. He said that the PR girls had asked him to be 'the club's Ambassador for Homosexual Tolerance, in keeping with our heritage'. They were confused when Achilles told them that if he wasn't an ambassador already, he didn't want to be one.

For a long time, Aisling didn't talk about this with Adam, because she had ignored all his warnings, and anyway, she was very busy at work. Eventually, though, she could resist no longer.

She sat on her roof terrace in the chilly late-July night, sipping gin and feeling guilty about running an outdoor heater. After a perfectly nice evening when they hadn't talked about football, she finally raised the subject and suddenly Adam was stressed and distressed, and he wouldn't sit down. He waved his glass around and said that things at the club were terrible. Adam was such a neophyte that this was the first disappointing season he'd had to endure. He didn't realise that the panic and soul-searching were normal, and then something would come right and you started winning again. 'I'm not worried about the results,' she said. 'It's the wages. How did you let that happen?'

'Are you serious?'

'It's your job, Adam.'

'I've been trying to tell you I can't do it by myself. I need you at KSC meetings.'

'What are they going to do next?'

'Whatever they want. They're making the Socialists just like everyone else. I told you this would happen.'

'No, you didn't. You said it was a sensible business decision.'

'Don't try that! I advised you very clearly not to do it.'

'Fuck off, Adam. This isn't my fault.' They had never been explicitly angry with each other before, and Aisling hated it. Adam had advised against the sale but he hadn't told her that things would turn out like this. 'I can't believe Esther isn't on your side. She's obsessed with "the soul of the club". Is it Will?' Adam nodded. 'He's a fucker. I'm sorry I landed you in this,' she said.

'I chose it, Aisling, and this isn't about you and me. It's about trying to save Kilburn.'

What had she hoped to achieve by getting Adam here tonight? There was nothing she could do and, anyway, she'd got her own life to lead. 'I don't have time for this,' she said, looking at her glass. Then, more defiantly, she added that it was difficult enough attending Rosslare Group meetings let alone KSC ones.

'You're the one who brought Kilburn up,' said Adam.

Aisling thought again about how much time and work it would take to deal with KSC's issues, and she decided that her worry wasn't about Kilburn after all. Her actual problem was that she was a good friend to Adam, and she was upset to see him being hurt. She said, 'If you love Kilburn, you must hate what's happening?'

'Yes.'

'So you should get out.'

'What?'

'If there's nothing you can do, you should get out. You should leave KSC.'

'No. I don't want to get out.'

'In which case you should be grateful to me for getting you the job,' said Aisling. 'You being there is unfair on me. It makes it harder for me to draw a line.' She was embarrassed by what she was saying but she didn't let on. Adam was furious.

At the European Championships in Russia, GB got knocked out in the semi-finals, and Italy won. It was all very anticlimactic.

The manager was pleased with the off-season, but there was one final task. He had to seal his authority by showing his arrogant team that no one was indispensable. He sold Mickey Faller and Pat Credence, but everyone knew their time had come. He would like to have made an example of Achilles, who was the main troublemaker, but Achilles was indispensable.

In the warm-up games, it seemed that Dave Guinevere was back to his best, controlling the tempo of Kilburn's play. But he'd been crap last year, and it was possible he could no longer handle the rigours of a full season. Moreover, he was still the GB captain, which made him a perfect subject for a demonstration, *pour encourager les autres*. On 5 August, the manager unceremoniously announced to his team that Dave Guinevere had been sold to Manchester & Stockport.

WHERE HAVE ALL
THE FLOWERS GONE?

There are five minutes to go in the first game of the new season, and the score is 0–0. The Socialists are playing Manchester & Stockport, who were led on to the pitch by their summer signing, Dave Guinevere. Could anything be more predictable?

Both Kilburn strikers, having edged as far up the pitch as the M & S defenders will let them, suddenly turn on their heels and run towards the ball, drawing their markers with them. The defenders have committed their momentum forward, and would be powerless to cope with anyone bursting through, but they see no one in front of them except the forwards they are following. Dave, until now, has strangled Achilles in midfield, overpowering him not with the control and skill he displayed in Italy two years before, but with simple power. Wherever Achilles has turned, he's found Dave's legs, arms, body, whatever. Now, with his vanquished opponent having drifted out of the game, Dave allows himself to cover for his beleaguered inside left and shepherds Jermaine Cole into a nothing position on the right. He hears Achilles' distant call, and he instantly knows what he has done. Without pausing to confirm, Dave spins and sprints back as Cole curls a perfect ball behind the defenders for Achilles to run on to, completely free, forty yards out from goal and ten yards inside the left touchline. The M & S keeper, thinking it's his only chance, hurtles out of his area in a forlorn attempt to intercept. Achilles skips nonchalantly past him, and runs the ball infield to make the angle certain, his golden boots dancing in the rose petals.

In the private enclosure, 26, who loves being called 26 more and more with the passing of the years, is glowing. The loopy Gardener guy said that all the paper confetti the fans were throwing was a problem for his poor, poor grass. 26 totally ignored him, because he was just being homophobic, but Adam – and you'd have thought *Adam* would understand, of all people – said the tradition had to stop. She turned the negative into a positive, though, and organised the distribution of petals instead. When Achilles and Zondi ran on to the pitch, the home stand erupted in fluttering colour, which was beautiful and meaningful at the same time. It's a real pity Dave isn't still at the club, because it would be amazing to have pictures of him and his model girlfriend in the programme, with the sick kids, though 26 just spoke to the model on the stairs and she was really stuck up, actually. 26 is sitting behind stupid Esther. She isn't jealous of the Chancellor and she understands that it's a sensitive situation, but she wishes Will would deal with Esther so everyone could know the truth.

Esther is confident about the coming season. Dave has played well today, admittedly, but you always expect a player to raise his game against his former club. Esther is also buoyant because Will, finally, has said that he can't wait for her any longer. The pair will become a public couple in two months' time, just as soon as a year has passed since she split up with Tom. Esther agrees with Will that anything sooner would be cruel to her still-mooning ex. It is part of her growing self-confidence that she can accept that Tom is still mooning. Esther loves the thing with the petals. She congratulates 26, who has been super nice to her recently.

Aisling and Nicky have been discussing Punty, Dave's model, who is sitting twenty feet away with the puffed-up opposition chairman. She breezed up the stairs ten minutes before the game and immediately started chatting with 24 and 26, seemingly unaware of all the stares. Presumably she's used to them. Aisling knows Punty's older sister, Chaz, or has met her at parties anyway, because Chaz went out with one of the registrars at Aisling's hospital. There's another sister, too, but Aisling can't remember her name. She knows people who remember Punty from Godolphin, where she played hockey and the cello, and who say she's lovely. Aisling looks across at Punty again, who had planned to go to Exeter Uni, apparently, until she was 'discovered' during her A-levels by a friend of her mother. Nicky asks Aisling if Dave could be any more of a cliché. When Aisling looks at Punty, and sees a younger model, it's not the same thing everyone else sees.

Punty is terrified. She knows what Dave thinks of her, and everyone else. She can see that he laughs at other people's jokes, but never at hers. It's not her fault that she loves him absolutely, passionately, without reason or reservation, truly and for ever.

Zondi is on the bench, desperate to play wherever he's needed. He can fill in anywhere apart from centre half or up front. He is frightened also, and his eyes are locked on the Tall Hunter, who has struggled with his rage all night. When the red mist descends on the Hunter, he can achieve great things because he will not accept that the world won't bend to his will.

Dave knew he would have to leave KSC eventually, like all the others he's watched leave over the years, but what happened to him was different. He should still be a Socialist. He was only sold to make a point, and it was his own fucking fault. He was the turkey who voted for Christmas. He'd fucking show them.

It makes no logical sense to do this by smothering Achilles, since Achilles is the one who argued for nothing to change, but this is not to do with logic. When Dave walked out of the home changing rooms at KSC for the last time, blank with shock, and collected his pathetic boots from the bootroom, which always and still smelled so strongly of mud, Achilles raced after him. Achilles obviously wanted to commiserate, but Dave said, 'Don't fucking gloat. I know it's my fault.'

'You know I wasn't —'

'Fuck off, Achilles.'

Dave is making Achilles pay for his pity. He's chosen, for now, to see Achilles as his preening nemesis, as the embodiment of KSC, who need to be taught a lesson. The club he loves and has given his life to is killing itself. Dave was the first player to be sold after the Socialists ended the pension contracts. The pension, like the wages, was a civilised symbol of gratitude. It's okay for Dave, but what if KSC signs some youngster and he shatters his knee five minutes into his first training session? Will he be looked after? The Socialists have changed, and Dave owes them nothing, and he will not be beaten today. All through the match he's smothered Achilles, and how could he, of all people, fall for that weary hobble towards the safety of the touchline? Achilles still has to come infield. Dave doesn't care how he stops the Argentinian: he'll hack him down and give away a penalty if he has to; he'll stop the ball with his fucking hands. A penalty is probably a goal, but probably a goal is very different from a goal.

In training, sometimes, when Achilles finds himself alone in front of goal after a particularly outrageous piece of skill, he will take the piss out of his teammates by stopping the ball on the goal line, sinking to his knees and gently heading the ball along the ground into the net. He's never done this in public, of course, but today, after patiently waiting more than eighty minutes for Dave to drop his guard, and having won the battle, something in him cracks and needs to crow. He glides to a halt and kneels into a shallow sea of pink. Dave's long legs tear the petals into little clouds, chasing down his prey beyond all hope of success. Achilles is a natural winner with a telepathic awareness of the pitch around him. He would never do what he is doing if there were any chance of being stopped.

A dozen photographs, each worse than the last, freeze the moment: the ball rolling gently into the net; Achilles' head on the way to its impossible final angle; Dave's boot against his cheek; Dave's vacant eyes.

PART THREE – GONE FISHING

Punty hacked open a coconut. She sipped the warm milk, passed Dave the rest and gutted the jodari. She stuffed it with garlic, spices and couscous, wrapped it in foil, nestled it into the ashy embers and strode down to the sea to cool down. She swam out to the raft, pulled herself up and lay on her back. When they'd arrived, she'd needed Dave's help to clamber out of the water, but Punty was whip-strong now. Her hair was like straw, and the sun and salt did awful things to her skin, but she didn't care. Drying out in the hot sun was one of her favourite things in the world, more luxurious in the dying day than in its baking heat. Working here, doing something of value for the first time in her life, was the most unbelievable experience. She knew it was temporary, but that's not how either of them behaved, because what's the point of wasting paradise?

She rolled on to her side, feeling Dave's eyes on her back, and watched the sun emerge from its own glare. She loved it when it was too bright to be seen, and even more when she could actually see it. Logically, it must be further away, but it felt closer. The first evening breeze grazed the top of her arm and she rolled again, pressing her belly into the platform, keeping as low as she could, seeing if she could steal another five minutes from the zephyrs. Her cheek was warm against the wood's smooth grain, and her eyes stayed fixed on the sun, willing it not to sink.

Eventually, she stood and stretched languorously, imagining how she must look silhouetted against the burning amber. She did her best, brave dive – the sea would wipe away the stupid tears – and she stroked strongly back to the beach, emerging with a perfect smile. Dave was asleep, fists knotted.

HOW DAVE FOUND PARADISE

Sheriff Road
15 October 2002

Dearest Dave,

I know you said you didn't want to be bothered, but I had to write. You can throw this away if you want. Maybe you already have!

Jed was very happy to help you. I think he was nervous (we all were!), but he says you have settled into the school very well, and the other teachers like you (and Punty!) very much. Of course they do. Jed says that the school is on the most beautiful part of the coast, and the people are amazing. He says that if there is anywhere that can refresh your soul, then it's there. I hope so.

We are here to help you if there is anything you need. Your friends are all worried about you because at the funeral and after-wards you seemed so closed off. You said you couldn't talk about what happened, but you have to! I hope you are talking to Punty – she could be good for you, if you let her. What happened was not your fault. I understand why you have gone away, everyone does. Me and Aisling and Punty's family have told everyone the two of you have gone to stay in Ireland, but we can't pretend for ever. Eventually, you will have to come back to England, and you can't just bottle it all up until then. (I have seen more of Aisling. She's nicer than I thought. I'm glad I didn't know that before!)

If you ever do want to make contact with anyone here, Aisling says she will pretend to take letters to Ireland but she will actually give them to me and I can send them to you via Jed's friend at the embassy. It's like being a spy! I think you should write, but I know you are stubborn.

So, I won't say any more for now (not that I wouldn't!) unless you reply. I know you are happy for me and Jed. You were right about how you and I always wanted different things, I see that now,

and I am happy for you and Punty. She loves you. You know that,
don't you? Don't hurt her, Dave. Don't push her away.

Achilles was a wonderful friend, but what happened to him was
a terrible, terrible, terrible accident, and everybody knows it. You
mustn't let it destroy your life because you know he wouldn't have
wanted that. You know that would only be making things worse.

I really hope you are all right.
All my love,
Sally

*

After Achilles' death, Dave couldn't speak to anyone, but he assumed
that would change at the funeral. He thought he would face the awful
moments with Zondi, and with Achilles' parents, and then he would
endure a dread mix of unspoken blame and understanding from the
Socialists. When he arrived, the first people he saw were Esther and
Will Beauchamp, who should have been the easiest to bear. He nodded
to them.

'You knew exactly what you were doing,' said Will. 'You knew you'd
never get the ball.'

'You don't look as if you feel anything!' said Esther, her face streaked
with tears. 'You killed him and you don't even look sorry.'

Dave looked at the people in the room, in couples, with friends,
united in their grief and secure in what they would do tomorrow, and
he felt like a leaf torn from its tree, whipped in the wind, its useful life
over. He disconnected from the room. The only person who broke
through was Sally, and she had to say hello twice. She knew he didn't
want to talk about it yet, but she said she was there for him when he
did, and she asked after Punty. He said he asked Punty to stay away
from him because he needed to be alone. 'That's exactly what you don't
need,' said Sally. Behind Sally was Jed. The American ran a network of
hospitals and mobile clinics that operated throughout Africa. Hollow-
faced, Dave nodded to him and Sally, and moved towards the garden.
Sally followed Dave, and Jed followed her. 'You can't not speak,' Sally
said. Dave didn't reply. It was not that he refused, it was that he couldn't
think what to say. Sally said, 'What do you want to do now? You've got
to talk this through. Are you going to carry on playing?' Dave shook

his head. 'What then, Dave? I'm not trying to be difficult. Someone has to help you.'

'I want to be somewhere no one knows who I am, but that's impossible, so thank you, but you can't help me.' He knew what he was asking, and how gracelessly.

Sally turned to Jed, whose gears were already turning. 'We only need doctors and nurses,' he said, 'but I know people in other organisations. I'm sure I could find you something, if that's what you really want, and you can commit to it. I can ask, if you trust my discretion?'

'I . . .' Dave started. He was blank for a moment, then he nodded. 'Yes please, I think,' he said. 'If you can, that would be . . . Thank you. I hadn't meant to put you under any pressure,' he said equally to Jed and Sally.

'I know,' they replied in unison.

Dave apologised again, as if that was the end of the conversation, but he couldn't turn back into the room, towards the people he knew.

Jed found Dave a job teaching on the Tanganyikan coast at a Catholic school whose principal was married to one of Jed's doctors. Dave would be expected to teach science as well as history and geography. On Sally's firm instructions, volunteer work was found for Punty in the hospital. Dave was presented with both placements as a fait accompli. He could have tried to dissuade Punty – she had a career to think of – but he didn't. Sally knew Dave needed Punty, even if he was too proud to ask.

And so, by the light of the African sun, with their feet stained red by the hot earth, Dave and Punty taught and worked. Then, in the long evenings, in air washed quiet of any distraction by the sounds of sea and forest, they learned Swahili, played cards, read and slept. They weren't hermits, but they didn't hunger for human contact. They spent some evenings with the doctor and her husband, a Midwestern couple who hadn't the faintest idea who Dave was. Maybe some football-mad local would have recognised him if his hair was still red.

In his sleep, every night, Dave would kick, jerk and moan, 'I'm sorry, I'm sorry. Fuck you too, *querido*.' Punty didn't tell him.

*

247

Nzasa
22 Oct

Dear Sal,

Of course I'll reply. I can't thank you and Jed enough for helping me.

The most important thing is you mustn't worry that I think it was my fault. I mean, of course it was my fault, but you mustn't worry that I think it was anything other than an accident. But it was such a terrible accident that I needed to get away. Tanganyika is extraordinary, and Nzasa is a paradise, somewhere completely outside the real world. Jed's Midwesterners are lovely (they had never seen the sea AT ALL before coming here two years ago) and the kids are brilliant. Time is the great healer. It was the space I needed, and even in six weeks I feel completely different. I needed to get the clean air in my lungs, and sit watching the sky. Cured is not the exact word, but that's how I feel.

I know it was you who made sure Punty came. Thank you for that as well. She is quite full-on after you and me, and our old-married-couple style of having a relationship, but she's good, funny, and she's game for anything that gets thrown at her. After all the image-obsessed crap of her life in London, she's loving the chance to engage with reality. Also, and this is cool, when she says, 'Jump!', people jump Sugarlump jump. Command is bred in the bone, I suppose. The children all love her, obviously. And the fishermen. And the other teachers. And Jed's mate from the Embassy. And everyone else. We get up with the sun, have tea before it gets too hot, work like maniacs and then eat fish that got hauled out of the sea ten minutes earlier. Punty's desperate to make sushi, but she hasn't a clue how. If you could send a sushi cookbook, that would be great. Maybe you'd have to send wasabi, too.

Punty wanted a computer and a phone, but I vetoed them. I'll deal with the letters (I can't believe how many people are writing to me – most are nice but there are some deranged people in the world), but that's more than enough for me. I know that pretending we're in Ireland must be a hassle, but please don't tell anyone where I am for now. I'll get round to it in time, but everything here is too perfect to ruin with that just yet. If there's ever been a time to be grateful for not having family to worry about me, then this is it. If

you need us instantly, you can always go via the school or the clinic.
The good doctor internets all the time.

Don't worry about me. I have come to terms with what happened.
This is a wonderful place, and I'm completely fine. You should visit.

Thank you again, and love,

Dave

COMPARE AND CONTRAST

Keats Grove
29/10/02

Dear Dave,

Sally said you wouldn't mind getting this. I don't know why I'm writing it though, unless it's because you're so far away it doesn't seem real. I've found sometimes in the past that distance removes inhibitions. Does that sound sane? I don't know. It's not that I have anything useful to say!

I'm so sorry about what happened. I was going to say something about knowing how you feel, but of course I don't.

KSC's doing okay, all things considered. Esther, who wept all over every newspaper, by the way, persuaded Strabis to hand over a shit-load of cash – emergency money, and it's hard to say this wasn't an emergency, however ghoulish it sounds – to buy Marten Vlocker from Cardiff, so Strabis is now the fans' hero and everyone's saying how lucky it is he's here to bail us out. Cardiff didn't want to sell Vlocker, but they've been playing like crap (not much I don't know about football these days) and he made it clear he wanted to go, and it was either now for a ton of money or at the end of the season for peanuts (whoop-de-doo for the Beckford ruling), so we got him. It didn't do us any harm that Vlocker goes out on the piss with Cole and Drayly.

It's interesting seeing all this from the outside. I have so much more perspective than I had even three months ago. The Kilburn chapter of my life is almost closed – it's only Adam still being there that ties me in. I worry about Adam. I tried to get him to leave again last month, but he's emotionally sucked into the club now and can't see reason. We argued about it, actually, which was horrible, but it was nothing compared to what happened about ten days ago, after Vlocker's first game for us, which was a 0–0 draw: Vlocker went to Flower & Scythe with Cole and Drayly, and got in a fight with some actor. The actor, who's a screaming queen and was showing off (I got all this from the guy who runs F & S, who's a friend of a friend from Oxford), told Vlocker that he wasn't fit to lace Achilles' boots. Vlocker asked who the fuck the actor thought he was? The actor said he was a fan, and people like him paid Vlocker's wages. The actor was playing to his gallery, and he demanded an explanation for Saturday's tedium, or something equally precious. Drayly couldn't resist, and he called the actor an ignorant fucking poof. There was a debate about homosexuality during which Cole, Drayly and Vlocker departed from, in PC terms, the racing line. Things got confused and Drayly ended up thumping the actor and giving him a shiner. Thank fuck he didn't break his nose, thank fuck the actor wasn't filming, thank fuck I know the manager of F & S, and thank fuck the fucker Horton offered the actor a puff piece as a bribe, so we've been able to more or less hush it up.

So, I did my bit to help out, but that's the end for me, and I thought that surely even Adam would understand now, but when I brought it up, he was furious and said I should be helping him, not running away. I said he was doing no good, so why was he torturing himself? He said that of course he was doing good, and the only way to help KSC was to turn up. He gave a 'for instance': Esther and slimy Will Beauchamp want us to play the rest of the season in a black strip, which obviously Achilles would have hated. Adam said he could stop this happening, especially if I added my voice on the Board. We had a proper shouting argument. He said I was betraying my heritage, and I called him a sell-out for sticking to KSC after the bar fight, and he told me to stop telling him how to live his life. In the end, he stormed off saying that he was going to start making rational business decisions for the good of KSC, and the first one would be approving the black shirts, which would make a fortune. The club made the announcement two mornings later, and also announced that the KSC/Clarion Foundation would henceforth be called the Achilles Foundation, and Achilles is being deified as its spiritual father, along with Will B and the fucker Horton. They did a grotesque TV press conference using Achilles' picture, and Zondi's, and they didn't even ask Zondi's permission, which beggars belief. It's money for a good cause, but Achilles hated going public about the charity. I hate it, in the way the end of a relationship is always *loose threads – you worry and worry at them until everything unravels. I'm angry with Adam, but I also feel sorry for him. He's being pathetic, and he'll regret it.*

What matters, and this is really why I am writing, is that Zondi seems to be okay. Sort of. He's always been quiet, and I don't know him brilliantly, so it's not that easy to tell, but I'm sure that it's the quiet of deep distress, rather than the quiet of someone cracking up. I'm almost certain. I go to see him, and we spend an hour or two watching television or a video. He's an amazing cook, did you know? Of course you did. But I think he's okay, and he said he hoped you were okay. I told him I was writing to you, and that he could write too if he wanted, and I think he might. He asked if there was anything I could do about the Foundation to take Achilles' name off it, and I felt so helpless. I don't have any control over what the club does, not that I ever did, really, and I'm sure it's a good thing, because we shouldn't live in an aristocracy, blah, blah, blah, but I wish I could have done something for Zondi. He completely understood that I couldn't. I don't know how someone who says so little can make you feel so comfortable. You just get the feeling he believes you are trying to do the best you can. Or that's the sense I get, anyway, but maybe it's wishful thinking. I could certainly do with someone thinking that about me, given how I feel about everything, especially about Adam being stuck in the middle of this mess.

I'm being overdramatic. Like I say, I do feel better now I've cut the cord. I've applied to be a chest registrar at the Brompton, which I probably won't get and don't necessarily even really want, but Nicky (I'm sure you've met her – she's the super-bossy one with curly dark hair) has been nagging like mad. I thought she'd be pleased when I told her, but she instantly said, 'Oh, the Brompton. Really!' or words to that effect. What she means is that I saw this guy for a few months (surgeon, forty-five, does triathlons, funny, relaxed, recently separated) and he's also just moved to the Brompton. This relationship was hardly a relationship when it was one, and it's over now, but Nicky obviously doesn't believe this. I tried to pacify her by saying I was thinking seriously about an old friend from college that she's been trying to set me up with (Jeremy, thirty-two, barrister, earnest), and she even got tetchy about that. She said that if Jeremy and I are still unsure (after six months of sporadic dates), we should both be

253

moving on. And then, and I'm not kidding, she said, 'The longer it takes you, the older you'll be when you have children.' Nicky's problem is that she's never been single as an adult.

This letter is turning into a bloody novel! All I wanted to do was say that Zondi is okay, and to prepare you for the fact he might send you a letter. I don't know if you want to be prepared for something like that, but I would, so that's why I've said it.

Sally says you're finding some peace, and I hope that's true, and that this letter doesn't disturb it. You don't have to reply, I won't be offended.

Love,

Aisling

*

Esther thought Will was wonderful in the wake of Achilles' death, so supportive and kind, and taking charge of everything. He was the perfect mouthpiece for the club, eloquent and moving even though he couldn't get through an interview without noticeably holding back tears. It was especially important because Zondi refused to speak to the press. Will loyally said this was Zondi's right. It was also Will who said that the club had to make an obvious tribute to Achilles' memory, and suggested the black kit. It was an amazing and sensitive idea. Adam tried to stop it at first, saying that it was not what Achilles or Zondi would want. Will asked Adam how he knew. Adam said that Aisling had been speaking to Zondi, and that Zondi wanted everything to be as private as possible. It was typical of Aisling and Adam to secretly try to take control of everything – Adam was probably just jealous that the black shirts weren't his idea. Will stayed totally calm. He said that if Zondi had objections, then they must be respected, up to a point, but didn't the club have a right to mourn? And also, maybe this might salvage something positive from the horrific event. Will was sure the black shirts would be popular with the fans, and the money from selling them would go to the Foundation, which he suggested brilliantly could be renamed in Achilles' honour.

Will was wonderful, but their relationship seemed to be cursed. The tragedy was yet another thing that got in the way of them getting together publicly. Will said that it would be inappropriate for them to do anything immediately, and maybe, if Achilles' memory was to be properly respected, they might even have to wait until the end of the season. 'Do you agree?' he asked. 'I hate waiting, but I'm worried about how it would look. It might look as if we were being unfeeling towards Zondi, but if you think the thing between us is more important than showing him respect, then I will forget Achilles in a heartbeat.'

'Of course we must wait,' she said.

Esther was afraid that Adam and Aisling would block Will's plans out of jealousy, but then Adam and Aisling had a fight, and afterwards Adam completely changed his tune. At the next meeting, he said, 'Okay, I've done the maths. We'll shift, conservatively, fifty thousand black shirts. That's a clear profit of eight hundred grand and that money'll go to the Foundation, right?'

'It's not that we don't feel Zondi's loss,' said Esther.

'I understand. I'm a businessman, not a priest.' Adam even accepted the other idea – which one of the Stationery Office girls had come up with and which Will passed on to Esther – that for the rest of the season all the players should wear Achilles' name on their backs, rather than their own, which would be a beautiful gesture. Adam looked funny about that for a moment, but he accepted it.

Calum masterminded the shirt announcements and the Foundation's name change. The TV advert, which would raise the Foundation's profile as well as sell shirts, was amazing. Against a black background, starkly lit, Will's face looked straight into the viewer's eyes. Underneath was written, 'Will Beauchamp. English of Huguenot descent. Straight. Protestant.' Then: 'Seung Park. Korean. Straight. Buddhist; Dirk Volendam. Three-quarters Dutch, one-quarter Surinamese. Straight. Atheist; Terrible Zondeki. *Xam*. Gay. Animist; Louie Cohen. African American. Straight. Muslim.' Then there was Achilles' face over the words 'Achille de la Rue de la Pierre au Diable. Argentinian. Gay. Roman Catholic.' The picture faded into one of all the Socialists, arms linked across each other's shoulders. In unison they said, 'Kilburn, United.' One final fade to the new Achilles Foundation logo, above the slogan 'For All Our Futures'.

It was too much to expect that the Socialists would be unaffected on the pitch. Even the most diehard fan accepted that this was completely different to Mr Brown's death, when KSC had a settled team. The Socialists had to rebuild. Marten Vlocker replaced Achilles like for like at the point of the central diamond. KSC played with almost frantic freedom, losing 3–5 and 3–4.

The manager told Esther that he found it hard to watch. The players were doing whatever they wanted, with no sense of where each other would be. Esther nodded.

Flair could come later. The manager imposed a rigid 4-4-2, not with the KSC's usual diamond but with a flat four across the midfield. This meant Vlocker had to restrain himself, and play close to Will Beauchamp. Vlocker didn't like it, but when he was dropped for running out of position once too often, he got the message. A team must play as a team. The next two results were a 1–0 victory and the 0–0 draw that led to the bar fight in Flower & Scythe. Will told Esther that playing like this was okay while the Socialists were regathering themselves, but the manager needed to realise that, in the long term, he couldn't treat Vlocker like this, or give Cole so little chance to express himself. Esther agreed, completely. Will explained that the Flower & Scythe fracas only happened because the players were frustrated. He explained it to Adam too, when Adam wasn't happy about covering up the fight. 'Look,' he said. 'I understand you don't like this, but this wasn't gay-bashing. Those boys joined KSC, remember, the gay club. Cole and Drayly played with Achilles and Zondi, and it was never a problem.'

'The greater good, mate,' agreed Calum. 'Just think about the greater good. Anything that hurts the Foundation is bad for the people the Foundation can help. It's that simple.'

This all made obvious sense to Esther, but she worried that Adam would not understand because he was gay. She needn't have. Will could persuade anyone. Will said it might be a good idea to move Craig Drayly from figureheading a kids' literacy programme to fronting one of the AIDS groups. Adam only looked strained for a moment before he agreed. There were problems when Drayly made some inappropriate jokes at a dinner, but he was a boisterous young man who didn't know any better, and they were only jokes. It was incredible he could make them when he knew he should be on his best behaviour, but Esther increasingly understood that you couldn't expect twenty-year-old lads to be angels.

Will's other idea was that forcing players to do 'personal development', was not only treating them like children, it was actually selfish, in a way. If players wanted to learn something, they could always do it in their own time, with their own money. If the club was going to mandate that they spend time productively, that could be more time spent on extra work for the Foundation. After all, Marten Vlocker was never going to be a concert pianist or an astronaut, but he could help kids achieve such goals.

'I understand, Will,' said Esther, 'but it's a tradition, and —'

'This is your chance, Est. While everything's changing. You can work out what traditions are good ones, and why they are there, and put new ones in place if you have to. The Socialists are there to help society, and society's always changing. This is how you get to keep the Rosslare legacy going. I'm so proud of you,' he said, and held her hand.

*

Nzasa
8 Nov

Dear Aisling,

First, thank you for writing. I could have coped with an unannounced letter from Z – I'm pretty strong – but I appreciate the thought. Also thank you for the ongoing Great Irish Deception. The cloak and dagger feels ridiculous sometimes, but all those letters that have been forwarded! Most are nice, but I'm glad the nutters don't know where I am.

I understand what you say about distance and inhibitions. Things seem less real. Certainly, for something that was a huge part of my life for so long, KSC seems another planet, and I don't think about it at all. It's part of my past now.

Nzasa is paradise. I'm sitting on our veranda and it's starting to get dark, which means I have twenty minutes before I have to go inside the insect doors and turn on a light (the Tanga mossies could carry away a small child). I should be learning about the liver and kidneys – I'm teaching science, hilariously enough – but it'll only take an hour and I've got all evening, or at least until Punty gets randy.

I know what it is you hate about what's happening to KSC. I've had a lot of time to work this out, both over the years and now. It's to do with the private and the public spheres, and how we're all supposed to jump around like performing monkeys making the faces people expect (when a monkey looks as if it's smiling, it's baring its teeth in anger – you know this?). KSC isn't the club I joined any more. Mr Brown would never have bought Cole and Drayly, who are self-obsessed wankers, and he'd never have bought Vlocker, who's an arsehole. I'm not surprised they got into that bar fight. I hate what football is becoming, and KSC can't escape it any more. The best way of explaining, and I know this sounds bad but you have to let me finish, is that Mr Brown wouldn't have sold me when I was sold. I'm not going to go on about it, but it's important if I am going to explain. Mr Brown sold players as soon as they weren't worth their place in the squad. For this reason, KSC didn't make as much money selling them as they would have done if he'd sold them a year earlier. It was a combination of hardness and loyalty. When I was sold, at least a year before I'd have lost my place, maybe two years, that was disloyal. I'm not saying that that's what was behind how I played against Kilburn, or that anyone is to blame except me, but I was angry and I'll leave it at that. KSC decisions used to be based on internal considerations only.

The old KSC was like a monastery; the new KSC-plus-Foundation is a mission (or it's pretending to be a mission, anyway). The monastery was aware of the world, but it was inward-looking and private. The charity and the self-development were all about making us be as good as we could be. Mr Brown and your dad created a little model society, but Mr Brown's ambitions were limited. He remembered we were a football team, and he didn't send us out to change the world. I know this can be seen as selfish – Calum Horton is a fucker, but he isn't an idiot – but everyone can <u>always</u> do more, and there has to be limit, because you have to live your life as well, or what's the point? That team was amazing to be part of, and nothing will ever be like that again.

All this sounds sanctimonious, but it's me trying to understand what's happened since Mr Brown died – it's not how we thought at the time. We just did what we did, and I think, as a result, we became better people. I don't know any better people than the Socialists I played with under Mr Brown. We could do it because we were protected from the world. I think that the example we set was a good one, and did good, and by sending out good people it had a good effect, but I would think that, wouldn't I?

Anyway, Mr Brown's KSC was great, but, like all things, it was stuck in its time. You aren't allowed to be a monastery any more – people have a 'right to know', and light burns off the magic, but people don't mind because they think the light's an absolute good. So the Socialists will never be what they were, and it's pointless to go on about it (ironic, given the length of this letter). Missionaries were often troubled people who didn't live up to their own ideals, and they did harm sometimes, but some of them did good too. That's what we have to hope KSC does, but it's not the club I grew up with any more, so it's time for me to let it go. Also, football's not the game it was, if it ever was. It's getting horrible now, and it makes people ugly. Maybe it always was, and I was in denial because I was good at it, and actually I wasted my life making something rotten worse. Everything football touches is sullied. You are right to wash your hands of it, and you have to try and get Adam out too. You must patch up your fight, because there's nothing as important as friends, and a few mistakes don't make someone a bad person.

I don't remember Nicky, but she sounds funny in a hard-to-deal-with kind of a way. I'm hardly the best person to be giving romantic advice, but I can see Nicky's point if it's really true that you've been dating this guy Jeremy for six months and nothing's happened. Unless it's because of that surgeon? Beautiful young surgeon with older married surgeon sounds almost too much of a cliché to bear, but then I'm a footballer living with a model. Just because it's a cliché doesn't mean it's wrong. But if you say it's nothing, then maybe the combination of him and Jeremy is stopping you looking for someone better? Ignore advice at any price, that's what I call good advice.

Time to go inside to escape the mossies. Right. That's done.

I'm going to wind up. The KSC I grew up with is gone, and I can't do anything about it, but at least I can do something about myself. Do you know your sister got angry with me at the funeral for not crying? ~~As if I~~ I know you didn't need to see me cry to know what I was feeling. I know Z didn't. ~~The idea that~~ It's crazy that I had to leave ~~because I couldn't bear to spend that time somewhere where no one believe something existed unless it was displayed~~. Here I can deal with it in my own way. Also, the school is refreshingly old-fashioned. The kids are super well behaved, and they learn maths and grammar till sums and subclauses are coming out of their little ears. The difference between them and scrotes like Craig Drayly is unbelievable.

I know Z will understand all this without my having had to say it, and I hope he writes. I still haven't spoken to him, did you know? I wrote to him immediately, just a few words saying that I didn't have the words to express what I felt, and that all I could do was trust him to understand. I thought I'd speak to him at the funeral, but I couldn't. I only just managed to stay in the room. Z will be okay. Remember what he's been through. He's a lot stronger than he looks.

This has been an interminable letter. You are presumably eating your hands with the dullness of it. Thanks for writing, though. I really appreciate it.

Love,
Dave

LOST

Dear David,

Thank you for what you said in your note. I am sorry I did not reply sooner, but I was lost and the world has been noise.

People are very kind. Aisling visits, which I like although I have nothing to say to her, and she must be bored. She comes because she is tied to KSC tightest of all of us. People forget about blood.

I had to stop writing this for two days after the last line because I was not ready. I do not know what to do. I wish I could stay lost, because I would not have to face the outside then, but Achilles would have been angry, and so I must find the road back. I cannot imagine what shape the road will take.

With you and Achilles gone, after everything else, the club is like a bus with no driver, running down the hill full of people who do not know how to get off. Some are happy because down the hill is easy, but it is a road to a cliff. The Serpent is near the front, hissing at anyone who wants to take the driver's seat, but his eye is always on the open window next to him. He has hypnotised the manager, who thinks he is driving, but he is like a child many seats from the front playing with a plastic wheel and stamping on air. Adam and Esther are hypnotised too. I wish I could speak like Achilles, because then maybe I could make them see, but I cannot. I am off the bus, but I do not want it to crash. It breaks my heart. Aisling thinks she is off the bus, but she is only in the doorway. Maybe I am only in the doorway too, or being stupid like usual.

Esther came to see me also, but only once, because it was expected. She was too scared to come alone, so she brought the Serpent, and she wanted to touch me while he kept speaking, speaking. He asked me to forgive you, and I said I had. He said I must say this to the reporter Calum Horton, to speed the healing, but I told him I would

not. I said that you know in your head that there is nothing for me
to forgive, and all that must happen now is for your heart to follow,
and nothing I can say will make that faster. Esther did not under-
stand. She is not like Aisling. Maybe I am a fool about the blood.

Aisling says you wrote a letter that sounded hysterical. I should
not say she used this word because it will make you angry, but I do
not know another way to say it, and I think you must let me speak
because of who I am, so I say this: it will pass and the world will
be less bright and sharp. It is the same for me, but different also.

I have bought a dog. She is a girl dog, but I have called her Mr
Brown, because she is clever and fat.

I miss the stars you are seeing,
Zondeki

*

At four o'clock every day, most of the kids walked home or played on
the beach. But several, more than a few, were met by black BMWs, or
white Mercedes, or huge 4 x 4s. These children were driven up the hill
to satellite televisions and swimming pools, French chefs and Japanese
air conditioning. The school, St John's, abutted the hospital, which was
a gleaming white complex carved out of the emerald forest. The complex
was almost exactly halfway between the village and the houses up the
hill. Dave and Punty could have joined the Americans in the residen-
tial compound, but they both preferred to live by the sea.

Nzasa was once one of many similarly sized villages in the area, but
it was not like them. It stood on the main coast road, and also on one
of Tanganyika's three trunk roads to the interior. The coast road detoured
to it when a straight line could have taken it directly past several other
villages. This was because President Nagape was born in Nzasa. He sent
his immediate family to schools abroad, but a number of his favoured
cousins, close followers and staff had homes in the village, and their
children went to St John's. The hospital and school served a wider
community, but they were sited here because of the dignitaries. The
quasi-Western conditions helped attract volunteers, and the connection to the regime smoothed out paperwork and permits. Jed's organisation believed that the time spent serving Nagape's people was an
acceptable cost of doing business.

It was five o'clock and Dave was at home. He sat on his chair, pretending to read, watching the kids from behind his shades. Two months into his time in Tanganyika, he was now well reconciled to the fact that he wasn't in paradise. When he arrived, he was still raw and his first impressions were overexcited, even though he should have known better. That's probably why Aisling thought he was hysterical. A football, made of paper, coconut leaves and tape, hit his shin. Half these kids were in his class, and Dave was interested to see how they behaved away from the school. One of the boys approached him apologetically.

All is vanity. Dave flicked the ball up with his toe, and started to juggle, just with his right foot at first, but gradually getting more elaborate, foot-to-foot, foot-to-head-to-foot, a-bit-higher-while-crossing-legs-then-back-to-upturned-right-instep and then, finally, instep-to-suddenly-extended-left-foot, where he caught it nonchalantly between the crook of his foot and his ankle, and proffered it to the entranced boy. The next day more children came to the beach, and the day after some of the kids from the Nagape entourage came as well, bringing a proper ball. Dave didn't want to let them down, so he demonstrated a little, and helped the ones who wanted to learn tricks. They got bored quickly, though, because further down the beach was a real game to be part of. The game was chaos, and Dave began to referee. A few days later, fifty kids were turning up, boys and girls, and the game became impossible, just a pointless, frustrating melee. As the light went, and the game ended, he asked them, 'Do you want to be in a league?'

'Yes, Mr Hector!' the children chorused.

He hadn't been himself when he chose the pseudonym. Or he'd been too much himself not to edit. Either way, it was a stupid choice. Every day, at least once, it stopped him still for a moment. 'Sorry,' he said. 'Some sand in my eye. When you get here tomorrow, I'll explain how it will work.'

'Aiiiii! Tell us now!'

'Tomorrow. I have to have my supper.'

'Aiiiii!'

'I mean it.'

'Yes, Mr Hector! Goodbye, Mr Hector!'

Dave pretended to be upset at what he had let himself in for. 'It's great to see you passionate about something again at last,' Punty said.

'But?'

'You keep saying, about football, that —'

'That's the game in England,' he said. 'This is totally different. Look at the kids on the beach. It's not the same thing at all. This is *pure*.' He was excited, and it was infectious. He said it was vital for his authority that he make a good first impression, and Punty teased him for being pompous, and they started giggling. Dave cannibalised his wardrobe for the forty sashes he would need, in five colours. He started, dramatically, by taking a carving knife to his dinner jacket: 'I'm not going to the Christmas Party again – why do I need this old thing!' Punty responded by hacking apart a bias-cut Taka Imamura, and then they got really frenzied. It was their best night yet.

When the kids arrived at the beach the next day, Dave said, 'This is what I'll do. Two days every week, Tuesday and Thursday, we'll have five ten-minute games, eight a side. Players can be substituted any time, but only eight on the pitch at once, okay? The rest of the time, you can play like you did before, okay?'

'Yes, Mr Hector!'

Dave took the five best players and told them to pick players in rotation. 'Stop,' Punty ordered, and they stopped. They looked at Dave, who nodded. 'Alphabetical order,' said Punty. 'Chop-chop.' She walked along the line, numbering them off, one to five. They corralled themselves into their respective groups, and she handed them back to Dave, who was smiling proudly.

'Off you go,' he said to the kids. 'I want you back in ten minutes with team names, and I want each team to pick their own captain.' He said this looking at Punty, warning her that this time he was right.

*

Dear Zondi,
Thank you very much, for everything you say.

I like the sound of Mr Brown, though I thought it was always Achilles who wanted a dog and you who said that he couldn't have one, because you knew who'd end up looking after it. This is a time of gathering for all of us, in our ways; we must never forget the past, but we have to look at the future too. Every day we make decisions that push us one way or the other.

I think you would be surprised if you came to Nzasa (and you are always welcome). I reacted badly to you calling me hysterical, but thank you, because it was a short sharp shock, and helped jolt me into being calmer. I went through a delusional few weeks when I arrived, thinking that Nzasa was some kind of idyll, cut off from the world, which goes to show that you never really grow out of your dreams, which is actually a pleasing thought. The village is attached to a big politicos' retreat up the hill, which is fine, frankly. I'm not <u>really</u> naive enough to believe there is anywhere outside the world any more. I don't mean everywhere's the same, obviously. The change of place and pace has cleared my mind amazingly. Understanding things in the heart, as you put it, is vital, and all the things we used to talk about – why the Socialists were different and what made it special – being here has shown me the answers much more clearly than I could see them when we were stuck in the middle of the mess that everything turned into after Mr Brown died. The other thing that has calmed me down – predictably or unpredictably, take your pick – is football. I mistook the money and the grime for what football truly is, which is kids playing on a beach.

What you say about the bus I can understand. Snaky Will is not the cause. He probably even thinks he is, but he'll keep doing what he does, thinking he can escape whenever he wants, but the world is entropy, and he can't avoid it any more than anyone else. He'll always want more, and he'll never get any joy out of what he does, so I feel sorry for him. By which I mean, in the interests of honesty, I feel sorry for him with my head – my heart thinks he's a twat. Anyway, the hill is too steep, and the bus is going to crash whatever we do. For a while Mr Brown slowed it down, but that's the tragedy of it all – you can work, and work, but in the end you have to hand things on, and who knows whether you hand them to a wise man or a fool? This is what I understand now with my heart: the world is too big for us to engage in grand plans, as if we know what should happen to everyone else. The people who try are the idealists, and some are okay, obviously, but that's the road to Nazis, Communists and all the other fundamentalists trying to make the world the shape they want – they think there's a single standard of truth, but there isn't. What

KSC was all about, under Mr Brown, was making sure we were all as good as we could be. If we all did the good we could, not by going out and preaching, but just doing it, we made ourselves better people, and that made the world a better place in a small, dependable kind of a way. Now, KSC is different. It's bigger and it's still a good thing, I suppose, but it's pretending it can affect the big things – poverty, and literacy, and whatever – and it can only ever scratch the surface. They're for governments and professionals. We might have been doing little things in the old days, but they were good things, and we mustn't spend our lives trying to control other people.

I've started a football league for the kids. They're so keen, and right from the start I'm being strict about how they must behave on the pitch, and about working as a team. These are great lessons to learn. Sport is so pure, its essence is, that when the world is not interfering with it, it really is a better place. There are tensions, obviously, but the beach is somewhere the ones from the village and the ones from Nagape's huge family are all on a level playing field (not that it's that level!).

So, you see, I've found what I needed to find. A world small enough to remind me that it's the little things that matter. I'm trying to compete with you on poetic expression, but I'm failing.

All my love to you, and think of the future. You know it's what he would want,

Dave

(I nearly didn't write this, which would have been cowardice: I called myself 'Mr Hector' when I arrived, because I didn't want to be recognised. It was stupid, and I'm changing to my real name now, which is proving as cringe-making as taking the pseudonym was in the first place. I tell you so that if you ever hear I did something this insensitive, you'll already know. Sorry.)

KILBURN UNTIED

Nzasa
18 Nov

Dear Aisling,

Thanks for the letter. It's probably for the best you didn't get the Brompton job, however much you're not seeing Surgeon Man any more. This house officer thing at Tommy's – how does it work? Being a reg is a job not a qualification? So you're qualified to apply to be one, but you're not one till you get a reg job?

I think you're right not to be going to the Christmas Party. I'd completely forgotten that it would be coming up. Things like that seem so unreal out here. I can see how it feels weird not to be going after all these years.

Zondi did write. I've just replied to him in fact (I'm getting my correspondence out of the way in one fell swoop, because El Courier is coming to dinner with us and the Good Doctor this evening).

On which subject: I'm really sorry your gran's been hassled, and you're absolutely right – the idea of pretending to be in Ireland all year was crazy. It's incredible that Esther hasn't twigged already (thank fuck for Will taking her mind off it!). I'm sending a letter to Sal in this batch about telling people where we really are and asking them to leave us alone.

You don't have to apologise about calling me hysterical. I see how I might have seemed a bit unhinged, but I'm completely calm now. As I wrote to Zondi, which wasn't as hard as I feared, it's all about understanding how little you can control, and how it's not worth trying. The problem is all the fundamentalists who think they can make the world the shape they want. There are all kinds of these bastards, from free-market ones, to Islamic nutters, to scary American Christians (I wrote that for balance, but I'm more frightened of the Muslims), to all these far-right loonies cluttering up European politics. What I thought when I read your letter about all the reality-

267

TV voting, and stupid public polls on the news, it scared me somehow. Your jokes were funny, don't get me wrong, but it made me think that even democratic fundamentalists are dangerous. Where does it all end? We can't have a society where everyone gets a chance to decide on everything, because how is some harassed fucking house-wife in Kilmarnock supposed to formulate foreign policy?

End of rant, but my point is that people are losing their perspec-tive, and they think they have the right to be anything, and then they'll get upset when they can't be, which they can't. It's narcissism, and the press panders to it, and all this searching-for-myself, pseudo-religious bollocks panders to it as well. It pretends the world is easy and compre-hensible, but it isn't. That's what I am trying to teach these kids here – I've started them in a football league, to show them that they can't just do what they want or everything gets ruined. They have to play by the rules. When you accept that, you stop trying to control other people all the time. End of my rant again, but really this time.

Punty had a load of 'I'm spiritual not religious' baggage to get rid of when she arrived, but I think I've hammered it out of her. It wasn't hard – she gets things pretty quickly, but she's had a sheltered life. She reminds me of Sally in lots of ways. She's bright, and she's great with people, but she's never paid much attention to how the world works, so she can be naive about it. I think she's enjoying getting her eyes opened. Sport's one example. She did the team-picking for the football by random, instead of having the kids choose things in order. That is definitely as fair, and it meant no one got hurt by being last. But then, the next day, she said it would be best if I refereed in such a way that everyone won the same number of matches, and that I should award prizes for fair play but not for winning the league, because winning isn't what's really important. I think she even said winning isn't the point, though I might be making things neater in my head. The whole point about games is that winning _is_ the point – that's what makes fair play important. Fair play makes winning harder. It's _valuable_ because it _costs._ It's a sign of how much I like Punty that I thought what she said was sweet, though it helps that she realised it was bollocks as soon as I explained.

She's unbelievable with the kids. Did I say this before? Also, I'm pretty sure she's getting broody. She's only twenty-three, but that's quite old to be childless out here. Now I've noticed it, I find I don't mind *the idea. It would be nice not to be an old man when my kids are grown up, and Punty would be a great mum. This might just be a good time for both of us. There's a time to get, just like there's a time to lose; we must trust ourselves and each other to know the difference.*

I know what Sally would say – 'Don't hurt her because what if you suddenly fall madly in love with someone else?' – but that's only because Sally found the One. I'm very happy for her, but that doesn't happen to most people. Anyway, it's just as likely Punty finds the One as I do. She says <u>I'm</u> the One, but she also said she's thought that a few times before, so she obviously doesn't mean the same by it as you and I would. If we were to have a child, I wouldn't be rushing in blindly. I do feel responsible for P coming here, even if she's enjoying it and it's good for her, but I would only have a child because it was the right time for me too, because it takes two, and because we have decided to find a way to make whatever it is we have work.

Dinnertime.

Love,

Dave

(I can't believe you still haven't dealt with your spat with Adam. I was actually quite annoyed when I read that in your last letter. The longer you take, the harder it'll be. Don't let things fester.)

*

Adam was in Esther's office, waiting for Louie Cohen. Esther flapped busily between her desks picking up bits of paper and moving them around. Here and there, she furrowed her brow and made a note, or tutted and shook her head. The computer pinged, and she sighed as she dealt with yet another important email. Adam let his phone flutter silently in his pocket.

It was cold. Adam watched the Gardener and his team scatter something on their precious turf. The Gardener swore that this labour-intensive process was the only way to keep the pitch going through the winter. If he couldn't have an extra laying, or up-to-date under-soil technology, then he was not going to be responsible for bruising the grass with hard, heavy wheels, not unless he had to. Adam suggested a hovercraft, and then, realising what he'd done, emphasised that he was joking. The Gardener didn't like jokes about grass.

There's nothing in a name. The Bursar had an MBA; the Stationery Office wouldn't know a sheet of paper if it hit their computers in the face; even the Manciple had his spreadsheets; and up and down the gardeners went, broadcasting away, medieval serfs obsessed with soil science.

The arguments with Aisling had cleared Adam's mind of clutter. The old KSC was great, but you have to work within your environment. It's no good being the best dinosaur in a world of rats. Now that KSC had worked loose of its customs and restraints, Adam could see how suffocating they had been. The players began to breathe more freely, and they began to win again. You couldn't forget heritage, but you had to use it or it would use you.

Adam raised KSC's ticket prices closer to their competitors'. He licensed player dolls, auctioned off relaid turf and courted commercial partners. It was his *job* to maximise profit for the shareholders. It was his *mission* to increase the value of the tiny cuts that went to the Trust and Foundation. In his more fanciful moments, Adam saw himself as a combination of money launderer and Robin Hood, but it wasn't just about the Foundation. Football was messed up, but there was something amazing at the heart of it, a dream of a better world, which wasn't there in the City. It's not that he didn't believe that people acting in free-market self-interest created societies and met needs, and all the rest. It's just that the atmosphere at Kilburn Park still sent shivers through him.

Louie arrived, bouncing with zeal. Adam sat down, went through the formalities and then asked to hear Louie's idea. 'It's "Socialists", man,' Louie said. 'It's all wrong.' He currently favoured a black suit, black shirt and black tie. It was certainly imposing. Louie refused coffee. He wanted to explain and he didn't want to waste any time. He sat forward, towering over the pygmies. Adam turned his chair towards the window. 'Football is global, man. "Socialist" sends the wrong message. I've been talking with Phil Maroon, and he says we're missing a trick. We got a great story, but we can't get it out there. It might work in Britain, with your irony and all that, but in the rest of the world, if you call yourself a socialist, you're a socialist.'

'You didn't think that.'

'I'm special, man. I always seen further. I never thought there was anything we could do about it before, but there is.' Up and down went the Gardener. Up and down. Adam refocused, sharpening up Louie's accusing reflection. The 'Kilburn, United' advert had been phenomenally successful. Money had rained down on the Foundation, and volunteers had flocked to Foundation programmes. In their turn, these volunteers, celebrities included, featured in new versions of the advert, side by side with the players, and the cycle began again.

'"Socialists" is just a nickname,' Adam tried.

'"Social Club" is as bad. You know I'm right, man. This is killing us abroad.'

'We've never been bigger across Europe. Wouldn't we confuse our fans ther—'

'I'm talking about America, man. That's where the money is. Will asked me why we couldn't raise our profile there, and then the next day Phil also talked to me about it, and it all kinda clicked. America's where we can do good for the Foundation, and where we can spread the message. If we reach as many people as we can reach, we raise every penny we can raise, and then we help the most people we can help.'

'Will's right,' said Esther. 'And Louie. Everyone knows I'm the most committed person at this club to the Kilburn heritage, but maybe now is our chance to make the difficult decisions so we can move forward not backwards. We were called the Socialists because then "we were all Socialists now", but we can't keep explaining that to people, and it's English people as well as Americans. We're always having to explain it. "Kilburn United" is a way of saying the same thing in modern language and, also, the free publicity we will get by changing the name, especially since the adverts, will be worth tons of money to the Foundation. It's because of the adverts that we should do this now.'

'The fans won't like it.'

'The *English* fans. And anyway, they won't desert the club, because we have the best fans in the world, so only ones who don't really love the club or who don't understand will leave. And also, people are naturally conservative, so they don't like change, but they will get used to it.' These were Will's words, Adam presumed.

Up and down went the Gardener. Surely there came a point when the last rope tied to the past would be cut, and the tent would collapse? Or maybe the last rope would be cut, and the balloon would soar.

Adam walked out of Kilburn Park at five o'clock. Changing the name made plausible commercial sense, and Donald would leap on it, but

Adam knew in his bones that it was not a good change. But if Donald and Esther wanted it, then it would happen. If Adam campaigned publicly, he would lose credibility and influence within the club, where he might still actually do some good. The only thing to do was bite the bullet, stay inside the machine, and fight the battles that could be won.

Stung into action by Dave's letter, Aisling arranged to have lunch with Adam at Café Topaz on the edge of the Heath. It took longer than she expected to finish her rounds, and Adam had finished a coffee by the time she arrived. The meal wasn't relaxed after the past few months' frost, but they made an agree-to-disagree truce. They also agreed not to talk about Kilburn, but Adam said there was one thing he had to mention, and told her about the name change. It was unfair to focus her anger on him, so she bit her tongue. She suggested a stroll before she got the train to Tommy's.

They walked between the ponds and up the hill, and Aisling made jokes about Nicky's latest diktats. As they turned into a little wooded bowl, they saw Zondi with Mr Brown. The dog was clearly in charge, waddling self-importantly through the leaves and up to a tiny girl in a red plastic mac. The girl was mesmerised by Mr Brown's calm, appraising stare. Eventually, Mr Brown nudged her, and the girl gave her a nervous pat. The dog nodded, and moved on. Zondi followed, and, at a guilty distance, so did Adam and Aisling. Mr Brown chose who would pat her. Twice, passing walkers reached down uninvited and the dog veered away. There was something endlessly comical about Mr Brown.

They should have talked to Zondi. He would have known what to do about 'Kilburn United', or at least have something sensible to say. But, after following him, Adam said he couldn't ever speak to Zondi without being embarrassed. Aisling could have done, but she agreed that it wouldn't feel quite right.

When Nicky heard about the truce, she informed Aisling that she was maturing at last, especially in respect to that stupid football club, and put it down to her own good influence. This was so irritating that Aisling called Adam and asked if she could go to the Christmas Party.

*

David, David,

Are you sitting down?

Now?

If you're not sitting down now, it's not my fault.

From 1 January, the Kilburn Social Club will, officially, be no more. Some unlikely change of heart or policy to the contrary, we will be renamed 'Kilburn, United'. With a fucking comma. It's unbelievable, it honestly is, completely surreal. Everything at the club for two months has been about how we have to grab the tragic chance we have been given, how we must change, transform, renew and revivify. How it's 'now or never' to sweep away the unnecessary clutter. The announcement will have been made by the time you get this, so you'll probably have heard, and you didn't need to sit down after all. All the drama is making me overdramatic.

The drama is relentless, David, it honestly is. I'm living in a soap opera. The Christmas Party was nuts. <u>Everything</u> is nuts. I know I shouldn't have gone to the party. When I called Adam to ask him if I could go with him, it was the day after we'd made our peace at last. We'd only just agreed that we would be friends and we wouldn't talk about football any more, so he naturally thought I'd gone mad. Maybe I had. I just couldn't not go. I've never not been, and I still own five per cent of the club. It was my last one, though, I think – for the first time I felt like a spectator and not a participant (when I told Nicky that afterwards, it slightly calmed her down). The weirdness of me and Adam being at the Christmas Party and trying not to talk about the Socialists paled into insignificance pretty quickly.

The disgusting Will is still stringing Esther along, which is horrible to watch, since he's shagging the (increasingly misnamed) 26, who arrived on Will's arm painted bright orange and wearing heels that Errol Flynn could have used as swords.

Esther, and so help me God I was so angry about this I almost killed her when I found out, was with puppydog Tom, claiming that they were just friends and affecting surprise that anyone might see a problem with it. The sainted Fucker Horton, friend of the powerless, was there with some minor comedienne. He was premiering a goatee which didn't make him look like any less of a twat. He's thick as thieves with Will B, and they persuaded Esther to let a couple of photographers in to the dinner this year. Served them right what happened.

I liked seeing the guys – Carlo and Dirk asked after you, among others – but Esther was pissed almost instantly, and she was horrendous. She told me I was being a bitch for lying to her about you being in Tanga, and then she said that if you are doing voluntary work you should at least be atoning properly by working for the Foundation. She's heard you turned down the interviews, and she thinks you're being selfish. Then, thank fuck, Will arrived and she started making doe eyes at him, and brushing against him with sly little looks as if she thought 26 was blind or – it suddenly comes to me in a moment of clarity – as if she didn't know about Will and 26, which is possible, since Esther only sees what she wants to see. We sat down (fabulous beef, since you ask), and she wasn't too bad until the photographer got to our table, at which point she stood up and made a speech crapping on about esprit de corps, and how it was so appropriate that everyone was wearing black, as if this was something new. She made everyone toast 'The General', and then she made us toast Achilles. The photographer took all these pictures of people pasting their official sad faces over skew-whiff drunken grins. The only pictures they could use without looking as if they were taking the piss were the ones of Louie and, of course, Will B. Louie hasn't got a clue what's going around him, but he knows how to put on a show.

The excitement hadn't even begun. I took Esther to powder her nose and to tell her to get a grip, which she didn't take well, and 26 stormed in after us. She and Esther started shouting and screaming. Esther said 26 was cheap and common and Will was with her because he needed a date that no one could take seriously. 26 said Esther was a deluded sex-maniac bitch who refused to accept that Will had chosen someone else. Then they jumped on each other. They literally had a fight in the ladies' loo. Me and a couple of girls I didn't recognise pulled them apart, and then made a human wall between them while they repainted themselves, glaring at each other in the mirror. I don't really know 26, but it seems she's no less deluded than Esther. She went straight to Will, holding back the tears, and demanded that he tell Esther that they were in love, that they had *been for months, and that Esther should look elsewhere. She was trying to hiss it out, but it was more like a shriek, and everyone could hear. It was a fucking train-wreck, even before Esther ran over. Dirk and Carlo went straight to Tom, by the way – <u>that's</u> esprit de corps.*

Anyway, back to the plot. Everyone wanted to see how Will got out of this one. (Fucker Horton looked like he was loving it too, incidentally, so that's a love that only runs skin deep.) The cameras were going crackers. Will had to say something, and he stayed cool, I'll give him that. He gave a little nod to one of the massive security men, who started rumbling towards him, and you could see that 26 was terrified that she was going to get ejected (a thought which never crossed Esther's mind). Will said that emotions were obviously running high at the club right now, it was perfectly understandable with everything that had happened, and everyone was hurting. He said that it was only right that people express their pain over the loss of Achilles (Esther and 26 looked as confused by this as everyone else) but that some pain should only really be shared within the family that was KSC. He got the security guy to take away the photographers, clever boy. Then he said, 'That's it, everybody. Show's over.' People didn't know what had gone on, and they sort of went back to their business while Will took his harem into the lobby, one under each arm. Only he and Esther returned.

I ran out the opposite door, and dashed round the corridors till I got to reception. 26 was being consoled by 30, crying as if her cat had died, her face in white-and-tan stripes like a boiled sweet. They looked at me as if it was my fault, but I said I knew Will was a bastard, and my sister was an idiot. I asked what the bastard had done. 26, and I'm paraphrasing and leaving out the more colourful bits, said that fucking Will had fucking used her, the fucking fucker. He tried to say that tonight wasn't the time for this, but 26 had fucking made him. Instead of telling Esther that he loved 26, he told Esther, who was a total bitch, that he loved her completely, but it was true that he <u>had</u> been sleeping with 26. Will wasn't proud of it, but he did it because he was only a man, and needed release. By doing it with 26, who didn't matter, he was staying away from temptation. 26 couldn't believe her fucking ears, especially that the Bitch was upset, which was fucking hypocritical since everyone knew the Bitch still fucked Tom whenever she got drunk. The Bitch was the biggest fucking Bitch in the fucking world, etc. This went on at some length. I half-wanted to stay with her, because she's the one who's been worst treated in all this. And Tom, obviously. None of it's my fault, but I felt guilty, and listening to her, I got in a little rage of my own. When I went back into the room, I found Will and Esther and I told them that if they didn't sort themselves out, they would pay for it. Don't ask me how I thought I might make this happen. They just looked at me. That was the worst bit of the night, from my own perspective, which goes to show how selfish I am. Adam and I left soon after. The fighting brought us closer together. Probably it's what things were like during the Blitz.

There were a couple of stories in the papers the next day (Voice, obviously), but Fucker Horton wrote about what a pleasant evening it was, and how things were being blown out of all proportion. He then went on about 'the tragedies of the drunken lovelorn', and how risky it can be to have a few when you're in the presence of an object of mistaken desire. He turned it into a joke, and I bet it would have been funny if you were an ignorant reader. 26 has had to leave the club, but Adam's made sure she's all right for work, because he's brilliant, I know he is, even if I wish he'd see sense.

There's one other thing. I know you said you didn't need a warning about Zondi writing, so you probably don't need a warning about this either, but I had dinner in town with Sally yesterday (because she wants to show how over the past she is, which I find hard, but she means well). Monica and Jed were there and we were rounding up what we knew of how you were, because we're your friends, not because we're obsessive stalker ex-girlfriends in any way because we're NOT, David, we're not – it's perfectly NORMAL to have pictures of you all over the flat and to wear your old playing shirts in bed (maniacal laughter). Anyway, in the middle of pudding, I said you were obviously fine, because you're thinking of having a baby. Consternation, etc., as Sally and Monica went into shock that you could have written such a thing to me. Basically, they think it was the height of insensitive emotional fuckwittery, and I reckon Sally will be writing to you about it. They were genuinely het up (it was *quite sweet, actually). Whatever they say, I knew what you were saying, and I'm absolutely fine.*

For all the ranting and raving, things are good here. The job at Tommy's is good hours, and it will be better for weaning myself off inappropriate liaisons with older colleagues than working at the Brompton would have been. And yes, I apply for reg jobs as and when, especially if Nicky is in the room.

Also, I'm a millionaire aristocrat.

Love,

Aisling

(What you said about winning and fair play – I'd never thought about it like that, but of course you are right. I wish I'd had that argument in my armoury for when Mum told me I was too competitive at Monopoly.)

BRIGHT-EYED

c/o Doctors-in-Africa
Nzasa
Tanganyika
18 December 2002

Dear Sally,

I hope you do not mind me writing to you. Dave writes all the time and now I am getting into it too – Mutter loves getting the letters! (Mutter's my mother. We are a stupid family with names, and you can understand why I prefer Punty to Punctuality?!) Before I start, I must say thank you so much to you and Jed for helping Dave and I to be here, and for helping to keep anyone from finding out so he can have space to Heal his Spirit.

Space is very important. That is why we don't have the internet or anything. Dave says that we are so used to instant communication like email and mobile phones that we have forgotten the joy of letters, and of the different amount you think when you are writing them, and the excitement of waiting for the post to come. I told him he had obviously never waited desperately for a reply to a text message from someone he fancied! But it is true. He banned us from having a mobile or a computer out here, and now I am really excited when the letters arrive!

I also understand now why he doesn't want the internet. He gets all these letters from people anyway – people blaming him or saying it wasn't his fault, or even just asking for autographs. I suppose pop stars get things like that all the time, and I used to get some from my agent, but she always weeded out the horrible ones, and Dave insists on reading everything. I know we had to say where we are, but we've already had loads of people ask us for interviews and all we want is to be left alone.

Writing letters DOES make you think about things. For instance, yesterday, I wrote to Mutter about the politics of Tanganyika! Dave would have been proud, because he would think I was getting into politics, but it was really only because you have to explain the politics to explain why Nzasa exists and what it is like. Dave is always trying to teach me things, about philosophy and global economics and population shifts and demography. It's because he doesn't have any grown-up students out here I think! Did he used to do it with you? I think it's sweet, so there's no doubt, it must be love!

Of course it's love, and in my opinion, if you love someone, you have to love them completely. It means I have had much more than my fair share of heartbreak in my life, because when I give my heart to someone, it is theirs until they decide to let it free. I am always the one to be broken-hearted. It's the way I am and I couldn't change it even if I wanted to, because I always want to believe that nothing will ever end. I thought when we came here it was because Dave needed to get the tragedy out of his system, and we would be in Africa for six months or a year at most, but now it looks as if he's going to stay for longer, and he hasn't said anything, but he expects me just to stay with him. I thought he'd be bored of me but he isn't. I thought that it was okay for me to put everything on hold for six months because my man needed me, I have never had a long holiday like this, and it would be a wonderful experience while it lasted. I don't want to stay here for ever, but Dave still needs me. I don't know what he writes to you, but he has a great pain in his soul because of Achilles. Ever since we got here, he says he has slept well, better than in England, but the truth is that every night he cries and kicks and I have to hold him. It is funny, but the things that happen when he doesn't know about them have made me closer to him than all the talking. I love him for what he has been through, how deeply he has suffered. It is just being honest to say that you are part of that suffering, not that it's your fault, because I know you were only following your heart when you left him, but Dave needs me, and I can be his strength and shield while he recovers from his sorrows, so being here for him is an unbelievable gift I can give him, because I am young enough to recover when he decides to end it. But how long will it be? I think I can stay another year at least, but after that, I do not know. Maybe I am wrong, and he really will love me in the end. I have started to think he might. I don't know what I would do then.

Dave is more sensitive than he pretends. That's why I'm writing to you. He will never say it himself, but he was really hurt by what you wrote in your last letter when you said he was cruel to Aisling when he wrote about babies (we aren't going to have one, don't worry!). I know you meant it kindly, but he has spent ever since worried. He says Aisling understood, but I know Dave really well now, and I have to say that you really hurt him. That's all I want to say about that.

His sensitivity also shows in answering so many letters. He understood that people would eventually have to know what he was doing, and he is very grateful that you have tried to keep the location private (and it is not an easy place to visit!) and told people that we don't want visitors, but I think maybe you could have waited a few more months before sending all the mail, even though he asked. Even the nice ones make him cry, and then there are the horrible ones, and the stupid ones, and all the ones asking for autographs. He doesn't need to be reminded of what happened all the time, but he won't say because he's so grateful to you.

I do not mean to be a complaining cow! The people here are amazing. They are so open and honest compared with at home (especially if you're a model!) and they have a spirituality which is mind-blowing. There is a sense among the villagers (not the rich ones from the big houses) that life is about the moment you are in. They know that it is more important to fish and cook and laugh and be happy than it is to go to school in order to get into Nagape's thieving government, who are really wicked. It's incredible to be here and see the difference between the houses on the hill and the ones on the beach.

Dave hates Nagape, and his 'kleptocratic cronies' (I know what kleptocracy means now!) and he worries that however much he teaches the kids in school they will be as bad as their parents. To take his mind off it, he started this little football league on the beach (I was surprised he could bear football, but it's been part of his life for so long that he can't let it go). The ironic thing is that now all the rich kids come and play, maybe even more than the village kids, but Dave keeps on with the league anyway.

I'm glad your album is selling well. Dave found it hard to listen to, obviously, but there is no way he could have avoided it for ever, and he would have thought that was cowardly anyway. He said to me when we listened to it that you just have to face these things, but it didn't make things easier, obviously, and it's not up to me, but I think you could maybe have waited a bit to have made him listen to some of those songs! I didn't write this to upset you or anything, just to say that although he says he's okay, Dave isn't, and I'm trying to look after him.

    Love, and Merry Xmas!

    Punty xxx

*

Sally replied to Punty's letter with icy calm. She explained that Dave was sometimes insensitive, and when this happened he had to be told. It was the honest thing to do. *On the subject of honesty*, she added, *it is very important you tell Dave where he stands. I was never honest with him about what I wanted and what was important to me, I see that now. He and I are close friends, but we were always too different to be any more than that. If you are not careful, there is a danger he will think you two are more compatible than you are, because he is desperate for security, especially after what happened. I worry that he will simply assume that everything between you is perfect (maybe it is!), so you must make it very clear to him what you think and want, so he doesn't deceive himself and make it worse for both of you in the long term.* Punty didn't appreciate being lectured and didn't reply.

At last, thought Aisling, Jeremy was going to make his move. For the first time since the ridiculous protracted courtship began, he had invited Aisling for dinner without any encumbering theatre or gallery to take up most of the evening. Like all her friends, he laughed when she was late. Jeremy was six foot two inches tall and his brown hair was always too long. The day after he had it cut, it looked like he should get another haircut tomorrow, and it continued to give that impression until he got round to having it cut again. He had a long face, handsome in an awkward, gawky way. She got the feeling that even when he was working on a brief at home, his ironed shirts were tucked into his jeans. He was the kind of man who made sure that imperial cities had sanitation, and worried about the fate of the natives without understanding anything about them.

He kissed her in greeting, as always, and they ordered. 'I fancy you,' he said abruptly. As an opening gambit, it was so gauche that she had no reply. 'I think it's time we did something about it,' he clarified.

'I don't know.' She looked at the menu. Nothing thrilled her.

'We know each other quite well now, don't you think?'

'Yes,' said Aisling. 'And still nothing's happened.'

'We've been learning about each other. That's what sensible people do.'

'Is it? Doesn't that take the excitement out of it?'

'How's your approach working for you? We're not teenagers any more.' It wasn't exactly Ovid. 'Is it David?' he asked.

'No. I don't know.'

'What does he think of you?'

'I don't know.'

'If it's him you're waiting for, shouldn't you find out?' He was relentless. 'At least I understand what I'm getting into. You and I get on, and we want similar things from life. I know you aren't perfect, and that this won't be an easy conquest, but there are things in you I value, seams that I can tell other people haven't mined. I think we might have something, and I want to find out if we can make it work.' He'd marshalled his forces carefully. 'I'm not expecting you to cave in, but I want you to know that I'm ready for a long siege,' he said.

When they left the restaurant, two hours of clarification later, Aisling's defences were still holding. Jeremy kissed her chastely goodbye at Charing Cross tube and said, 'I know this is not how you would choose to be wooed, but I'm not someone who charges in and lays waste. I advance slowly, and I know what I'm doing.'

For comparison's sake, mainly, she met up with her surgeon for the first time in months. She used to find that he cleared her head, but this time he just made her tired and when she said this was definitely the last time, he said, 'Okay,' and they went their separate ways to work. As if anything could have been more predictable, she met Nicky at the hospital door. Nicky disapproved silently. 'It's more complicated than that, Nicks . . .' She stopped. 'Later, can we?'

Nicky was just finishing a night, so they agreed to meet at seven. Leo would cook, Nicky said.

That evening, after a day spent pondering, Aisling anatomised

Jeremy's comical footling, which Nicky didn't find funny. Aisling's own reaction to it was still negative, but with unfathomable undercurrents. She added that she wouldn't be seeing the surgeon again, and, as if an aside, gave the latest news from Nzasa. Aisling worried that Punty was finding it difficult to adjust.

Nicky looked down, biting her lower lip. 'What is it?' Aisling asked.

'Oh, come on, A,' said Nicky. 'What's going on with you and David?'

'Nothing.'

'Not good enough.'

'I don't know.'

'Don't know what he thinks or don't know what you think?'

'Both.'

'Work it out, now, Azzabelle. And bin Jeremy.'

'Just bin him?'

'Yes.'

'Is there a faint chance that one day you will stop lecturing me?'

'Me?' said Nicky, and lightning didn't strike her for some reason.

'Scoff!' called Leo from the kitchen.

Aisling wasn't an idiot. She knew the letters to David were an issue for her. She was sure, deep down, that the letters were an issue for him too. He must have realised, on one level, that Punty was wrong for him, and vice versa, but what if they both got trapped by their circumstances, settled for each other, and made each other unhappy? It wasn't Aisling's job to rescue David, any more than she would try to rescue any of her friends – which she might if she could, after all – but if her letters to him did mean what she feared they meant, then this was different. It was easy for Nicky to say, 'Sort yourself out,' but Dave was over there, she was over here, and what if she'd manufactured a mad crush out of unobtainability and distance? Then it would be unforgivable to interfere with him and Punty.

Aisling was a great believer in the power of jealousy, and in her next letter she explained about the final end of the surgeon, and said that she was thinking seriously about Jeremy's advances. *He makes sure of what he's getting before he proceeds,* she wrote, *and maybe there's something in that approach.*

David replied a week later, quicker than normal. She saw the envelope, and she couldn't open it. She showered, and made coffee, then sat down. *You sound like you don't know what you want,* Dave wrote.

You have to let Jeremy know where he stands, because it seems from here that you're leading him on, which is unworthy of you. Then he added, *Punty and I have discussed things. We're definitely staying in Nzasa for another year.* Well, thought Aisling, that could hardly have been more clear. She was annoyed that Dave felt the need to sound so like a school-teacher, and her instant reaction was to break off the correspondence.

The next day, she invited Jeremy for a drink, and she said she was ready to give it a go.

The six weeks around Christmas were the low point of Kilburn's season. For a month and a half, they played as if they didn't know each other. Tom, who had always found space so naturally in front of Achilles, was especially anonymous. He constantly ran offside, his first touch was terrible and his instinct a memory. Commentators excused this as under-standable, given the circumstances of this season, and fans gritted their teeth for the same reason.

Will Beauchamp missed a week after being bruised in training by a clumsy challenge from Dirk Volendam. His first day back, in a session led by the coach, Dirk clattered him again. As Will lay writhing, he turned his head towards the manager's office window, and gave it a look which said, 'I told you so.' The boss had been watching sceptically, but as soon as Volendam started moving towards Will, intent clear even from fifty metres, the manager had been heading outside. He arrived to find Will gingerly brushing himself down, and the players in two sullen camps. 'You're like a bunch of fucking babies!' he shouted. 'Get in a fucking line.' They didn't like it. 'Get. In. A fucking. Line. This is a football team, not a fucking girls' school. I don't care who any of you are fucking. I don't care if you're fucking everything that moves, or if you're a monk, or if you're a poof. What I care about is that on my fucking football pitch, you behave like a fucking football team. If you don't, you're out. Do you understand?' Silence. 'Do you fucking under-stand?' Some yeses, some nods. 'Right. Get on with it. Volendam, you come with me.' From the corner of their eyes, the players watched the huge centre half face the boss with dumb insolence. Afterwards, Louie asked Will what had happened. Incredibly, Louie was serious.

'It's about the Christmas Party.'

'What about it?'

'It's about Esther. They're angry about me and Esther.'

'But I thought Tom was going with Esther. What happened?'

'You did notice the screaming fit in the middle of the dinner?'

'You said it was because people were upset about Achilles.'

'No. I was just ... Esther and I are ... Esther and Tom have never really been together. I mean, they fancied each other, but it was never serious.'

'I didn't realise. I thought Tom —'

'Between you and me, mate, Tom has been using Esther, really. For years. You know his shyness is just an act? But Esther and I, we started to realise last summer that me and her have something special, and then we were waiting for the right time to tell people, and it didn't seem appropriate after the tragedy.'

'I understand. But why —'

'Suddenly, because she finally decided to break free of him, Tom got jealous. Some of the others have taken his side, and that's why I've been having a rough time in training.'

'Dirk kicked you deliberately?'

'Yes, Louie.'

'Man!'

Now that he knew the facts, Louie was determined to sort this out. A football team has to be a team, and that had to come from mutual love and respect. That was what had brought him to Kilburn. The manager shouting at everyone wasn't the way it should be. Louie drove home slowly. The change in Tom was obvious to him now, and there was no time like the present, but it was important – respectful even – to put on a suit. This was a business matter. Louie's flat was well serviced and spacious, right in the heart of East Kilburn. He liked the utilitarian feel of the huge television and banks of speakers, the unused chrome kitchen and the black-and-white photographs of Martin Luther King, Malcolm X, Muhammad Ali and – and this he couldn't explain, but he'd seen it in the shop where he bought the others – the dome of St Paul's wreathed in the smoke from the Blitz. His wardrobe contained six black suits, all bespoke and all, to Louie, very different. He chose the Barker & Osbourne, soft and sharp at the same time. It was professional but unintimidating. He wore a white linen shirt and no tie. Before going, he sat down to think. His sofas were black and long. They would seat eight in reasonable comfort; a depression was worn into the left end of the right-hand one. It's not that Louie couldn't be sociable if he wanted, it's just he was focused, and he wasn't frivolous. He wasn't friends with his fellow players, necessarily, but they had a good working relationship. He sometimes wished things were different. He would have liked a girlfriend.

Louie knew he mustn't be angry with Tom just because he'd been deceived by him. What mattered were straightforwardness, forgiveness, tolerance and a determination to be stronger tomorrow. He should speak about this subject on Monday night after the match between St Brendan's Youth Club and the boys he helped coach in east London. Coaching was Louie's new venture. Previously, he had concentrated on the front lines of the fight against fundamentalism and bigotry, but one of the women from the Foundation, who was a Christian, as if that mattered, suggested he watch this Bangladeshi football team in Bethnal Green. The kids were crazy about the game, but drifted away at fourteen and fifteen, and started hanging around the streets in closed little gangs. Louie's presence dragged some of the recent departees back to the team, and he enjoyed the contact, saving kids he recognised.

He would have liked a girlfriend, but women were probably frightened of him. Maybe they feared he would make them cover up, but if Louie were a woman, he'd have probably found a way to be Muslim without covering up, because that would have been a powerful demonstration of how variegated Islam could be. Being Louie Cohen was about being an example.

Tom lived north of London. His street was almost silent and the houses were enormous, set off the road behind great, thick-trunked trees, lawn verges and hedges in various states of repression. Some had gates with intercoms, but not Tom's. Louie parked round the corner, so that he could enjoy a small moment of peace as he walked. Behind a hedge, Louie paused again. Tom would be surprised to see him. Probably not happy. That didn't matter, but Louie had to be prepared for it. He adjusted his suit, ran his hands over his head, and walked to the door.

'Louie!' said Tom. 'Er . . . Come in.' Tom didn't have a clue. He obviously thought Louie hadn't seen through him. 'Are you okay, mate?'

'I'm fine.'

'Can I get you something? I was just about to eat. I could heat up double. It's . . . it's good to see you.'

'No thanks.'

Tom's lounge was a mess. He'd paused a video game, the screen locked on an unconvincing cityscape seen through the windscreen of a pink car. To the right of the television, a sliding glass door opened on to a swimming pool and a grass tennis court.

'Sit anywhere,' Tom said. 'Just clear out the magazines. Are you sure everything's okay?'

'I'm here for a reason, man.'

'Okay.'

'The team can't carry on like this. You know you can stop it.'

Tom shrank back, but he'd brought this on himself. 'You got to let her go, Tom. It happened six weeks ago, it's in the past. You got to get past it. You got to stop the others ganging up on Will. We're a team, man.'

'I didn't ask them to do anything,' said Tom.

'You know you could stop them. Esther's a good woman. Don't you think she deserves some happiness?'

'Of course she does.'

'Well, back off her, man. You're ruining her life.'

'But . . . I've not said anything, but I can't help being afraid for her. I'm scared he's using her, and she'll get hurt.'

'You're jealous, man. She doesn't need you confusing her. You've done it for too long.'

'But. Yes, I know. I'm sorry. I'll . . . I'll stop.'

'I've come out here to make sure you do. I want you to tell the others. It's time to leave her alone. Let her move on.'

'I will. I'm sorry, Louie. I promise I will.' Tom seemed ready to agree to almost anything, which proved he was in the wrong. Louie didn't have anything else to say, and he stood up. 'Is that it?' said Tom.

'It's all I had to say. Now it's up to you.'

'Are you busy? I was going to watch a video, and I really am just heating up food – I've got loads. It's the chicken curry. I could call Seung and Fliss – I'm pretty sure they're not doing anything.' Louie had the same curry at his house. Every few days, the kitchens at Kilburn Park sent the players home with meals in boxes and bags. Part of Louie thought of staying, but it would compromise his message, and this was all about the good of the team. He said he had some things to do. As he showed Louie out, Tom said, 'I'm really sorry, mate. I honestly didn't realise. I'm such a twat, I'm sorry, but I'll sort it out.'

'Good,' said Louie. He was right to leave, because it showed Tom how serious he was. He drove home with an empty sense of a job well done.

Two days later, after some light set-piece work, Dirk Volendam hauled Louie aside. 'What did you say to Tom?' Dirk demanded.

'Don't push me around, man. Don't mess with me.'

'Don't be scared. I have sworn never to use my special training.'

'What special training?'

'Never mind. What did you say to him?'

'We're a team, man. We can't fight over a woman. I told him to let her go.'

'Let her go?'

'He's ruining her life. She could be happy with Will.'

Dirk looked at Louie in disbelief. 'Are you serious?' he asked.

'Deadly serious. She's a good kid —'

'Shut up. You know Tom. How can you?' Dirk explained the story of Will and Tom from a completely different angle. It made sense of what Louie thought about Tom, but if it was right, then Will was lying to him; which was inconceivable. Louie didn't know what to think, but he wasn't going to let it rest. None of these people were honest to each other, so there was this area of doubt in which distrust and intolerance could arise. He needed every side of the story, and then he'd sort it out.

He went to Will, who said, 'Of course, Dirk would say that, wouldn't he?'

He went to Esther, who said that she and Will were perfect together, and they had known for nearly two years now. She completely forgave him for sleeping with 26 because, after all, he wasn't a saint, and it was only until the time was right for them to be together. He asked about Tom, and she got angry. 'Tom's got a vendetta against Will just because Will's the better man. I didn't realise but Tom has always been passive aggressive. He was always hanging around, suffocating me, making it impossible for me to speak to anyone else.'

Louie returned to Tom, who was horrified that he'd behaved so badly, even though he hadn't realised he was doing it.

Louie went back to Dirk, who said that this was all bullshit. Will had Esther on a string, and Esther used Tom because she was a selfish fucking bitch. Dirk was scary when he was angry, especially when he was trying to hide it.

On the pitch and in training, from enough of a distance, everything looked fine.

KSC couldn't officially change their name until the end of the season, but that didn't stop the transformation beginning, de facto. All new replica kit was initialled KU – the comma was unworkable – and the manufacturer sold old KSC stock to memorabilia enthusiasts, so no one lost out.

Socialist legends crawled out of the retirement-home woodwork to wail about betrayed heritage. Will and Louie were always present to explain that the new name said what the old name originally meant. Will repeatedly added, smiling his most reasonable smile, that the people who wanted to cling to 'Socialist' were like the old duffers who complained that 'gay' had been demeaned by its appropriation by the homosexuals. The storm was only in a teacup, and one positive side effect of doing it now, during this turbulent season, was that it would not be an issue hanging over the next one, when the club would be able to focus on the football again.

Louie proclaimed the united front with fervent intensity, but he seemed to be on edge every time Will spoke. Will congratulated him on how well he was doing, but suggested that he could tone things down a notch, maybe. It was vital that he sound convincing, which shouldn't be hard since this was his idea, but the Brits (Will laughed self-deprecatingly) couldn't deal with so much certainty at once, and they might think Louie was protesting too much. Louie bit his tongue.

The first reporter found his way to Nzasa. Dave walked straight to the school, phoned Sally and set in train the contingency plan he had prepared. Villagers and co-workers knew what to do, and the reporter got nothing but a polite refusal to comment. The reporter filed the next day, but his guns were spiked by Dave and Punty's dignified statement, in a competing paper, that they had explained that they didn't want any publicity and that they sincerely regretted that their privacy had been invaded. Any piece written by a visiting reporter had received no cooperation from them or from any member of Jed's outstanding organisation, with which they were proud to be associated.

Punty took this opportunity to finally reply to Sally's letter. *Thank you for your help about the reporter,* she wrote. *It's funny you talk about honesty, when you still live in the world of celebrity, where no one is honest at all. Being in Nzasa has made me understand about reality for the first time in my life. Dave has calmed down and stopped trying to explain all the time that KSC is a mission and that fundamentalism is inherently totalitarian, and all that Western bullshit. He is escaping from the need to be analytical all the time, and I can help him with that.*

Although I say thank you about the reporter, she added, *in my opinion, it would have been better for us to ignore him completely. It was Dave still clinging to the old world of image and all those things instead of letting it be. He's getting better, but he's not completely better yet. As for insensitivity and honesty, maybe Dave can be clumsy sometimes, but he isn't the one who lived a lie and then left her fiancé on the eve of their marriage.* Sally would have replied immediately, but she and Jed were on their honeymoon.

Tom told Zondi about Louie's visit. Zondi heard Louie's loneliness in the gaps between Tom's words, and Zondi was ashamed because the loneliness was obvious and it must have been for years. Zondi invited Louie for food one night, after training. Not a dinner party or anything formal, just food. Zondi cooked roast beef, because no one would expect that on a Wednesday. He wanted to cook the special beef that Achilles' father sent him still, but that was not halal.

Louie filled the doorway. He was in a black suit, of course, and under it, because it was casual, a black polo shirt. When he saw Tom, he said, 'I'm not here to be told off, man. I'm not a kid. I might have got it wrong about Esther, but I'm not —'

'Sorry, don't worry, no,' said Zondi. 'It is nothing like that. All it is, in all these years, I have not seen you ever aside from football. You are right what you say to Tom and the players. We should be a team, even though I am not ... We must look after each other. I ... There are other people coming. It is just food.' He was painfully awkward, worse than usual. This was going to be a disaster. He went to the kitchen, like a coward, but the doorbell saved him. He had thought very hard about who to invite to put Louie at his ease. Aisling might have been too much, somehow, as if he were making a point, so he settled on two young women he knew from St Brendan's. One of them organised the youth team, and she raved about Louie's Bangladeshi boys from Bethnal Green, so that was at least something for them to talk about. The other brought her husband, an ichthyologist, whose favourite thing was to meet new people and tell his stories about tuna. Zondi watched the Yorkshire puddings nervously through the oven's glass door, knowing there was nothing he could do for them now, that they would just have to make it on their own. He heard the other room start to liven up. Louie wasn't asking questions, but he was answering them more freely. When Zondi went to bed, the stars above his bed looked as if they were in the right place.

Ten days later, Tom invited Zondi to dinner, along with Louie, Seung and Fliss. When Seung arrived, and God knows how late he'd have been without the apologetic Fliss dragging him the sixty yards from their house, Zondi asked Seung what the possible menu included. Tom rolled his eyes. Seung said that KSC had sent them home with lasagne, beef bourguignon and a red prawn curry this week. Tom played along. He said that, who knows, he could have frozen something from last week, maybe the chicken pilaf or the salmon and pasta bake. Or maybe, just maybe, he might have made something himself. That got a big laugh. Zondi could see Louie trying to adjust to the banter, still after all this time.

Tom, in triumph, produced a fisherman's pie. Zondi immediately went through to the kitchen. It was gleaming, but there were no boxes. 'You'll find nothing, mate,' Tom said. 'A good cook always cleans up after himself. First rule.'

Zondi asked, 'Is this nutmeg?' and, 'How do you get the cod so delicate but keep it from crumbling?' and Tom replied that he wasn't going to give away his secrets. Tom, Seung and Fliss found Zondi's refusal to let go hilarious. Zondi felt a foot on top of his. It was Louie, who gave him a warning, almost a wink. Then, suddenly, Louie sat bolt upright, eyes fixed on his fork. 'This is a scallop, man!' he said. 'It is not halal.'

Tom's face went white. 'Jesus,' he said. 'I told the chef it needed to be halal. I'm so sorry. What can I —' Louie was grinning. 'You bastard. You absolute bastard. Yeah, okay. I got the chef to do it, but she only agreed because I'm so charming, and she gave me three options, so it's not like I had no input. You've got to admit I had you going. You're such a bastard, Louie.'

Driving back towards Kilburn, after a silence, Louie said, 'I suppose it's my turn next?'

'Oh no,' said Zondi. 'It's not like that —'

'Okay, man, okay, I'm sorry. I didn't —'

'This is not about turns, I mean. We are friends. If you want us to come round, we will enjoy it very much.' Louie was quiet, unsure. Zondi kicked his mental head for his carelessness. Three evenings later, he knocked on Louie's door. 'I saw your light on,' he said. Louie was in suit trousers and a white T-shirt.

'Would you like a coffee?' Louie said. Zondi paused. 'Not if you don't want to . . .'

They went inside. 'Thank you,' said Zondi. 'What are you writing?'

'I'm thinking about marriage,' said Louie.

Louie's untouched home made Zondi so sad that he almost drank the instant coffee. In the end, he compromised by not saying anything, and just left it on the floor getting cold. He persuaded himself that this was better than drinking it, because it proved he had only visited to see his friend. Louie said he didn't like what was happening to Kilburn, but he couldn't explain. He was angry with Will Beauchamp because of Esther and Tom, and he wanted to believe that this was not what Will was really like, that it was only because of love, which made men do strange things, but Louie didn't sound convinced.

Another dinner, not long after, cooked by Zondi, fussy and delicious. It was ostensibly in honour of Aisling finally becoming a registrar – she'd be at the Charing Cross for six months – but really it was Zondi trying to introduce Louie into their circle. Aisling was amused that Zondi had adopted Louie as a project, but she was on her best behaviour while the American was in the room, even when he told everyone why 'Kilburn United' was better than 'Kilburn Social Club'. He explained with excruciating clarity that it was a name that said what it meant. Adam asked Aisling what she thought, but Nicky changed the subject before she could answer.

Later, with Louie gone and Leo watching *Newsnight*, Aisling nibbled spare delicacies while Nicky crashed around at the sink and Zondi flustered nervously behind her. Aisling said, 'I tell you who I think would be good for Louie, I thought it about halfway through tonight. Did you meet Monica Dylan ever? There's definitely something —'

'Where's Jeremy?' said Nicky loudly, as if Aisling weren't speaking. 'I'm just asking.'

'I think he's working.'

'You *think*?'

'We don't live in each other's pockets. We're both busy.' It was folly to think the reg job would get Nicky off her back.

Nicky turned round, and stood with hand on hip, in a pose Aisling once christened the Nicky the Irritating Teapot. 'While I'm speaking my mind, for once,' she said, 'I'm really annoyed with you, Adam.' Adam had been sitting quietly in the corner with his cup of tea, and he was off balance. 'You know what I mean.'

'I really don't.'

'Azza's doing brilliantly keeping out of Kilburn stuff, and you kept trying to bring her into it all night.'

'I asked her one question.'

'You shouldn't still be at the club. It's impossible for her to make a clean break until you leave.'

'It's fine, Nicky,' said Aisling. 'Don't make a big thing of it.'

'How many times have I told you that Kilburn's the best thing that's ever happened to me?' said Adam.

He didn't deflect Nicky. 'You said you were powerless. You said you hate what's happening. It's time for you to break whatever this emotional tie is, you and Aisling both.'

Aisling told Adam later that she was fine, and she thought that was that.

Middlesbrough won the league, Everton snatched a Champions League spot and Cardiff had to be satisfied with the FA Cup. Kilburn's mid-season slump ruined any chance of a European place but, everything considered, eighth was respectable enough. There were enough flashes of brilliance from Vlocker and Cole for the fans to be confident about next season.

Adam heard through the grapevine that the FA needed someone to oversee their business-development unit, especially with another round of Panther negotiations coming up. He applied for the job and he got it. 'You don't have to jump because Nicky says, "Jump!"' said Aisling. 'You don't have to do this for me.'

'I'm not doing it for you.'

'If you're leaving Kilburn, why not go outside football? It's all fucked.'

'I don't think it is. It doesn't have to be. I can do more for Kilburn at the FA than I can working with Donald and Esther. I feel responsible for what happens at Kilburn Park, but with the FA it feels like someone else has buggered up, and I might be able to help. Does that make any sense?'

'Are you serious?'

'Yes. This is a great job, which I want to do. Helping you out is a bonus.'

'Thank you,' said Aisling, but she felt betrayed.

*

Sheriff Road
1 June 2003

Dear Punty,

I don't want to get into an argument with you, and I'm sorry for not writing back sooner, but Jed and I have been travelling.

On the subject of me and Dave splitting up: yes, that was awful how it happened, and I am sure it must have hurt him very much, but it was the right thing to do and it was an honest mistake. I had not understood what I wanted before. Think if I had said nothing and it had happened later, when we were married and maybe with children? Everything would have been even more terrible then, and we'd have been even more unhappy. Dave and I were very good friends who fancied each other. I never knew what love could be until I met Jed, and when you meet the One, you know it. You say you love Dave, but is he the One? If you can even consider coming home without it tearing you apart, then he can't be. It is not a criticism to say that you are emotionally immature perhaps. You remind me of Aisling. I have seen her a couple of times recently (she wants my friend Monica to go on a date with one of the Socialists is why she got in touch, but Monica will never let someone else set her up!). I think I will never exactly be friends with Aisling, but I understand her. I hadn't noticed it myself, and I am not a class warrior or anything, but Monica pointed something out the other evening (she said it to Aisling's face when we met up! Monica has no fear!). She said that you and Aisling are both beautiful girls who have never had to work for anything in your lives. You are both lovely people, and Monica means that because she never says anything she doesn't mean, but you need to learn that life is a struggle for other people. You cannot behave as if all your decisions are right just because you are the one who is making them and no one has ever criticised you for being selfish before. Aisling said she could understand what Monica meant, and that it had taken her a lot of time and experience to learn things. You have to be honest with Dave. To be truly in love with someone is not just a matter of feeling you need to be with him the whole time, and 'needing' each other, and being 'passionate'. You have to share his outlook, so that you can get through the hard times.

I felt the 'passion' with Jed, but we share each other's 'outlooks' also. I can't explain, and it's something I never felt with Dave, however close I was to him. Can you honestly say you and Dave want the same thing? Are you sure he is not agreeing with you on the surface, but using his agreements to weave a cocoon he thinks he will be safe in, but inside which he is someone completely different, struggling to get out. That was what he was like with me. You must be honest with yourself. You mustn't say you love him if actually you don't and you think it is going to end, because he might think that it means you want to be with him for ever. I'm saying this all as a friend, I honestly am.

You say that everything in Africa is real compared to the celebrity world, but one of the things Dave taught me is that all our worlds are real, if we are honest about who we are in them. It's a cheap shot to say someone with no material things has a more real life than someone rich. They are different lives, but they are both real, with wants and aspirations. One might be easier, I know, and luckier, but it is still real. Does Dave talk about this with you? If he doesn't, think about why this might be maybe.

Aisling and Monica got along very well when they met, which is funny because they used to not be able to stand each other. I think it's because they both swear so much! But also, Aisling is still troubled, which comes from her terrible sadness from years ago when she felt she couldn't bear Dave's child, but she is making progress and coming closer to understanding herself. That is the important thing I am trying to say. You have to understand <u>yourself</u> before you can understand other people.

So, let's be friends. If you are going to stay with Dave, you must stay with him. If you are not, and this is not a criticism, you must tell him so that he understands where he is. Otherwise, you are only looking after him while it _suits you_. Married life is wonderful, but it has to be with the _right man_.

Think about it, and be careful.

Love,

Sally

BOOKENDS

Keats Grove
4/12/03

Dear David,
I might look like a little slip of a thing, David Guinevere, but I am brave and strong, and the reason I know this is that I got through the fucking Christmas Party without killing my sister or any of the other people I wanted to kill, who were, believe me, legion.

Yes, yes, I know, the Christmas Party. What was I doing there, you wonder, since I've barely mentioned football since Adam jumped ship for the FA? Well, it was Hank's fault. He gets tickets, natch, and he somehow doesn't seem to have noticed that I haven't been to any games this year, or that I no longer discuss Kilburn at RG Committee. Out of the blue, a fortnight before the dinner, I got home and he was stuffing something through my letterbox. It was good to see him, he's so lovely, and it was pissing down and he was in his funny navy coat and oilskin hat (he looked, now I drag it into my mind's eye, quite a lot like Paddington Bear). I pulled him inside, anyway, and opened the letter. He was bright red by now. It was an invitation to join him at the dinner, but it was weird. Let me go and get it – I can't remember the words. Here it is. It said, 'Your family has been very generous to an old man, and it is a poor gift in return for me to give you the offer of my companionship for the evening of the Kilburn Christmas Party this year. It is an even poorer gift for someone so much in your debt to insist that you accept my gift, but I do insist. I have always your interests at heart, as the Rosslares are dearer to me than anything now that Abigail has gone before.' You've never seen anything so cute (he's got beautiful handwriting, by the way), and he stood there wringing his oil hat. I had to say yes.

So there it was – I was going to the Party. Nicky the Irritating Teapot was predictably irate. I told her that I can hardly pretend that Kilburn doesn't exist, and at some point I had to face up to it.

It's like the first meeting with an ex-boyfriend, I said, and the more I think about it, the more I think that's a good analogy. When I told Jeremy, he did a sad wise face as if I was a silly thing who will learn what's good for her in the end. I really don't know why I'm still going out with him. We have a perfectly nice time, and he's attentive and caring and all that, but it's not going anywhere. I've probably only kept on so long because otherwise Nicky would have said I didn't give it a fair chance. Anyway, Jeremy knew what he was getting into.

Also, the new job is a nightmare. It's good to be back at the Royal Free, but A & E is so gruelling, and it's no better now than it was when I was an SHO. This is definitely the last time I'm doing it. So, I was actually looking forward to the Party, just to do something different.

It was unfuckingbelievable. I prepared by doing a crash course in what's happened at Kilburn since the summer. I don't know if I am your only source for club news (Zondi?), but the season started dreadfully, and about three weeks ago the manager got the boot. He was replaced by Billy Krenabim, if you can imagine such a thing (I admit, I had heard this before I did my crash course – you'd have had to have lived in a cave not to).

In the light of this, darling Esther decides we need some great display of unity, to remind the world what Kilburn is all about, as if the fuck-up and traducing of the club isn't basically the doing of her and her fuckwit new husband. Consequently, we all get a letter two weeks before the dinner telling us that 'in this Difficult Time' (I am not making up the capitals) it is up to us, as Women, to show our Menfolk (Menfolk!) how to stand tall. We are all told to report to Esther's fucking dressmaker, because she thinks it would be a Powerful Symbol for us to wear Matching Outfits. I phoned Esther to tell her what I thought of this, and she said that most of the girls had already made their appointments, and they thought it was a brilliant idea, and what kind of message would I be sending out if I didn't do it too? That I thought I was better than everyone, that's what! And, she said, that would be okay by Esther, because then Everyone would Know (and this time I'm adding the capitals, but she fucking pronounced them).

The worst thing is, she was right. You can't be the only one wearing something (or not) without everyone looking at you. I thought of ducking out, but there's something about Hank. I bit the bullet and made an appointment.

I'm not going to give you even three guesses what we were wearing: the same brown dresses Esther wore five years ago, with numbers and, grim, grimmer, grimmest, the names of our partners on the back. Those of us with non-playing dates had to choose our own numbers. I was in the shop with some idiot girl who said she was sooo jealous 'cause I could pick 69! Which would be sooo funny! I chose 72, because that's when I was born, and what can you do? (Incidentally, Donald's wife – you know they got married in July, the week after Esther and Will? – chose 69, much to the general glee. It didn't stop D trying to grope every girl in the room, and they had their usual fight.)

(D's a rat-faced twat, but he's good at his job. He was hanging out with Strabis, who was crapping on about how impressed he was by Donald's decision-making. He also praised Donald for being able to 'see past the pointless aspects of the Kilburn heritage'. He was trying to needle me, and he was staring at me to see how I'd react, but I didn't give him the satisfaction. It was water off a duck's back anyway. It's his club now and he's welcome to it. The Group's what I care about, and even Adam admits that Donald is doing a decent job there.)

Esther made a grisly and rambling speech about how moved everyone had been by the tributes and silences held on the anniversary of Achilles' death. She even paid tribute to you, saying you had shown your devotion to the Kilburn Ethos by trying to atone by working for charity. She basically repeated that Calum article I told you about, right down to a tearful bit about the broken-hearted Zondi, whose dignity showed everyone the meaning of True Love. I'm not saying she hadn't worked herself into a pitch of genuine sincerity, but it was still excruciating.

The one positive thing that came out of the evening was that Louie might be getting together with Monica, though, to be honest, it'll be more vice versa if it happens. Zondi and I were right that they'd hit it off (and Sally was wrong, incidentally, not that I get competitive when anyone questions my judgment!). They seem very different, but they got on brilliantly. Louie avoided preaching,

Monica didn't say anything inflammatory, and they persuaded themselves that they were the only straight-talking people in the room. I don't know if it's going anywhere, but I hope so. Not just because I'm competitive. In a way, this is more about them than it is about me.

I love Esther, she's my sister, but I basically hate almost everything she ever does. Her dress didn't even say, 'Beauchamp', it said, 'Mrs Skipper'. If you're the one who's different, you're the one who everyone notices, blah. She can't be more of a twat since they got married, but she seems more of one. Slimy Will seems more slimy. He touches people all the time in this creepy way that he thinks is masterful because it's gentle. If he isn't unfaithful to her within a year, I'll eat my dress, and it won't be much loss, because it's not as if I'm ever going to wear it again.

Oh good grief, almost forgot. Talking of touching – when Tom arrived with his date, some perfectly nice girl, Esther went straight over to them and gave him a big hug and held his hand while she talked earnestly to him about something, all without acknowledging the poor girl at all. Tom was mortified and he didn't know what to do. I went and dragged Esther away on a pretext that I suspect was brilliant but whose details I forget, at which point she said I was completely immature and couldn't I understand that former lovers could be just good friends with no baggage.

It was funny, and you know which way I mean, to be at the dinner and Dirk not be there (you know we've loaned him to Spencer?). The team has always changed. You, Zondi, Achilles (I'm crying about him again, like I do every time I don't just say the word but let myself think for a moment, and I bet you are too now I've said it) were much bigger changes, but you three left in such a huge way. Dirk just suddenly wasn't there one day. He was one of the guys as long as I remember, and now he's gone and you don't realise how much he'd been there when he was there. Torquil hung around Tom at the party like a great lost elephant child.

Zondi's dog is still funny. That's all I'm saying because I know I've said it before, and there's no way to explain unless you've seen her.

You were right about the anniversary of Achilles' death. I was very careful not to say anything about it, just went to Zondi's and ate with him quietly. He said he only realised about the date last week, and he thanked me for my kindness. Thank fuck Esther didn't have a minute's silence at the dinner.

Oh. Another thing I couldn't not know before the dinner, however much I've been avoiding Kilburn, is the latest misery from the KU Football Club's merchandising machine. It's a clothing range with the slogan 'FCKU'. I hate to admit this, and I hate the idea, but it's pretty clever and it's worked like a charm if all you want to do is sell shirts and pretend that you're doing it for the sake of the billionth of a per cent that goes to the Foundation.

They are already gearing up for the general election. It's beyond tedious. You can talk about clashing ideologies all you want, and I'm sure that's what Tanganyika's like, but if you can tell the difference between the candidates here, you're a better man than I am. Calum (God rot him) put it well actually (I can't believe I always read his column). He said they've run so hard towards the middle ground that it's like they clashed and fused into a completely indistinguishable two-headed mass with one brain and two faces. Calum's obsessed with the end-of-history idea, like I said, and I know you don't like it, but from here it doesn't seem stupid.

I'm glad the Sharks won this round of the beach-football league, and not just because I know they are secretly your favourites. I like the sound of the one-legged kid who's their manager. You seem really settled out there, and that's a good thing. Do you think you'll ever come back?

I'd better send this – the sick need healing.

Love,

Aisling

*

Four months before the Christmas Party, back in the summer, Adam arrived at the FA. He spent a couple of weeks feeling his way around. From the outside, he had found it hopelessly in thrall to the big clubs (like Kilburn) and he joined to help change that, if he could. His new colleagues said he was dreaming. They could barely get the Premiership fuckers to come to the table, let alone strong-arm them into doing anything contrary to their own narrow interests, even with the situation in the lower leagues so desperate. It looked as if a couple of second-division teams would go into receivership this year. If football was a good thing, which Adam firmly believed, then at least part of that must be in not letting these poor relations fall by the wayside. He toured troubled pitchsides in small Scottish towns and on the Fens, and he developed a picture of football finance that was very different to his hands-on experience. Armed with this, and knowing precisely how little he'd be asking the big boys to sacrifice, he was ready to talk to the clubs. He started, logically, with the new Bursar of Kilburn, a middle-aged woman, slightly overweight, but very appealing in a short-haired, mumsy way. She was unbelievably defensive. She said, 'Esther Rosslare has prepared me well, I'm afraid you'll find.'

'Excuse me?'

'She said you'd ask me to make Kilburn a leader, and get the club to do uneconomic things for the good of other clubs who should learn to be more efficient. You couldn't get KU to do it when you were here, and you can't push us around from within the FA, I'm afraid you'll find.'

'I don't want to get off on the wrong foot.'

'Nor do I, Mr Greswell. So long as you realise that Kilburn United is a well-run business, we shan't have any problems.'

'There's nothing wrong in taking a lead, sometimes.'

'I'm afraid you'll find, Mr Greswell, that it's the front soldier gets the sword.'

Adam knew enough about organisations to know that durable change requires painstaking effort. Adam learned his new colleagues' ways and prejudices, and they were impressed with him. He got on particularly well with the Governance Director, a former lawyer from Perth whose route into football had been as circuitous as Adam's. She was furious about the game's murky corners, and extremely patient as she cast light on them. 'Complete change, these past ten years,' she said. 'I got here in 2000 and the stories from the old hands would have frozen your blood. It's better now, but there are still crooks like Krenabim around.' Corruption was better than it had been, but there were still fortunes changing hands in baroque deals involving 'agents' who did nothing but who happened to be the manager's son, or cousin, or whatever. In November, when Kilburn appointed Krenabim as their new manager, the Governance Director made Adam feel like it was his fault. 'All this work we do, and idiots like you and the BBC keep hiring him as if he's endearing! We should drum bastards like that out of the game. I can't believe you let them do it.' She was venting, but Adam was still embarrassed. 'You should warn Kilburn about him. He'll cost them.'

In December, Salford, Vale Athletic and Newcastle Town all went into receivership. They had fought hard, each buoyed by the other's fingertip survival, but once one went, they all went. Adam did what he could for them. Cardiff's Chief Executive said they had failed because of incompetence, but some other chairmen and clubs were more generous. Everton lent Vale a million pounds, interest free, along with three of their youth squad. Actual, visible, tangible financial failure made fans around the country think differently about rumours that their clubs were short of cash.

Adam didn't do anything about Krenabim until the Governance Director told him that Billy Krenabim's nephew was going to be paid three hundred thousand pounds for sitting on a phone in Clapham when Acol Mutrix finalised his move from Tampa Freebooters in January. During an evening game at Kilburn Park, with Zondi as moral support, he spoke to the Bursar for the second time. 'How good's Mutrix?' he asked.

'I'm afraid you'll find that it's not really your business, is it, Mr Greswell?'

'I'm still a Kilburn fan.'

'In that case you will know that Mutrix is the brightest young star in the American game.'

'He's very young.'

'I'm afraid you'll find that Mr Krenabim knows what he's doing.'

'How do you know how he's going to develop? He sounds very arrogant. He says he won't be happy in the reserves, but he's obviously not going to be up to playing in the Premiership yet.'

'I didn't know you were such an expert, Mr Greswell, compared to the former England manager.'

'That's not what I'm saying.'

'Mr Krenabim says you have to speculate to accumulate. You have to take a few risks to get one superstar.'

'He's taken a lot of risks, is all I'm saying. We've got the biggest squad in the Premiership.'

'Are you lecturing me?'

'No. It's just that with the broader financial situation in football, I worry about paying so much in wages.'

'You can leave your worries at the door when you come here, I'm afraid. You can worry about getting us more money from Panther instead of giving handouts to little clubs like Stockport, can't you?' Adam thought back to what he must have been like after five months at Kilburn, and shuddered.

Zondi watched Adam talk to the Bursar, trying his best. He was sorry for his friend. He also saw Esther approaching, and he joined Adam before it happened, not that he would be able to help. 'Oh!' said Esther brightly. 'A secret meeting! How exciting.' Her head darted, full of cunning accusation, like /*Kagga*, the sister of /*Kaggen*, who thinks she is so clever but everybody pities her.

'Congratulations,' said Zondi.

'Of course, I haven't seen you since the wedding! Yes, isn't it beautiful?' she said, holding up her sparkling hand. 'They're South African,' she added.

'Oh,' said Zondi. 'Good.'

'So, to what do we owe this pleasure? What's the big secret?'

'There's no secret,' said Adam.

'Good,' said Esther. 'There shouldn't be any secrets. After all, I run the club!'

'Adam was offering financial advice,' said the Bursar.

'No, no, no. I'm sure he was very persuasive, but I know what's going on!' Esther went up a tone. 'I knew something like this was happening, and I've been waiting for you to come out in the open. This scheming is going to stop right now.'

'We're not scheming.'

'I'm not stupid. Why have you come here behind my back if you're not scheming?' Poor /*Kagga*. Even when she was right she turned people against her, like when she told the stuck-shape people after the Sundering that they would die of thirst unless they threw spears at their mother, the Rain. 'Do you think Will and I don't know what you're doing?'

Zondi looked at the floor.

'Honestly, Esther —' Adam said.

'Don't. I knew you'd turn Tom against me, but now you and Aisling have got Louie in your little net.'

'This is nothing to do with Aisling.'

'It's pathetic. Louie was completely on board with me and Will. Kilburn United was his idea, but now suddenly he has all these doubts, and he's Tom's best friend, and you're having cosy little dinners all the time. Do you think I'm blind?' said Esther.

'I'm sorry that you feel like this,' said Adam. 'I am simply worried, as a Kilburn fan, that you're spending more than you can afford. It's the first time since Manus arrived that the club's running in the red.'

'Mr Kinsale has made the funds available to Billy Krenabim.'

'I know, but the result is you *need* Kinsale now. You can't get by without his money. That's a very risky position to be in.'

'Strabis Kinsale is a very generous owner, and trusts us to make the football decisions, unlike some.' Adam had said what he had to say, so now they could leave. Zondi thought that Adam might possibly have been grateful for his support, even though it was silent and useless.

On Boxing Day, Aisling went to La Thuile with the friends she'd skied with every year since going to Oxford, who didn't include Nicky, thank God, who tried it once and broke her arm. She didn't ask Jeremy, because the relationship was on its last legs and it wouldn't be fair to encourage him. She was unbelievably tired after the first six weeks of this A & E rotation, and she didn't make things better by spending her nights having a pointless affair with one of the ski party, a fund manager based in Lucerne.

When you're skiing, you can think a lot. You can think, for instance, that if great sex with a decent guy is making you feel like shit, you should probably not be doing it. You can wonder what it means about your sickly relationship with a boyfriend you've not treated very well. You can also think about the football club that you haven't been able to get out of your mind since you went to its miserable Christmas Party, and speculate that this kind of obsession isn't helping you in any way. You can compare your relationships with both boyfriend and football club and wonder how critical their conditions are, how responsible you are for them, and what you can do to revive them. You can remember how you once thought that your job, as a doctor, was to try to save people however critical their condition, and to carry on trying until there's no hope left, but that you've come to realise that being a doctor sometimes means knowing when you can't help. You can decide that fighting for a relationship is within your powers, but fighting for a football club would be a doomed and destructive gesture-slash-leap-in-the-dark that would consume resources that you simply don't have.

And then, having made this decision, you can return to your boyfriend and grind on for busy, knackered months. You can turn up to vote in early May, having been convinced by Dave that Labour's inevitable re-election is a good thing and not the result of a choice between two cut-outs listening to the same focus groups. A week later, finally free of your nightmarish job in A & E, you can feel the weight disappear from your shoulders as you board the plane for Aspen, to go skiing again with the same people and without the same people. But this time you do not feel so embattled, and you can resist the fund manager, and you can sleep, glorious sleep. In spite of this, you are skiing again, and the memory of the last time and all its decisions and revisions are clear in your mind. You can think you were right about abandoning the football club, whatever Strabis Kinsale says about your heritage, because there's nothing you can do, but you can recognise that your decision to stay with your boyfriend was a decision made by someone who decided she was too busy to make a change that needed making, and that's a ridiculous way to go about anything. So when you return to a baking day in early June, you can be ready to do what must be done. Also, you can feel guilty that it's taken you so long to do this, and you would be right to. You can arrive last thing at night, have a brief conversation with your doomed boyfriend, arrange to meet him tomorrow, and sleep like the wind.

When Aisling woke, she thought she felt fresher then she'd felt for years, and she went to the first day of her new rotation at the Charing Cross. One of her new colleagues had birthday drinks, and she couldn't not go, at least for the start. She lost track of the time. When she reached the restaurant, shiny in the sultry evening, Jeremy had been waiting for twenty minutes. 'I don't mind,' he said. She ordered lamb and he had his usual monkfish. He asked about the new job. She said it was fine and asked about his, looking straight through him, waiting for the right moment. 'Sorry?'

'I said, "You're not listening." What are you thinking about?'

'It's nothing. I was listening. You were talking about the client fancying the solicitor.' He couldn't catch her out that easily, but it put her on her guard. 'I saw the PM on *Newsnight* yesterday,' she said. 'He was good.'

'Really?' said Jeremy. "What happened to the 'identical politicians all listening to the same focus groups'?"

'I said that months ago!' Aisling replied. 'I then spent weeks saying that I'd realised it was bullshit.'

'Not to me.'

'Are you sure? I really thought we talked about it.'

'We didn't. We never talk about anything you care about.' She said that it must have been because she was so busy, but it wasn't much of a defence. Whenever they had a disagreement, Jeremy positioned himself as the plaintiff, made it obvious that she was guilty, and then forgave her. Because she was usually guilty, she had to take it with good grace. 'Why did you change your mind?' he said. 'Was it a letter from Dave?' Oh. She should have seen that coming. Jeremy was setting her up.

'Please don't get jealous. Dave explained something and I agreed with him. It's a sign of my great maturity that I don't always have to be right,' she laughed. Jeremy didn't.

'We never talk about football, either.'

'Uh?'

'Say what you like to other people, Ash, but I know you've thought of trying to rescue Kilburn. Why did you never talk to me about it?'

'I never thought about that. Not really.'

'We both know that's not true, but I will say this – you have to let it go. There's nothing you can do. If you were ever in a battle with Strabis, then Strabis has won it. Getting Kilburn back is a fantasy. If you try to do it, you'll be abdicating your responsibility to live in the real world. There, I've said it.'

'That's exactly what Dave would say,' said Aisling, which brought Jeremy up short, but that was the first and only point she'd scored all night, and it was cheap. 'I'm sorry,' she said. 'We've got to talk.' She started by telling him about the affair in La Thuile. She hoped that he would dump her, because she couldn't think how to end it herself without saying things that made her sound like a bitch. She thought that this was kindness.

Jeremy smiled sadly and said, 'I knew about him, Ash. I'm not an idiot.'

'Didn't you care?'

'Of course I cared, but we both know that you've never committed yourself to this relationship. If you had, then it would have been different.'

Aisling was angry that he took her infidelity so lightly. 'What kind of a person do you think I am?' she asked. 'Do you assume I sleep with anyone?'

'I assume you don't know what you want. I don't think you're a bad person.'

'Could you be any more patronising?'

'I've been waiting a long time for this conversation, Ash.'

'Why?'

'Because you weren't ready for it until now, and you're worth it.' Aisling didn't know what to say. 'I'm your friend,' said Jeremy. 'I've been watching you sleepwalk, and have all kinds of nightmares, and I've been waiting for you to come out of it. I can be your rock, if you'll let me. You can't see it, but you need something to cling to. That can be me.'

'I presumed you'd dump me,' Aisling said.

'You hoped I would, you mean. I'm not letting you go that easily, but it's time for a change, darl. It's time for you to see you've been running around for too long with no idea where you're going. You need someone who can give you the strength you need to stay still. You need to get rid of the silly stuff, and concentrate on what matters.'

'I . . .' said Aisling, but he put a finger to her lips.

'No. I want you to have time to think before you say anything else. I look at you, I see a frightened girl. I don't want that girl to say anything hasty that she might regret or be too proud to take back. You need a rock. You always have. Think about it and you'll see. I'll go home tonight, and give you some space.' He removed his finger, reached down and squeezed her hand. They danced an awkward gavotte over payment and goodbyes. Jeremy hailed a cab and offered it to Aisling, but she said she'd take the tube. He climbed in and headed for Fulham. The night was suffocating, the air fit to burst. Aisling wanted to be walking near her flat and for the rain to drench her.

She was on the steps down into the station when a swollen drop hit her foot. She swivelled and ascended, ignoring the surprised looks from those who had hurried gratefully for shelter. The slow plocking of the first fat rain was unbearable, each droplet splashing into a visible little crown. The air smelled tropical, and she threw back her shoulders and strolled alongside Green Park, the pavement deserted. She didn't head for the corridor of sheltering plane trees in the park, because this was not about running away. The rain teased, dying, then started again. She didn't flinch from the drops on her face because she had tensed herself not to. There were still dry patches on the flags, but then, suddenly, from every side, lightning flashed and thunder rolled and, as if the sky had never been closed, she was soaked to the skin. The splatter around her feet was so intense that it felt like she was walking in two inches of water, and the air was so saturated that she could hardly breathe. On her right, cars, their engines muted by the rain and the walls of splashing spray they sent up at her; on her left, the rain's thud into thirsty earth. She smoothed her hair back once, and it was plastered against her scalp. Her bag swung nonchalantly against her side. She could replace the book tomorrow.

I've felt guilty about this affair all these months, she exaggerated, *and he doesn't care! Or is it that he forgives me? Is that kind of forgiveness a good thing? Do I really need a rock?* She had never thought like this before.

Taxis slowed down in the corner of her eye, but she ignored them. Someone walking in the rain like this could look bedraggled and desperate, but she beaconed assurance. Lightning forked straight ahead of her, thunder crunched behind, and then thunder and lightning crashed together. Involuntarily, in the first wisp of noticeable breeze, she shivered.

He had said they never talked about the things she really cared about. And there, right there, was the rub. What did Aisling care about? What did she think about alone at night? Aisling thought about Dave, and she thought about Kilburn, two things she couldn't control, and she could care all she liked about them, but they didn't care about her.

She was wearing silver sandals with little heels, and the sole of her right foot slipped against the slick leather and she went over on her ankle. Not badly, but badly enough to stop her for a moment, and turn her round, since she was at Hyde Park Corner already. Not so badly she couldn't hide it too, though now she had to concentrate to saunter. The last thing she needed at this moment was a fucking prince riding to her aid. She also didn't need the slow drive-by and leering hoot. She wouldn't believe people didn't know how to behave, she thought they just chose not to. Walking towards the tube was completely different from walking the other way. The rain was more mundane and pushed clumps of hair forward and over her face. Aisling didn't let it change the easy shape of her stride, and tilted back her head. She could have stopped a taxi, but for some reason that would have felt like she was screaming for a prince, so she went underground. Her soaked top looked painted on, and even if it didn't, every man there would still have given her at least a second look, but she stood as if she were alone in a minor art gallery she was visiting out of duty to a friend.

A young couple lit cigarettes and stood defiantly. Aisling walked over, unaggressive, and said that smoking wasn't allowed on the tube any more. There was enough of a crowd to make her feel safe, but she liked to think she'd have done it if there hadn't been. The couple stubbed the cigarettes out, surprised at themselves. Aisling gave a grateful smile and returned to her place.

The train came quickly. If she was the girl Esther thought she was, Aisling would have soaked a seat. It wasn't a long journey anyway. She refused to inspect her book, but she took her eyeline out of those of the other passengers and looked at her reflection in the door. The lipstick was fine but the mascara had run, making a dark mess of her eyes. It was quite rock star, or sluttish, like something you might see in a photo shoot, but not something Aisling would have ever done deliberately, because it would be a lie. Jeremy was a decent man, and he might have been graceless in company but was that really import-ant compared to the fact that he was always there for her? However independent you thought you were, there came a point when you realised you were not an island, and recognising this was not an admis-sion of weakness. She would commit properly to Jeremy, the result of an active choice rather than choosing not to choose, and she would give the experiment six months, during which period she would not dream idly or plan exit strategies, and during which she would work on the compromises that would be needed for her to love him. Maybe this was what she needed. Aisling turned back into the carriage, and straightened her left leg, taking the weight off her ankle and cocking her hips, pretending not to notice the frank stare of the old guy nearest her. She had goosebumps and the water was puddling around her feet.

The 2004–5 season was fast approaching. Esther showered, and dressed in black. She put on her glasses, looked in the mirror approvingly, and took them off. They were a brilliant idea of Will's, even though she didn't need them. He got her to try on a pair one evening when they were out for dinner with some of his friends, and he said they made her look more authoritative (and sexy, not that that mattered!). He wondered if a pair might help her at work. People did seem to treat her in a more businesslike way now. She put them back on, re-entered the bedroom and kissed Will. He didn't ravish her. She didn't have time to be ravished anyway. The car picked her up. It wasn't a long walk to the ground, but she was in heels, and she'd earned the few perks that went with all the hard work. The chauffeur said something about something, but she took out her papers and sipped busily from her vacuum coffee mug to show she hadn't even had time for breakfast, so she certainly couldn't chat today.

The car wasn't moving but Esther wasn't really in a hurry. Today, she hoped, would be a huge day! She took off her shoes, and pressed into the soft carpet, slipping her feet inside the sheer of her stockings. Outside, people scurried and bumped, trying to catch up with their lives. It was so messy. Life was about being prepared, one step ahead, and she had finally got there. The car window was like a magnifying glass or a television screen showing images from a smaller, more primitive world.

The car reached Kilburn Park, spat out its passenger, and sped underground to park and drink irritated tea. Esther stood for a moment looking up at the great sheer cliff of the North Stand, swathed in scaffolding. Some of the original brick would have to stay, because it was part of the club's history, but there would be a gleaming glass superstructure to house the new restaurant and hospitality areas, as well as the . . . the . . . Esther was almost embarrassed to think the words, but she smiled. The old white letters which had spelled out 'KILBURN PARK, HOME OF THE KILBURN SOCIAL CLUB' had been sold off in an auction which had raised thousands and thousands of pounds to be shared between the Social Club Trust and the Achilles Foundation. The stand would be ready for the start of the season, the developers promised.

She felt a righteous thrill at the thought that she was following in the footsteps of her mighty ancestors, and maybe (probably?) doing more than any of them had done, individually. Her forebears had simply been building on what went before, but she had faced a crisis. She was the one who had realised that the world had changed. She was the one who had made the club both a private business and a credit to its heritage. And she had done this in spite of the fact that, for two years, Adam Greswell, secretly working for her jealous sister, had tried to stand in her way with his quibbles and stupid ideas, but he was gone now and soon Kilburn would be great again. This was where she could make a difference. She hadn't voted in the general election last month. What was the point wasting your time with grubby politicians who never change anything when you are making decisions that change the lives of thousands of people? Hundreds of thousands, actually, if you thought about the fans. Millions, maybe.

She swept through the main door, nodded to the receptionist and made her daily pilgrimage to touch the Hallowed Turf. She passed through the chocolate-and-cream passageways to the changing area. Her heels clacked dully on the rubber floor. She peeked into the home dressing room, empty of course, and into the bootroom. The sharp smell of leather overlaid an ineradicable bass note of something else. Esther had never really wondered what the other note was. For her it was simply part and parcel of Kilburn Park.

Outside, on the pitch, the Gardener was on his knees. He seemed to be listening to the ground. He noticed Esther, and turned away. Esther didn't mind any more. You couldn't say yes to everyone if you ran a football club. Of course they all thought their own sections were the only thing that mattered, but Esther had always said that the important thing was to have perspective. That's why the main decisions came from her. She walked out into the sun, and turned slowly around. The seats were a sea of brown, with letters massively picked out in white. The North Stand had replaced 'KSC' with 'KU', and the South Stand would follow. The West was teeming with workers who were replacing the old white stripes with the word 'UNITED'. The East was still striped. Esther had not decided on what to change there. The Stationery Office was coming up with ideas, but the verdict would be hers.

When the scaffolding was removed, the new superstructure would be magnificent. Its crowning glory was a pod housing the media centre on one side and the Achilles Foundation on the other. The Kilburn Social Club Trust remained in its old building down the road, but the Achilles Foundation didn't have a home until this Magnificent Gesture.

In gratitude, Calum had insisted on calling the rooms the Esther Rosslare Complex. Esther accepted the honour on behalf of her family. When Aisling heard about that in a Rosslare Group meeting, she looked sick with jealousy. No other Rosslare name was part of the building – other rooms were called after famous players and managers – and it was high time that the situation was rectified.

Esther looked up to her office window. Donald was there, gazing down. She hated that he treated it as if it were his own. She went back through the dressing room, up the players' stairs to the bar, and then through to the offices. She walked along the line of Rosslares who had presided over the club, from Kevin all the way to Manus and herself. Adam had tried to insist that Aisling be featured, but it wasn't appropriate – she'd been in charge for too short a time, and only nominally anyway, and she'd hated it. The problem was only resolved when Will asked Aisling, in Adam's presence, whether she wanted a picture. Esther was frightened she'd be arrogant enough to say yes, but Will was clever, and Aisling said no.

Esther went to RG Committee meetings these days merely to make sure her sister didn't do any mischief behind her back. She told herself that she didn't fear Aisling any more. Actually, she pitied her. She increasingly wondered whether Aisling's real problem was that Esther was more successful with men now too. Aisling had a boyfriend, but a drippy barrister was hardly the same as Will Beauchamp! Poor Aisling, then, but that didn't mean Esther could relax her vigilance. She knew her sister too well.

Esther's picture was on the wall, even though she hadn't *officially* been running things for long, because she had really been the power behind the throne for all of Aisling's time, and she was the first Chancellor of the modern era, so it was important symbolically.

She stopped in front of Manus's face, as she sometimes did. The photograph was beautiful, her father's fine features hauntingly black and white as he turned towards the camera. Esther didn't know how she knew he had just turned, but she knew. She let her gaze lose focus, and shifted half on to tiptoes so the lines of her face fitted more exactly with her father's. She was like a Russian doll version of him, every feature the same but smaller. He would have been so proud of her now.

Esther's was the only portrait in colour. The first woman, the first in colour, the first Chancellor. The new era updating the traditions of the old.

'Hi, Esther,' said Donald as she entered. He was wearing too much of his horrible aftershave, as usual. 'I like the glasses. Sexy secretary. Very you. I saw the Bursar outside, shall I get them in? I'm in a bit of a whizz.'

The new Bursar was not, in Esther's opinion, attractive, which Esther had no problem with. Her credentials were excellent – she began her professional life in consulting and then spent ten years with Deltacom. Donald picked her, on Strabis's recommendation. Strabis felt, and Donald and Esther agreed, that it was best to have someone with no football background, so that the division of labour could be as clear as possible. The only problem had come a few weeks ago, at her second Board meeting, when she said, 'There's something I feel I really have to bring up, I'm afraid. Adam Greswell has spoken to me a number of times.'

'I told you he was in my sister's pocket!'

'I'm afraid you're right, Miss Rosslare, but he seemed very worried about the financial health of the club, and while I rebuffed him to his face, I felt I would be remiss not to produce a few projections for you to look at.' The Bursar handed over some sheets full of mumbo-jumbo charts. 'As you can see, we are not in an unhealthy position, thanks to the money from the FCKU range and ticket sales, but we are exposed. Eveything's predicated on getting the top whack of TV money, and also on getting the gate receipts and telly cash for European games. If we're not bringing in that money, we'll be seriously short.'

'We'll be getting the money because we're the most successful club in Britain,' said Esther. 'You're worrying about nothing. We can't pretend to be a small club.'

'I'm sure you're right,' said the Bursar. 'It's just that Mr Greswell – and I feel I have to pass what he said on to you, given your historic position – is worried that should anything go wrong, and should Kilburn United be exposed, it would be dependent on the generosity of its owners.'

'Strabis Kinsale has backed this club to the hilt,' said Donald. 'I hope you aren't suggesting anything else.'

'I am sure that's right, I really am, but I am relatively new to this post, and we are hopefully making a new commitment which will have a knock-on effect on our large squad. I felt it was my duty to present the facts.'

'Thank you for your diligence, Bursar,' said Esther kindly. 'Billy Krenabim is preparing for his first real full season in charge, with his players. It takes time to bed in. With him and Will, we will soon be in our rightful league position, you don't have to worry about that.'

'I hear troubling things about Mr Krenabim. Adam told me —'

'Billy Krenabim is a football man, Bursar. Adam Greswell is not. Trust me on football matters.'

'Absolutely, Miss Rosslare.'

That had told the Bursar, which was vital because Esther didn't need distractions. She was on the verge of the first great mastercoup of the new era. Donald read the paperwork, because it would require a commitment from Strabis, but it had all been okayed in principle. He skimmed through, nodded at Esther, and said, 'Good luck. Strabis is very excited by this.'

Three hours later, Esther heard the Bursar shout in triumph, put down her phone, rush from her desk, check with Esther's secretary that Esther was free, and bustle into Esther's office. Esther held up a hand to indicate she was completing a serious task, clicked at her keyboard, seemingly at random, and looked up. The Bursar said, 'He agreed! We've got him!'

It was supposed to be impossible to get the best Spaniards to leave Spain, people always said, but Esther had done it. Juan Vales, the Spanish captain! The superstar hero of Rojo Madrid, who had played up front for his hometown club ever since he was sixteen and broken every scoring record in the Spanish league! And he was joining KU! Kilburn managed to steal him away cheap because Rojo had let his contract run down to a single year, certain that he would never desert them. But at the European Player of the Year Awards, Vales had quietly told Will and Billy Krenabim that he wanted to cap off his career with one final challenge. Naturally, Vales said, there would need to be a financial incentive, in terms of wages, but he couldn't see that being a problem, since Kilburn would be saving so much on the transfer fee. The papers had only got their first hint of the story earlier this week which is why some of them were writing jealous pieces that Vales was past his best, but that was rubbish.

The Bursar had been worried that Vales's wage would have an effect when it came to negotiating other contracts. Will reassured Esther that he, for one, would happily stay on his present contract whatever Vales was paid. Esther told the Bursar that opportunities like this came so rarely in football that you had to take them and sort out the details later, and Strabis was behind her. The Bursar accepted that it was a football decision, and her job was to make it work financially. The structure of the payments, where the club and Vales both paid the same agency, which Billy Krenabim held shares in, seemed odd to her, but Krenabim said, 'Beauty of football, darling! It's not like any other business. We need Chinese walls in our heads sometimes!' Krenabim was a good guy, if naive, decided the Bursar. He was a Jack the Lad, shrewd rather than business-schooled.

The favourites won every single match before the second round of the 2004 World Cup. On the evening of 3 August, Australia, fresh from their easy group, held Great Britain to a goalless draw in São Paolo, and when Gilmour Hyde clipped the winning penalty past the hapless Stephen Brown, he cued three days of insufferable Antipodean bonhomie. Australia lost to Nigeria in the quarter-final, who lost to Brazil in the semi, who lost to Spain in a distraught Rio. Juan Vales was captain, but the Spanish were really led by little Milagroso Nuñez from Cadiz, thirty-one now, pudgy-looking with a comical moustache and helmet of dark brown curls.

Two weeks later, Vales arrived for training at Kilburn Park. He immediately told the rest of the team how he, Will and Billy Krenabim had engineered his transfer, and they should all be grateful because it would guarantee that everyone got better wage deals next time round. Louie Cohen told Will he was scum for selling out Kilburn. Will turned the other cheek, with a smile.

Towards the end of the next training session, Carlo chipped in a delicate hanging cross. Will timed a run that would leave him a free header unless Louie intervened. All Louie needed to do was get enough of a fist on the ball to deflect it past Will. It was not as if the pair were charging dangerously towards each other, their full weights committed to the moment. So when, at the last instant, Louie dropped his fist beneath the ball and into Will's cheek, it was a stiff jab he delivered, not a haymaker. Will's head jarred back. Blood erupted around his eye, but this was training and so, instead of rolling around clutching himself, he flipped straight back to his feet, flailing into Louie, ripping four-limbed like a cat. Louie fought back.

For a moment, it seemed as if everyone was going to join in, but Will was dragged off Louie, alternately spitting with rage and feeling above his eye for the size of his future scar. A shocked Billy Krenabim told the protagonists to cool down and come to his office, together, in an hour. He almost sent them both off to get changed, then thought better of it, and kept Louie where he could see him.

'I have to go to fucking casualty,' said Will.

'It is just a cut,' said Volendam, returned from his year at Spencer and training well enough to force his way back into first-team consideration. 'The doctor can deal with it.'

'We'll see about that. I'm not being scarred because of that cunt. If I have to be stitched in the face, I'm getting someone from fucking plastics.' He walked, tight with rage, to the changing room. Some of the watchers were satisfied. Will never lost his temper.

By the time he'd been to the hospital, been stitched up and returned, he had smoothed himself. He was waiting for Louie outside Krenabim's office. 'You're a superficial, self-centred, self-glorifying cunt with as much idea of your vindictive fucking religion as a pig,' he said.

'The terrorists are not believers.'

'Don't be fucking stupid. I don't give a shit about your half-cocked Islam, and I don't give a shit what you think about me, but hitting me today was fucking stupid. This vendetta your little friends have with my wife is pointless. Esther and I won. I won't fight you again, however much you goad me, and I hope you stay at Kilburn because I'm a rational person, and you're a good player with the right image. But if one of us goes, it'll be you, and don't you fucking forget it.' Will turned and knocked without waiting for a reply.

Krenabim wasn't going to sweep this under the carpet, where it might fester. He was a manager of men. He was someone people loved, and who helped them love each other. 'Boys?' he asked.

'It was nothing,' said Will.

'Don't come the muffin with me, Will. We go way back.'

'You know me too well, gaffer.'

'It's my job. Louie, mate?' said Krenabim. Louie was sitting slightly

319

further from the manager, at an angle. Krenabim could tell that the American felt awkward and wrong-shaped. Krenabim wanted him to be happy.

'It was an accident,' said Beauchamp. 'He hit me by accident, and I overreacted. Training-ground passion. It's healthy.'

'I was there, Will.' They were like kids. They had to be able to come to you, but they had to know you saw through them.

'Okay, boss. I should know better than to pull the wool.' Will was a good boy really, thought Krenabim. 'Me and Louie don't like each other. I'm prepared to believe his fist was an accident, but we really don't like each other, so that's why I reacted like I did. I think Louie is an arrogant twat, and I am sure he thinks the same about me, and he's friends with Aisling Rosslare, who's always trying to undermine my wife. I think it's pathetic, and I rise above it, but when I thought he was making something physical of it, I overreacted. I'm very sorry. It won't happen again.'

'Why not?'

'Because I'll be ready for it next time, boss. I'll control myself. Not that Louie would do anything deliberately, I'm sure, but I'll control my own reaction.'

'He abused my religion,' said Louie. 'Just now, outside. He is a hypocrite.'

Will shrugged, palms up, and shook his head with a small, tight smile. 'This is the problem. We're never going to agree. He thinks I'm a hypocrite, and I think he's one.'

'Why?' said Krenabim. This was beyond his experience. When he managed England, he used to be wary of Dave Guinevere, and Will was a bit the same.

'It's the Islam crap, gaffer, especially in the current climate. Louie says he's a Muslim, which is a misogynistic, narrow-minded faith, and —'

'It isn't.'

'I don't think Louie's narrow-minded, or misogynistic. I think he's modern and self-centred, and he isn't prepared to let religion get in his way any more than I am, but at least I'm honest about it.'

'Progressive Islam —'

'There is no God, mate. We aren't responsible to higher powers. We have to take the world as it comes and make the best of it. Louie's no worse than all the Catholics on the Pill or the Anglicans fiddling the Scriptures to fit their convenience, but they're not the ones bombing us. He's an egotist clinging to a religious fig leaf, and that's hypocritical.'

'I don't want this to interfere with your football,' said Krenabim. Will laughed and Krenabim had to pretend he'd been making a joke. 'Who else is involved in this? What can I do to sort it out?'

'It's honestly not important, boss. We don't have to like each other. That's what tolerance is all about. The whole point about KU is we *look* united, and we can do that.'

Will held his hand out to Louie, who felt he was melting into the background. Louie had to take the hand, only to find it limp and insolent, the fingers soft, almost stroking his palm as Will smiled at him.

*

Nzasa
1 Aug

Dear A,

Hey, etc. Things are still idyllic, mostly, though Punty and I have been bickering, and the bright class of nice kids has gone its merry way, and the next lot are no fun apart from Abdie-the-one-who-memorises-poems, and the others hate him.

The bickering isn't that important, by the way. It's the natural result of her having to nurse me through the malaria, and having to listen to everyone tell her that she'll get it next, because everyone does, and it's a rite of passage. Since I got better, she's spent all her time off at the hospital pretending to be busy, because she's needed the space. Relationships are give and take and ups and downs, and that's why it's a good thing that you've decided to put proper effort into Jeremy. It'll pay off, I promise.

I'm not surprised that Zondi's upset that Kilburn bought Vales, who's an arsehole who wouldn't piss on you if you were on fire (which is an image I am very pleased with, as you can tell). It's only because he hasn't had the imagination to do anything really unpleasant that Rojo have been able to keep him looking like a good guy. He's been trying to whore himself to someone else for the last three years, and if Will suddenly pretended to notice, then there's something in it for Will or I'm Dutch. How much is Billy's bung? is the other question. (Not for you, obviously, because you don't run a football club.)

There really is nothing much else to say, since all I did for two weeks was lie in bed. Errr . . . Oh. It was the big Sharks–Owls game yesterday (2–2), and they sang a song to welcome me back after the convalescence. That's about it.

I think Punty bickers because she's not made for the jungle and finds it hard to be cut off from everything. I'm not ready to come back though. While I was ill, when we ended up being forced to talk for hours, I mentioned children again, and I realised that she didn't want to have them in Nzasa. Where that leaves us, I don't know, because I don't want to come back.

That really is it. I'm writing because it's been a while, but I have no news.

Love,
David

MISSION OF MERCY

Maison Terrible Rue
14 August

Dear David,
Thank you for your letter, and Mr Brown thanks you for scratching
behind her ears.

An interesting thing happened last night. It was an event for the
Achilles Foundation which I was invited to. I must go to them, like
I must write out the name of the Foundation, because he made me
not be a coward about little things, and I will honour him always
if I am strong enough. I thought I would go alone, but Aisling knew,
and she was there and also Adam. I felt guilty that they put in this
effort for me, but I was happy also.

It was the evening you would expect, with announcements of who
will get money this year, and which other famous people have joined
the Foundation, and how many volunteers we have now placed with
which organisations, and some prizes and cheques (I had to hand
over one of these also, which I was a muddle for and felt stupid).

Strabis Kinsale was there, and he came to the table with us sitting,
and he said to Aisling like he was making a joke but not with his
eyes, 'I didn't expect to see you, Lady Rosslare. I thought you'd given
up on your heritage.' It was horrible how he spoke. Aisling made a
joke back that was also not a joke, and Strabis Kinsale smiled which
I did not like because it was a real smile, and I do not know what
it meant.

Then, immediately, also came William the Snake, with his stitches
in his face. Also there was a young waiter who I have to mention
who was listening, who was an Asian, I think a Pakistani maybe,
with a new moustache he couldn't quite grow yet. Will said to Louie,
'I didn't mean to offend your faith, mate.' Louie started to reply, but
Will said, 'It's just that you talk about Islam, but you turn up here
with your popstar girlfriend, even though Muslims shouldn't listen

to music, and she's hardly wearing any clothes, which I love, mate, but I'm an atheist, I just don't get it. Do explain it to me, please.' He was even more horrible than Kinsale, because I knew what he was doing in front of all the people and cameras, because he was smiling and holding out his hand. Kinsale looked at him like someone who approved. Louie did nothing except shake his hand, and there were many pictures, and Will said also, with more nodding and grinning, 'I love how you're so predictable, mate. You people can't face the truth about the modern world, and your first resort is violence. I suppose I should be grateful you didn't bomb me.' Will is clever to know what to say, because Louie is very ashamed of when he punched Will, because he wants to be an example. Monica was quiet in all this, which shows that she is older too now. When Will went, she said some things to do to him which were funny but I cannot remember them.

But after the end was the main thing, when we went outside. The young waiter was there, and he came over to us. Louie thought he was going to ask for an autograph, but instead he spat on Louie's shoes. The waiter was in jeans now, and a hooded green jersey, and he looked very scared, but he didn't run away. Louie was not angry. He asked the boy why he did it. The boy said, 'You are not a Muslim.' Louie said he was not a fundamentalist. The boy said, 'Islam is the truth. You either accept or you do not.' Monica told Louie not to waste his time and the boy said, 'Listen to your Christian whore,' and he spat on Louie's shoes again. He was shaking now. Louie said he wouldn't fight, and the boy said, 'You have no faith. You are a label. You are without substance.' Louie started to say about his group, and reformism and progressive Islam, but he was confused and the boy said, 'I am a Muslim. The Qur'an is the truth.' Then Aisling said about the Qur'an contradicting itself, but the boy said she was ignorant and asked her to show him the contradiction, which she could not do, so he said that she would burn and he would not spit to cool her. I have seen boys like this in my life. He has learned some things, and he knows them so strongly that he can feel like he is right when he says them in an argument. Now we all stood quietly until the boy went away.

Louie did well in this, and I think it makes him feel better about fighting Will. He said to me while we walked that he was scared to ask, but could I please tell him the difference between him hitting Will, and a fundamentalist bombing an embassy, and what I did in South Africa. I could not tell him properly, because I am stupid like this, but I tried to say something like that in Louie's dream world, everyone <u>chooses for themselves</u>, and that was my dream too, but the fundamentalists have a different dream about them <u>choosing for everyone else</u>. I fought because there was no other way in South Africa to make the government listen to me as an equal voice, and everyone has the right to be an equal voice. The fundamentalists fight because they can't bear that other voices are equal to theirs. This is what I have thought when I have tried to understand it, but I am so clumsy. I said he should write to you about it because you are more clever, and so he will, I think. I said that him fighting Will was not like either of these, it was because Will is a bad man. Even so, I think the boy upset him very much, and also he is upset very much about Will. He says he must do something about Will, and although I have said he should not, I think he will try.

My other thing is this. You say Aisling has made the right decision about Jeremy at last, but I do not know. All the rivers flow to the sea, but along the way they meet and join, split and remingle. Jeremy thinks Aisling will change to be like him, and he is patient like an engineer slowly forcing her course to his. I hope (and think also) that the force of her flow is too powerful and she will find her own way and he will have to follow her, or maybe she will burst her banks and wash him away, but now she is like a trickle. It is important to know who you are and what it is you want.

Your friend,
Zondeki

*

Dave read Zondi's letter to Punty. They were lying in the huge hammock, Dave crossways with his back to the house and Punty with her head on his belly and feet up towards the point attached to the palm tree, ear to Dave's skin, gazing down to the flaming sea. It must look great, thought Dave, but it felt wrong, with neither of them comfortable.

'He doesn't agree with you about idealism,' said Punty.

'What? Yes, he does.'

'He said you can't compromise.'

'No. He said . . .' Dave rechecked the letter. 'Human rights are one thing, but we were talking about idealists who try to force other people to join them. Like Jeremy with Aisling.' Punty turned her face into his belly, but not to kiss him, more in irritation, as if she wanted to bury her head. 'What is it?' Dave asked, putting his hand to her shoulder. She shuddered at his touch and shook off his hand. 'What is it? I always said Jeremy wasn't right for her, and this is why. I tried to be positive in letters when Aisling said she was not going to entertain any doubts for six months, because Jeremy wants to turn her into something she isn't, and —'

'Fuck off, Dave.'

'What?'

'You've told me how to think ever since we got here. You're always telling people what to think.'

'No, I don't. It's not the same,' he said, but already he was screwing up his eyes against the light. It was a very specific silence, a meaningful gap in conversation, and he should have been thinking of things to say but instead he wondered whether the effectiveness of the silence was increased or decreased by the heavy crashing waves and the rustling trees. 'Is that really how you see it?' More silence.

An hour later, they had cooked and eaten. Dave was rereading, letting a familiar murder wash through his mind, giving his subconscious space to process. Punty was cross-legged on the floor, painstakingly mending a fishing net for one of her friends in the village. It took her five times as long as it took the villagers, but they'd been doing it all their lives and she'd been doing it for five weeks. Dave presumed that it gave her a similar kind of active downtime to his reading, and it normally relaxed her, but not tonight. Eventually, she looked around and said, 'When we met, you didn't just want to read about stuff, you wanted to do it. You were amazing. I'd never met anyone who was more alive than you.'

'You met me at a weird time. I wasn't myself.'

'Yes you were. You were angry, and you did something about it.'

'Punty!'

'There's nothing wrong with that! What happened to Achilles was a terrible accident, but it doesn't mean you should give up!'

'I . . .' He didn't know what to say.

'When we came here, I thought you were going to make up for it, because I thought you'd never give up, ever. I thought you'd do something amazing, and I know you want to but you're too scared.' He didn't trust himself to speak. 'You're the biggest idealist I've ever met.'

'No, I'm not.'

'Why didn't it work out with Sally?' Parts of him were being skewered, but Punty didn't know which parts. She went on, '"Football is a perfect little world, where everyone has to play by the same rules"?' There was something almost plaintive about how she said it.

'I don't force them to play. I'm showing them something. It's a parable.'

'I'm not criticising you! It's brilliant what you do for them, and you should do more of it, be part of the community, not teach them crap about Europe and trade.'

'I'm trying to be a responsible teacher.'

'You're indoctrinating them. You're teaching them all these things they'll never need to know because you hope they'll change the world, but it's never going to happen.'

'They've got to know about the world.'

'They have to know about *their* world, Dave.' She picked apart the tangled knot she'd been half-heartedly trying to tie. 'I don't think I can do this any more.'

'You want to go home?' Punty shook her head. They went back to what they were doing. Dave couldn't concentrate. He thought he'd faced down the part of himself which couldn't trust anyone to know better than he did.

Two uncomfortable days later, he asked Punty what he should be teaching the kids.

'I'm not telling you what to do,' she said.

Her self-righteousness was irritating, but he persevered. 'Seriously, P. I can't teach them nothing about the world. That would be irresponsible.'

'Why? The ones on the hill will grow up to be crooks and the ones from the village will be fishermen.'

'Everything won't always be like it is now,' said Dave.

'Not if people like you keep trying to change everything. These people are happy.'

'They're hungry, and they're ignorant.'

'Only by your standards.'

'How come they all want televisions?'

'Because of people like you.'

Dave didn't carry on. She would come round. He wasn't forcing anyone. He was just trying to tell them the truth as well as he could, to prepare them.

Krenabim's new-look Kilburn began the season in dominant form. After a month, the club went top of the league for the first time in three years. Juan Vales had scored four from five starts, and Will Beauchamp, Marten Vlocker and Craig Drayly were outstanding. To an ignorant observer, this was the team that had risen from the tragic ashes of Mr Brown and Achilles.

Sitting in the dressing room, Vlocker, Cole and a few others still sported heavy pieces of gold, but things were changing. The younger players were starting to smarten themselves into little clones of Juan Vales. Carlo was almost completely mutated. Vales himself sat back exquisitely, soft shirt and careful stubble, schoolboy stripy blazer and neat jeans, looking like a rock star. Dirk Volendam sat on the other side of the room in beige cargo trousers to his calves, a tight white T-shirt and slippery little trainers that transformed him from a thirty-five-year-old footballer into a forty-one-year-old computer-games designer. Will Beauchamp wore a calm suit and no tie. He could have been a banker relaxing at the end of the day or a writer going to a meeting. This befitted his role as someone allied to the gang, but not part of it. Louie had asked for a moment of everyone's time. He stood up to speak. 'It's great we're winning, hey!' he said. 'We all love to win, am I right?' He paused, demanding assent, which was granted in embarrassed grunts and nods. Louie pulled a sheet from his pocket and squinted at it. 'Yeah. This is an important time. Now, I been thinking a lot, and I talked to Dave Guinevere, you know, I mean I wrote to him, and I got a letter back this week. The thing Dave said about Kilburn is that it's a mission, not a monastery, do you see?' Drayly, looking at Cole, stifled a giggle. 'A mission has to try to do good, and tell the world about it, and we all have to be good examples.'

'Yes, sir,' said Drayly. More giggles.

Beauchamp said, 'Come on guys. Manners.'

'I'm saying that . . .' This was all so clear in Dave's letter. 'Okay, here's an example. A monk doesn't have to justify himself to anybody except God, and his society trusts his behaviour to be above reproach, but in a more public context, then —'

'What the fuck?' said Vales, his whispering interpreter having struggled along a couple of beats behind. Half the room laughed.

'I'm trying to say that things change over time, you see, and we have a responsibility, because this is not a normal football club, Juan. We have a mission. People follow what we say, and so —'

'What the fuck?' Laughter.

Louie turned over his sheet of paper, determined to carry on. Beauchamp wondered why some people found it so hard to see the levers that would move a situation one way or another. Louie tried again: 'We have to live up to what we say. Kilburn has ideals, and we —'

'What the *fuck*?'

'*Listen to me!* What we do is important. We talk the talk, but we have to walk the walk. Can't you understand? Or else it's —'

'Fuck off, Cohen.' Vales stood up. 'I am footballer. I play football, I eat, I party, I fuck fat English mingers.' He gave a mocking bow to his acolytes, and swept from the room.

'Don't worry about him,' said Will soothingly. 'It's a language thing. Do carry on.' He was looking at Cole and Drayly, quietening them but letting Louie hear his condescension. Now was the time to start things rumbling if he wanted to be out of Kilburn in the New Year. Will was in his prime, but that's when you have to start planning for the future, when you still hold the aces.

'I'm not blind, Will,' Louie said. 'Dave said you were a cancer. He said this would be hopeless while you were still here.'

Speaking carefully to the room, Will said, 'I'm sorry to be the one to say this, because I know Louie still listens to him, but Dave Guinevere is a bitter man who thinks he's better than the rest of us. He couldn't handle being sold, and because he couldn't handle it, he went crazy when he played against us, and Achilles died, accidentally I'm sure. And he couldn't handle being rejected by a woman, so he ran into the arms of a pathetic model half his age. He's weak, and I don't take him any more seriously than I take people pretending to be Muslims. I've had enough of your sermons, Louie. Who's coming for a drink?'

The older players were embarrassed by the vehemence of Will's tirade. It was certain to accentuate the divide that was already forming. With Louie were Tom Benjamin and Dirk Volendam, along with the injured Torquil and a couple of the other long-timers. Seung was gone, snapped up cheap by Racing Bilbao, and Will Laird had been sold to UEFA Cup winners Hamburg for ten million, so that took out two of the old guard, but a handful still remained. Will Beauchamp half-led the other camp, but he was also withdrawn from it, posing as a man aloof.

Louie made a careless error in the next match, which Kilburn drew 1–1 with Spencer. Afterwards, an interviewer asked, 'Louie, Kilburn's winning run has finally come to an end. Are you gutted?'

'It's just a game, man,' he replied.

'But —'

'What I'm *gutted* about is hypocrisy. What I'm *gutted* about is people demanding *respect* and then behaving as if the rules don't apply to them. People who talk about *honesty* and *charity*, but who lie and scheme for their own gain, and I'm not naming names, but those people know who I mean.'

'So . . . You're gutted about those first dropped points?'

'What?'

'Do you think Kilburn can go through the season undefeated?'

'This interview is over, man.'

Louie intended his outburst to be a shot across Will Beauchamp's bows, a warning that he must behave or he would be publicly shamed, but his words had a much bigger impact than that. The British public had given football a decade of almost unstinting good will and it was time for a readjustment. Unfortunately for Kilburn United, its puffed-up rhetoric made it an easy target. Louie's much-repeated interview was the catalyst.

It's easy to criticise the press, since their sudden 'revelations' about the likes of Cole, Drayly and Vales were stories that had been common tabloid knowledge for years, but the press weren't telling lies. Vales was a venomous shit, and why should he be treated like a saint because he dressed well and spoke quietly?

Will Beauchamp played the crowd perfectly. He was sorry that these things had been publicised, because he loved Kilburn, and the game itself. 'But,' he admitted, 'maybe it's for the best. The real sadness is that these stories are true. There's a canker at the heart of British football, and maybe casting light on that canker will help burn it away.' People, Will accepted, had a right to know which of their heroes had feet of clay.

Juan Vales didn't understand or forgive this public repudiation, and nor did Cole, Derkin and Drayly.

Calum Horton was impressed, and told Will so. He asked if Will had something for him in this, something a bit classier, maybe? Soon after, Calum wrote a piece based on a deep throat within KU who told him that the players were seething that Louie thought he was better than everyone else. Louie, after all, was earning twenty grand a week, lived in a huge house and kept three cars. He should be worrying about what his fellow Muslims were doing in the world outside football – not that the source was alleging Louie had any sympathy with terrorists – instead of complaining that a few young men got high-spirited once in a while. Louie might make a good public show, said the source, but his fellow players thought he was a hypocrite.

A few weeks later, another interviewer asked Will if the dressing-room ructions had died down, and he replied, 'Yes, thank goodness. The two sides have trouble seeing each other's point of view – the older guys want to stick their heads in the sand and the younger guys only care about money and women – but I've been able to act as a kind of honest broker, and patch things up.' The two sides, still wary of each other, had already begun to close ranks against Will, and this now intensified. His response was to give an exclusive interview to Calum about the divisions in the club. He said, 'The bare minimum we should be able to do is to get together on a Saturday and give the fans, our employers, a hundred per cent commitment.' When pressed as to whether some players were not giving this commitment, Will refused to be drawn, but he did say that the situation was exacerbated this year by the new transfer regulations, which made it impossible to buy or sell players until the January window. Kilburn lost twice in a row.

At least, wrote most reporters, *Will Beauchamp is doing his best*. Kilburn United might have been out of form, but Will was covering every inch of turf in an obvious solo attempt to change things. But by the day of the Christmas Party, they'd lost four of their last seven matches and lay fifteenth in the Premiership.

Billy Krenabim came under pressure. Esther had to make public pronouncements in order to clear things up. She said after the first two defeats that she had every confidence that Krenabim would turn things around. The day of the Christmas Party, after two more losses, she repeated herself and also, subtly, questioned the commitment of some of the players. 'As others have pointed out,' she said, 'the disadvantage of this transfer window is that it makes certain players lazy. They'll all start playing properly in the run-up to January. It's clear that only our most committed players are performing to their full potential. The others should be thinking very carefully.'

'So you're saying there's going to be a clear-out?'

'You must make your own mind up about what I'm saying,' she replied coyly.

The Christmas Party fixture was against Manchester & Stockport, who were also struggling. Whatever else happened, Kilburn would surely win this match, but there was a special edge to the annual speculation that this might be the year that broke the spell. The dressing room was less charged than the terraces. Carlo showed Drayly a photo of the Range Rover he was having customised.

Krenabim said, 'Today is a day of destiny, boys. Three points today changes everything.'

'We're not idiots, gaffer,' said Will. 'We'll start winning again when people get a fucking grip. We'll win when dickheads stop focusing on their fucking cars and start to show some fucking desire.' He was nothing like his normal icy self. He ripped the photo from Carlo's hand and tore it to pieces. 'We need *everyone* to run themselves into the fucking *ground*. People are coming off the pitch hardly fucking sweating and I've had enough of it. This is a great club because we've always loved each other, and played like people who loved each other.'

'Will, I know you're —'

Vales's interpreter had caught up, and the striker slammed his hands on the bench with a huge 'Bullshits!' and a torrent of Spanish.

The interpreter spoke, 'Football teams are not lovers. Players do not have to like each other. In Spain, I do not like many players, and you lie if you say you love other players, Will fucking bastard, but we all want to win. What we need is for all players, for you, fucking Will Beauchamp, to play properly in their place in the side.' Beauchamp threw his hands in the air.

'Easy, everybody,' said Krenabim. 'You're both right. Will, everyone could learn from the effort you've been putting in the last few weeks, but you're trying too hard. You're running so much, you're not always in position to play the easy balls. It's not just Juan – other people, I won't name them, have said the same thing.' Will glared as if he'd been knifed in the back. He had managed to put himself in a place where no one would support him.

Kilburn took the pitch silently. They played excellent football for half an hour, skipping the ball around the puffing M & S. Beauchamp held his position, Vales and Vlocker switched and tormented, and Tom Benjamin poked home from two yards at the end of a move lasting twenty passes. Shortly after, Vales tried one trick too many, and was dispossessed. Will Beauchamp, covering behind him, was caught just for a moment on the wrong foot and was bypassed. It was the most unfortunate moment possible, since Carlo had overlapped confidently up the left and there was a huge gap behind him. M & S fired the ball into it; their centre forward was there before the labouring Volendam and he crossed instantly to his partner. From their first chance of the game, M & S scored.

This seemed to enrage and inspire Will Beauchamp. He was every-where, lifting the game by the scruff of its neck. He took three huge shots from thirty yards, stinging the keeper's hands with two of them. He overlapped down the right. He found himself space on the left. M & S might have had more space to play with in Will's absence from the centre of the pitch, but they were so busy containing him that they couldn't use it.

At half-time, Beauchamp's teammates rounded on him. He'd been told what the fuck to do, and he'd done it for most of the half, so what the fuck was he doing now? He should fucking sort himself out. They'd been exhilarated to finally be playing properly; they despaired at slip-ping back towards the rut; they raged at the one not doing his job; they were desperate to win again.

In the stand, Esther was hopeful. Kilburn were clearly the better team. All they needed to do was show patience and commitment, and their quality would ensure they got the result they deserved. But it's hard to be patient when you have been losing. Will was playing the long, risky balls that were so brilliant when they came off but which often ended up at the feet of the opposition. Commentators had said he was trying too hard, and she had, two weeks ago, very gently wondered if there might not be something in this? He was only human. It was only natural that he would also be affected by the losses. Will was furious. He said that all the players were turning against him, and she was just as bad. He said she was trying to suffocate him. Football was the most important thing in his life, but not the only thing. He'd never said anything like this before and his anger came out of nowhere, but it seemed so cold and well prepared. His problem was that he cared too much.

There he was now, making a typical run, exchanging a one-two with Vlocker and arriving late into the box. He only had to slip the ball to Vales, but he took the shot himself and it slid agonisingly outside the right post. Vales shouted, but Esther watched Will ignore the Spaniard and race back to where his team needed him instead of wasting his energy in petulant display. There were still ten minutes to go.

Kilburn continued to press forward. Drayly's crosses swung just wide of Vales, or just in front of Benjamin. Drayly was crossing too early, and under pressure, because he was unable to find the simple little pass inside that Will used to provide – Will was now racing into the box himself, hunting the goal.

The M & S keeper collected a cross and overarmed the ball down the left flank. The receiver sent it up the line to the lone striker, who held it for a moment and switched it back inside to the most attacking midfielder, ten yards inside the Kilburn half. It was a neat quick break, but Kilburn had it contained, three defenders comfortably covering the two men. M & S kept the ball, switching it around briskly, thirty yards from goal but not threatening, when Will, tired from having sprinted all the way from the opposite box, made a tackle he didn't need to make, mistimed it fractionally and conceded a free kick in a dangerous position. It was only because of their dreadful form that Kilburn hearts leaped into mouths. Louie arranged the wall and waited. The defenders picked out their men. Nick Chouksey, preparing to take the kick for M & S, could feel a scriptwriter toiling in his favour. Three seats to Esther's left, she heard Zondi whisper to Adam. 'This will go to the top left,' he said. 'If he hits it clean, Louis can do nothing.' Chouksey hit it clean.

In a superhuman final effort, Will almost inspired a recovery. With the ninety minutes already gone, he slipped an inch-perfect pass to Cole, who flicked it over the advancing keeper, and the score was 2–2.

No one could say Will hadn't done his best, but in the end it was not to be.

'You're pathetic, man!' Beauchamp didn't reply. He had no allies. Louie would not let go. 'You're an arrogant a-hole,' he said. No reply. 'You know what you did.'

'Fuck off, Louie. I ran myself into the ground; I almost scored three times; I set up the equaliser. You're the one who let Chouksey put it in the top-left corner, which is the only place he ever aims, as everyone in this team knows. I'm sorry I gave away the free kick, but it was fucking childish of you to let it in to spite me.' No one gave that any heed. 'Didn't see much of you today, Juan,' he said.

'Fuck off. No one pass to me. Fucking cunt.'

'Don't call me that.' Will stepped forward, toe to toe with Vales.

'Cunt,' said Vales. Will made a tiny motion as if to butt him, and Vales rocked his head back and punched. As the surprised and aggrieved party, Will was perfectly free to hit back, and he punched three times before he was dragged clear, each time aiming for the nose. He felt the bone give way with the second. The third was for luck.

As they stood apart, Will said, 'Fuck you, pretty boy. He hit me first, you all saw.' To get into one fight with a teammate who has struck you out of hatred, confusion and disappointed loyalty may be regarded as a misfortune. To get into two, etc. 'Don't look at me like that, you fuckers. He hit me first. Just like you did, Cohen.' No one showed him any sympathy. When footballers watch the video of a foul, they know what has really happened, whatever lies they tell. They know when someone has tripped another, even if contact seems minimal. They know when a clattering tackle is mistimed rather than vicious. They knew Will had baited Vales. Will always knew what he was doing.

Aisling left the ground. She was watching today because she was going to the Christmas Party. With Hank again. When he invited her, she ran it past Jeremy. He smiled magnanimously and said, 'You don't have to ask me. You're the one who thought it was a good idea to bin Kilburn.' That wasn't true. Jeremy always told her to wash her hands of the club. Was that all a manoeuvre to strip her of her rooted loyalties, to make her easier prey? She shouldn't have thought such things. Jeremy went on, 'All I ever minded was when Kilburn got in the way of us. Do you think Hank has a little crush?' She laughed at that. She said Hank wanted her to do her duty. 'You went above and beyond your duty for that club,' said Jeremy. Aisling was four months into her commitment experiment and, most of the time, it was great. She always used to prefer theatre to football, so you could say that Jeremy had helped her get back to who she truly was. She arrived home wanting a lazy bath and a slow change, but Jeremy surprised her with champagne and roses. He was thoughtful.

After Vales and Will had left, Krenabim spoke to the sullen, mutinous dressing room. He said, 'Lift yourselves, boys. I don't give a fuck that we haven't won on the day of the Party. Records are bullshit. A draw's better than a defeat, and the day you're in is the best day to make a new start. We clear our heads, we hold them high, we have a great bash, and we come back strong.' Everyone knows the words to these speeches. The skill is to make them sound as if they mean something, and Krenabim did. The players knew he was right, and Will had brought them into temporary harmony.

The Party started piano, but champagne is an excellent agitator, and unusual pockets of players huddled in righteous indignation. And more champagne, and pretty girls, and the need for release, and food, and wine, and this strange new truce. Krenabim, speaking with Zondi, Hank and Aisling, said Kilburn had turned a corner, and he had higher hopes than he'd had for a while.

When Vales walked into the room, nose reset and left eye puffing, the buzz dropped by a semitone. He always carried himself well, but his hauteur tonight was epic, and he strolled past Will and Esther on his way to Louie, of all people. Vales's date, well briefed, bristled for her chance to tower over Esther and ignore Will to his face.

Will had told Esther about the fight when he got home and Esther was angry with him for the first time. However much Vales deserved it, Will should have put the football first, today of all days. Obviously the feud with Vales underlay the way Will was playing. 'Not you as well,' he said, when she put her hand on his to talk seriously. 'I need someone to be on my side.'

'I'm on your side.' All evening, in gratitude, he stayed with her and the other Board members.

*

Three hours later, the room was hot with drink. Monica saw Vales and his interpreter heading towards Will and she grabbed Louie. 'Come on!' she said. Louie was torn, but he followed her. Aisling didn't want to look prurient, but this was clearly the evening's big excitement and, anyway, it was either follow Monica or stand around on her own. On reaching the group, the first thing she heard was Esther saying to Vales, 'You hit him first.'

'He provoked me. Ask Louie,' translated the interpreter. Louie obviously wanted to be somewhere else. In his letters, Dave said that the Christmas Party should have been stopped years ago, and Aisling saw what he meant. 'Tell them!' Vales said to Louie. Vales's date held him gently round the waist, leaning out and away so the plunging V of her dress casually flashed Will and Esther her entire torso. 'Tell them!' said Vales again.

'I don't know,' said Louie. Monica tugged Louie's arm furiously. Earlier, Louie told her and Aisling that everyone in the dressing room had been sure Will started the fight deliberately. Louie gave in, and said, 'It was Will's fault, Esther. He provoked Juan.'

'Your husband is cunt,' drawled Vales, nodding to the interpreter, and carrying on in Spanish. 'Will Beauchamp thinks he is better than everyone else, but he is a child. He will not pass to me because he is jealous. He runs like a little fly, with no skill. He does not realise that other players are better than him. He persuaded me to this club, but he is a fool, and it is his fault we are losing. It is his fault we draw today. We all know it. If his wife was not boss, and if the gaffer was not weak, Will Beauchamp would not be picked.'

'My husband —'

'Everyone knows it's true,' said Vales's date. 'Everyone says he's lost it. I bet you know it too, but you're too scared you'll lose him to say anything.'

Esther started, 'My husband is worth ten of —'

But Vales was ready and said, 'He hits you? That is it, no?'

'That's not fair,' said Aisling.

'Thank you, Aisling,' said Will. 'At least *someone* will speak up for me.' Aisling should have said that this also wasn't fair, and one champagne ago, she would have, but if Will felt abandoned by Esther, then that was probably no bad thing in the long run. Esther gulped, and ran off. A moment later, under the glares of the others, Will followed her.

'She's —'

'She's my sister,' said Aisling, spinning to Vales's date, 'before you say anything. Let's not talk about this.'

'Fuck Will Beauchamp,' said Vales. 'Fuck Kilburn.'

Aisling wanted to cry.

By this time, Zondi was making his way across the leopard's shoulder. His best shoes poked from underneath his coat. Achilles loved these shoes because they were so light and elegant. Zondi thought they looked ridiculous, but he still wore them because, more than any others he owned, they let him feel the ground. He wore them seldom, so they would always be a treat. It was important to keep walking.

He went to the Christmas Party to show he did not kowtow to terror, which was Aisling's joke. Aisling going back to the dinner was like a migrant creature. If she did not go one year, would she ever know the way again? It was a mild November. Zondi barely needed his coat. The migrant creatures are not good role models for a person. If Aisling kept returning to the same place for ever, would each return wear the old path deeper and deeper, so that she could not climb out of the rut she had made? Had Zondi colluded in this tonight? He did not know. He kept walking. Was Aisling still tied to Kilburn because of her letters to Dave? Was she trying to escape with Jeremy's help? Was Jeremy the right thing for her? Was he really her rock, or was he quicksand? Man is not a migrant creature. He must respect the bonds that tie him to his life, but the road is not a circle and if a man chooses to stop he will never learn where his road goes.

'Penny for them,' said Adam, walking alongside.

Zondi smiled nervously. 'Aisling must move on, maybe. I do not know.'

'I think she will. I think this is the last year. The club's not hers any more, and it's nothing like it was. She knows it really.'

When Zondi left the party early, he phoned Adam because the FA was near the hotel, and Adam often worked late. Adam said that if Zondi didn't mind waiting ten minutes, they could get a drink and talk about the Party.

After Zondi called, Adam took off his tie, put it on again, and then took it off. His legs ached. He'd started running, and the day after his legs always ached. Still, he felt better for it, and, though this was not important, he looked better.

Zondi was pristine, as if he were on the way to the Party rather than from it. It had taken Adam a long time to realise how much effort Zondi put into looking pristine, and now he felt slovenly rather than casual. Zondi explained that everyone had finally turned on Will, as Zondi had predicted. 'Esther?' asked Adam.

Zondi shook his head. 'She is still trying to be with him,' he said. It was late, and they left the bar after one drink. Adam put his arm out for a cab, but Zondi said, 'Come,' and turned north. Adam assumed he was being taken somewhere. It took him a while to realise that they were walking to East Kilburn, which was a habit Zondi hadn't yet shared. When he worked out what they were doing, he was incredulous but he said nothing.

'We are at the leopard's neck,' said Zondi.

'Uh?'

'I am a foolish person. I have made London a leopard in my head, and I know all his spots, so I am never lost. This is what I am like.'

'You're never lost?'

'On foot. In most of London. If I know which of the leopard's spots I am walking to, which I often do not.' He smiled. 'It is not as good as an *A–Z*. It is like with the stories of animals.'

'Is Louie still a rhino?'

'Also Will is still a snake.' They walked on. 'I worry what Dave says to Aisling. His story is the Tall Hunter who will never be satisfied, and if Aisling does not escape from him, then . . . I am a foolish person.'

'What do you think I am?'

'I thought you were the Bower Bird, but not so stupid,' said Zondi.

'I am flattered.'

'No. Stupid would have been better than what I thought then. It was when you let Esther think that you and she . . .'

'I remember.'

'You are a lion.'

'No, I'm not.'

'No.' Zondi was embarrassed. 'These are not for real. I only do it in my head, to remember the stories.'

'There's nothing wrong with that.'

'But I do not really remember the stories. I make them up.'

'I believe them,' Adam said, and then, as they approached the nape of the leopard's neck, 'Have you got any new ones?'

Zondi could tell him about Juan Vales, who was the prideful Elephant Bull, pushed out of his herd and blundering into a new one whose bull was also fading. But he wanted a happier story. He walked silently through two squares, thinking. Zondi's friends were used to these withdrawals. 'When Mr Brown was here, Kilburn Park was like the *Mz'lnkadze*, the first waterhole, before the Sundering, which was when people got stuck in their shapes for ever. When the people of the First Time drank at the *Mz'lnkadze*, the other people could see what shape was their essence, and it didn't matter, but that was how people knew what shape to be when the Sundering came. Mr Brown was the old, fat River King, because even before the Sundering people had to have justice. The River King could see all the shapes that were then and would be in the future, and he knew he would die and the Sundering would come, so he tried to teach the Lion to see, and . . .' He stopped. 'This is not the right story. All my stories are sad. I do not know why I tell it.'

'It's beautiful.'

'For my people, there was no King before the Sundering. Kings came later. This is just a stupid story.' They walked on. The new shirt was cool against Zondi's skin. At least, this year, for the first time, he had only bought one new shirt. 'Achilles was not a lion. It is only now that I can't . . . Achilles was a butterfly. He tried to pretend to be a lion, but he couldn't.'

They reached Adam's house first. Adam said goodbye and went in alone. He didn't want to push his luck.

Back at the Party. Strabis sat opposite Aisling, ostentatiously delicate with her as they cracked their spoons through the golden sugar lattice. 'I am very disappointed,' he said. 'The club's soul seems to have gone, somehow, inexplicably. What do you think?' She knew not to react. 'You must be so glad you aren't responsible,' he carried on. 'I imagine it would be heartbreaking if you thought you were. Esther seems happy, though. Do you know, when I see the decisions she makes, I sometimes wonder whether your sister really understands the Kilburn heritage.'

'Fuck off, Strabis,' she said. The corner of his mouth flickered.

*

Still at the Party, half an hour later. 'You don't understand what I'm going through,' hissed Will to Esther, apparently oblivious to the other people in the corridor. 'You don't seem to get that I'm trying to keep Kilburn afloat on my own.'

'I do understand, Will. I do. You're amazing.'

'You're the same as all the others.' His anguished voice rose slightly. 'You think I should try less hard. Well I can't, and don't think that if I stop, things will be better. The others are using me as an excuse because they don't like me, because I show them up. You don't understand anything, none of you do.'

'Will. We mustn't do this here.'

'Oh yes, sorry! Your precious reputation and your precious fucking dinner and your precious fucking club. Nothing must harm Kilburn United.' Esther was unprepared for this. Aisling was watching, probably laughing at her. Will wasn't finished. 'Some day you'll have to wake up and see that there's only so much loyalty one man can give to something that gives him nothing back,' he said. 'Or to someone.' He turned and left, every inch the wounded party.

Esther stood stupefied. She stared blindly and stumbled under the foyer neon, and, although it took Aisling only a few seconds to reach her, in each of these seconds Esther felt more like the victim of a prom-night prank in an incomprehensible American high-school movie. Aisling's pity was more than Esther could bear. She ran away.

Will was nowhere to be seen. She took a taxi to their home, but he wasn't there. He eventually turned up at three in the morning, crying like a drunken crocodile. She was waiting for him, stiff with terror. He glared balefully, shook his head and went to the spare room. When he woke up, looking like he hadn't touched a drop the night before, she was still there, as if she hadn't moved, as if she hadn't walked to his door every half-hour.

'Everyone turned against me,' he said. 'I needed you to be on my side.'

'But I am,' she wailed.

'I don't know,' he said. 'I'm going for a walk. Clean yourself up.' He was like a different person. When he got back, and she was showered, dressed and hurriedly remade up, he said, 'I'm serious, Esther. I can't stay at Kilburn if everyone's against me.'

'I'm not against you.'

'I'm sure you're not. I'm sure it was just last night, but you seemed like you were on their side.'

'I'm not. I'm on your side.'

'It can't be just you anyway. You're not enough. I'm in my prime. And I'm the only player whose image keeps Kilburn's head above the muck. I need some sign that people value me, or why am I killing myself to keep this club alive?'

The next day, in her office, Esther tried to consider this rationally. Will had two and a half years left on his contract, but it had been negotiated eighteen months ago, and wages were skyrocketing. He was one of several players who, although they were well rewarded, lagged significantly behind their market value. Juan Vales's huge salary, inflated by the lack of a transfer fee, threw this into sharp relief. Esther had pointed all this out to Will before, but he always demurred, saying that he and Esther didn't need more money than they had, he would only give it away and, more importantly, he didn't want to take advantage of his position as her husband. He must, and he laughed at himself saying this, be Caesar's wife. He was wonderful.

But now he said he didn't feel valued. Money wasn't important to him, but it might possibly be a way of showing him that the club cared. She called on the Bursar. 'This is very embarrassing for me,' she said, closing the door behind her.

'Coffee?' said the Bursar. 'I don't know what it is, exactly, but I've always found people can unburden themselves to me.'

'It's nothing like that,' said Esther.

'I don't mind. Some of my friends say it's because I'm so comfortable in my skin, but I'm sure that's not right. I think it's because I'm efficient but also sensitive, that's all. Are you okay?'

'I'm perfectly fine.'

'You can tell me.'

'This is not about the Christmas Party. There is no problem between Will and me. That's what makes this embarrassing.'

'I was sure you two would be fine. I didn't listen to anything anyone else said. I'm so glad. So what is it?'

'It's Will's contract.'

'Oh. I see how that would be embarrassing. I suppose the best thing to do is leave it to me,' she hinted, 'because of the conflict of interest? He's one of the ones we have to do next summer, isn't he?'

'I think you should do it now.'

'Really? Why?'

'It's not for me to say.' The Bursar could be obtuse at times.

'Well, maybe we should wait until next summer then, because —'

'I think we should do it now,' said Esther, very carefully. 'Before January.'

'Oh. Because if we don't . . . I see. Really?'

The Bursar sounded doubtful. She thought Esther was doing this because of greed when she was actually doing it for the club. 'Really,' Esther said.

'Oh.'

'I think if it wasn't for me, Will would already have left because we pay him so little, actually.' As she spoke, Esther realised finally that this must be true. 'I'm sure it's only a matter of meeting the market rate,' she said. 'If you think that he is paid any less than that.'

'Ye-e-e-e-s,' said the Bursar. 'Money is tight, though. And the other players are bound to —'

'What would it cost to replace him? Even if we could find someone else as good.'

'No, no, I'm sure you're right.' But the Bursar sounded uncertain. This was the problem with employing someone who didn't understand football.

Will's secret deal with Rojo Madrid was this: in return for helping them offload Juan Vales, and assuming Will could free himself from Kilburn, they would buy him in January for not more than twelve million pounds, and on whatever wages he was earning at the time. Rojo badly needed a strong midfielder, and Will was particularly attractive because he wasn't playing European football, and so would be both fresh and available for the Champions League. Rojo also thought that the impossibility of Will renegotiating his wages before January would make it a neat piece of business.

After signing his new contract, and committing himself outwardly to Kilburn for four more years, Will was sweetness and light. He was malleable and attentive at home. He played responsibly, and KU began to win again. On 3 January, the first day of the window, he put in his transfer request, filed for divorce and held a press conference.

'Why are you leaving?' asked the Panther reporter.

'I'd prefer not to answer, if you don't mind. I recently signed a new contract, so I think anyone can see that it's not because I'm unhappy at Kilburn.'

'Is it because of your personal life?'

'I'm not going to expand on that, and I would prefer it if you didn't speculate. What is private and painful should remain that way.'

'Is it true that your marriage is over?'

'I have told you that I won't talk about that. I have nothing but the utmost respect and affection for my wife, but sometimes these things do not work out, and it's very upsetting, but we have to move on. I thought she could change, but it wasn't to be, and I don't want to say anything further about it.'

'What did you think she could change?'

'I've said that I won't discuss private matters in public. I would like to be given space to try to move on with my life. Thank you very much for your time, but I have nothing more to say.'

'Your wife is a very rich woman. Can I ask —'

'No, you can't. I know I speak for a lot of people when I say that I find this kind of prurience about money unpleasant and voyeuristic. Footballers are paid the market value for their services, just like everyone else. I will say, however, just to kill the story you obviously want to tell, that I am legally entitled to half of my wife's estate, but I will not claim it. This is not about money. The only exception, and I say it since it will inevitably become public knowledge, is that I will request half her shares in Kilburn United. It is, after all, a club I have given my life to, and which I am leaving only reluctantly. Pardon? No, sorry, I will not discuss private matters, as I have already said. Holding the shares is how I want to demonstrate my loyalty to what I have always thought of as the best fans in the world.' The fans admired Will's dignified refusal to talk, but they could read between the lines, and they were outraged at Esther on his behalf.

The Bursar was very stressed. Esther was watching Will's press conference in her office. She had only just told the Bursar that Will had moved out of their home the day before. Krenabim had immediately phoned to say the club couldn't afford to let Will go. He ranted that Will was under contract, which he only signed a month ago, he'd settled down on the pitch and he was obviously unhappy about leaving, so he must be persuadable. He said that everyone, except for Esther maybe, needed to work flat out convincing Will to stay, starting from right now. Esther strode back to her office. The Bursar agreed with Krenabim in principle, but she had to deal with Esther, and Esther needed to be calmed down. The Bursar ordered food and wine from the kitchen, and set them up in the boardroom. Periodically, the Bursar would venture some small, definite movement and say something like, 'Right. We must work out what to do now.' Each time she did this, Esther broke down again. Maybe the Bursar would have been more careful if she knew that Esther had not slept or eaten in forty-eight hours.

'It's obvious,' said Esther. 'We make the bastard stay. Even if he doesn't play. He's planned this for fucking years but he can't get away that easily.'

'I know it must seem like that,' said the Bursar. 'It would be easier if I knew what it is he isn't saying, what the problem was between you two?'

'He's a bastard,' said Esther. 'That's the problem. Nothing was wrong between us.'

'People don't just —'

'He's a fucking, fucking bastard. I finally understand exactly everything he's ever done. He made us give him a pay rise so he could walk out on us. He's a bastard. And he pretends not to want money, but the shares in Kilburn are where my money is. He's such a fucking bastard. If he thinks he can get the better of me, he's got another think coming.' She clenched her jaw and said, 'I'm going to tell everyone the truth. I'm doing a press conference of my own.'

'I really think —'

'You can't stop me. Get the Stationery Office to sort it out. I want to do it this afternoon.'

'Certainly, Chancellor.'

The Bursar hurried away. She called 24, who was now twenty-seven and had been promoted to Head of Stationery, and told him what Esther was demanding. Then she looked left and right, as if someone might be hiding in her empty office, and said, 'Come via *the stairs*.'

The Bursar rushed to the stairwell. She wore a sensible brown blouse and a grey skirt. Her hair was neatly bobbed. Her shoes were calculated to give an efficient but casual impression. All this meant that when she bustled, it was because she had a reason. She intercepted the Head of Stationery in the stairwell. He wore tight black trousers, smart shirt, golfing sweater and little red trainers, like someone wearing a quarter of four mutually exclusive outfits. The pair locked eyes, and the Head of Stationery jumped up the last four steps nodding assurance that he was up to this.

'This is an incredibly hard time for her,' the Bursar said. 'This is where we support her, whatever she needs. We have to help her, and make sure she's okay. Do you know what I mean?'

'I think so.'

'It's vitally important that we present a calm and united front. It must not seem as if personal affairs are upsetting the smooth running of the club. Okay?'

'You want me to stop her doing the press conference?'

'Absolutely. You can't let her do it. I've said what I can, but public relations is your job, and I can't stop her, because she has to think I'm on her side, whatever happens. She mustn't speak to anyone until she's calmed down.'

'First question,' said Esther, alone behind the microphones, squinting into the flashlights. At the back of the room, the Bursar tried to catch the Head of Stationery in her glare, but 24 ignored her. This wasn't his fault. No one could have stopped Esther today.

'Your husband has indicated that personal issues underpin his decision to leave Kilburn. Can you comment on this?'

'He's lying.'

'Can you expand on that?'

'He's a liar, and he's lying. He has been planning this secretly for ages to get his hands on my money.'

'But he said he doesn't want your money.'

'My shares *are* my money.'

'Not all of it, surely.'

'Why are you all on his side? I should have expected it. How many women are there in this room? It's typical. He's left me for no reason. He secretly wants to go to Spain. We've already had a bid from Rojo Madrid, so they must have known all about this. He probably has a woman there or —'

'Are you alleging that he was tapped up by Rojo?'

'Of course he was. It's obvious. It's obviously a plot to ruin Kilburn United.'

'That's a pretty serious allegation, Miss Rosslare. Are you sure you want to accuse —'

'Anyone can see that he has been disloyal to me and to the club. Anyone can see that Rojo's bid is suspicious.'

'What about the fact he has just signed a new contract with Kilburn.'

'Can't you see that was just a tactic to put everyone off the scent? It's so obvious.'

'Will you let him go?'

'Of course not.'

'How can you keep him if he doesn't want to stay.'

'He's signed a contract. He can't get out of it. He'll just have to make the best of it.'

'Returning to the personal issue your husband referred to, if I can —'

'I told you. There was nothing wrong with our private life.'

'You had a very public falling-out at the club's Christmas dinner.'

'He knew what he was doing even back then. I understand it now. It was all part of his plot. The way he played and behaved, he was trying to turn everyone against him, so that he would have an excuse to leave, and when he shouted at me that evening, *for no reason at all*, it was to make everyone think there was a problem when there actually wasn't.'

There was a silence. Esther had prepared carefully for the camera, but under the lights a few stray hairs had escaped and stuck in the dampness of her brow, and they combined with her wild eyes to give, in close-up, a frantic impression. After what might have been only a couple of seconds, a voice asked, 'Are you saying that Will Beauchamp deliberately isn't playing to the best of his ability? Are you suggesting —'

'Of course she isn't saying that,' said the Head of Stationery, finally taking control, after increasingly wild gestures from the Bursar. 'You are twisting the Chancellor's words, and taking advantage of her in a difficult time. This press conference —'

'I can speak for myself, thank you very much,' said Esther. 'I am not an idiot. I know how my husband's mind works.'

'Seems like it!' said an unidentified voice, and there was a wave of laughter.

'I know my husband. I know exactly what he's done to me, and to this club. He's a traitor, and he will not be allowed to leave under any circumstances. That is what I called you here to say.' She swept out of the room, Bursar in attendance. The Head of Stationery tried to calm things down, but the conference had been carried live on Panther, so there was a limit to what he could achieve.

Will refused to respond. He said that he didn't want to reply to accusations that surely couldn't have been meant seriously. He added, with great dignity, that he was only too aware that certain people, when they got emotional, couldn't really control what they said or did, that they might say and do terrible things simply because it felt right at that particular moment. These people might regret their words and actions later, and he had been as understanding as he could, but when such behaviour recurs and recurs, the burden ultimately becomes intolerable. 'Whatever is said and done in the heat of the moment,' he said, 'I just want to say this: I am not the disloyal one.' He refused to elaborate.

Privately, however, Will's lawyers conveyed a threat of legal action over Esther's slander. Kilburn had no choice but to sell him. At least they got a fair price. The fans rounded on Esther.

In the immediate aftermath of the Christmas Party, Aisling was desperate to help Kilburn. However, she was acutely aware that this was exactly how she had felt after the previous year's horror show, and she was afraid that she was simply reacting to Strabis's needling, so she forced herself not to act. Now, however, six weeks later, as she watched Will Beauchamp's schemes unfold, the scales fell from her eyes. The Kilburn Social Club was part of what her father had left her, and she had let it go because it was too difficult for her to think about. She failed it, and her family. It was time to redeem herself. She didn't know what to do, but she was on the nearest thing she'd get to a nine-to-five rotation in the next few years, so there would never be a better time to get her head round it.

She needed to tell Jeremy but she wanted to get Nicky over with first.

'You don't mean it.' Nicky was pregnant, sipping cranberry juice over lunch.

'I do, Nicks. I really do.'

'The six months are nearly up,' said Nicky, smugly.

'Oh, for fuck's sake.'

'Leo told you, right at the start, and I agreed with him, that six months was an exit strategy masquerading as commitment. You're coming to the end of it, and you want an excuse. This has nothing to do with Kilburn, and we both know it.'

'This is not about Jeremy,' said Aisling. 'I'm not leaving Jeremy.' She was furious. In the hospital that afternoon, Aisling found her mind racing. Nicky had never understood her properly, but speaking with her always clarified Aisling's thoughts. As she cut through the hard fat around a plumber's heart, ready to excise, rebuild and renew, she thought, *This is all I ever wanted to be, but I shouldn't be here while I'm thinking like this.* The operation went fine, but she felt like she was using someone else's hands.

That evening, Aisling explained the situation to Jeremy, marshalling analogies and arguments she'd been practising all day, fully prepared for the possibility that he might, in light of her decision to focus on Kilburn, finally call a halt to their relationship. Instead, he laughed. 'You've learned a lot arguing with me,' he said.

'Yes. So, you see, if I decide to do something – and I don't know what I can do – then you would still be my rock, I suppose.'

'Ash, I understand that you'll never be happy until you've tried this, but you shouldn't give up surgery while you're doing it.'

'I have to, Jem. I have to do it properly, or I might not see it through.'

'So long as you're sure, darl. As far as I'm concerned, you including me in the decision is what matters. It means I'm part of your life, and your plans. That we're a team.'

'Yes,' said Aisling. 'That's great. That's brilliant.'

In early February, Punty told Dave she was leaving him, and was going to live with a fisherman called Abid. In his deepest heart of hearts, Dave thought she and Abid would make a good couple, but that was a long way down.

*

Dear Zondi,

Well, we could hardly have been more right about Will Beauchamp's plans. He can't have predicted Esther's telly rant though – he got lucky with that.

Also shitty: season eight of the Beach League looks set fair to be at least as depressing as season seven. I thought it couldn't get worse after the introduction of coaches, but now the games have been moved up the hill. Minister Tonta, as a 'special treat', built a beautiful grass pitch in his grounds and presented it to the league last week. I fought a losing battle to keep everything in the village, but there was nothing I could do. Tonta even wanted me to change the league's name, but I wasn't having any of it. He got his son Paul to ask me. The boy approached me after a kick-around on the beach, which is where the kids still play for fun, and said, 'My father thinks it would be a touching gesture if the league was renamed after him in honour of his generosity in building the pitch and contributing to the ongoing fucking up of something that was, in its tiny way, rather wonderful.' I have paraphrased slightly. Little Paul, to be fair to him, looked shamefaced. He kept looking over his shoulder at the goons who were watching him. I put on a show of listening, for their benefit, and I said I wouldn't change the name. I was very grateful, I said, but could he please tell his father that Englishmen are very obsessed with the past and I didn't want to change the name of the league because of <u>history</u> and <u>tradition.</u> We've only had one round of fixtures, but the games are sixty minutes now, professional referees travel up from the capital, and only the Chickens have no hillside family sponsoring them. Consequently, I have bought the Chickens a strip myself, and I coach them. This is tolerated because they are so useless, since any family with half a brain insists its skilful children play for a team which might provide some kind of life-changing patronage. I do not blame them for this. I almost hope someone would take the Chickens off my hands. I'm not sure I can be bothered any more.

It must seem from my letters as if the whole of Nzasa is mad about football, but there are exceptions. The shining one is this amazing kid. Jonathan Ngwere, who's a bright boy and is desperate to go to university in Dodoma and become a teacher. I like him, but I never thought much about him till a few evenings ago when I was hanging around the beach and I saw him playing football with his sister. Jonathan's about five ten and stocky, and he's pretty athletic-looking, but most of the kids are. I suppose, in retrospect, I recall noticing that he was one of the strongest swimmers, but he's never joined in with games. And then, like I say, a few evenings ago, I watched him teasing his little sister by dribbling an old paper ball around her, and doing tricks like you wouldn't believe. I asked him why he doesn't play with the others, and he said he didn't have time because of schoolwork. This time last year I would have tried to persuade him into the Chickens, but now I was just incredibly glad that somehow he's escaped the system. He's a genius, though, and if I noticed it, I dare say one of the other teams will get hold of him and up the hill he'll go. At least it won't be my fault.

Okay, okay: Punty. I meant to get this out of the way at the start, and then when I didn't I thought I'd say it at the end, but I'm just going to say it now. I got your letter this morning, and thank you very much. It's nice that you and Aisling think it's not my fault, or say you think it isn't, but this has happened twice now. I don't know what more I could have done. I don't know what to do now. I don't want to come home or see anyone and I don't want to waste my life. I don't know what I want, basically. I suppose I should write more than this, but I haven't got anything else to say. I genuinely hope she's happy with Abid.

On this basis, you will be pleased and excited to hear my advice about Adam, which is that he's shy and can't believe his luck, and that's all. He can't presume to step into Achilles' shoes (which we both know is not the situation) but you're going to have to make the move. It's as simple as that.

You're right to be nervous about Aisling. This idea of her taking a break from medicine to sort Kilburn out is unhinged. There's nothing she can do to save it, now. Things might have been slower if she'd not sold it in the first place, but it would only have been a more lingering death. We must get her to leave it alone.

Enough, already. Is the world really Hobbes, and Machiavelli, and Nietzsche, and all the other depressing ones? Is it moral cowardice to pretend that it isn't? No, it isn't, and I don't really think that way.

I've just been dumped, remember. I'll be fine in a few weeks. It's not all bad news, anyway. This afternoon, the Chickens beat the Sharks, against any reasonable expectation, and to the well-hidden but surprisingly profound glee of their coach. Stifling industry and well-worked set pieces, as if you hadn't guessed.

    I am thinking of you, and thank you,
    Dave

ANOTHER DAY IN PARADISE

Kilburn Park

2 March 2005

Dearest Dave,

You must be surprised to get a letter from me after so long! I am in my office at the stadium, and the night sky is blue-black outside. It is probably only me in the whole of Kilburn Park, apart from the security people. There are times when the night can feel like it is a liquid weight on your head, enveloping you in its horrible milky darkness, and there are times when it can be a mysterious time of enchantment and possibilities! What is tonight? I wonder.

I have only just heard about that bitch Punty! All I say about that is sorry, but I am not surprised what she did to you. Loyalty is a very rare gift. You are blessed with it and so am I but there are very few people like us. If I may say this, because I know my sister has tried to get you in her gang but you have to remember that I know my sister better than anyone, and Punty always reminded me of a younger version of Aisling. There, I've said it. She and Aisling cannot settle down with anyone because they are too weak to make the necessary commitment. Since you've been gone, I have realised a lot of things, like I intimidate people, for instance. I have noticed that people won't meet my eye when I am angry or speak my mind. This is what happens to an intelligent woman who is not afraid to be counted. This probably comes as a shock to you, I know, because when we were such good friends, I was as quiet as a church mouse! I know you must be very bitter about women, Dave. You have been lied to by my sister, abandoned by Sally, and now deserted by Punty. I promise that we are not all like that, and that there is something better than all this deception. Somewhere, for you, there is the someone you can trust, and who will be devoted to you and your equal. Somewhere there is that person for all of us, it is Fate, but it is VITAL that we don't let Fate walk past while we close our eyes.

So prepare for another shock, Dave. Back when we were so close, I loved you madly from afar! Looking back at how you spoke to me, I think you probably even quite liked me but never said anything because I gave you no encouragement. How funny that seems now! The reason I say it is that it is more important than ever for both our happiness. My defining characteristic is that I probably know my own mind. So listen to this, Dave Guinevere – I still love you, and I always have loved you! What I felt for Will was never serious, just what happened when I was deceived, which will never happen again. And I, unlike some, would never deceive you. Never!

Will has betrayed everyone. I am still in the office because Kilburn United is in Crisis. You probably do not care about all these things, lost in desolation as you must be, and also on the far side of the world, but I know you always believed deeply in the Mission of this football club. I understand that our disloyalty to you, in which Will was to blame as he was for so much, was really why you left England, and that the tragic accident was just the storm that broke the camel's back. I do not know how much you are aware of the world of business (but since you are so clever, you probably know everything!) but the bad season Kilburn United is having means that everyone says the club is under financial pressure. Strabis Kinsale has always been very generous, but he is suddenly reluctant to buy new players for us at this moment in time, probably because he is shocked by what Will did.

The crisis – which would have made me fall apart before, but now I am dealing with it perfectly calmly – got worse because of Will, who is a spy and traitor as well as a bastard. When he betrayed me, he took half of my shares, out of greed, and now he has found a new way to stick the knife into my heart! Three days ago, he told me he didn't want the shares. He asked me if I wanted to buy them (my own shares!), as if he didn't know I spent all my money on them in the first place and couldn't possibly afford them. He said that this was what he thought, and that he would have advised me not to buy so many in the first place because the club is overvalued, which is why he wanted to get rid of them.

Then, yesterday, Aisling came to see me at home, which she never does. I should have known it was some disaster. First she told me about Punty, which was how I knew about your great Sadness (which could be an opportunity?), and then she told me that she had bought the shares from Will! It was then that I realised that they must have planned this whole thing from the start. All the time, Will was secretly working for her so she could take the club away from me, just like she's always taken away everything I really wanted, because she cannot bear to see me happy, even for a moment. The worst thing was that when the news got out, everyone assumed she was helping Kilburn, and supporting me rather than stabbing me behind my back.

Actually this wasn't the worst thing. The worst thing was that when she came round, she said she had been speaking to Adam, who said that Kilburn was overextended and not achieving the success on the pitch we need to sustain our wage bill, and we will obviously not qualify for Europe this year, which will be the final straw. She claimed (she lied!) that Will had first offered his shares to Strabis Kinsale, and Strabis said he didn't want them and suggested Aisling. This means, says Adam, that Strabis is preparing to dump Kilburn. Obviously, Aisling should pay for new players and help, since she now has twenty per cent of the club if you add Hank, who must all be part of this, but she said she had now spent every penny she has, because the Rosslare Group is cash poor (which is a stupid thing to say when it is so valuable). I understand perfectly now that she is trying to make the club unstable and frighten off Strabis so she can buy it for a pittance.

But I will not be beaten by them. I will never believe another thing she says. The Bursar agrees that we may have to sell a couple of players and renegotiate the more extortionate wage demands – which were only raised because of Will's conspiracy against me, of course, on Aisling's instructions (and probably Adam's?) – but she doesn't understand football like I do, and I have worked out that Kilburn can survive if I finally give it my full attention which Will has always kept me from doing. It's obvious that the club is still worth the same as before, since the players are the same, and the ground is the same. I will not be tricked into giving up my birthright.

I am listening to classical music. It is very beautiful and relaxing. After putting this all down on paper, everything is much clearer to me. Dave, you and I are fated to be together and I will wait for you for as long as it takes for your wounds to heal. I have learned that

*the best way to rise above terrible personal times is not to run away,
but to lose oneself in work. Kilburn United desperately needs someone
to help me rescue it, someone who understands its Mission and
Heritage. We both know you are the person to do this. We must
protect my father's (and The General's) legacy from the looters. Then,
working together with me, I hope you will finally overcome the
damage that has been done to you, and admit your deeper feelings.
But, as I say, I am prepared to wait, because I have enough strength
for both of us.*

    More love than you have ever known,
    Esther

*

Aisling slumped in the soft chair, the yellowing walls leering around
her, trying to stay awake. She rested the cup of awful hospital coffee
on her lap, but she didn't remove the lid. The plastic-tasting pastry, its
apricot furrowed like a great golden thumb, perched on her knee. This
was her last night shift until she'd dealt with Kilburn.

When Punty left Dave, Aisling asked Zondi whether Dave might be
persuaded to help her. 'I do not think this would be a good idea,' he
said. 'He will not be careful at this time, and . . . I do not think so.' She
was sure Zondi was wrong. Zondi asked, 'What does Jeremy think?'

'This is not about Jeremy, it's about Kilburn. I've always wanted Dave
to help. It's just now there's nothing to stop him doing it.'

'You will not be able to force David to do what he doesn't want to do.'

'Good,' she said. 'If he comes back, it'll be because he wants to.'
Aisling respected Zondi's opinions, more than anyone's probably, but
you had to be your own person. 'I know you think he's the Tall Hunter,
but this is different. Honestly, Zon.'

'I cannot predict him,' Zondi said.

Aisling sipped her coffee and kept it in her mouth to soften the next
bite of pastry.

Two days later, to celebrate Aisling's rebirth as a 'Lady of Leisure'
(Jeremy's phrase), Jeremy decided to cook for her, Leo and Nicky. He
always cooked when they had guests. He left chambers mid-afternoon,
and met her at Waitrose. Jeremy thought cooking was a great way to
spend quality time together. He arrived half an hour late, which meant

he and Aisling coincided perfectly. Jeremy fussed over his list – two large aubergines, six organic tomatoes, one small jar of salted capers, etc. – and Aisling thought, as she had before, that he never cooked anything that could be produced from the usual kitchen detritus. She worried she was the same.

Aisling meandered down the aisles in Waitrose. With Hank's shares, and her own, she had twenty per cent of the club, which was the threshold for being able to veto some, primarily football, decisions. Strabis didn't mind letting her get hold of this veto. He clearly wasn't interested in the football side of the club, which only made her more determined. She had spent a month meeting with financial experts, usually with Adam sitting in reluctantly, going over the implications of various schemes. Louie, Zondi, Tom and even Carlo had helped her understand what the Socialists were like under Mr Brown and what was different now, what was important for success on the pitch and what was merely nice. She wouldn't take any concrete action until she could articulate a precise goal and had formulated a plan for achieving it. She was going to prove wrong everyone who'd ever said she never followed through. Jeremy still said she could count on him for as long as it took her to get this out of her system. Her correspondence with Dave had been, thus far, unsatisfactory.

'You have to go to Sainsbury's,' said Jeremy. 'They only have capers in vinegar here.'

'That'll be fine,' said Aisling.

'I love you,' laughed Jeremy. 'Do you want to go to Sainsbury's while I pay?' She bit her tongue but she went.

When they arrived home, there was a message from Nicky to say she'd agreed to cover for someone tonight at the last minute, but Leo and little Daniel would be on time. Jeremy was angry because he'd bought food for four, and this threw out his plans. He thought it didn't show, and said, 'Typical! It's no problem. I should have known I'd never get three of my flaky friends in the same room at once! You don't know how lucky you are to have got hold of the last reliable man!'

While Aisling chopped onions and garlic, Jeremy lined up the ingredients in order. 'That was so you,' he said. 'The recipe says "salted" and you think "vinegar" will do just as well.'

'That's not what I think, actually. It's . . . Well . . . I don't really. I mean, I really don't. I just wasn't thinking.'

*

'How's the work?' asked Leo, who was half an hour early. He was five feet seven inches tall, and had an aureole of strong brown hair rising around an increasingly prominent bald spot, and he usually sported a few days' worth of heavy stubble. He was scruffy and barrel-shaped, with a ready smile and easy laugh. His eyes were active above the laugh unless his dimples joined in, in which case they closed with joy, and he guffawed. Little Daniel looked frighteningly like his father, and he slept all the time.

'Pretty good,' Jeremy said. 'I'm defending . . .'

He told a long story while Aisling and Leo sipped, Leo impatiently. When he broke, Leo said, 'And you, Az? How's the rescue mission.'

'It's going okay.'

'Details! Come on, do you have a scheme yet?' Leo, so long as Nicky was not staring at him, was riveted by Aisling's plans. There was an enthusiastic small child in Leo who would never really go away. 'How's Esther? Any closer to sanity?' Aisling shook her head.

'Remember that she's Aisling's sister,' said Jeremy, in a concerned voice. 'I think we should talk about something else,' he continued. 'Food's ready.'

The stew was amazing, as usual, and maybe Jeremy was right about the salted capers, but it was impossible to know. If you never go outside the recipe, cooking is easy, but is it really cooking? Is cooking just reading with actions, or is there something more? Is the real skill making something as delicious when some of the ingredients aren't to hand? Aisling knew she wasn't thinking about cooking, and she pretended to herself that what she was really thinking about was relationships: viz. there was no skill in being like Sally and Jed – it was easy for them because they lived next door to the world's best supermarket, and had a perfect kitchen, and knives like razors, and identical palates, and everything. The *skill* was in making something delicious out of discordant ingredients – out of Jeremy's overpowering sweetness and her own tendency to become acidic. By the time she'd worked through this, Leo bubbling away in the background, she had almost persuaded herself that this really was her subtext.

Leo and Jeremy were discussing Brasenose friends, as usual. Leo had a wicked sense of humour she noticed only slowly when they were younger because she was being careful not to lead him on, and he brightened Nicky whenever they were together. Leo's mind wasn't on the discussion at hand. He kept glancing at Aisling, and she thought he was trying to tell her something. After a little pause, he mentioned that a guy in the year below him and Jeremy now got comically self-righteous letters published almost every week in *The Times*. The letters, which could have been written by a particularly pompous Trollopian vicar, were funny in and of themselves, but Jeremy didn't get why it was *so* funny. The point of Leo's story was that, at Brasenose, the one thing that everyone knew about this guy was that he deflowered half the college's Christian Union. Jeremy either never heard this titbit or didn't remember it, and Leo squinted at Aisling. She pretended not to understand, because there was nothing wrong with the fact that Jeremy was above gossip. Leo was very perceptive, though.

When Jeremy left the room, Leo asked, 'What are you doing, Azza? What's really important to you?' She deflected him by saying, 'Kilburn.' He played along, because this was hardly something they could talk about with Jeremy next door. 'Are you sure you should be thinking about Kilburn with Strabis Kinsale circling?' he asked.

'I'm sure.'

'Okey-doke, but what are you going to *do*? It's not as if the club's in any danger, or as if Strabis is struggling for cash. He won't let you have it unless he's getting something in return, and you're not going to give him the Rosslare Group, so . . .'

'I've got sort of a plan.' He asked what it was, and she said, involuntarily looking to the door, 'Not today. Not until I've worked it out properly, I mean.'

'Okay, but we know he really wants the Rosslare Group, and he's trying to use Kilburn as a way in. You've got to be prepared to let the club go, if it comes to that.'

'That's never going to happen.'

'Ash —'

'He couldn't beat my father, and he won't beat me. Don't worry about it, Leo.'

'What are you trying to do? You can't turn KU into what it was. We've eaten from the tree of knowledge. We know the players have clay feet.'

'I don't agree.'

'Really? I mean that. Really?'

'Everyone looks like they have clay feet when reporters start digging around their private lives.'

'Only if they have clay feet. If there was nothing to report, what could we do?'

'You're so fucking prissy.'

'You're the one talking about getting back to the old days. If things only looked great because the players got away with murder, then what's the point?'

'They didn't. There was a time when KSC *were* what they said. Mr Brown was . . . Do journalists have to be so fucking cynical?'

'If the players were so wonderful, there's nothing a journalist could have said.'

'Tell that to Calum fucking Horton.'

Jeremy was back in the room, and by now he'd put his hands protectively on Aisling's shoulders, with the tips of his thumbs and the inside of his index fingers grazing her neck. She wanted to shake him off. He said, 'The things Horton said about Ash were hardly in the public interest, were they?' – and they're into this again. Leo got very worked up that his vocation had become something his social circle felt happy vilifying. Out of nowhere, he asked if Dave was staying in Nzasa.

'No, no, Leo,' said Jeremy. 'I told you, not tonight. You haven't run this past Nicky, have you?'

'I'm sorry, Az,' Leo said. 'I've got a thing I thought you might be able to help me with, or Dave might, if he's still out there.'

'That's enough, Leo,' said Jeremy. 'I'm keeping Aisling out of your sordid clutches.' Leo looked annoyed and he left soon after. Jeremy abased himself. He said he didn't know what he was thinking, letting Leo raise his stupid plan, but Leo could be so persuasive if you weren't on your guard. Aisling asked what Leo wanted, and Jeremy smiled, 'I forbid it, hon. I should have realised that they're all the same. I'll take you out tomorrow, somewhere special, to make up for this.'

While Jeremy slept, Aisling thought about how much she had gained from their relationship, which didn't take long, and the next morning, when he tried to kiss her, she couldn't. She told him it was over. He quickly marshalled his forces, yielding territory here, demanding concessions there, struggling to establish a new border. It was hopeless. There was nothing he could do if she wasn't willing to treat with him, and she wasn't. 'I'm sorry, Jeremy,' she said 'I've tried, but it's not right.' With a dangerous sense of liberation, she phoned Leo.

*

Nzasa was too small a place for Dave to avoid Punty, and he was too proud to try. All the same, he was sickened by her saccharine maturity, her tendency to clasp his hands in hers and ask whether he was all right. She insisted on wearing 'native clothes', as if everyone in Nzasa didn't want jeans and T-shirts. She looked ridiculous. 'You'll fly home in a year,' he said.

'You've never understood me,' she said. 'I don't need my old friends and I don't care what's happening in the West. I wasn't alive before Tanganyika. Nothing was ever real compared to being here and what I feel about Abid. All I want to do is work with my hands, and be there for him. You always say we should focus on the little things and try to make life better bit by bit, but I'm the one doing it. Life is about being at peace, and you aren't. I'm sorry, but I have myself to think about.'

Dave could not articulate what he felt when he saw Punty with Abid. Jealousy was certainly part of it, and loss. Also despair. Outwardly, he carried on as normal.

Dave was shocked and upset at what Aisling was up to. It would be better to put Kilburn out of its misery rather than have it besmirched by a tawdry struggle, rending and snarling for life, red with nature's tooth and claw. He was glad its name had changed. He didn't care if Kilburn United died. It was just another football club. The fans would find somewhere else to go. Everything dies.

Dave would still have told you that his life was satisfying. Routine is therapeutic, and time is the healer. He rose, taught, read, ran, cooked, ate and slept. He didn't shun his fellow expats, but he withdrew part of himself. They saw and understood. He resented their understanding.

The Chickens won four and drew three of their first seven matches of the season. Ten days ago, Minister Tonta sent poor little Paul to inform Dave that the Eagles had fired their coach and the Minister himself had selected Dave to be his replacement. Dave said that he meant no disrespect but that he had made a commitment to the Chickens, and he could only reconsider that commitment once the season was over. Paul looked terrified.

Minister Tonta agreed that Dave's loyalty was a marvellous characteristic, and so on and so forth. To reward him, and the Chickens, Minister Tonta declared that he would henceforth sponsor the Chickens as well as the Eagles. They would be allowed to train on his grounds, and after training they would of course be fed at the big house, and driven home, and everything else. To signal his commitment, he would remove his second son, Robert, from the Eagles, and place him with the Chickens. Tonta made his announcement at the end of last Friday's game. Dave wanted to refuse, but the joyful little Chickens ran around as if their heads had been cut off. Dave really couldn't see what he could have done differently, unless he had played to lose. Would it have been worth doing that if it had saved the Chickens? Once you are playing to lose, is there anything about you that is worth saving? He wasn't reflective, he was furious, but he thought he hid it while he was teaching.

A school day ended, a successful day in which Dave had managed to describe the nature of blood cells without feeling too much of a charlatan. Two of Minister Tonta's men were waiting on the dusty street for Jonathan Ngwere. The Minister's local sly man, who was pale and fat, asked Jonathan if he wanted to hear some very special news.

'Yes,' said Jonathan cautiously.

'The coach has seen you play football with your sister, and told the Minister. Now Minister Tonta wishes you to join his Eagles!'

'I do not play football.'

'The coach is insistent. This is a great day for you, no?'

'I do not want to.'

'The Minister insists. You must come with us and meet the coach.'

'I have to go home to my mother.'

'You are to come with us,' said the Minister's other man, who was tall and thin. Neither of these were hard men.

'Is there a problem?' asked Dave.

'The boy is to come with us to the Eagles.'

'Do you want to go, Jonathan?'

'No, sir.'

'Then you don't have to,' said Dave, stepping between Jonathan and the Minister's men.

'We have orders from Minister Tonta,' said the sly man, bristling, and Dave punched him in the face. He hadn't expected to, but he didn't apologise. He stepped towards the shocked man and hit him again. The sly man fell to his knees, looking for help. The other had his gun out but Dave didn't care. He was ready to carry on, to grab the gun if he had to, aware of the stunned faces all around. He was protecting the rights of the individual, he told himself. 'Tell Tonta that if he wants Jonathan, he has to come through me,' he said absurdly.

When Jonathan's mother heard, she dragged her son up the hill to apologise to Minister Tonta and beg forgiveness, because this was a wonderful opportunity. Minister Tonta sent Dave a gloating note. It said that bygones were bygones, and so on and so forth, because it was clear that Dave was not himself at the current time, but please to be aware that the period of grace was not indefinite. Dave was embarrassed by his counterproductive quixotism. Punty congratulated him for finally making some progress and committing himself to protecting the Village against the Hill. He couldn't say anything to her.

Adam and Zondi arranged to see a film. Adam worried how he would know when the time had come, if it did? How long would be the gap between too soon and too late? He wanted to ask Aisling, but she was all over the place. Adam was worn out trying to protect her from herself.

Zondi was waiting in his huge coat. He saw Adam, walked over, took him by the hand and walked him straight past the cinema. Zondi's hand was small and hard in Adam's, warm and dry and definite. Adam did not normally think in adjectives. They only held hands for a few hundred yards; they both hated the display. Adam knew the way home on foot by now. Sometimes Zondi would tell a story but often they said nothing.

Holding hands in bed, looking up at the stars, Zondi said, 'The stars say we are lying with our heads to north, and it is December.'

'It must have taken you ages.'

'I did not get everything right first time. Also I have made it neater. I have made the ones I like bigger. I do not mind that they are wrong.'

Adam said, 'I recognise Orion.'

Zondi paused, and Adam wondered if he had said something wrong. 'Orion is our hunter too.'

'The Tall Hunter?' Zondi nodded. 'That's amazing.'

'Yes.' Zondi's forearm was light as a twig over his, Zondi's side hot against his flank, but not uncomfortable. 'The three, in a triangle, near the corner of the room? Those are the arms of /Kaggen. His head is the small star above them, his back is the two next to each other, and the big one is his feet. He is on the edge of the others, looking in.'

'Where is the Butterfly?'

'The middle. The four bright stars are his head, his tail and the tips of his wings, and the many little stars are the pattern of his wings.'

'He is —'

'In the African night, it is not just the little stars. He has clouds of other stars behind. He is not always in the middle of the sky, but he always feels like it.' Zondi's hand stayed calmly in his while he spoke.

'Thank you,' said Adam, and felt the fingers tighten.

The afternoon after his stupid fight, Dave lay face down in the water, breathing through his snorkel and watching small fish eddy in the rolling tide. You could see them better if you were closer to the shore, but out here there was enough field of vision that he often saw one of the gun-barrel-blue barracuda flick in from the deeper water, snatch a hapless victim and swagger away in a flurry of disturbed sand. There was nothing sinister about his enjoying this moment. People like to see action. A few times, he'd seen sharks approach the shore. They were only three or four feet long, and the locals weren't worried by them, so neither was he. He'd always been able to quell his fear of sharks, anyway. Even in Australia and South Africa, fear was statistically inane.

He should head back to shore. However much sunscreen he wore, and however long he'd been in Tanganyika, half an hour in the late afternoon was all his skin could stand. He swam lazily past the kids, who were whooping and skidding on the bodyboards he'd bought them. When he did so, Punty complained that they'd obviously always body-surfed before, and why was he interfering with these new boards? He said that they'd also died of cholera and malaria before, and why was *she* helping the doctors interfere with *that*? That had been years ago, but it was only at this moment that Dave realised Punty was humouring him when she eventually agreed. Fuck her. Bodysurfing didn't work when the waves were too big or small, or if you weren't skilful. Bodyboards were better in almost all circumstances for almost all the kids. He'd stayed in the water longer than usual because he was putting off writing to Aisling. Zondi had written to him and said, 'Aisling will not listen to me or Adam. You are the one she might listen to.' Then there was Esther's letter.

Dave dug his feet into the hot sand, trying to dry them before he got to the house. The fine grains fell away as he banged them with his flip-flops.

He didn't go inside, but stood with his hands on the rail, looking over the sea, feeling the grain and knots of the wood through his soles.

What would be good for Aisling in the long term? What would be good for him? Kids were playing football on the beach, laughing. He wanted nothing to do with football. This morning, Jonathan said to him, 'Thank you for trying, Mr Guinevere. I know there is nothing you can do. Maybe it will be easier to be a teacher anyway if Minister Tonta is on my side, maybe?'

'Maybe, Jonathan.'

'Yes. Thank you, sir.' Jonathan was a great kid, like most of them, but they were so unprepared. It was Dave's job to ready them for their lives, and how could he do that if he didn't have an idea of what the world should be? How far do you help people; how far do you let them make their own mistakes; are you ever responsible for someone else? How long had he been standing still, brain in neutral? The sun set fast in Nzasa, but not that fast, and the red disc was almost gone.

He cooked a simple supper, and poured a Coke. He laid out a sheet of heavy paper and sat, pen in hand. He was tired. He folded his head on to his arms to think. There was nothing new in his head. *Dear Aisling*, he began. He asked her straight off if she was sure about Jeremy. *I understand how Jeremy feels right now. There's always been a similarity between you and Punty.* He left it at that, thinking he was being measured and businesslike, and moved on. He reiterated that saving Kilburn was a pipe dream, and he wouldn't help her keep it alive. He said he wasn't being driven out of Nzasa by Punty. He wrote, *I can make a real difference here. I teach mostly kids from the Hill now, but they're the ones who'll be in power eventually.* He added, unable to help himself, that in Punty's opinion all the kids needed to learn was how to fish and farm. *I explained to her the other day that there's no point in that,* Dave wrote. *Global trade rules mean they can't sell what they produce. Punty said my whole problem is that I always try to make things more complicated than they are. She said they don't have to sell their fish to England, they have to sell them to the next village, and global trade is irrelevant. I called her an idiot, she said she didn't have to listen to me, and she walked off. I nearly followed her, but I won't argue with her outside the house. The only thing I can't bear is people's pity, and that would be worse if people thought we were fighting.*

Dave stood and stretched. He hadn't meant to be so involved, but if anyone deserved a full and precise explanation it was Aisling, so he carried on: *I couldn't leave it alone, for some reason. I went round to hers in the evening, and I tried to persuade her by agreeing that she was right, but only in the short term. She behaves as if now will last for ever, but it's building in the sand. In the end the tide will come, and the world will break through, and her dreams will wash away. She said I was being depressing, but I'm the one trying to give Nzasa the tools to deal with the future, because tomorrow always comes.*

Dave stopped there. He didn't tell Aisling how Punty had replied. 'I understand you're hurting,' she'd said. 'I'm very sorry, but what happened was best for both of us. You'll see that one day, and everything will look better. Perhaps you would help yourself by not seeing so much of me?' Dave, as usual, was too enraged to reply.

Then Dave described the fight with Tonta's men, and looked at the bruises on the back of his hand, the little cuts from the sly goon's teeth, the red deadened behind a thin film of antiseptic cream. He felt better for having acted, but the feeling was illusory. *It's my job to prepare the kids*, he wrote, *but only in the schoolroom. The world doesn't need paladins taking matters into their own hands because they don't like what it's become, and I have to control myself. I want to fight all the time, as if that's an answer to anything. Kids like Jonathan should use their talents as best they can, whatever I think. I'm not coming home to where people might listen to me. I'll do less damage here.*

Dave finished off, wrote a reply to Esther, which was less difficult than he expected, and wandered to the hospital to put the letters in the bag. Nzasa would struggle on, for five years or fifty, until all the things the villagers clung to had disintegrated. Then they would have to change, find a place in whatever new world came. If there was no space then, then at least the struggle would be over. That is how Nzasa seemed to Dave. He wanted everything to be different.

*

Nzasa
10 March

Dear Esther,
I was very surprised to receive your letter.
I think the most important thing for me to say first is that I am very honoured by your feelings about me, I genuinely am, but I am afraid I do not feel the same about you. I think immediate honesty

in these cases is always the best, so we can move onwards without any misunderstanding.

You say you are not still upset about Will, but from a distance I can't help feeling that you are. I am desperately sorry about what he did to you. My disagreements with him were public knowledge in the end, so there is no point in my saying that I can't believe it turned out badly, but I am absolutely sincere when I say I'm sorry. I am so far away that I can't be sure about anything, but I imagine many people think you're being paranoid about what he's done. I believe most of what you say. I think he's a sly and scheming man, who married you for money. It's pointless to speculate further, because nothing can be proven. I say it so you know that I, unlike many others I imagine, think you are justified to feel persecuted.

However, and this is very important, I think you're wrong about Aisling. She's not trying to do you out of Kilburn United (I still find 'United' hard to write) – she is trying to rescue it. She hates what Will did as much as you do. I'm not saying she's always cared about football, we both know that's not the case, but in the last few years, she's started to see, as you have always done, that the club was a special part of your family's legacy.

The crucial word in that last sentence is 'was'. This is so important, Esther. I've tried many times to tell Aisling, but I don't think she's listening, that football is changed for ever. It used to be separate from the world, a little, but it isn't any more, and probably that's a good thing in some ways, but it is bad in others. There's no use whining about it, because it's happened and there's nothing any of us can do. I've advised Aisling to get out of Kilburn, and I advise you to do the same thing.

I also have to say that Punty is nothing like Aisling. Punty ignores the world because her life is all very nice, thank you. Aisling wants to try to put the world right, even if what she wants to do would be a mistake. Punty and I are absolutely fine. You mustn't think I am too upset. I worry more about you.

You're young and there are so many other things you could do that would be worth your time. The Foundation is not a bad thing, though it tends to focus on the quick, flashy fix rather than the real problems. If you want some advice on causes you can get involved in that might really make a difference, you have only to ask. It's all the long-term ones that count: trade agreements, water, diseases that rich Westerners don't get, education and equalisation of economic opportunity. I'm not a prophet. I'm only saying the stuff that everyone knows but won't commit to because they're too scared that if they start trying to solve the real issues, they'll never escape. That's why I'm staying in Nzasa. These kids will run the country one day, and if I can persuade them that some time, one day, there will be a reckoning, then maybe they will be the ones who break the cycle.

This letter got more lectury than I meant it to. All I meant to say was that I am very grateful for what you said and sorry I do not feel the same, and that Aisling is not the villain of the piece. It's history, money and power, and you can't fight them. I hope that these difficult times do not dull the many things about you which I have always valued.

Your friend,

Dave

GRASPING

David (or Cassandra, as I have taken to calling you),
I have my fingers in my ears and I'm making blablablablablabla
noises to stop me from hearing what you're saying. You can tell me
till you're blue in the face that I'm wasting my time, but this club,
in my hands, with my money, is better off than it would be in any
other way. We both know it. You're always saying that we have to
do the things we can, make the things around us better, and this is
something I can make better. I know I have to try at least.

We also both know I'm not like Punty, and you only wrote it
because you were red raw. It wasn't nice for me to read, though. I
should be big enough not to mention that, but I'm not.

What did you write to little sis, by the way? She came screaming
round here with your letter two days ago, saying that it was proof
that you were part of the conspiracy. She said she had smoked you
out of your sordid little burrow by pretending to be in love with you
to see what you'd say, and no doubt you had boasted to me about
it, but her plan had worked perfectly, and now our 'evil scheme' is
doomed and we'll be sorry. I don't think you have much influence
with her any more.

I shouldn't joke. Esther has really lost the plot, and I feel sorry
for her. If I thought for a second she wouldn't go berserk, I'd suggest
she went to see someone professionally. Donald called me last week
to say the Board needs to replace her. I don't know how that's going
to happen.

Strabis Kinsale is up to something unrelated to the football club,
which is why he let me get hold of Will's shares, I suppose. The
Group is in decent shape but short of day-to-day cash, and I only
managed to buy the shares because the programmer people at
Knight Soft have had another good year. They've been designing

combat-simulation games for so long that they have a sideline in the software that makes sense of all the electronic data coming into tanks and helicopters, and we've just got a big defence contract. I could have explained that better, but you get what I'm saying. (In fact, you get it so much that you are already preparing some response about how the pampered West uses technology to distance itself from battle – that it is all easier to deal with if we treat it as unreal. If you tell me you are not thinking this, I shall know you are the shifty liar my sister says you are. Of course, the stuff about distancing ourselves from war is completely true – I read it in Fucker Calum's column so it must be – and it makes me feel odd. I never saw myself as a profiteer before. Every little helps, I suppose.)

I take childish joy in pointing out that you and the Fucker think alike, and I do it because I'm annoyed with you. I'm tired, I'm getting into something huge, and I'm scared, but I know it's the right thing to do and I want you on my side. You say you're happy out there, but that's not how it comes across. I can't believe you're satisfied in Nzasa. It's not enough for you. For Punty, maybe, but not for you. I don't mean this in a terrible way, but I'm not shocked about Punty. I wouldn't be your friend if I didn't say this, but you started seeing her on the rebound from Sally, and then you went to Africa, and you two were stuck together with no one else you could really speak to. Of course that made you closer, but think back to what you thought of her before you went away. Did it ever cross your mind before you went away, even for an instant, that she might be for life? We get things wrong when we are young or under pressure, and it's hard to take them back. I don't have to say the rest.

When I say 'be careful', I'm speaking to you as a friend who has some perspective. And don't say that you are trying to do the same thing when you tell me to run away from Kilburn – the cases are completely different. You've had an awful few years, and if you sit back from yourself for one moment, you'll see what an impact they have had on how you look at things. I've been writing to you for a long time, and I know you. You say the world doesn't need paladins, but if you're not trying to make the world better, what's the point in anything? That's why you had that fight. You were showing those kids there's another way, and it might look as if it had no effect but

370

they'll all remember it. There's a place for people who are prepared
to be an example. Everything you've done in Nzasa screams that you
think this way, and when I hear you trying to deny it, it makes me
wonder how the hell it is that <u>you</u> are worrying about <u>me</u>. You think
you're not coming back, but I've got other ideas, Davey, and I'm not
taking no for an answer.

    Life, be in it,
    Aisling

*

Kilburn's problems in the boardroom and within its squad took a predictable toll, and the club finished seventh in the league. Billy Krenabim wanted out. After making a gentleman's agreement with Torino, he publicly criticised Kinsale for being mean and Kilburn's players for being lazy. Kilburn (and everyone else) had seen Krenabim do this before and refused to pay him off. Eventually, he was forced to resign. His statement read that he loved Kilburn and that he would always support the team, but he'd been hired by an incompetent organisation and he deserved better.

The Board met late in May. Present were Donald, Hank Tam, the Bursar, Aisling and Esther, who might have been ejected from the Chancellorship but whose shares still commanded a seat. The Chancellorship would probably stay vacant. Only Esther had ever really misunderstood what the role had been created to do. The Bursar presented a gloomy report. Because Kilburn weren't in Europe, there was no chance of meeting next season's wage bill. Moreover, the new stand left the war chest in a parlous state that the sale of Will Beauchamp had only just covered.

'Strabis will have to pay,' said Esther.

'Well,' said Donald, and looked around. Everyone except Esther knew what he was going to say, and she only didn't because she couldn't take a hint. 'It's not that he doesn't want to help – he wanted me to be very clear about that – but he also wanted me to convey that he won't be treated like a fool.'

'Who has —'

'He wasn't blaming anyone. I think, if anyone, his argument is with Billy Krenabim, but he said the club must take responsibility. He wants

Kilburn to stand on its own two feet for a period, and if it doesn't, he might have to walk away. He would regret doing so, but he regards this as tough love.'

Esther was shocked. She turned to Aisling and said, 'This is you, isn't it? How did you get him to do it?'

'It's not me,' said Aisling.

'You should give the money then,' said Esther. 'You want to be the owner, so you should behave like it.'

'I don't have the cash. You know I don't, and I will not try to raise it while Strabis still controls the club.'

Donald watched, almost pitying. Strabis was trying to lever Aisling into selling chunks of the Rosslare Group in order to fund Kilburn, or to borrow against Group assets. If he could persuade her to haemorrhage enough cash, he might finally be able to make a move for the Group. Strabis had told Donald that, should Strabis ever succeed, Donald's expertise would be considered a valuable addition to Quo Vadis?, but Donald retained some residual family loyalty. He stopped the cat fight with a decisive 'Bursar?'

'I have been considering our options in case this —'

'You knew?' squealed Esther. 'Everybody knew?'

The Bursar continued. 'The most obvious course of action,' she said, 'is to rationalise certain assets, renegotiate wages in upcoming contracts, and refrain from buying new players over the summer.'

'You're so blind!' said Esther. 'We're a football club. Everything depends on our results. We can't economise! It's so obvious. We make money when we win. Strabis knows that.'

The Bursar said, 'There is truth in that. If we behave like a small club, we don't attract players, but the problem is —'

'Exactly,' said Esther. 'That's what I said.'

'For fuck's sake, Esther,' said Donald. 'Can't you hear between the lines? If we don't tighten our belts, and Strabis lets it happen, Kilburn's going bust within a year. Even if we do tighten our belts, and we qualify for Europe next season, we might still go bust. You bought too many fucking players and you pay them too much.'

'We're all responsible,' said the Bursar.

'Very noble, Bursar, very fall-on-your-sword. But the decisions weren't so insane when it looked like we'd have a successful season, and before Esther's private life fucked that up the arse. That wasn't our fault. I don't blame Strabis for washing his hands. We can't pay our wage bill. We certainly can't buy new players.'

'The squad is larger than we need,' said Aisling.

'Yes,' said the Bursar, looking gratefully away from Donald. 'That's a very good point. We have a squad large enough to cover a Champions League run, but we're not in the Champions League. Maybe we could trim now, and when we're back in the Champions League, we expand again?' She looked around for someone who might support her. 'What do you think, Aisling?'

'I'm still learning,' said Aisling.

*

Nzasa

31 July

Dear Aisling,

So. Here it is. This is my last letter from Nzasa.

Your scheme worked a treat. Leo charmed the socks off everyone here (including me). Everyone believed that he was an old friend, and then he flew home and stuck the dagger all the way in. That's a large chunk of this year's aid budget for Tanganyika fucked in the higher cause of Leo's circulation, or, as he so touchingly calls it, 'the Truth'. I suppose it might conceivably affect the way Nagape behaves, though it's more likely to change the way the EU and UN deal with aid, and, to be frank, it's not even likely to do that because turkeys don't vote for Christmas. Leo can dream of a better world, but the longer I spend here, and the more I see people running for a seat on the gravy train, the less likely it seems. People will die of hunger because of what Leo wrote. Maybe he's right that people were dying anyway. Maybe I, as you knew would happen, am being chucked out of the country. You've grown fucking cunning in your old age.

Punty's pregnancy has nothing to do with me coming home. I'm angry with her for being too scared to tell me about it until it was obvious, but it is what it is, and I wish her the best in her deluded choices (I don't mean Abid). If I sound bitter, it's because I am. Zondi told you I was dangerous, and my first response was to be angry with him. My first response to everything is to be angry, and yes, I know, it's because of what's happened to me here, but I'm writing this so you can never say I didn't tell you. I'm coming home, but I can't spend time with you. I have my own agenda, and I'll do things my way or not at all. I don't guarantee that I'm what you expect, or want, or will like. This is your last warning.

I've packed. I've said goodbye to everyone. I'll be in the car with the courier who'll get this letter to you at about the same time I could have delivered it by hand, but I've written so many while I was here that it seemed the appropriate way to end this chapter.

That's it. I'm off.

Dave

DAVID COMES HOME

Strabis Kinsale thought he would probably let Dave Guinevere manage Kilburn. It looked as if Aisling had manoeuvred very deftly to force Guinevere out of Tanganyika, but her suddenly saying that Dave would take the job if he were offered it made Strabis suspicious. He couldn't be certain what had brought Guinevere and Aisling together, or what they were planning. Guinevere was apparently still volatile after being dumped by his model. If he was functioning on emotion, that could be useful. Strabis wanted to meet Guinevere face to face. Know thy enemy, he thought.

The moment his private morning hour was over, his secretary knocked and brought in a message. It was from Guinevere, who demanded a meeting no later than tomorrow. Strabis nodded and spun his chair slowly towards the window. *No later than tomorrow?* He was not impressed by amateurs trying to flex their muscles. Moreover, he didn't need Guinevere. He would have the Rosslare Group in the end, inevitably, and he was in no particular hurry.

On the other hand, of all his various strategies for attacking the Rosslare Group, the most elegant was to enmesh Aisling in Kilburn United. Allowing her a little victory over Guinevere would help that. The only danger was that Dave might turn around the club's fortunes. Strabis didn't think that was possible, but he didn't underestimate his opponents. He buzzed his secretary and told her to set up a lunch at the Danton Grill. His secretary returned a few minutes later saying that Guinevere would prefer somewhere more private, preferably Strabis's office, preferably first thing in the morning. Strabis said this was fine. You lose nothing conceding irrelevant territory.

So, at six the next morning, Strabis stood in the window of his office, bright sun slanting across St James's Square. He didn't register Guinevere until the man was almost at the stairs of Quo Vadis?. He'd heard that the footballer's hair was grey now, but his mind's picture had somehow not adapted. He didn't face back into the room when Guinevere was announced, interested in what the other would do. Almost immediately, Guinevere said, 'I'm not here to play games.'

Strabis turned. 'Of course not,' he said. Guinevere's hair was more distracting than he expected. It made him ageless, harder to fathom. 'You wanted to see me?'

Dave was not nervous, but he was taut. 'You decide whether I get the job, yes?'

'Yes.'

'You know I was chucked out of Nzasa? I didn't want to leave.'

'I thought so, until you said you'd take this job. Now I'm not sure.'

'Fair enough.' Guinevere shrugged, just with his hands, and collected himself. 'How discreet are you?'

'This sounds like the start of a game.'

'I don't have time for bullshit. I'm asking you a straight question.'

'I'm discreet.'

'If I take this job, I intend to relegate Kilburn United, and I need a free hand.'

Strabis didn't expect that. Surprisingly, it excited him. 'Are you serious?' he asked, and then immediately added, 'No, okay. My first question is: why? Is it revenge on Aisling?'

'No.'

'Okay I'm just going to say, since we *are* playing games, whatever you pretend, I'm taking everything you say with a handful of salt.'

'Nothing I can do about that. Like I say, this isn't a game for me.' Every time Guinevere spoke he took a half-step forward, making himself bigger, his body and strangled voice failing to hide the demons. Strabis noticed such things. 'Kilburn's fucked,' Guinevere said. 'We both know it, and you're doing what you can to speed it up. You won't sell it until it's screwed because you only bought it as a way to get at the Rosslare Group, so that's that.'

Strabis was surprised that Guinevere had come out and said it, but it was hardly news, and it wasn't provable. 'So?' he asked.

'It won't work,' said Guinevere. 'You don't understand Aisling. She'll never sell the Group.'

'You're wrong. She'll sell.'

'Fair enough, Mr Kinsale. It doesn't matter to me. But, if you're right, then Kilburn being relegated will be perfect for you, because at that point you can either get rid of Kilburn Park or bankrupt the club, and

Aisling will sell up to prevent either of those things. I happen to think that when Kilburn falls off the edge, and there's nothing she can do to save it without selling the Rosslare Group, Aisling will let it fall and you'll have wasted a lot of time and money. But whatever we think about what happens afterwards, we both want Kilburn relegated.'

'I know why I do,' said Strabis. 'You've given me no good reason for yourself.'

'I care about Aisling. I care about Kilburn, too, but it's fucked, sooner or later, whatever happens, so I want it to be sooner. That way, Aisling can get back to her life.'

'She'll hate you for it,' said Strabis.

'Probably, in the short term. Anyway, that doesn't make it wrong. I'm the only person who can do this without it dragging on for a few years, and if it drags on, I think it makes her bitter and twisted, and I don't want that. She chose a life away from this shit, and she should be allowed to lead it.'

'Do you love her?'

'No.'

'Does she love you?'

'No.' Well, thought Strabis, that was bullshit, but a lot of the rest might well be true, or at least true enough to be getting on with. Guinevere was acting on impulse. Strabis trusted his own judgment concerning Aisling. He could manipulate her so she'd never let Kilburn go.

Guinevere listed his demands. He wanted twelve million for transfers; he wanted a commitment that the club would reintroduce the equal wage, without bonuses, as soon as that could be made consistent with existing contracts; and he insisted on total authority with respect to all aspects of training. He wanted no assistants. He would keep a physio and a doctor, and that was it.

Guinevere left, and Strabis informed his secretary that he needed half an hour alone. He was unfussed by Guinevere's style. Strabis would base his decision on what was good for him alone, and if it looked to Guinevere as if Strabis had succumbed to an ultimatum, that was to Strabis's advantage, because it meant Guinevere couldn't read him.

It was an easy decision. Hiring Guinevere would please the fans, and it would tie Aisling tighter to the club. In addition, if the timescale with respect to Kilburn were accelerating, Strabis had some other cleavages in the Rosslare Group that he thought he could exploit. He dug out Esther's phone number.

At a special meeting of the Board, Esther learned that Dave had joined her sister and stuck his knife in her heart again. An hour later, her mobile rang, with an unknown number. It was Strabis Kinsale! He said he had a matter of extreme importance to discuss, and said he would pick her up from her house at seven that evening.

Why did he want to see her? It couldn't be a coincidence that it was today, so it must be to do with Dave somehow. Strabis hardly seemed to notice her usually, because he was always so haughty and concentrating on Aisling, like everyone else. He was very handsome, which was irrelevant, because she must remember to be on her guard, because her father said Strabis was dangerous, but her father hadn't been perfect. Strabis had been a good owner for Kilburn, whatever people said about his motives. He'd been very generous, even if he had always done everything through Donald.

Precisely on time, he knocked heavily on the door, even though there was a bell. He was a perfect gentleman. Esther looked in the mirror, and she saw a cool and sophisticated woman of the world. She was underdressed, if anything, the way Aisling always was. She opened the door. Strabis wore a beautiful dark-blue wool suit in case Esther dressed up, so he could put her at her ease. He kissed her, quite near the edge of her mouth, the beard and two-day stubble rough against her cheek.

They went to the Bitter Lemon by black cab, not Diabolo. Strabis didn't need to be furtive. A beautiful girl with too much make-up greeted him excitedly at the restaurant, and pouted breathily that his table was ready, of course. Strabis hardly looked at the pouting girl, just thanked her in an off-hand way while he took Esther's coat and handed it over, then guided her through the busy room, his hand lightly on her shoulder. She recognised several faces in the room, and carried herself even more erect. Strabis pulled her seat aside before the waitress could get to it, and tucked her gently in. He was too refined to bring up business in the early stages.

They swapped stories while they ate. Esther chose peppered salad and grilled snapper with a lime salsa. Strabis ate truffles and venison. He ordered Esther a white wine which he said would complement her meal perfectly, and it did, sharp against the spicy freshness of her food.

He drank a pale red. The waiter brought them a dessert menu. There was a pause while Esther examined it.

'I've brought you here to apologise,' Strabis said.

'About what?'

'I didn't realise what you felt about Dave Guinevere until Donald reported back from the meeting. I've been extremely busy, and when I heard he was prepared to manage the club, I presumed everybody would be overjoyed. Had I known you objected, I would have met with you beforehand. It was unforgivably careless of me. You are, after all, the soul of the club.'

'That is very kind of you.'

'It's nothing, Esther.'

'Are you going to make me Chancellor again?' she blurted.

He tilted his head, thinking. 'I strongly considered it.' Her face must have fallen. 'Don't be disappointed. I want you for something much more important.'

'Really?'

'Really. But first I am going to tell you something, to show I trust you. The time has come for me to take over the Rosslare Group.' Esther gulped in shock. He just said it like it was nothing! He just said it! 'I've never made a secret of what I want. I'm a straightforward man.'

Esther couldn't speak. She looked into his frank grey eyes and felt powerless. 'I won't let you,' she whispered eventually.

'That's very brave,' said Strabis. 'It's what I expected. But I want you to think of something before you decide to fight me. What is the Rosslare Group about?'

'It's about . . . It's . . .'

'It's a financial conglomerate, Esther. It exists to make money. It has a particularly generous scheme for its employees, but that depends on the Group making money. Do you think it will make more money under me or under your sister?'

'You?'

'Yes, of course. I don't pretend to understand football like you do, but I understand business. I find it as hard to watch the Rosslare Group being misrun as you must find it to watch the mess others make of the football club.' It was so true! Strabis gave a predatory smile, but Esther didn't mind because he was a predator. It didn't make her helpless. It was the struggle of life. He wanted to prey on the Rosslare Group, and she must make sure the Rosslare heritage was not destroyed. He had strength and ferocity, like a wolf, but she had quickness and cunning, like a gazelle. 'You will fight me over the Group, I understand, but can you see now that I'll be straight with you?' Esther nodded. 'Good. What I want you for is nothing to do with the Rosslare Group. I want you to be my ambassadress in Board meetings. After going over your head, Donald has forfeited my trust. In the future, he will not be able to make decisions for me unless they are okayed by you. I care deeply about Kilburn, whatever anyone thinks, and I am determined that you have your say. Are you prepared for this?'

'Yes,' said Esther, and smiled. 'Aisling will be really angry!'

'Really?' said Strabis. 'Well, I can't help that.'

Esther's head was still spinning when Strabis walked her to her door. 'I've had a wonderful evening,' he said. He bent down, and as she put her hand around his flank and pressed up, he kissed her firmly and briskly on the mouth, turned and left.

PART FOUR – THE
2005–2006 SEASON, OR
EIGHT YEARS IN THE LIFE
OF THE KILBURN SOCIAL
CLUB

KILBURN AGONISTES: SOAP, FARCE OR TRAGEDY?

by Calum Horton, 20 September 2005

Heard the one about the bitchfighting aristocrat sisters playing chicken with the future of a billion-dollar business? Don't you love the fact they went loopy after being spurned by separate England captains? You might not give a fish's tit about football's preening layabouts, but if you aren't gripped by the soap opera that is the Kilburn Social Club, you've got ice in your veins, because it's got everything – heroes, villains, sex, death, toffs, financial scandals and madness. You couldn't make it up.

Unless you live in a cave, you've heard bits of the story, but even seasoned watchers have struggled to keep up during the frantic months since the return of the prodigal, the tortured ex-hero who came home to make amends for his past but who is driving the club into the dust. For newbies, here is the potted version.

The Kilburn Social Club was founded in 1881 by the Rosslares, a bunch of Irish aristos who made their name and fortune snuggling up to the English and starving their tenants. These mighty hypocrites built KSC as an 'urban mission' to hammer home the pious Anglican ideals of Queen and country, and make the working classes play sport so they would be healthy enough to butcher unarmed Africans in money-grubbing wars.

The club was a founder member of the FA. It survived the transition to professionalism because the Rosslares squandered blood-gotten riches on enticing top players down from Scotland and the north. Kilburn, ridiculously nicknamed 'the Socialists', became one of the richest and most successful teams in the world. The team had faux-egalitarian gimmicks and pretensions – everyone was paid the same – but the club's origins were in rapacity, business, exploitation and empire, and the gimmicks were lip service to a false heritage. Footballers were almost all working-class heroes, and the club that gathered the smug exceptions was KSC. Sometimes the team was successful, and sometimes not, but it survived perfectly well until the deaths of Manus, sixteenth Viscount Rosslare (1993), and John Brown, Kilburn's most successful ever manager (2000).

Enter Manus's bickering daughters. Stage left was Aisling, the new Viscountess, a flittering social butterfly who treated the coffers of the Rosslare Group like a private bank. Stage right was the football-crazy Esther. It has evolved into a drama worthy of Shakespeare.

Aisling didn't care about football, but she liked footballers. After a one-night stand with Dave Guinevere, the self-satisfied academic and journeyman England captain who lifted the World Cup, she conceived and aborted a loveless love child. Perhaps we should pity her, because this sad, private act has borne such bitter fruit. It is doubtless behind her current wild behaviour. Esther, who loves the game at least, did her best to run KSC while Aisling clung to the reins. In retrospect it is clear that Aisling was clinging to Guinevere. As soon as Guinevere got engaged – to a pop star, of course – jilted Aisling jettisoned the club in disgust, selling the family silver to make a quick buck.

Kilburn was bought by Strabis Kinsale. The playboy entrepreneur pretends he's a Kilburn fan par excellence but he's another grandstanding buccaneer wallowing in football's mucky glamour. Kinsale's priorities were vividly demonstrated when he bought the club. He ensured himself complete command of Kilburn's finances, and even seduced the football-mad Esther Rosslare's support by allowing her some small control over what happened on the pitch. Her twenty per cent of the club came with a veto over crucial footballing decisions. No one doubts Esther's commitment to Kilburn, but she was hopelessly out of her depth. Kinsale's interest in football was nothing to do with the game. It was all about PR for Quo Vadis? and gladhanding his fellow celebs. As soon as it started costing him big money, what would he do? Can you hear the beat of distant drums?

Dave Guinevere grew old and tired, and Kilburn sold him. The pop star left him at the altar and he took up with a posh model young enough to be his daughter. During his first match against his old club, in an act of rage-fuelled recklessness, he killed his best friend, Achille de la Rue de la Pierre au Diable, better known as Achilles, one of the greatest players and greatest gentlemen the game has ever known. In horror, Guinevere ran away from England to teach as a volunteer in Tanganyika. This self-glorifying atonement was hardly beset by discomfort – instead of choosing the distant jungle, he taught the sons of Tanganyika's notoriously corrupt government in a 'village' full of up-to-date luxuries such as a modern hospital, satellite television, mobile phone coverage and Internet connections.

With Guinevere on the lam, it was left to others to pick up the pieces and secure Achilles' legacy. I played my own small part by taking the charitable Foundation I had created with Will Beauchamp, Dave Guinevere's successor as captain of Kilburn and England, and renaming it in Achilles' honour. The club ran smoothly, but only because Esther had jumped into bed with Will Beauchamp. However badly she treated him behind his back, his advice kept her from making a fool of herself. Beauchamp helped the club ditch its embarrassing 'Socialists' tag, and 'Kilburn United' was born. The club finally started paying its players according to their worth. Under Beauchamp's stewardship, Kilburn was dragged into the twenty-first century.

Then, out of the blue earlier this year, Will Beauchamp signed for Rojo Madrid and left the club he loved. He was too dignified to cast the first stone, but he simultaneously announced that his marriage to Esther was over, and speculation was rife that his wife, amorously linked with many players over the years, had finally gone too far. With Will gone, Esther and Kilburn were in disarray, and Esther had to be removed from the business.

Re-enter the glamorous Viscountess. Will Beauchamp decided to sell the Kilburn shares that reminded him all too painfully of his tragic marriage. Esther was unable to buy them. Strabis Kinsale didn't care because he had all the shares he needed and he didn't want to expose himself to what was increasingly looking like a bad investment. And so Will, motivated by loyalty to a family that has shown him so little in return, sold to Aisling. The big question, of course, is what was Aisling up to?

She was doing it all for Dave Guinevere. Tied by the invisible thread linking her to her unborn child, she still held a demented torch for her runaway lover, and now she threw millions of pounds into a black hole. I am told that from the moment she bought Will's shares, she was begging Guinevere to return and manage Kilburn, and this summer she finally got her man. But he didn't come back because of her, and she certainly hasn't got what she wanted. He won't even speak to her.

Guinevere's beachfront idyll fell apart when his model realised she was stuck with a jaded roué who, like some colonial throwback, had no interest in the village he'd chosen to make his home. She left him, married a Tanganyikan, and has found her heart's content as a valued member of the local community. This did not persuade Guinevere to leave Tanganyika, but it did make him careless. In July, as a favour to Aisling, he hosted this newspaper's Leo Harry, and introduced him to his corrupt government cronies. Unbeknownst to Guinevere, UK Development Minister Michael Strickland was on a family junket in Tanganyika, and Harry was working to expose Strickland's role in the serial misappropriation of British aid money. When the Strickland scandal broke, Dave Guinevere was expelled from Tanganyika. He scuttled back into Heathrow two months ago, tail between his legs, and immediately told Lady Rosslare that he would take the job at Kilburn. She thought her dreams had come true.

The sports pages – the last bastion of romantic dreaming in British public life – had a field day, and they were nothing compared to the sentimental lunatics that support Kilburn. Esther held a press conference, saying that Guinevere was a traitor who should never be allowed near the club, which was just the latest bout of her increasing dementia. Esther no longer owned enough shares to veto Dave's arrival.

'Guinevere knows the club,' say the sentimentalists. 'He's succeeded at the highest level. He's brilliant, articulate and popular with the fans.' Guinevere stoked those fires with a speech about restoring the club's values and ethos, and returning it to the glory days of the Brown era. Guinevere took control on a tidal wave of optimism.

Four matches into the new campaign, and all these hopes have crumbled. After a dismal pre-season, which nervous pundits suggested was 'part of the rebuilding process', Kilburn have lost all four games and are playing as if they'll never win another. Moreover, they are doing this with a squad full of international superstars that most of their competitors can only dream of. What went wrong?

In the euphoria that surrounded Dave Guinevere's Lazarus-like re-appearance, Kinsale and Lady Rosslare allowed him to sign a contract which gave him complete control over who joined the club and who left. He said that previous managers were hamstrung by decisions from footballing incompetents on high. As a result, he made decisions that these footballing incompetents could have told him were financial madness. He broke the club's transfer record to sign Milagroso Nuñez from Cadiz, an excellent player but even older than Juan Vales, last year's fading Spanish import. Then, in quick succession, he brought in Rodney Norman, a second-division striker famous for being fat, and Jonathan Ngwere, a Tanganyikan teenager Guinevere had watched playing on the beach.

These bizarre decisions remind old-time fans of John Brown, who discovered greatness in strange places, but Brown was a unique genius. Cynics suspect that Guinevere is blindly aping his great forebear and the suspicion is confirmed by his insistence that Kilburn United change its name back to Kilburn Social Club and reinstitute its equal-wages policy. Not content with this, he sacked the club's coaching staff and he now makes his players run their own training sessions while he, half hermit, half Canute, sits in his office drinking tea. Guinevere is heading for a breakdown, and he's taking the club with him.

Esther Rosslare has begged the Board to sack him, but she's been bitten by the very provision that once gave her a say in major decisions – Princess Aisling has gobbled up the twenty per cent of shares she needs to veto footballing changes, and yesterday, while I was writing this very piece, she made the following extraordinary statement: 'Dave Guinevere has, and always will have, my complete confidence. He is the only person who could take this job on, and as far as I am concerned, this is an appointment for life. I expect some small-minded critics to worry about short-term difficulties, but it is my belief that his success will not be measured this season, or maybe even next season, but at some point in the future. I am prepared to wait for as long as it takes.'

Will Aisling, drunk on love and loss, really stick with a ship's captain who seems hell-bent on running his vessel into the rocks? It is a compelling human drama, and although I called it a soap opera at the outset, it is, without exaggeration, a modern tragedy. It might look, to weak-minded watchers who think the ship will turn around in time, like a romance, but this is the real world. Aisling Rosslare and Dave Guinevere are classic tragic protagonists, characters of enormous potential undermined by hubris – the insolent pride and fatal inability to see that they have overreached themselves and lost touch with reality. In their vanity, they have made mistakes with shattering, inevitable consequences, which cling to them as they stumble to their doom. As sure as fate, the day is coming, sooner rather than later, when their worlds turn upside down and they realise what they have done. Then, and only then, and then only maybe, might there be a cathartic purging of emotions.

Their tragedy is subsumed in several wider ones. It takes no great mind to see football's hubris. The game has always deluded itself with its own invented pomp and glamour, but the fatal moment came a decade ago, when the fool's lucre from Panther Digital rushed madly in. The cashball has been overpumped, and it is about to burst.

This is the backdrop against which Aisling Rosslare plays Lady Macbeth to Dave Guinevere's Scottish King. They believe that they, standing alone, can put their fingers in the money dyke, that they can command the waves to wash around their castle in the sand.

Old Socialists pray the Rosslare Group's crock of gold will bring back the glory years, but Guinevere and Rosslare are on a selfish quest for redemption that has nothing to do with any dream of making Kilburn great. They want to clean the Augean stables, but neither of them is Hercules, and Kilburn is not the stables, it is just one stall of shit-strewn thousands. It is impossible to clean up Kilburn without diverting a river through the whole ordurous mess.

Tragic protagonists often win our sympathy, at first. The arrogant Guinevere was a national hero who tore his life apart by killing his best friend. Aisling Rosslare was a vacuous socialite who was never told she couldn't have whatever she wanted, and who learned her lesson by making a decision she couldn't take back. I understand them and see what made them, but as they shred their lives, they are also destroying the hopes and dreams of countless others, and they forfeit any right to our sympathy.

That doesn't mean it isn't gripping. You don't leave *Macbeth* at the interval.

Calum Horton is the author of the forthcoming Kilburn United: Betrayal of a Legacy, *published by* Clarion *books. The* Clarion, *First for Football.*

JONATHAN NGWERE'S YEAR

Before he left Nzasa, Mr Guinevere asked Jonathan to come to England to play football. Jonathan thought this must be a joke, but Mr Guinevere said it was not. It would be a mistake and a disaster, but the amount of money was unbelievable, and how do you say no, especially if your mother is Mrs Ngwere? Mr Guinevere said, 'Don't be scared, Jonathan. Stay true to yourself and you'll be fine, I promise.' Mr Guinevere was Jonathan's favourite teacher. Mr Guinevere ordered his mother to stay in Nzasa, which made her angry, but Jonathan was grateful.

Jonathan sat in the middle of the aeroplane, which was like halfway between a bus and a big noisy room like the waiting room at the hospital, but more organised. He was prepared for the white and steel of Stansted airport, and the glass, because the hospital in Nzasa was like that, and the government buildings in Dodoma. The crowded halls were full of people from everywhere in the world, which was new for him, but also not a shock. The car that drove him would have not raised anyone's eyebrows back home. Jonathan had been too shy to ask to look out of a window when they flew over England, and so the view from the car was his first surprise. The UK was tiny with an enormous population. Jonathan had therefore pictured an endless city, because there could be no space for anything else, and yet, as soon as the car was away from Stansted and on to the big road, it was passing through great, huge fields on either side, of all different colours of green and gold, with hardly any houses at all. 'We are driving to London?' he asked.

'Yes.' Mr Guinevere understood. 'It's beautiful, isn't it?'

'It is so neat,' said Jonathan.

'It's an old country. It's careful with land.' The fields lasted fifteen minutes only, and then it was the city he was waiting for. As they drove through the stone valleys, Jonathan was disappointed that they felt familiar from films and pictures. Mr Guinevere said, after they had been stopping and starting in the full streets for half an hour, that they were now on the property which was owned by the Rosslare family, who started KSC. It was a marsh once.

The house he was to stay in was not big, and with less gold decoration and oil pictures than the houses up the hill in Nzasa. Also it was joined to houses next to it on either side, and the garden was a thin strip at the back. The television and stereo were small compared to Minister Tonta's, but Jonathan didn't mind. If his mother had been there, she would have complained. Jonathan's mother was a nurse, and she moved to Nzasa from Dodoma when the new hospital was being built. Jonathan was already nine then, and little Sarah was six. Eliza was not born. His mother came to find a rich man from the new colony on the hill, but she was too old and she settled for Jonathan's father, the only father he knew, who was the Head Gardener for the Minister of Justice, who was Nagape's nephew. His mother always complained that she had settled for second best and should have waited, because many men found her beautiful. It was an insult to live only halfway up the hill, she said, even though they lived not on the hill at all, but just at the end of the village closest to the hill.

Everyone was very welcoming to him. First, two players called Dirk Volendam and Tom Benjamin showed him the places in Kilburn to go to, and the training ground and football pitch also, which was frightening. He asked them what it was like when it was full, and Tom said, 'Amazing.' That day he had to have pictures taken with Mr Guinevere and also another new player called Rodney Norman, who was very nice and quite fat. Jonathan was excited but scared, and then it was worse when he saw on the sports channel on his television that many people said Mr Guinevere had made a mistake to buy him and also Rodney Norman, who was good in the second division but not up to the Premiership. This confirmed Jonathan's fears, and he could not stay in his house because he felt so bad.

It was still light although seven, and he walked down the road to the place called Hampstead Heath. He walked between two brown-green ponds. The one on the right was surrounded by fence, but in the left there were, it seemed, a hundred people swimming like sick white fish. Behind the pond were little hills and trees, and more people sitting under them with books. Many of the people were girls. Some were bathing with their breasts exposed. Jonathan couldn't believe it, but other people seemed to think it was not strange. Jonathan untucked his shirt to hide his erection. Jonathan was hot in leather shoes and long grey trousers, because this was England so he expected cold and rain. The trees on the Heath had little leaves and although they were not planted in rows, they seemed to have been organised. Everything was less glossy than home, the colours not so intense and the sun paler, as if it were coming through glass, as if the whole Heath were inside. It was less beautiful than the jungle, but it was a nicer place to be.

When he arrived at his house again, there was a huge black man waiting in a huge black 4 x 4. 'Hey,' said the man. 'I was worried about you. I'm Louie Cohen.' The man was another one from Kilburn. 'Get in,' he said. They drove to the house of an also new player called Milagroso Nuñez, although his first name was not really Milagroso – that was just what he was called. Louie and Milagroso were both very excited about the return of Mr Guinevere, and about Kilburn. They spent all of two hours explaining about the club, and Jonathan hardly said anything. Milagroso said he had always dreamed of joining KSC, but it was impossible while Dave Guinevere and Will Beauchamp were still there. 'We're gonna make it what it was, man,' Louie said. 'You don't know what it's been like, but Dave's gonna sort it out.' He told Jonathan about a man called Mr Brown, and how he made Kilburn Social Club into the best football team in the world, and how it was a special and unique community. Then Mr Brown died, and there was a tragedy, and Dave left, and the club lost its way and its mission. It turned its name into Kilburn United instead of Kilburn Social Club, but now the name was changed back again. Louie said, 'Kilburn United was my fault, man, because I didn't understand, but we've got another chance. We can make it right. Dave Guinevere understands, and you, my friend, are the proof.' Louie explained about how Mr Brown chose players no one else could find. Louie told him not to worry about anything the newspapers said, ever, because they had to fill their pages. Louie said that he trusted Mr Guinevere absolutely. Jonathan, for the period he was with Louie and Milagroso, was convinced.

His third type of greeting came after he met the rest of the squad two days before training started. Mr Guinevere sat everybody down in a bright room with blue chairs, and he said, 'Hello, everybody. Some of you know me, and some of you don't. This is an unhealthy club, and you and me are going to deal with that, and we're going to do it together. You've all played enough football. Your problem is taking responsibility. So, starting today, you're running your own training. Here's the rota. Everyone takes their turn. No fear, no favourites, strictly by the alphabet.'

All the players looked around. They were not certain if this was true or not true, but then Mr Guinevere left. Louie Cohen said, 'You heard the gaffer. Let's do it. Let's make sure we're ready for it, okay?'

While they walked out, there was more doubtfulness, but Mr Guinevere was a hero for many of them, and he was famous for being clever, and also he was 'the gaffer', which meant in charge.

One of the young players, who was called Jerry Cole, said to Jonathan then, 'Hey, Jonny mate! Tonight we're going to show you and Roddy a proper welcome, Kilburn-style.'

Louie Cohen said, 'Let them settle in, JC.'

Jerry Cole said, '[Bad word] off, Louie. You've given him your lecture. We're going to show him how to have some fun. You're in the house on Denning Road, yeah? Be ready at eight, yeah?' Jonathan was scared of how to do the right thing when two people disagreed, but he didn't want to say no to a friendly person so he said he would be ready. Cole picked him up and took him into the centre of London with some other players, who were Vlocker, Drayly, Vales, Norman and Derkin, and later an American man called Phil Maroon, who had eyes like blue stones behind milk. They went to a private club called Flower & Scythe, where they wouldn't be bothered about Jonathan's age, Cole said.

In spite of what Louie said, Jonathan still feared that Mr Guinevere had made a mistake to buy him, and these others must surely think it also, but they treated him as a friend. He had never got drunk before, but Cole said Jonathan wasn't going home until he was pissed. After almost no time, just three drinks of beer, he was explaining that he wasn't good enough to be here, and that everything would be a disaster. The others laughed.

'What's Guinevere like as a manager?' asked Derkin.

'He is brilliant. The Chickens were —'

'Chickens!'

'Yes. I was for the Eagles, but the Chickens nearly beat us, even with no good players.'

'He sounds like a genius.'

'Oh yes. He is a genius. What is this drink?'

'He won the Tanganyikan Kids League —'

'Just Nzasa. It was the league in our village.'

'He's a genius because he won your village league?'

'With the Chickens, who were very bad players.'

'Not like you?'

'No. I was the best player, but I was only in my team from halfway through the season so we did not win overall. Things never go well for me in the end. It is because I always think there will be a catastrophe which I cannot avoid. Mr Guinevere says I need some fighting spirit from somewhere, it is all I am lacking, but —'

'This will help,' said Juan Vales, holding a new drink. Cole and Vlocker looked at Jonathan eagerly.

Carlo Derkin, who was quieter than the others, said, 'He's had enough, Pedro. Let's get him home.' But Jonathan did not want to go home, and the next thing was that he woke in his bed. Derkin was asleep in the chair next to the bed, and there was a smell of vomit.

When Jonathan got to the ground later, it was like he was a popular boy. Also, playing with these people was not a disaster. He was faster and stronger than everyone else. Also, the pitch was no better than the one Minister Tonta had built up the hill. Jonathan tried hard because it was his duty, and also because when they saw he was not terrible his new teammates were even more friendly, and they always invited him with them when they went out. He did not mind getting drunk, because he did not remember what happened and he never felt bad the next day.

Some players did not join the group which went out. Dirk and Tom said he should be careful because Vales and his mates were not good people, and because drink affected your fitness and that's why footballers were sensible about it these days. Cole and Drayly and the others said this was because Dirk and Tom were old and boring arseholes. Jonathan believed you should not criticise your teammates, but everything was so new to him.

Jonathan especially did not like it when Cole criticised Mr Guinevere (it was called 'slagging off'). Last year, the team had two coaches every day, and a coach for fitness and one even for goalkeeping. Now there were people to massage them after training and to doctor, but no one for training. It might have been okay if the gaffer was there, watching over them, but he wasn't. The big problem, the others said, was that no one knew who the gaffer would pick, and in what formation. It was stupid, said Cole, and the players thought it would come to an end when they started losing friendlies. When Rod Norman had his turn to run the training, it was horrible. Rod was funny when they all went out in the evening, and he pretended to laugh about being fat and useless. But the first day they met, at the beginning, Rod said to Jonathan that this was his big chance, and you only ever get one. He was going to turn over a new leaf. It was like Moon Face in Nzasa, who was so scared of having no one to play with that he pretended not to care that everyone teased him. Moon Face and Jonathan were friends in private, and Moon Face always said that tomorrow he would admit that he was learning to read and wanted to live in Dodoma and work in an office, but Moon Face never did it. Rod tried to be serious when he ran the training session, but no one listened. Then he started joking, and everyone laughed, but they stopped after ten minutes, and grumbled that Norman was a decent bloke, but he was an idiot, and what was the team doing wasting its time like this four days before the start of the season, and what the [bad word] was the gaffer playing at? It disrespected the [bad word] players, who deserved [bad word] better. The next day was going to be Jonathan's session. He asked Cole what he should do. 'Whatever the [bad word] you want, mate. This season is [bad word] before it starts.' He pressed Cole, who said, 'Listen mate, you're a [bad word] good player, better than that lazy [bad word] Nuñez, but you're not even going to be playing, because the [bad word] gaffer isn't [bad word] watching. He'll be gone in a month, believe me, so if I were you, I wouldn't [bad word] worry.'

A month into the season, Jonathan emailed his parents: *Dear Mother and Father*, he wrote. *It is obvious that Kilburn is not succeeding on many levels, and so on and so forth. On Saturday we lost our fifth time in a row, which is the record for a worst ever start in the season for Kilburn. Everything is terrible, as I foresaw. Today was the first time I played, even though only for the last twenty minutes, when we were already 2–0 behind. The problem is the gaffer. Mr Guinevere was good in Nzasa, but the Premiership is too 'high pressure', and he has 'lost the plot'. Louie Cohen, who is the American I said about, says we must give him time, but my friend Jermaine Cole says that Louie is living in the past, like the gaffer. (Jermaine is always called 'JC' or 'Jerry'. I am called 'Chicken' but it is friendly. My friends are JC, 'Carlo' (who is Carlo Derkin), 'Smithy' (Will*

Smith), 'Useless' (Rodney Norman), Marty V (Marten Vlocker) and 'Craggy' (who is Craig Drayly). One of our friends is 'Pedro' (Juan Vales), who I secretly do not like. Another friend who is Phil Maroon is just called Phil. He is not a player. He is, it is hard to explain, like a friend and a servant also, and a businessman too. Football is so much money and so complicated, so Phil is the one who deals with the money and makes sure we are okay in our careers. He always comes with us in the evening if we go out, and he does not drink so he can look after us. I tell you this so you know I am safe. It is good when we go out, because we are young and we have a right to enjoy ourselves, because it is only natural.

It is also team spirit, but only half of us have it. The gaffer wants everyone to have team spirit, but my friends are always arguing with the older players like Louie and Dirk and Torquil (it is said 'Torkil'). It is worse than when I was first in the Eagles with Bang-Bang and Abdul. It is all the gaffer's fault. I do not like to think this, but a newspaper article today explained everything that is wrong. Mr Guinevere has had many tragedies, and he is not capable of the pressure and the new way football is done, like my friends have said before but I did not want to believe them. But the problem is that Mr Guinevere cannot be sacked because there is a woman in love with him who is one of the people in charge of Kilburn. She will have to see reason soon, everyone says.

I said to Phil Maroon about this, but he said not to be worried. He said that it was a 'crying shame', but I was to remember that Kilburn was not bigger than football. He said that I had nothing to fear, there are many other clubs, and if KSC goes 'tits up', he will still look after me.

I have sent you the details for my bank account, and the papers which let you sign for the money. I hope Sarah and Eliza are well, and that they are enjoying school. Please ask them to write to me about the new teachers.

Jonathan signed off and put on his new clothes he had bought with JC, because it was Saturday night.

Four days later, the Socialists faced high-flying Everton in a mid-week game. Louie Cohen was in goal. Blackie and Volendam were in the centre of defence. Carlo and Craig Drayly were the wing backs, and this unit was experienced enough to cope with the chaotic pre-season. In front of them was Milagroso Nuñez. Jonathan was mystified by the former Cadiz star. He never seemed to leave his tiny area of the pitch. His nickname didn't derive from any flair – it was given him by his first teenaged teammates back in Spain, and it stuck. It also fitted with his public image. One story Jonathan read said the police once had to find him on a Sunday afternoon because he forgot there was a game. He was located on the beach with a bottle of wine and a beautiful Norwegian dentist. He was profusely apologetic, arrived at half-time, and turned a 0–2 deficit into a 3–2 win. The other players against Everton were the 'academy graduate' Ben Sweetman on the left, Marten Vlocker at the point of the diamond and Rodney Norman up front for the first time alongside Tom Benjamin, which made Juan Vales angry. Will Smith started at right midfield. Mr Guinevere told the press that Jermaine Cole was being rested because Kilburn had a strong squad, and it was important to rotate.

For the first time, Jonathan thought, Kilburn played with good organisation. It was not perfect. Only Milagroso would pass to Rod Norman, who was unprepared for the pace of the game at this level.

After twenty minutes, Vlocker received the ball in space, played a one-two with Nuñez, released Sweetman down the left and arrived in the box to meet the subsequent cross with a header that hit the back of the net before the goalkeeper had time to move. Everton replied strongly, but the Kilburn defence held firm, and Benjamin almost scored on a breakaway, lifting the ball over the onrushing keeper but an agonising foot wide of the post. At half-time, the dressing room was buzzing, and Jonathan watched JC grow mutinous. Mr Guinevere made bland comments about how happy he was that things were starting to come together, and said everyone should just keep going like they were going. As they walked back through the tunnel, Mr Guinevere asked Cole and Jonathan what they thought. 'We're [bad word] lucky,' Cole said. No he didn't. He said 'fucking lucky'. The word didn't embarass Jonathan any more. It was just a word.

'I agree,' said Mr Guinevere. Jonathan thought the manager was smiling inside, but like a wild dog in the forest.

'Normo is totally off the fucking pace.'

'Everyone has to learn.'

'What about Nuñez then? It's not *his* fucking first time.'

'I thought he was playing well.'

'Look at the fucker! He's standing around while everyone else works their fucking arse off! What about Jonathan? He's brilliant, and he can run for fucking ever.'

'Okay. Point taken.'

After ten minutes of the second half, Will Smith danced around his man, dummied to cross, skipped inside the centre half and was hacked down. Benjamin scored the penalty. Five minutes later, Dave sent Jonathan on to replace Nuñez. As Jonathan stripped off his tracksuit, Cole whispered, 'Prove yourself. Show the fucker.' When Milagroso left the field, he shook Jonathan's hand but he looked angrily at Mr Guinevere. For the rest of the game, as Everton fought back, Jonathan felt powerful, as if he was everywhere at once, making tackles, intercepting passes and releasing his teammates. But it wasn't enough. Everton started to find space higher and higher up the pitch, and they sent a succession of good crosses into the Kilburn box. They scored with ten minutes to go, and again with five.

With a minute of injury time left on the clock, Everton were camped outside the Kilburn penalty area. They smelled a winning goal, but the opening wouldn't come. Finally, after an interchange down the right, the ball fell to midfielder Martin Clarke, just outside the box. He saw enough space to shape a curling strike around the oncoming Juan Vales, who was not exactly the bravest when it came to flinging himself in the way. Clarke caught the ball perfectly but it thumped into Jonathan's ankle, thrown across its path seemingly from nowhere. Clarke's teammate Charlie Kirkham should have been first to the ball, but Jonathan was on his feet already. He nicked the ball away from Kirkham, looked up and spun a pass hard off the outside of his right foot through the gap between the central defenders, and into the path of a clever run by Rodney Norman, who had only the keeper to beat. Norman's first touch was clumsy. The ball bundled forward. Norman would still have got there first but he was too eager and he tripped over his feet. The final whistle blew.

In the changing room, Drayly, Vlocker and everyone else, but especially Cole, said, 'Great game, Chicken. Bad luck.' They said nothing to Norman, who couldn't laugh. Dave Guinevere said, 'First point on the board, guys. Well played, Milagroso, but I thought you looked tired.'

'I was not tired. You know I was not tired.'

'You weren't tired because you didn't fucking run anywhere,' said Drayly, to laughter.

Four months later, early in January, Jonathan was full of doubts.

Dear Mother and Father, he emailed. *You will have been pleased to hear that we won the FA Cup game today, which was a hard game against*

Sunderland, who are a team from the top of the division below us. Mr Guinevere played only the young players like me. He said that it was his plan always to do this, but there is more to the story than meets the eye, which I can tell you but you must not tell other people.

Because the season has been a disaster, Phil Maroon and my friends . . . Jonathan paused. They *were* his friends. They were the people he went out with and spoke to at training. You did not stop being friends with someone because they did something you disagreed with and, besides, they knew so much more than he did about how football worked. He continued: . . . *have decided that they deserve to be at clubs which value them, and give them respect.* His friends hated being left on the bench, which was only natural. Led by Juan Vales, they were particularly vitriolic about Milagroso. Jonathan had increasing qualms about this. Frequently, the Socialists would be leading or holding their own after an hour, at which point Mr Guinevere would replace Milagroso with Jonathan. The papers and his friends had all been very complimentary about Jonathan's performances, but when Milagroso was off the pitch, KSC found it harder to control games. Sometimes Jonathan's energy made up for this lack of control, and sometimes not, but Jonathan found himself watching Milagroso more carefully. One thing he noticed: Milagroso was always furious when he was substituted. In fitness sessions, Milagroso was never the quickest, but he never stopped either.

Because of the bad atmosphere and results, Jonathan's friends had all handed in transfer requests in the January window. Mr Guinevere said they couldn't leave. Phil Maroon said that Mr Guinevere couldn't force stars to play when they didn't want to. Maroon's players, who were Craggy, JC, Marty V and Benny Sweetman, all faked illness on the day before the FA Cup game. This was the real reason why Mr Guinevere had to pick the young players, whatever he pretended.

Jonathan was ashamed even to write about this to his parents. He deleted what he had started to type, and he wrote merely that they must not worry, because Phil Maroon said that Kilburn was a great shop window. *Mr Maroon says that if I play my cards right, he can get me a 'stonking' deal with Cardiff, where he knows the important people. He will talk to them, and if I'm not interested when he comes back to me, that's fine. He will do this because I am young and do not have anyone else looking after my interests, and it makes him sick the way players get treated.*

This sounds like I am ungrateful to Mr Guinevere, but I am not. He is 'out of his depth'. In two games over Christmas, he took off my friend Marty V, who is the best player for Germany, and put on to the pitch Rodney Norman, who is a 'clown', even if he is a nice guy. The guys don't blame Rodney because he agrees he is rubbish and it's not his fault he gets put on. He says this in a funny way, and so we know it is the fault of Mr Guinevere. Do not worry. I still want to be a teacher, but I am very good at football, and I deserve to have the market price for my few years of playing career because it can end at any time, like one of the old players who was from Kilburn called Will Beauchamp (it is said 'Beechum'), who snapped a ligament in his knee this week in a game in Spain, and everyone here was very quiet when they heard because they all know it can be anybody.

This email was similar to many he'd sent in the past months, because he couldn't think what else to say.

By the start of April, the Socialists were still struggling in the league, but they had reached the semi-final of the FA Cup. Mr Guinevere had refused to sell his mutinous senior players, and he had continued to pick the club's youngsters for cup games, 'saving' the stars for the league.

When KSC won their quarter-final, Phil Maroon looked unhappy. Maroon took Jonathan aside and told him slyly that a moneymaking cup run was not necessarily *convenient*. Jonathan refused to understand what Maroon was saying. Maroon was his friend, and was the friend of all his friends, and Jonathan would not be able to make other friends now because of how he had behaved this year, so he dug his head in the mud.

April was very wet, and London was a different green to Nzasa. The forest leaves at home were green-yellow, but the trees and grass here were green-blue. It was a fresh colour, and he was interested especially in it being new after everything died in the winter.

An ordinary Friday, Jonathan emerged from the changing block with Jermaine Cole. Zondi had been watching with the old man Hank, which embarrassed Jonathan because of how his friends spoke about Zondi and Hank, who were nice to him. Walking to JC's car, Jonathan pretended not to notice Zondi until Zondi called to him. JC patted Jonathan on the back, and said he'd wait in the car. JC didn't understand why Jonathan had to obey, because JC didn't come from a culture where he had to respect his elders. JC said Jonathan needed to get over that shit, but it was difficult. Jonathan approached Zondi. He was wearing a long-sleeved T-shirt that cost a hundred pounds, and another T-shirt over it which cost a hundred pounds also, and a beige zip jacket that looked cheap but was made in Japan and cost two thousand pounds, and jeans that cost six hundred pounds and shoes with pointed toes that cost four hundred pounds. The clothes were cool, and they were not much of the money he earned. He had to look good, the others said – it is what people expected. Zondi asked Jonathan how things were going, and Jonathan replied, 'I'm not getting enough pitch-time, man.' Jonathan heard the inflections grafting themselves into his speech as if by magic. He was not in Nzasa any more. It was his old self that didn't fit in.

'How is training?'

'It's a farce, man. The gaffer doesn't care. He's totally lost it. It's every man for himself, man.'

'That's how you're playing, Jonathan.'

Jonathan didn't need this hassle. He was only getting a few minutes every game to prove himself. It was easy for Zondi, who was finished playing, but Juan Vales, who was also old, said that football is so quick that if you blink, you've wasted half your career. Jonathan said, 'We going down, man. I got to show what I can do.'

'You show what you can do by playing for the team,' said Carlo Derkin, who was suddenly at Jonathan's shoulder, though Carlo wasn't looking at Jonathan, he was looking at the old man, Hank. Carlo said, 'You want to get picked up by a gaffer who understands who is playing for the team and who is playing for himself.'

Jonathan was taken aback. 'It's all right for you —' Jonathan began, and was interrupted by a sharp double blast from Jermaine's car horn. 'I should go.'

'I'll give you a lift,' said Carlo.

'No, man, JC is driving . . .' but Carlo was waving Cole off. 'We're going to JC's, to watch a DVD. You know.'

'I know. It can wait, mate. We need to have a chat. Do you mind, guys?' Zondi and Hank nodded to them, and it seemed the old men were happy for some reason. Carlo and Jonathan got into the car, and Carlo spoke to his steering wheel: 'I'm fucking sick of JC. And Drayly, and Vales, and Vlocker, and Smith. I can face training when Dave and Zondi aren't here, but when they watch, it's fucking embarrassing.'

'I don't understand, man.'

Carlo pressed the button, and the Aston started. Carlo revved the engine and thudded both hands into the wheel. Then he switched the car off. 'It didn't used to be like this,' he said. 'We didn't used to go round someone's house to watch sex on a fucking telly. We played as hard as we could to win, for our mates and the fans, because that's what the game's about. We weren't better players than we are now.' Jonathan wanted Carlo to drive to JC's house. 'Dave's lost it. It's not his fault. It's because everything changed here while he was away. This shit would have worked before, with the old players, but not now.'

'That's what JC says, man. That's why there's no point.'

Carlo said, 'JC doesn't get it, Jonny. If the Socialists are fucked, we'll have to go somewhere else, but if you play like JC and Marty V, you'll go somewhere like here, where they buy good players just because they're good.'

'But that's the best —'

'Listen to me, Jonny. Look at the teams who win the fucking league. They play for each other. They're not like we used to be, but they're not full of people doing their own thing. They might sign Coley, because they've seen him knuckle down, but they've never seen you do anything but show off.'

'Phil Maroon —'

'Phil Maroon's a wanker.'

Jonathan did not want to listen to Carlo, because if he did, he would not allow himself to have fun and be free for the first time in his life. He was a young man, and what was wrong with watching sex films with JC and the others? It was natural, and he should not be ashamed (but he was). Being ashamed was only one of the private things that Jonathan tried to keep hidden, like thinking that Milagroso Nuñez was the best player at Kilburn, and Jonathan did not blame Milagroso for hating Dave now. Anyway, what did Carlo know about what was right for Jonathan? It was easy for him, he was reaching the end of his career, but how would even a wise manager see how good Jonathan was if he got no time on the pitch? Carlo drove north at last. Jonathan said, 'Phil Maroon believes in me. He is as powerful as any manager, he says. He told me he will get me a team for definite.'

'Think about what I said, Jonny. Someone will buy you, but you don't get many chances to find the right team, and Phil doesn't give a shit about that, even if he knows what the right team is for you, which he doesn't. When I'm old and knackered, I won't give a shit about the last few years, but the time Dave was skipper was fucking amazing, and it's not just 'cos we were winning everything. I've been a tosser to Dirk and Torquil, but if I was in trouble, I'd go to them before I went to Jermaine Cole, every fucking time.' Carlo pulled up outside JC's electric gate, and said, 'I'm not coming in, mate. But think about it.' Jonathan nodded. Then Carlo said, 'You should watch Milagroso.'

Inside JC's house, Jonathan felt himself shrink. When they had been sitting for an hour, and Jonathan was phoning a Diabolo to take him home, the doorbell rang. 'It's Maroon,' said JC. 'I told him to fuck off, but he said he was coming round. I'll bin him.'

JC went to the door, and the others could hear him open it and greet the American reluctantly. 'You okay, Coley?' said Phil.

'Yeah, fine. What is it?'

'Hey, we're buddies!'

'Yeah. What is it? I've got stuff to do.'

'It's the FA Cup, Coley. It could be a problem for us.'

'We're not even playing in the Cup.'

'If Kilburn win, it insulates Guinevere.'

'Give a shit, mate. We'll be gone.'

'It's prize money, and it's European football next year. If Guinevere and the Princess are still crazy, they might be able to cling on to some players, whatever division they're in. You see what I'm saying, buddy? That a risk you wanna take?'

'There's nothing I can do about that. I'm not on the pitch in cup games.'

'Well,' said Phil Maroon, 'I think we could do something about that. I could set up interviews, if you want. Maybe you could say something like . . . Wait. Are the others in here? Who's listening to this?'

JC, Marty V and Craggy all spoke to the press about Kilburn's progress in the FA Cup, and the upcoming semi-final against Cardiff. Cole's comments were typical. He said, 'The FA Cup has been a real bright spot for the fans in a difficult season,' and 'It's been brilliant to see the kids playing so well, y'know, a breath of fresh air,' and 'Of course, it's the business end of the cup now, and Cardiff are a great side, so maybe the gaffer will need to bolster the team, who knows?' and 'Yeah, I'd love to play in the semi-final, given the chance,' and 'People talk about money, but silverware is all us players really care about,' and 'There's only a few games to go till the end of the season, so I don't think it would be a problem fitness-wise, but that's the gaffer's decision.' Some reporters said the kids should be given their chance, but most reluctantly agreed that Guinevere's duty was to his fans, and he had to put out the best team for the job.

Jonathan prayed that Mr Guinevere would resist the pressure, but when the team was named the day before the semi-final, it was the old players, and JC smiled. Jonathan looked around the room while Mr Guinevere was finishing his talk, and he saw the eyes of Louie Cohen and Milagroso Nuñez and some others go cold. Jonathan was sad for Mr Guinevere's weakness.

SONG OF THE BALL (PART 3)

FA Cup Semi-Final, Kilburn Social Club versus Cardiff City, 23 April 2006, Ibrox
Kilburn Social Club 0–1 Cardiff City

Listen to the roar! ME, in the semi-final of the FA CUP! I knew I was destined for greatness! This is Ibrox, half the home of Celtic-Rangers, but today there is the brown crowd for Kilburn and the red crowd for Cardiff. The Brown are lit by the Great Ball, and the Red are lost in gloom, and so I hope and pray for the Brown of course, but I do not mind so much as I should, because I am in the LIGHT!

Wow, wow! What I tell is only the main-centre-drive of what I experience and know and think and feel, a tiny sliver of the whole. Every fraction of every thing within this bowl of noise is within my fleeting compass, and how can I express this, but no matter because the wonder! It is so bright! I want to bounce! I want them to see me fly and bound and sing and soar!

I am the latest. I am Top of the Range, with a 32-panel double microfibre cover, with a lining including a high-tensile lamination system using four layers of pure polymer microfibre along with a micro-cellular foam layer for added compression and softer heading. I have a top-of-the-line 70–80-gram (size five) Air Tight Butyl Bladder for excellent air retention, and he pushes firm against my inner skin. I have a Three Year Shape and Stitching Guarantee. I am Hand Stitched by ADULTS, but my stitches are small even so. The stitching: vital to a ball's performance, the best-quality waxed and twisted polyester threads are used to give permanently tight seams. This helps reduce airflow drag, which in turn increases speed and distance. I am Made by Dusseldorfballen. I fly like No Balls Before Me. The goalkeepers with their sticky gloves fear me; my pure polymer microfibre is made to tack to the gloves, but the gloves cannot control me. In olden times they tried to catch and possess us, but my high-tensile lamination system interacts with the air, and I veer and swerve beyond the dreams of my forebears, and the gloves are happy if they can punch me away, and instead of being trapped I soar free, and I thank Dusseldorfballen that I was made this way, and not of olden Leather, so porous and so heavy, so earthbound and easy to grasp.

Nothing is so piteous as the claim that all (who pass Quality Control) are alike. The Great Ball put me *here*. She could have put me anywhere else, or she could have put anyone else here, but She did not. It must be a Sign. The less fortunate think I am stupid, but I am not. What you do and when you do it are as much who you are as how you were made.

Marten Vlocker tickles me forward, and Tom Benjamin taps me back to Juan Vales and also Craig Drayly and Jermaine Cole and the other stars are playing, thank goodness! I knew it would be them! The other balls said that the old man Guinevere would select his little players, and take the glory from my day, but my Air Tight Butyl Bladder told me that it would be All Right in the End, and it is. If I am good today, I will . . . No! What am I thinking? I must not be distracted! This is my Match Day and we have but one. Juan Vales's boot caresses me again, little strips of rubber on top of the soft leather flap over the laces clinging to my skin and forcing me to curl as I fly, softly into the path of Jermaine Cole, who taps me and dances, confusing the fat red legs of a Cardiff, who falls, and then I am skipping forwards again, revelling, but more fat red legs slide in, and I am thumped into touch and back from an advertising hoarding which suggests the purchase of sportswear from a company I will not name because it also makes balls, but its balls were not chosen for the FA Cup because its high-tensile lamination system was deemed too plasticky, and its balls flew so wildly they were not in control. I am free and graceful, but I am still in control. If I were a hat-trick ball, then I would be in a glass case and signed, and even Sold at Auction, and . . . No! Forget the future. I will not be in it so what do I care?

Oooh! I am kicked hard and high into the red section of the crowd, where I bounce and spin from hand to laughing hand, uncatchable as soap. Finally I am returned to earth, and Carlo Derkin takes me, and launches me to Juan Vales, who flicks me gently just over the halfway line, which was waiting to stain me with his white blood. I will do anything I can do for Juan Vales. Others claim that balls have influenced games by the power of their will, and I believe them. It is impossible that the Great Ball endowed us with this moment only to render us impotent. Who could believe such a thing? Vales kicks me towards Drayly, but not quite hard enough by mistake, and Drayly tries to reach me but he does not try quite hard enough also, and although I strain, and I am sure I nearly reach Drayly, it is not enough this time and I am at a Cardiff foot.

For forty minutes, often this happens. Vlocker is caressing, and I feel as if I know his will, and his foot feels certain, and yet, inexplicably, I never fall where I am needed by another Kilburn. Milagroso Nuñez makes me go where he wants, but he is cautious and I want more. I want what Vales and Vlocker nearly give me, again and again, but always they are in error, spinning me too far, or a tiny angle wrong. And yet, when I feel their boots soft against my skin, I do not feel mistakes. How can this be? I should feel everything! When the heavy feet of the defenders make mistakes, as they always do because the good players do not play in defence, it is obvious immediately that they have erred. Their faces ripple with annoyance, too fast for silly men to see, but I see and know, and their donkey legs also ripple as they must change direction to deal with the donkey things that they have done. But with Vlocker and Vales and Cole and Drayly, their faces do not ripple, and it is as if their mistakes are not mistakes. I cannot understand this, unless they are trying deliberately to . . . No. I will not believe that, though I have heard balls whisper it these few weeks.

The balls who whisper such things are jealous lying cynics, and not to be trusted. The game is pure and shall not be sullied. Even a bad game is two sides fighting the good fight, with one rule to bind them all. I will not believe otherwise. And yet I feel the leather false-footed.

It cannot be half-time! I am hardly begun, and I have wasted precious moments on doubting! How am I so foolish? Surely no other Dragonfly ever has been such a fool, but maybe all have been? How do we ever know? And yet I feel in my air that I must have been a Dragonfly before. This is what we Dragonflies believe. We are spiritual, not like the Anti-Fanatics, with their upcast, world-despising eyes. We believe in an embracing world, and in the permanence of our Selves. Why do we depart from our bodies when there is still air within? It *must* be because we are reborn. But why am I wasting my brief now on this? Am I unwittingly Conservative? No. I sense everything, but it is so fast. I thought that sensing everything would make it last for ever, but the rush is horrible. This is why I think these cynic thoughts about the Kilburns. It is normal surely to feel fear, but I must put it from my mind. I must concentrate on the now and only the now.

A small red-hat girl asks her father if Cardiff will win because Kilburn are no good any more. She is high in the West, in FF57 and her father is in FF58. I am angry, but deepest in the air within my air I know I'm angry because she's right. Why should I care? The Kilburns are just a place for Dragonflying, but they are Legendary and Historical, and I must have indeed done well in my previous lives to have earned this moment, and who knows where I may next be reborn, or if this is such a Legendary and Historical Dragonflying that beyond this is . . . What? I do not know. I do not have a proper idea of Heaven. I certainly do not want to wander the world a perfect sphere of air insensate. What *joy* in that? I want to Dragonfly for ever.

Is this why I think these bad thoughts? Do I wish to perform badly, and so be incarnated to a lower ball? But how can it be if we do not revel in our greatest moment? And what if the greatest moment is our reward for all the others, and ends in the last and realest death, and I am throwing it away in all my doubt?

They're back! Already! Already, and I am rolling.

Juan Vales to Marty Vlocker to Jermaine . . . *No!* I am intercepted and kicked along the red left wing, where the Cardiff pretends to shift outside, and Craig Drayly moves the wrong way, even though the dummy was *obvious*, and the winger darts inside, and Cole and Vlocker have been slow to return and there is an overlap, and a cross and a clear strike later I billow the corner of the goal, touching first one strand, then another, then another, then another and so on, the nylon stripping microfibres in their thousands that will have no noticeable impact on my flight, as far as concerns dull-witted men.

High in the crowd, in brown, the blonde woman who is an owner of Kilburn gasps and looks to the white-haired Guinevere, who stares back grimly, and her hand goes to her mouth and she turns away, incomprehensible meat.

And I am rolling again. I do not want to think of the woman or Guinevere. She looks at him again and he doesn't look back but I sense all, and I know that although he is pretending sadness, there is in him deep-down elation, as if this were for him some lower simulacrum of my Dragonflying, an apotheosis and immolation.

I sense all the other things too: the lying Kilburn feet as they fluster and flurry and fuckup; the Cardiffs growing more confident with every ebbing of my air; the anger of the Kilburns on the bench, staring at their manager's back; and my fury to have given up myself for something I do not understand for all my sensing. But you too are a spectator, so I know you and what you need me to say, and I have said it, and at last the referee looks at his watch and raises the whistle to his lips, and Guinevere sighs out all his air, it seems, though he is not unhappy, and I am not unhappy either, and it is the end.

JONATHAN NGWERE'S YEAR
(CONTINUED)

Two shocks happened before the end of the season.

The first was when Will Beauchamp started to be seen around Kilburn. He was still limping, and if it were any normal player, said the others, he wouldn't be able to think beyond his fucked career, but Will wasn't normal. JC hated Will for some reason from the past, and so did some of the others, but Will spoke to them all after the FA Cup semi-final, and suddenly they all said Will was their agent now, not Phil Maroon, and they started playing better. Will Beauchamp arranged to meet Jonathan too. He said it would be best to meet at Jonathan's house, with no one else there, but Jonathan was nervous. He did not know who he could trust, and so he thought about who at Kilburn was the most honest person, and he decided it was Louie Cohen.

'What do you want me for?' said Louie. 'You're one of Coley's gang.'

'I am not,' said Jonathan. 'I do not want to be. I do not know what to do.' Louie was still, and then he nodded.

Jonathan did not need to tidy his house. A woman came in every three days to scrub everything, even though nothing was ever dirty. Jonathan had bought many things, but he did not feel as if they were his. He even had a car in a garage waiting for him to pass his driving test.

Louie arrived when he said. Jonathan gave him a glass of water. He wanted to apologise for being on the wrong side with JC. Instead, he said nothing. In the end, Louie said, 'You know Zondi?'

'Yes. A small amount.'

'He likes you. He says Dave was right to bring you here.' When Louie said 'Dave' his lip curled.

'I am glad,' said Jonathan, tentatively.

'Yeah,' said Louie. 'I love Zondi, but he's not always right. He still trusts —' The bell rang. 'Don't commit to anything,' said Louie. 'Will's clever.' Jonathan nodded and went to the door.

Will Beauchamp was in a grey suit and a white shirt with no tie. He was on crutches still, and his hair was the kind which was messy in a neat way. Jonathan was worried what he would say when he saw Louie, but Will said, 'Hi, Louie mate. You well?' Louie said nothing. 'Okay, I see. I want you to know, mate, I have no hard feelings. This,' he indicated his leg, 'has taught me a lot.'

'I know what you're like,' said Louie.

'You still basing that on things Dave Guinevere told you? How good a judge does he seem these days?' Louie looked like he had been slapped. Jonathan offered Will a drink, and Will said he was fine. He and Louie sat opposite each other.

'What do you want?' asked Louie.

'Jonathan is a special player, and I want to represent him.'

'No,' said Louie.

'It's your decision? You think he should be with Phil Maroon?'

'No,' said Louie.

'What do you think, Jonathan?' asked Will.

'I do not know. Mr Maroon is . . . He . . .'

'I know what he did before the semi-final. I know he's also told his boys that relegation would be good for them. He's an idiot, and he'll get you all in trouble.'

'I never —'

'I know you never, but you'll be tarred with the brush, or you would have been if I hadn't sorted it out. Coley and the others are playing to win now, aren't they?' Jonathan looked down. 'Aren't they, Louie?' Again silence. 'Yes, they are.' Will's voice was smooth but hard. He said, 'They don't like me, because I'm a bastard, but I speak their language. I'm cleverer than they are and they know it. You don't have to like me, but I'll get paid when you get paid, remember.'

'Mr Maroon says that he has special contacts. He says he has a deal for me if . . . if we get relegated. He says . . .'

'Phil has set up a deal that would take you to Cardiff for four million, of which he'll cream off a million, in exchange for persuading you to take twenty thousand a week, when I can get you forty, and I'll do it by taking my proper cut.'

'How do you know this?' said Louie.

'My contacts really *are* special,' said Will. 'Do you not believe me?'

Jonathan could see that Louie believed Will, but was still unhappy.

Jonathan believed Will also, but did not like him. He wanted to not be with Will or with Phil Maroon, if there was a way. He said, 'If Coley and Pedro play properly, we will not be relegated. Then you will not get any money from transfers.'

Will paused very slightly, and something passed between him and Louie, but Jonathan did not know what it was. 'I'm building a proper business,' Will said. 'I want people to know they can trust me. In the end, I'll make —'

'Bullshit,' said Louie.

'I beg your pardon?'

Louie turned to Jonathan. He said, 'Will is running around chasing up Kilburn players because he's certain we'll be relegated.'

'Why?' said Jonathan. We still have four games, and we are playing properly now, so —'

'Because of the sainted Dave Guinevere,' said Will. Jonathan did not understand. 'I'm surprised Louie noticed, because he's pretty gormless, but David is trying to screw Kilburn. I don't know why, presumably some fight with the Princess, but everything he's done this year has been about fucking you up. Why do you think Milagroso keeps being substituted, or that Dave picked JC and the others for the FA Cup semi when he's bright enough to have realised that Phil had got to them?'

'He was being weak,' said Jonathan.

'He was using weakness as an excuse.'

'I trusted him, man,' said Louie. 'I fucking trusted him.' Jonathan had never heard Louie swear.

'You can't trust Dave Guinevere,' said Will, 'because he'll always think he knows better than anyone else, and he'll do whatever he wants. Whereas me, I'm in it for me. You know what I want, and what's good for you is good for me. If Kilburn stay up, I miss a big payday, but I'll live with that and it'd almost be worth it to see Dave fail. But I don't get personal. I play the long game. I'll let you think about it, but Louie knows I'm right. Come on board with me and you'll have the best career you can have. Full stop.'

The games went exactly as Will had said, with Mr Guinevere changing the formation and making substitutions which hampered the team enough to keep Kilburn from escaping the bottom three. Kilburn drew with Putney Bridge on the penultimate Saturday of the season, but they could still avoid relegation by beating Hearts the next week, who were one place and one point ahead of them in the table.

The Sunday evening after the game in Putney came the second shock: the first person to call Jonathan was Craig Drayly. 'Hey, Chicken,' he said. 'Have you heard?'

'No.'

'The gaffer's had a fight with the Princess. It's top fucking secret, but Will told me. She thinks the gaffer's fucking up deliberately, and she's gone mental. She's not letting the gaffer near us, and she's asked Will to take over training for the last game. It's fucked, man.' Drayly ranted on, and others made similar calls, all of them unsure whether to be excited or scared. Jonathan didn't know either until Will Beauchamp phoned to explain.

'I take it you've heard what's going on,' Will said.

'Yes, Mr Beauchamp.'

'This changes things.'

'Yes?'

'Of course it does, Jonathan. It might not be public knowledge, but people will hear rumours, and that could be very bad. Our reputation is crucial to us, mine and the players I choose to represent.' Will's voice was hard like always, but it was not smooth today.

'How did Lady Rosslare find out about Mr Guinevere?' asked Jonathan.

'That's not important. What's important is that we win on Saturday. You've heard that I'm running the show this week?'

'Yes.'

For the first time since he came to Kilburn, Jonathan learned what training should be with a proper manager. He still did not like Will Beauchamp, but Will said at the first session that he did not care who liked him, so long as they respected him. He also said, 'We're winning on Saturday. There's no way we're letting that fucker win.'

'The gaffer?' said someone.

'Yes,' said Will, but Jonathan thought Will had to readjust before he spoke, as if this was not about Mr Guinevere at all. But who else could it be? It did not matter, because for all of that week, Will explained about what to do to beat Hearts, and about who his team would be, which had Jonathan on the right of midfield. Nothing was being made public, because it would shame the club, so Mr Guinevere would be on the bench on Saturday, but he would not be allowed to talk to the team or to make substitutions, so he would be helpless.

Some of the players worried that they would be stuck at Kilburn if they stayed up, but Will told them that once Guinevere had gone, which would definitely happen now, the club would be fine. If they really wanted to leave, any sane manager would let them. But first they had to prove they were honest.

Before the game against Hearts, Jonathan saw Mr Guinevere standing in the tunnel. Mr Guinevere said, 'I'm sorry you've had to be part of this, but I hope you'll be grateful in the end.' Jonathan knew Mr Guinevere had suffered very much, but that did not excuse him and Jonathan turned his back. Will Beauchamp spoke very strongly, and Jonathan understood even more what the team had missed. Jonathan walked out of the dressing room taller and more determined than he could remember. He waited in the tunnel next to Louie Cohen. The face of the American was awful, because the club meant so much to him. Jonathan felt a peculiar need to reassure him. He said, 'It has been bad, but we will win today. I know we will save Kilburn.' Louie Cohen looked at Milagroso Nuñez with blank eyes, and Milagroso Nuñez looked away, his knuckles white.

WILL BEAUCHAMP'S YEAR

Will Beauchamp snapped his cruciate ligament making an unspectacular tackle towards the end of a messy January draw with Espanyol. He could probably have played again eventually, but he was getting on and he wasn't prepared to risk being past his peak.

All the effort Will had invested in his image was money in the bank against the end of his career, however that might come. The sympathy he received as a result of the injury did him no harm. He had already done some work with the BBC and as a columnist for the *Clarion*, and he would carry on with that, but he'd spent fifteen years watching with disbelief as incompetent fuckwits made fortunes out of football, and he was ready to show them how it was done. He had no desire to move into management and spend his life having to justify himself to lunatic chairmen and ignorant fans. Will Beauchamp was accountable to no one.

While he was convalescing, he realised what was happening at Kilburn. He was so surprised that he spent a week in front of videoed matches making certain. Then he decided to speak to Strabis Kinsale.

Strabis was shagging Esther. Will didn't care. Strabis was clearly doing it to needle Aisling, and Will supposed he should pity his ex-wife.

Will made his move at a home match early in March. Strabis wore jeans and a suit jacket, and an old-style Socialists scarf, produced to celebrate the 1984 European Cup win. Strabis's plan was working – Aisling spent her whole time glancing across at him. At half-time, Will found himself alongside Strabis, as if casually.

'Will.' Strabis was very relaxed. 'I was so sorry to hear about the injury.'

'These things happen.'

'Is this anything to do with Esther?' Strabis asked.

'No. You're welcome to her.'

'I ended my relationship with Esther last week,' said Kinsale. The pair locked eyes. 'So, William, what can I do for you?'

'I want to talk to you about the future of KSC. I'm sorry if that seems direct. We could meet another time, if you'd prefer.'

'No, it's fine. I don't know what I can do for you.'

'It's your club.'

'The papers will tell you that I'm using it as leverage to get hold of the Rosslare Group.'

'That sounds terribly cynical,' said Will. 'You are, of course, a fervent Kilburn fan.'

'I am. Fervent.'

'Since I can see that you are so fervent,' Will continued, 'you will also see that, in anything else I say, I am suggesting no impropriety on your part.'

'That's sensible of you.'

'As a fervent fan, like me,' Will continued, 'you hate what's happening to the club.'

'I hate it,' said Strabis.

'And, naturally, you would like to get rid of Guinevere because he's proving such a disaster, but Aisling has a veto.' Strabis nodded warily. 'Now,' said Will, 'we come to something that I can't prove. Dave Guinevere is trying to lose matches.'

'I know what Dave's up to.'

'I know you do, sir.' Will saw that Strabis was impressed despite himself. 'Forget I ever said that,' he continued smoothly. 'It was a slip of the tongue. What I meant to say was that *some people* might say that relegation would suit your business purposes, and a conspiracy theorist might even think that you were forcing Dave to do it somehow, but that's ridiculous.'

'Ridiculous.'

'Of course, as we said, because of your fervency. You are desperately upset, but your hands are tied.'

'So, Will, what do you want?'

'Well, sir, should there come a time when, despite your fervency, you grow so disillusioned with what has happened that you wish to divest yourself of your investment, and perhaps coincidentally divest it of various assets which might be used by a new owner to give her – or him, of course – breathing space, then maybe you would consider working with a partner who understands the ins and outs of European football. It might be especially helpful, in case Dave's appalling behaviour comes to light, to have a partner whose character is beyond reproach.'

'What about the players? Will they agree to be represented by you?'

'They'll agree.'

Esther arrived suddenly from behind Kinsale's back. 'I might have guessed!' she hissed. 'I might have guessed you two would have a bastards' convention!'

'Don't make a scene, Est,' said Will.

'You'd love that, wouldn't you!' she spat. 'You hate having to take responsibility for breaking someone's heart so they are able to be seduced by another bastard, who they never loved but were vulnerable to because they'd just been betrayed by their husband!'

'People are staring,' said Strabis, looking at Will over Esther's head.

'I don't care. Why don't you go and have sex with my sister in front of everyone, since that's what you obviously want to do.' She left, probably thinking she had handled it very well.

'Well,' said Strabis, 'that's Esther. Thank you for speaking with me. I'll have to think carefully about what you said, but we'll talk again.' They shook hands, nodded and separated.

In the lead-up to the FA Cup semi-final, Will watched Phil Maroon's players bleat to the papers, and he was surprised as usual that anyone could be deceived by the American's low cunning, and bewildered that Maroon would take these stupid risks. It played into Will's hands though. For the *Clarion*, in a piece to be published on the morning of the semi-final, he wrote:

I am saddened that my old friend Dave Guinevere has bowed to player power and selected the likes of Craig Drayly and Jermaine Cole for today's big game. They are great footballers, to be sure, but they have underperformed this season, and it seems perverse to drop the heroic youngsters who have done so much. In my days at Kilburn, the manager ruled the roost and the players did what we were told!

I do not blame the players. They have been led astray by the kind of person who traditionally chooses to become an agent in the modern game. These sharks are obsessed with money, caring nothing for the players' development or the good of football. I have slowly begun to think that the best way to give something back to the game I love might be to become a new kind of agent, someone who actually understands the game and has the interests of his players at heart!

Will and Strabis acknowledged each other during Kilburn's defeat at Ibrox but no more. Partly this was sensible, but also Will noticed that Strabis never moved more than a few yards from Aisling. Will wondered if Strabis was as uninterested in her as he tried to pretend. The thought set off warning bells, but Will proceeded with his plan.

Over the next couple of weeks, he seduced Phil Maroon's players, starting with Jerry Cole. He faced up to their historical suspicion and dislike of him, explained that he would get them more money more dependably than Maroon, pointed at his own bank balance for proof, told them that their image was vital, and ordered them to start playing properly. They worried that KSC wouldn't be relegated, but he said they would. They asked how he knew, and he didn't tell them. After the stunts Will had pulled while he was at Kilburn, this secrecy convinced them more than anything. Will was particularly proud of getting Jonny Ngwere to agree while Louie Cohen was in the room.

Then, in the box at Putney Bridge before Kilburn's penultimate game of the season, Will noticed an electricity between Strabis and Aisling that hadn't been there previously. Will needed to know what was going on and so, at half-time, he cornered Strabis. 'I presume you saw what Guinevere did,' he probed. 'Leaving out Drayly and making Cole play right back? Not picking Nuñez?'

'It's sordid,' said Strabis.

'So it is. Still, it suits your purposes.'

'What's that supposed to mean?'

'You know what I mean,' Will said. Strabis said nothing. Will had to keep the conversation going. He said, 'Remember, as soon as you want the players brought to heel, give me the nod and I can sort them out.'

'I don't need you,' Strabis hissed. 'What Guinevere is doing to Aisling is disgraceful, and you're trying to manipulate it to your own advantage.' Before Will could reply, Strabis went on. 'I'm telling you now that when we go down, I'm keeping hold of Kilburn, and I'll make it great again, and it will be me that did it. None of you bastards – not Guinevere, not any of these players, and not you – will have a place at the table, and there's nothing you can do about it. You're a manipulator, and that's not the kind of person I work with.'

Will was left gaping. So Strabis had really had some kind of epiphany involving Aisling. Will collected himself. Whatever sanctimonious bullshit Strabis was spouting, he had also said 'when we go down', so he obviously still wanted Dave to relegate KSC. Will was a clear-headed judge of his own advantage, but he calculated pride into the equation and he was fucked if Strabis was going to get away with treating him disrespectfully.

Strabis fancied Aisling, but could it possibly be reciprocated? Will watched the pair of them circle the room, hyperaware of each other, and he grew certain, however unlikely it seemed, that this was the case. He worked through the implications. If Strabis planned to keep hold of Kilburn, the club would be awash with money, which could only be good for Will and his players. But if that was the case, then why let the club be relegated?

The answer was obvious: Strabis couldn't admit to Aisling what he had done. If she found out that Strabis and Dave Guinevere were hand in grubby glove, it would punch a hole in their little reverie. This gave Will an idea. No one got the better of Will Beauchamp.

After the game ended 0–0, he advanced on Aisling and Adam Greswell. Strabis hurried towards them while, in a voice of unctuous regret, Will explained what Dave had been doing. Aisling's jaw slackened in horror. Will kept quiet about Strabis's complicity. He was showing he couldn't be pushed around, but he wasn't burning his bridges.

Adam was also shocked, but overlaid with something else, probably scepticism. 'I don't believe you,' he said.

'Yes, you do.'

'I . . .' said Aisling. 'It's impossible!' Will watched as she put the jigsaw together, and the colour returned to her face. 'What can I do now?' she said.

'There is something,' Will replied. He explained that if she handed control to him, he would ensure that Kilburn beat Hearts next week, as near as certain in an uncertain world. She said she needed to think about it, but that was the shock. When she came to terms with what Dave had done, she would let Will do whatever he wanted. Kilburn would stay up and Will Beauchamp would be the saviour, which would do him no harm, none at all. Strabis looked at him with grudging respect.

*

It took Aisling till the following evening to call Will and admit defeat. She practically begged him to take charge and do whatever he could. She said that neither she nor Strabis wanted a public scandal, so Dave wouldn't officially be sacked, but Dave would not be allowed to do anything to disturb Will's plans. Dave was banned from Kilburn Park and wouldn't be permitted to make substitutions during the game.

Will, though he said so himself, was inspirational that week. The focus and precision he brought to this warring group of players made him wonder if he wasn't missing his vocation by going into business rather than management. Maybe he should take the GB job sometime? It would be similar to this – dealing with talented players and egos when you don't have much time. Will watched videos of Hearts, worked out how to beat them, picked his eleven, gave his pre-match talk and climbed confidently to his seat. He revelled in the thought of thwarting Dave Guinevere. He'd done a remarkable week's work by most people's standards, but that's because most people can't see the strings.

Forty-five minutes were enough to convince Will that he'd been right to eschew management. His tactics were perfect, but a manager has to rely on other people and their weakness was frustrating. After ten minutes, Craig Drayly and Jonathan Ngwere interchanged up the right, and Ngwere whipped in a cross which was met by a weak defensive header. The ball fell to Juan Vales who shaped to shoot, cut inside his opponent's tackle, and passed the ball through three defenders to Carlo ghosting in from the left, who clipped the ball into the roof of the net. Kilburn were dominating the game, but while the lead was only one goal the crowd was still fearful. Will watched the fear extend to his players. When the half-time whistle blew, the Socialists, for all their supremacy, had not added to their lead.

ESTHER ROSSLARE'S YEAR

All the little men in Esther's life had been false dawns as she fluttered her eyelids to wake from the nightmare of her cruel past, and now, in Strabis, she had finally seen the sun! He was too honourable to make promises he wasn't sure he could keep, but actions speak louder than words!

Not that there were *no* words. Strabis explained to her how her life had been hamstrung by irrelevant things from the past. She had been the pawn of her family history, which didn't deserve her. Strabis told her about his own past, which showed that it is what you do yourself that is important. You have to know what makes you strong, and live your life the way you want. 'What makes me strong?' Esther whispered to him. He had laughed, and then he said, 'Trust your heart,' and then he made love to her amazingly, and she could tell she was also amazing by how he reacted, so then she knew!

From the start of the season onwards, Esther was, it was the word Strabis used to describe her, his 'consort'. He smiled when he said it, and she did too, because he probably didn't realise because of his foreign heritage, but a consort was really a queen. She was the queen of his heart. The only thing Esther would have changed, only a very small thing, if it were possible to criticise Strabis in any way, was that she would have said that it was dangerous for him to parade their relationship in front of Aisling. It was probably fine, because Strabis was so in control, but Aisling must hate it and it was the kind of thing where she might do something stupid or horrible, as if it were some kind of battle royal.

Actually it was already a battle royal in a way, since Strabis was trying to take over the Rosslare Group. Esther knew he would succeed eventually, and when Kilburn kept losing, because of Dave Guinevere and her stupid sister, who wouldn't admit that Dave was a mistake, it began to look as if the Socialists might be relegated, and then Aisling would have to sell the Rosslare Group sooner rather than later. That would serve Aisling right, in Esther's opinion. The Socialists hadn't been loyal to her, so she wasn't loyal to them.

In February, KSC won twice, but then a run of two losses and two draws put them back in the relegation zone. Strabis pointed out the pieces of body language that showed Aisling was nervous and doubtful (he was a master of body language!). He said that now was the time to pressure Aisling and so, before and after games, Strabis imposed himself on her, keeping her threatened and irrational. In the directors' box after Kilburn had just beaten Torquay in the fifth round of the Cup, Aisling was glowing with relief and she was somehow always near Strabis. 'Be‚careful of her,' Esther said, and she instantly regretted it. Strabis punished her by staring frankly at Aisling. The next time Aisling glanced his way, he raised his eyebrow in acknowledgement and Aisling flicked her hair, pretending to be embarrassed. Esther quivered.

For three awful weeks after that, Esther had to watch her sister ensorcell Strabis. He was so honourable that he told Esther what was happening, and he said everything was going according to his plan, but Esther knew that couldn't be true, because Strabis was withdrawing from her.

It sent a dagger through her aching heart when Strabis told her he was taking Aisling to his cottage, to 'scope out the lie of the land'. He said his schemes were all in place, and he needed to definitively confirm that Aisling would choose the Kilburn Social Club over the Rosslare Group, when it came to the crunch. He returned that same evening (thank God!), but the next morning, he said that their relationship had 'served its purpose', and it was over. It was a nightmare, but Esther had prepared, because she was a war-hardened veteran of love now. She told him the terrible truth, that Aisling was trying to seduce him so he wouldn't destroy her precious football club. She told him that even when he defeated her, Aisling would be too irrational to give up. She would even destroy the Rosslare Group to stop him getting hold of it. Strabis didn't believe her.

Everything was awful, but Esther would fight for Strabis, and she would win, because of fate.

Her six months with Strabis had cleared her mind of the irrelevant things that had always cluttered up her life. She saw that she had been a tool of men and family tradition, like women had always been, but exceptional women broke free in the end, because they understood the power of their sex, which didn't lie in being an adornment to a man, but in being his partner of equal strength and feminine wisdom, without whom he could never achieve his goals because he would always be prey to parasites and whores.

She regretted thinking 'whores', and it was not exactly how she saw Aisling, but she couldn't quite banish the word from her mind. Strabis's only weakness, Esther realised, was that he'd never known true love before, and so he couldn't recognise it. Strabis was vulnerable to Aisling's tricks because he was inexperienced. Gaudy, girlish Aisling was the typical kind of person people picked for their first love. Everyone is a fool the first time, and gets it wrong. You never forget your first love, even when you know it is crazy – just look at Esther and Dave – but you learn that it was a mistake when you find your true soulmate.

Most people get past it, anyway. Aisling was still obviously in love with Dave or she wouldn't be letting him ruin Kilburn. Maybe Aisling would never get past loving Dave (if Aisling could ever love anyone apart from herself!) because Aisling would rather live her life in denial than admit she was wrong. The only thing that frightened Esther was that Aisling might realise the amazing things that Strabis was offering her. Part of why Aisling was still obsessed with Dave was also probably because of the baby, because Aisling was a murderer. The younger Esther had gone along with the idea that abortion was a matter of choice and women's rights, but now when she thought of what Aisling did, it horrified her. Esther would never have committed such an atrocity, and it was yet another difference between the two of them. Aisling had betrayed her most sacred obligation as a woman. Woman was Mystery and Mother. She was the two Marys. To defeat Aisling, Esther must draw on both of these.

She did this by finding out where Strabis would be, and by always being unpredictable and entrancing in his presence. She was never angry, except for once when she saw him and Will talking and she knew that they were talking about her in bed, like men always do. But the rest of the time, she was in charge. Sometimes she was sad and remote, and sometimes she was vivacious and flirting with other people. After three weeks, Strabis phoned her and said he was coming to visit that evening at seven. He told her that he had had enough, which was frightening, but the main thing was to have provoked him into action.

At quarter to seven, Esther arranged herself uncomfortably on her bed, imagining she resembled a doll discarded, boneless, stringless, collapsed and alone. Not a doll, a corpse. A bleeding corpse cast from a speeding car along life's highway. From a Porsche. A corpse which had been tossed at speed, and which had rolled and fetched up beside the road. She crumpled herself into an even more winsome contortion, imagining the vultures circling. She pictured herself helpless and destroyed, waiting for the cruel beaks to peck her apart.

She prayed she wouldn't have to disarrange herself to let Strabis into the house. He still had a key (to all her locks!) but maybe he was too much of a gentleman to bring it with him. Her left knee twisted across her body, her shoulders pressed back flat on the mattress, her arms were flung akimbo, her left ankle was wedged under her right thigh. She hyperventilated, arching her back slightly. *Let the vultures try to peck my breasts!* she screamed inside, in triumph. *Let them try!* However close the vultures got, she knew that in the end, Strabis, like a giant eagle, would swoop to rescue her, take her in his talons, beat the weak away. She knew him better than he knew himself.

Aisling had infatuated Strabis to try to save her stupid football club. Aisling thought she was clever, but Esther was Cleopatra, Mata Hari, Garbo and the rest: the eternal, ultimate femme fatale, pretending to be weak but drawing Strabis into a net beyond his comprehension. Her back started to whimper, so she uncoiled and turned over, mirroring her pose, cascading her tousled hair off the foot of the bed, sucking in her belly.

Strabis knocked!

'Come in!' she shouted. She saw in the mirror that she looked perfect, the top of her right suspender tantalisingly visible, her shoe half-off.

'Esther?'

'Come in. You have my key!' she called.

'Just let me in.'

'You still have my key, darling.' She would make him come to her. Her breathing deepened, grew more urgent. He might leave. She counted to five, then got to her knees, and then she heard the key in the lock, and she quickly sank back down and rearranged herself. Moving showed how stiff she was, but it would only be moments now.

Strabis framed himself in the doorway, hands on hips. 'Get up Esther, you look ridiculous,' he said. She stood up and crushed herself to him, her whole body pliant in the way he could never resist. He pushed her heavily back on to the bed, and she stretched back, eyes closed. Nothing happened. She lifted her head, and he was still standing there. 'Come downstairs,' he said. She followed him meekly. He sat on the armchair, sinking into the dark leather, and she went to sit on him but he pushed her away again. He couldn't even meet her eye. 'There's nothing between us, Esther,' he said. 'There never has been. Stop embarrassing me in public.'

Esther's thumping heart wanted to say, 'Why?' but her wise head resisted. She sat down, composed, and smoothed her skirt, waiting.

'I never promised you anything,' said Strabis. 'I love Aisling,' he said, eventually. 'I love Aisling.' So, Strabis understood the truth about himself at last. It changed nothing in the long run. He had never spoken like this before, so considerate of her feelings. It was a sign he was maturing. 'I know you love me, Esther, so I have to tell you this as clearly as I can: I will only ever love once. I will devote my life to it, and I don't care how long it takes. I finally understand how you feel, and I'm sorry I behaved like I did, but you have to forget me.' It was as if he were stabbing her, even though she understood how he felt and how he would change in the end, because she had felt exactly the same about Dave, once upon a time.

'I will never forget you,' she said. 'And you won't forget me.'

'Don't threaten me.'

'Who's threatening who?' she said silkily. 'I know things that you —'

'I've not got time for this crap. I came to tell you how it is.'

'No! You owe it to me to listen. I am not just your lover, I am your partner. That will never change, whatever you think. I will always be here for you. I believe what you say, and I am sure you will win Aisling with your plan, I have always known it, and I knew you loved her. I am not the fool you take me for. I see you are wounded, and even if you don't love me, I can help salve your wounds, if you will let me, if you have needs. I won't leave you spinning alone in the winds of love. Come to me.'

'You're ridiculous.' And he left.

She sat alone for a long time. She was sure of eventual victory, but that didn't make this less painful. Love was always pain, but when Strabis tore strips from her, there was exultation, because she was tied to a rock and he was an eagle, and the pain was worth it because the flesh regrew. When the vultures pecked at you, the weaklings, they swallowed and gobbled, without honour, and you didn't regenerate because they were mean and greedy and to be pecked at by them was to have the dead bits eaten. But still when Strabis tore her, even though she knew she would regrow, it did hurt, and eventually he would tear so much that she would have to reveal his growing seed within, and she was prepared for his anger and his rage, but when she revealed it, and her little victory, he would begin to realise and transform, and eventually he would not peck at her, but at the chains, and carry her away. And leave her sister to the vultures.

She was super aloof from Strabis after that, not even deigning to talk to him. All the same, she noticed everything about him, so she noticed the change in his behaviour after the FA Cup semi-final defeat against Cardiff. He was suddenly calmer around Aisling, which meant that they must have come to some kind of arrangement. Esther could see by Aisling's insincere face that she had been a lying bitch to have got her claws into him. Esther desperately hoped that Kilburn would be relegated so that the only sane way for her to keep the Socialists alive would be to sell the Rosslare Group to Strabis. When Aisling refused to do that because of her stupid pride, Strabis would finally see that he had been deceived and understand everything.

Come the last match of the season, Esther was ready. For a start, she exploited the fact that Aisling, for all her so-called beauty, didn't take proper care of her appearance. Esther stroked her hair and smoothed her make-up, which was all part of being a woman and using the bounty given to her by Nature (a woman). Esther's day-old jeans slunk into a pair of soft white velvet boots. Esther added a mint-green shirt from Taka Imamura, a cream cashmere shawl and matching knitted cap from Relée. Esther had taken fathomless aeons to understand that if you don't value yourself, no one else will, and so, however modest she was naturally, she was forced to agree with her stylist that she looked amazing when she tried. Her joy was complete when she arrived at Kilburn Park to see Aisling still wearing normal jeans outside cowboy boots, and a new shirt, but only from Tagna, and a coat Esther must have seen fifty times before. Strabis nodded to Esther, but she ignored him mysteriously.

Hearts were owned by an Indian steel magnate with socialite children, and they always filled the room with champagne and the right kind of people. The younger Esther would have felt uncomfortable, that she was worthless in their company, but now she went straight to the daughter, whom she met all the time at events and balls, and they sparred about the prospects for today's game. The daughter wore Hearts' black and white, which was vulgar, but the girl was immature, so Esther forgave her.

Aisling was with Leo and Adam, like always, and couldn't stand still, as if there were nothing more important in life than football, as if it weren't just another branch of entertainment, a way for normal people to get away from their dull daily lives, and a plaything for exceptional people like Strabis to toy with in their more rarefied world. When Strabis ended up with Esther, Aisling would probably fall apart because she would realise what a terrible mistake she had made, and she would give up the club at last, and Esther would take control of Kilburn as well as everything else. Then Esther would make the club truly great again, not because she cared about the past or her family, but because she cared about the future. She would make it great in a way that drove daggers into Aisling's heart, and Dave Guinevere's. She would make it mighty, as a monument to herself and Strabis's love for her, and as a gift for their children, who would be grateful.

The game would start in twenty minutes. Strabis was talking to Aisling now, who was goo-gooing up at him, twisting her hair in her fingers. Esther put her hand across her womb, jealous despite her secret knowledge, and decided that two could play that game. She angled through the crowd towards her ex-husband. It was time for her to bury the hatchet. She exclaimed, 'Will!' took his hand, and kissed his cheek as a signal that he was no longer to consider himself *persona non grata*.

'Hi, Est.'

'Will. It's been too long! We can be friends, Will. That's what we should be, okay? Best friends?' She swayed towards him, because the room was noisy. If it looked intimate from a distance, so much the better. Will talked about his plans. When appropriate, Esther touched his arm in support. He kept looking around the room, which was incredibly rude, but that was just how he was. He never understood how to make a woman feel special because he never saw beyond himself. He was superficial, unlike Strabis, who was still lost in talk with Aisling.

Strabis committed completely, like she did, whether it was to a conversation in a room, or to a business venture, or to a woman. *Completely* didn't mean *for ever*, as Esther well knew.

During the first half, she was frightened that Will seemed to have saved the Socialists. But then, soon after half-time, Will suddenly stood up and pushed along his row for some reason, looking furious. Esther didn't pay it much heed until he emerged from the tunnel down below and headed straight for Dave Guinevere. Dave ignored him; Will put his hand on Dave's elbow; Dave shook it off. Will grew animated and Dave smiled. The tension and weirdness transmitted itself through the crowd. Will spoke to the fourth official, but the fourth official shook his head. Now Will tried to grab the electronic board which indicated substitutions, but the fourth official wouldn't let go. Now Will was back with Dave, pointing him at the fourth official and ordering him to do something, but Dave shrugged. Dave looked as if he could hardly keep from laughing. Will turned, and Dave said something quietly and Will spun back round, but then, quickly, Will collected himself. He nodded to Dave and sauntered to the bench, as if everything were going to plan. Esther enjoyed Will's humiliation. She realised then that Will had always been jealous of Dave Guinevere, probably because Esther had secretly preferred Dave, and her ex-husband was still working out his issues. Well, more fool Will Beauchamp. He'd had his chance.

A few seats along, Aisling still looked hopeful, which was pathetic, because she was doomed whatever happened. She would try to keep both the Rosslare Group and the Kilburn Social Club, and Strabis would see sense, and then he would destroy Aisling because he was too strong for her. It was almost funny, but when Esther looked at Strabis looking at Aisling, she didn't feel like laughing.

TERRIBLE ZONDEKI'S YEAR

Zondi bought himself a new shirt for the 2005 Christmas Party but he did not buy one for Adam. He thought about sad things but he was not sad.

The Socialists won earlier that day, and they were third from bottom of the league. Zondi was pleased that Aisling had brought Adam back to KSC. He and Adam were pained by what was happening, but Adam was not sad overall, because he was in the right place for him to be.

At six o'clock, Zondi and Adam walked the ten minutes to Aisling's house, from where they were due to be picked up. Leo let them in, because Aisling was still unready. Aisling had invited Hank Tam, who didn't look shy or uncomfortable, just quiet in the corner.

'I'm glad we won today,' said Nicky.

'Yes,' said Zondi. 'It was very traditional.'

'Jonathan Ngwere is the real thing, isn't he?' asked Leo, hesitantly.

'Of course he is,' said Nicky. Leo looked at Zondi, and Zondi nodded. 'Pay no attention to my opinion,' said Nicky. 'Is Azza okay?'

There was an uncertain silence. Hank broke it. 'Yes. She's okay,' he said. Then he clarified, 'She'll be okay.'

'I wish I could be so sure,' said Nicky. 'I persuaded her to ditch Jeremy, but I never meant her to do anything like this.'

'She didn't do this because of you.'

'You always say that, Adam, but who spoke to her? Who got Leo to drag Dave back to England?'

'Wasn't that her idea?'

'Whatever you think,' said Nicky. 'I'm just saying, look at what she's doing. Don't tell me you're not worried by Strabis letting this all happen, because we all are. This is what he does. I should tell her to stop.'

'She'll do what she wants,' said Adam.

He trailed off as Aisling skipped down the stairs. 'Shall we?' she said, too brightly. 'Once more under the bridge.'

Strabis funded the Christmas Party, and this year's was the largest ever, a glamorous gala as much as a private party. When Zondi and the others arrived, everyone was excited, but this was just a normal party of people who went to parties, and Zondi felt tawdry and tired.

In the middle of the room stood Strabis and his consort. Esther flittered breathlessly, now touching Strabis's arm, now casting triumphant looks at Aisling, now pandering to someone she had seen on the television. To the edge of the room were Louie Cohen and Milagroso Nuñez, along with Monica and Milagroso's latest beautiful girlfriend. Zondi made his way over to them. When Louie noticed, he turned half-away, which alerted Monica. At the sight of Zondi, she seemed to grow an inch even taller. He plucked up his courage to speak over the silence, as Achilles would have done. 'Hello, Louie,' said Zondi. 'Monica, you are looking very stunning.' He said to Milagroso, 'It is good to see you,' and then to the girlfriend, 'I am Zondi.'

Zondi wanted to talk, to show them how he valued them whatever was happening, but Monica could not contain herself. 'You've got to do something about her,' she said.

'It is not her,' said Zondi. 'David is the manager.'

'He's lost it, man,' said Louie. 'He doesn't know what he's doing. Something happened to him in Africa. I loved him – I love him, I mean – but he needs help. She's the one has to make the decision.'

'We're not blaming David,' repeated Monica. 'And I'm sure Aisling thinks she's in love with him, but if they carry on like this, the club's going to be ruined.'

'It is not what I expected,' said Milagroso. Zondi stood eye to eye with the little Spaniard. 'I did not know the gaffer good before, but I thought he was an honourable man and I want to still think this.' He was asking a question which Louie did not understand and which Zondi would not answer.

Monica looked at Strabis. 'That fucker makes me sick,' she said. 'He's using Esther to get at Aisling, and Ash knows it, but it's still working.'

In the following months, Zondi watched Milagroso and Louie speak often, draw conclusions and harden against David. Zondi wanted to apologise for his friend, but he could not.

It was late February now. Strabis was edging towards Aisling, who looked increasingly vulnerable. Wheeling his bicycle alongside Zondi, David asked, 'Where are we now? The leopard's ear?'

David knew that Kilburn Park was the eye, so this was a fair guess on his part, but it was the guess of a man who thought you could draw the leopard over the map of London and it would still look like a leopard. Even Adam thought like this. Zondi didn't put Adam right because, although he loved Adam, this was a thing Zondi could keep of Achilles. Achilles was the one who understood that the leopard covered every part of London, so that to be the leopard London could not be flat, but must be folded in upon itself and have a form that could not be pictured for the eyes. Zondi would never comprehend the need to see things in clear shapes, with edges, with an inside and an outside. 'It is part of the neck,' he said.

'But we can see the stadium. Oh. It doesn't work like that, does it? It's layers on layers, like origami pressed flat or something?'

That was not exactly right, but it was an interesting way to think of it, and Zondi did so, because he was scared to say his important questions to Dave. Eventually, he asked, 'Are you not worried what is happening to Jonathan?'

'He's making his choice,' said Dave.

'He's only a boy,' said Zondi.

'I know,' said Dave. 'I know.' He looked tired.

'Milagroso is angry. He and Louie.'

'I can't help that,' said Dave. 'People make their own decisions.'

In David's voice was the fear he was making a mistake, but there was also the pitch of things unsaid, the Tall Hunter buried beneath. They walked down the track to the training ground, as they had done, together and alone, how many thousands of times? Mr Brown was agitated, because the track was not a place she was allowed to do her naughties. Zondi let her off the leash, and she scuffled around the corner. When Zondi and David came around the edge of the admin block, she was emerging from a flowerbed like the cleverest dog in the world.

It took Zondi a while to work out that Carlo was running that day's training session, because it was so directionless. There was a burst of sharpness as the players registered David's presence, but Carlo lacked the charisma to drive his teammates on. David did not read people very well who were unlike him. Zondi leaned his elbows on the fence, watching Jonathan Ngwere and his fellow youngster James Simmonds laugh at something Craig Drayly said. In the far corner of the ground was Hank Tam.

Training finished and the players trotted off, no one breathing heavily. David strode inside, leaving Zondi to wander to where Hank sat heavily on his shooting stick. Hank had been given one of the heavy kit jackets that the players wore for sitting on the bench, but he preferred his old greatcoat and white wool hat. The cutting wind was baffled by the stand of conifers along the east side of the training ground. Carlo was the last to leave the pitch, and he stopped to talk to Hank. Zondi picked up his pace, straining to hear.

'. . . what I'm doing!' said Carlo. 'I'm not clever enough for this!'

'Dave Guinevere ain't doing this for fun, Carlo.'

'That's what I think!' said Carlo. 'I tried to tell JC and the others that he's up to something, but they won't listen.'

'What do you think of the others?'

'I don't know. They're my mates, I suppose, even if it's not like the old days. The others don't care what happens to Kilburn, though, but I care, just as much as Dirk and Torquil and Louie, but they don't like me because I don't hate Coley and stuff, but it's not Coley's fault, or Marty Vlocker's. We're just players. There's nothing we can do.'

'You do the things you can,' said Hank.

'So I just do nothing?' Carlo was trying to be cool, but he was a second-bravest dog. He was a following dog. Cole was the one Zondi needed to persuade, but he couldn't think how.

Hank took his right hand out if its glove. It was red-mottled and rough, with heavy dark veins. He put it on Carlo's shoulder, letting the warmth slowly push through Carlo's shirt. He said, 'Whatever Dave's doing, you can't change that, but you can do the right thing, say what you believe. Everything is all the small things.' He took his hand back, and struggled it back into the glove. 'You'll be all right,' he said. Mr Brown leaned against Zondi's calf.

Carlo said, 'Thanks,' and moved away, then turned back and shook Hank's hand, as if he were embarrassed but had to do it. He noticed Zondi, and nodded guiltily. Then he jogged off to change.

Zondi and Hank stood in companionable silence. Sometimes Zondi wondered whether, by now, they didn't speak because they were afraid that their shared understanding was too precious an illusion to risk. Within his cocoon of performance fabrics and heavy leather, after decades of acclimatisation, Zondi still felt the chill spreading up from his feet.

'Rodney Norman will be the first to finish,' said Hank. 'He pretends to be busy, because he thinks he doesn't belong.' Hank pulled a sandwich out of his pocket, and offered Zondi half. Zondi declined. They stood some more. 'Norman's is the yellow Porsche,' Hank said. 'He bought it the day after he signed. Never saw someone so happy. You suggested him to David, didn't you?' Zondi said nothing. 'You did a good thing there.'

Norman emerged, hair wet, full of bustle. Zondi said, 'Rodney!' and Norman came over apologetically, saying something about hurrying to cookery class. When he first told Zondi about his restaurant, he added: 'Got to have a trade for when the gaffer sees through me!'

'You're playing well,' said Zondi.

'I've had a bit of luck,' Rodney said. 'No, I mean, I'm *trying*. I'm trying really hard.'

'You're looking fitter.'

'I am, I am to be honest, but I'm nothing like Craggy or Jonny – those guys are freaks. I'm doing yoga, though. I'm doing it now, before I go to the cooking, to be honest. Flexibility. I'm not telling the others. They all do it too, but they'd laugh if they knew I was.'

'Keep working.'

'Yeah. I think I'm improving. But training is hard, to be honest, like it is, with no one in charge, you know, to be honest. I hope, you know, if the gaffer does see through me, I'll at least have done enough for someone to buy me in Div One. It'd be hard to go back to Div Two, to be honest.' Mr Brown nudged Norman's knee, and rubbed her cheek against his leg. Norman absently tickled the dog behind her ears.

'Rodney —'

'No, sorry, mate, and thanks, but I've got to dash now. Sorry, mate.'

Jonathan Ngwere emerged with Jermaine Cole. David would be angry at the interference, but sometimes it is important to know what is right even when your friends disagree. He called over to Jonathan, who would come because he still respected old men. Zondi hated to think of himself as old.

Zondi asked Jonathan how he felt things were going, and he replied, 'I'm not getting enough pitch-time, man.' Jonathan was warring with himself. They spoke for only a few moments and then Carlo Derkin arrived. They spoke some more. Jermaine Cole wanted to take Jonathan away, but Carlo said he would drive Jonathan. When Carlo and Jonathan left, they sat in Carlo's car for a long time with Carlo talking. Hank smiled to Zondi.

And now it was Sunday before the last week of the season, and the crisis was upon them. Will Beauchamp had told Aisling what David was doing, and Will was going to be in charge of the Socialists this week. David asked Zondi to meet him by old Mr Brown's bench on Primrose Hill. They were standing there now, in the dark.

Zondi bit another strip off his biltong, thinking. This was the crux of Dave's life, the pivot around which it all would turn, for good or ill. The Tall Hunter had hidden his spear, had pressed down his public hunger and walked in the wilderness, leading his people away from the right paths and into barrenness. The Hunter was trying to persuade them that the good hunting was gone for ever, because he wanted them to give it up and make their way to the town, or the fields, or anywhere else. This made him look stupid, as if he couldn't find any prey, which was painful for him, but he did it because he believed in his heart it was for the best. But now, at the very last moment, when they had been ready to give up, /Kaggen had come, and he was showing the Hunter's people a fat water-hole, surrounded by antelope. The Tall Hunter feared that if they made this one big kill, the wilderness would have been all for nothing, and he would have failed. The Hunter thought /Kaggen's waterhole was the wrong one, and the drinking from it would be sickly. Zondi feared what the Tall Hunter might do if his hunt came to the wrong end.

Mr Brown coughed. She started down the path and looked back. Zondi and Dave didn't move. Mr Brown coughed again. 'Does she want us to walk?' asked Dave. Zondi nodded, but he gave Mr Brown a suspicious look as he and Dave moved downhill. Mr Brown was very smug these days and her bottom waggled importantly as she walked. After thirty yards, Mr Brown suddenly doubled back and ran up the hill. She silhouetted herself against the moon, lifted her muzzle to the sky and howled. She looked back down the hill, and in case they had missed it, she howled again. Dave laughed. 'She's been watching too much telly,' he said. 'Can we go back up now?' He and Zondi returned to the top of the hill, and Zondi bent to rub noses with Mr Brown because it was a good joke and the dog was quivering with joy. Dave scratched her shoulders. 'Bad wolf,' he said, and Mr Brown made happy grunts.

Dave had chosen the best puppy. Zondi thought he would be good for Dave if . . . He *hoped* the puppy might be good for Dave in the way Mr Brown was good for him, but the puppy was only a dog, and it was Dave that Zondi worried for. He said, 'You want me to talk to Milagroso and Louie?'

'Yes.'

'Have you tried?'

'It's you they'll listen to.'

'You have known this could happen.' Milagroso might have understood if Dave had explained at the start how Strabis was destroying Kilburn. Dave wanted to do everything himself, but the Tall Hunter did not have the power he thought he had. He needed Milagroso's help but Milagroso felt angry and betrayed, and Zondi might not be able to persuade him. If you shut something out for too long, then when you open the door in the end, maybe what you are waiting for will not be there any more.

'I think Louie also,' Dave said.

'No.' Zondi looked ahead into the night and felt as if the bottom of the hill was rushing towards him, turning the incline into a cliff, his toes hanging over the edge.

The next morning, Zondi spoke to Milagroso on the side of the training field, Will looking on suspiciously. Milagroso said, 'I know what the gaffer done,' he said. 'And I know you know. This is bullshit. This is wrong.' Zondi tried to explain but there was no point. Milagroso could not accept being a dupe. Will ran a good session. As the players left the pitch, Milagroso spoke animatedly with Louie, and they both looked at Zondi. Zondi was ashamed, and not because he had failed David.

Standing aside from the jostle and scrum in the suite before the match against Hearts, Adam said, 'Strabis really loves Aisling, doesn't he?'

Zondi said, 'I think so, but I do not know. He is very clever.'

Adam said, 'If we lose today, and Strabis chooses to let KSC die, there's nothing we can do.'

'I know,' said Zondi.

Zondi visited David in the tunnel at half-time because David would be alone, and Zondi pitied him.

In the second half, Milagroso was constantly losing the ball. Will saw it and understood. He went down to the touchline. The rule was in place about David making no substitutions, but Will had no official status so he couldn't make them either. Eventually Will gathered himself and returned to his seat. Will did not understand why Milagroso was doing what he was doing, because Will had never loved what KSC used to be.

HANK, CALUM AND
MILAGROSO'S YEAR

On the Monday before Kilburn's final match, with Will Beauchamp in charge, Hank thought the Socialists looked sharper than they had for years.

Hank feared Saturday even though he should surely be past the age when a football team could depress him. He had been buffeted at the edge of the void and his faith had held him fast, but he was weak and old now, and maybe this was the puff that would topple him over. He leaned back and looked upwards, exposing his neck and feeling the cold wrap around it like a scarf.

An arc of swallows peeled against the bright grey sky. They had been very early this year. The swallows circled once and were gone. Hank waited. At almost the same moment, on different paths, a crow soared high over his left shoulder and two gulls hovered low into the wind from his right. Hank saw the gulls much more clearly than he could see them. He saw them as if he were a young man, and they were floating stationary over the stern of his boat, feet from him, stray feathers flickering, waiting for something dead. There were so many gulls in London now. Zondi was here today, but he hadn't spoken to Hank. He just waved and waited on the far side of the pitch. It must be something important, something to do with Dave. Hank loved Aisling as he would have loved his own granddaughter, and he loved Dave Guinevere too, though Dave was acting like a man Hank couldn't love. The session ended, and as the players left the field, Zondi pulled Milagroso Nuñez aside, and spoke to him, looking at the floor. Milagroso was surprised to be having this conversation, and twice he gestured angrily towards the absent Dave's window. It is the saddest thing when a man goes so far off his track that he can never return, and you understand the person you once knew is gone for ever, and that it would be better if the person who he is now would disappear, before even the memories grow sour.

Hank hit his hands together again and concentrated on the birds, because there was no point in these thoughts. All he could think to do was wait for Milagroso to emerge from the changing room. When he did, Hank said, 'Mr Nuñez.'

'Sir?' said Milagroso, courteous as a conquistador.

'Zondeki is a good man,' said Hank.

Milagroso didn't reply immediately, but he didn't rebuff Hank. 'It is not what I expected,' Milagroso said. 'I dreamed of the Socialists in my young career, but there was Beauchamp and the gaffer so there was no place for me. I thought that now . . . It is not what I expected.' There were almost tears.

'Zondeki is a good man,' Hank repeated. 'So is Dave Guinevere.' He looked at the sky. 'I trust them,' he added.

'Thank you, sir,' said Milagroso.

It was half-time against Hearts. Calum scanned the directors' box lazily. His protagonists rolled along furrows that Calum felt he had personally ordained. Aisling was panicked and hopeful, tied by an increasingly visible string to Strabis Kinsale. Esther, as usual, was done up like a pretty thirty-something in a beautiful twenty-something's clothes. She would never see what was in the mirror, never have any idea of who she was or where she fitted in. It was more pitiable than pitiful. Calum wondered who would be next for her, and what she would think she was like then. Some people are not made to be happy, and there it is.

Five feet to his left, Strabis walked past Aisling, who watched his back with obvious greed. Calum caught her eye. 'You and him, Ash?' he said innocently.

'Never!' she said. 'Absolutely never! He's a self-obsessed arsehole.' If there was one thing Aisling had in spades, it was the capacity for self-deception. Calum teased her for a while. He didn't mind when she ran away. Today he was content to observe and ponder, to fit the last elements into what had been a fantastic plot, and when he wandered back to his seat he felt genuinely excited that the ending was uncertain, and satisfied that all the possibilities would suit him.

He revelled at the conflicted crowd, the fools who thought they were a sea but didn't realise that each one was an island. Their shared mood, so called, was cobbled together from misunderstood mumbles and nods as they looked hopefully at each other, trying to build bridges. Everything they thought about Dave, and football in general, came from fragments of tribal tradition, commentary, punditry and journalism that had coalesced into received wisdom. Not a few of these were things that had managed to filter from the words of the few genuinely astute observers of the game, naming no names, and down into the hackneyed opinions of the dullard quotidian media.

The ball skewed from Milagroso Nuñez's too hasty boot and off for a corner. Louie caught the cross and cleared it upfield. There were ten minutes left of the season. Calum, after chatting with Will earlier in the week, had boldly predicted a Kilburn escape, and he nestled back comfortably into his seat.

When Will appeared on the touchline, Milagroso wondered whether he would be substituted after all, and he was almost grateful, but Will could do nothing. Now, there were eight minutes to play, and Milagroso had kept his options open. He looked towards the bench. Who do you trust?

With a minute to go, subtler alternatives exhausted, Milagroso gave away a penalty. The other Socialists raged at the referee out of habit, but Milagroso couldn't join them. He walked to the edge of the pitch, unable to raise his head. He took a step back, and haltered forwards two steps. It looked as if he was staggering. The ground didn't seem level. The crowd inhaled and Milagroso glanced across at Dave, whose face was in his hands. The grass grew in front of Milagroso's eyes, as if it would snake around his calves and cling and drag him under.

AISLING ROSSLARE'S YEAR

It was a cool Monday evening at the start of March. The awful season was drawing to a close and Aisling was more frightened of Strabis Kinsale than she pretended.

The days were pale with watery sun. It rained every night, but the city retained a veneer of grime. It felt rinsed, not washed. Strabis phoned Aisling yesterday and said he must meet her, discreetly, and would brook no refusal. He was due to arrive in ten minutes, and Aisling had just returned from the hairdresser's to find Nicky waiting. 'You're seriously going to do this?' Nicky said. Aisling didn't deign to reply. 'He's dangerous, Azzabelle. Not sexy dangerous. Don't get distracted.' Nicky had some ridiculous theory that Aisling wanted to seduce Strabis to put Esther in her place.

'I'm not a little girl,' Aisling said. 'Pour me a glass of wine. I have to change.'

Nicky followed her upstairs without pouring the wine. 'Where's he taking you?'

'I don't know. He told me not to dress up.' She and Nicky decided on a skirt and her best suede boots, with a pink work shirt to offset any suspicion on his part that she thought this was a date.

'He's up to something.'

'Of course he's up to something.'

'He's a dick, Aisling.'

'I know what he is,' said Aisling. It was after seven, and Strabis hadn't arrived. She should have predicted he wasn't a gentleman. She slowed down.

'He really believes his own bullshit. He thinks girls fall for him because he's some kind of fucking superman, not because girls fall for rich, good-looking dicks.' Aisling agreed but, for what it was worth, if she did take Strabis's mind off Esther, she'd be doing Esther a favour. Esther wouldn't understand, but that was Esther for you. Nicky said, 'I'm seriously worried about you.'

Aisling didn't need this distraction. She was good with make-up, invisibly good when she wanted, but the mirror was full of someone trying hard to look careless. 'Please can you open the white in the fridge?' she asked. 'I promise I won't go nutty with drunken lust. I'll be down in two minutes.' Nicky left, shaking her head. Aisling stood in front of the mirror. She could wear something sexier, but that wasn't her plan. It was nearly half past now. Who was this guy? She changed her bra, and when she put her shirt back on, she left one more button undone. The doorbell rang as she walked down the stairs. 'Stay in the kitchen,' she hissed. 'I'll call you later.' She opened the door, and Strabis kissed her cheeks. He hadn't shaved or brushed his hair, and he was wearing a suit with no tie. Aisling stood with her toes pointed inwards.

'Do you need a coat?'

'I don't know,' she said, hating her coyness.

'Bring one in case.'

Strabis hadn't apologised for being late, and he guided her to the car with his hand, as if she couldn't find her way. Under normal circumstances she would have bridled.

The evening at his cottage was surprisingly enjoyable.

In the lead-up to the FA Cup semi-final against Cardiff, Aisling desperately wanted David to resist the media and the bullying from Cole and Drayly and pick the kids. He didn't, and Kilburn lost.

Five days later, Strabis took her on an Adventure. It was very exciting.

The next evening, she made dinner for Zondi and Adam. She tried to behave as if her life was going to plan. At seven o'clock, she was pouring a second cup of tea. Zondi had gone to the kitchen to refill his coffee. Mr Brown waddled over to Aisling – Zondi had been fretting about Mr Brown's weight, which was cute – and bumped her nose into Aisling's leg, then cocked her head. Aisling patted her distractedly, and with a movement that was incredibly either fast or subtle, Mr Brown took Aisling's hand gently in her mouth. Aisling looked down and Mr Brown, attention gained, let go and looked back at Adam. Mr Brown gave a small, agitated bark.

'I've never seen her so antsy,' said Aisling.

'Nor me,' said Adam.

Mr Brown barked again, distressed that this conversation was going on over her head. She took Aisling's skirt and tried to pull her out of her chair. Aisling pushed Mr Brown towards the kitchen, and pointed. 'He's in there, Mr B. Go find Zondi.' A reproachful harrumph and the dog walked off.

'Cole was appalling against Cardiff,' said Adam.

'And Vlocker. I know.' The defeat had left its usual weight in her. 'We'll get through this together,' she said, not for the first time.

There were dark rings round Adam's eyes. Thank God the Bursar (the real Bursar, who is called the Bursar again and not the Manciple) had never relinquished the reins, though maybe that should have been 'chains'. The Groundsman had stayed too. He was happier than ever, not that you could tell if you didn't know him. If Kilburn went down, there would be fewer games ripping apart his precious grass.

Zondi was taking for ever over the coffee. Adam was gazing at the bus pictures as if he'd never seen them before. Though, to be fair, Aisling saw them every day and she wasn't bored yet. They were two huge photographs, six feet by four. Each was centred around a red double-decker bus, the N16 and the 189 respectively, and each turned a dynamic street scene into a frozen moment that felt as composed as a still life, and what you took out of them depended on what you knew of a thousand unknowable stories. The woman in the headscarf running to catch the N16, who had just given up and was dropping her hand in desperate defeat. The two laughing black girls, jaunty in pink and blue velour, hair elaborately slicked and pompommed, white trainers shining, palms wild. The grey-brown-haired woman, can of beer in her left hand and right outstretched towards a fast-walking young woman in a neat coat and a rucksack, who was veering in surprise. The Chinese man in the front left seat of the top deck of the bright-inside N16, hunched forwards into his mobile, arm sweeping down and across his orange parka, mouth wide and cheeks sharp in anger, or maybe just emphasis. Aisling changed her mind about him often. The driver of the 189 was looking at her lap, eyes closed. There was no sign she hadn't just been shot dead or had a massive stroke, and then the picture would have been very altered, because the bus was moving briskly and the High Road was busy. Aisling made different journeys through the pictures every time she looked, but they almost always ended in the same place, which was her favourite secret thing. On the left-hand side of the road, the other side to the approaching 189 in this photograph taken by a stranger five years ago, hidden by the bus and only visible in the reflection in the window of the mobile-phone shop, Aisling herself was walking away from the camera. No one else had ever noticed. You don't always see everyone in the picture.

'You've got to take Strabis seriously,' said Adam.

'You think I don't?'

'I'm worried that if everything fucks up, you won't be able to walk away from Kilburn. The Rosslare Group —'

'. . .is my first responsibility,' she finished impatiently. 'Yes, Adam, I am aware of that, actually.' Aisling wished Adam had more faith, because when he talked like this, he chipped away at hers. No one privy to her innermost thoughts would have accused her of not taking Strabis seriously, but there was no point in letting it show.

'Zondi!' Adam called. 'What's taking so long?' There was no reply. 'Zondi?' he got up, not really worried. Aisling got up too. 'Zondi?' They set off after the exact same beat. Adam was halfway through the door, moving too fast, when he bumped into Zondi coming the other way. Adam, gangling, was thrown off balance, and barely stayed on his feet. Zondi was unshifted, and he twisted his smile with quick pride between the others, the edges of his mouth forcing dimples almost into his ears. Adam and Aisling were confused, and Zondi nodded down at his hands. He was cradling a puppy, straggling wet and grey, eyes scrunched. Zondi scuttled back into the kitchen, where Mr Brown was on her flank, straining and looking up at them reproachfully. She had five pups and they looked like they came from five different litters. Zondi still hadn't spoken. He sat down and crossed his legs, taking Mr Brown's head and resting it on his lap, where it sat lax and panting happily. He scratched her jaw. 'You are not fat,' he said. Mr Brown muttered back, but it was hard to know what she said.

'Who's the daddy?' asked Aisling, looking at the litter. 'It could be anything.'

'I do not know,' said Zondi. 'I have never seen her . . . I have never seen. Naughty Mr Brown!' Adam and Aisling laughed. Mr Brown grunted smugly.

'What do you do now? Can you move them? Do they have to see someone?' Adam phoned a vet. The vet told him that there sounded no earthly reason to make a house call and persuaded Zondi to accept this, although Zondi was at best unsure. Aisling opened champagne. They were all giggling, and she hopped up to sit on the counter, swinging her bare feet. Adam stood, the top of his shin against Zondi's shoulder, and while Zondi's left hand continued to scratch Mr Brown, his right arm, holding the unaccustomed glass from which he took tiny sips, hooked Adam's leg. The last shaft of evening sun bathed the couple golden, looking at each other and lost in a private place for away from Aisling, and her heart was bursting, perhaps with joy.

Some time later, a taxi took them away, carrying Mr Brown and the puppies all wedged into an open half of Aisling's biggest suitcase, lined with a duvet. Aisling poured herself a glass of wine. Mr Brown had saved her from Adam's lecture, but Adam wasn't going to say anything she didn't know. The easiest thing would be to give up on the Rosslare Group and focus her energies on KSC. There would be no public humiliation in conceding to Strabis, but Aisling was not governed by what the public thought. She wanted to keep the Group because, within her own private cosmology, it symbolised responsibility to her past and her family. These were exactly the same words she'd use to describe the Socialists, but there was no use pretending that she felt equally about the two organisations. She had invested so much of herself in the football club now that she could never let it go. On the other hand, she *could* imagine a life – an easier one – without the Rosslare Group. She might not have been able to five years ago, but she could now, and thinking like this didn't necessarily mean she was going to give it up, but it was a fact. Things change. So many things change, particularly at a football club, that maybe the last few years had accelerated her learning in this regard. That and being a doctor. She stared from the back window over her garden, and she asked herself who she was trying to kid. Nothing had accelerated her learning – she was simply getting older and, like everyone else, she'd learned to face the world turning. People slip in and out of your life, and the stars at the centre of your sky wax and wane.

She thought again about her Adventure with Strabis the day before. He had finally revealed himself and Aisling still hadn't come to terms with it. This morning, Aisling's bathroom was very bright, and she had spent twenty minutes examining wrinkles that were no longer crinkles. It was the first time she'd ever done it seriously. This afternoon, she had sat in the Committee meeting noticing the grey at Donald's temples and the sallow sink in Miss Skewbold's cheeks, a young old woman, not an old young one any more. Hank had looked the same as ever, but he was older to start with, and maybe Aisling wasn't so used to judging old men yet. There were no fixed points, however much you yearned.

She looked at herself again in the bus picture. That girl didn't care about football. She was probably buying wine to take to a dinner party. Everything changes. Aisling's relationship with Kilburn had changed and rechanged, and what would it be in five more years? She hung her head, and then re-erected it, because you could only be the person you are now. Later in the evening, she took a photo of herself, champagne glass raised, the 189 in the background. It took her five attempts to get a shot she was happy with. She printed it out, and she looked at the massive, heavy picture, wondering how to lift it from the wall. Then she shook her head – there was always an easier way to get what she wanted and she had always been able to find it. She slipped her hand behind the 189 and stuck her new photo to its back.

After Kilburn lost to Putney Bridge, Will told Aisling and Adam what Dave had been doing all season. She was sick to her heart, but she didn't let it show.

At half-time in the decider against Hearts, Aisling's chest was a block of panic. Calum Horton saw her watching Strabis, bated her about it, and when she responded, he bore down on her, leering from behind his stupid little glasses, practically licking his lips. Aisling hid her revulsion.

'I see you're supporting Hearts,' she said.

'What? Oh. I'm in black. Well, I always wear black, so —'

'Always?' she asked, wide-eyed.

'You know I do.'

'I'd never noticed,' she said. Little victories. Through the swirls of smoke and shifting crowd, Zondi was quiet and alone by the window, five yards away from Leo, Nicky and Adam. He and Adam were the only people on earth that Aisling envied. Zondi's quiet was self-sufficient, but he wasn't calm. His pupils had been small all day.

Behind Aisling, the steel magnate who owned Hearts laughed so loudly to his entourage that she turned their way. 'He's a wanker,' said Calum. 'Typical fucking pirate latching on to football and trying to steal its soul – he'll drop it like a hot brick now the fans are starting to moan. Although, God knows, football needs all the rich men it can get.' Calum looked pointedly across at Strabis, and Aisling's head had to follow. A champagne cork popped and the magnate's daughter whooped. 'Must be like a mirror,' Calum said, nodding at the girl. Aisling was upset that football needed rich men, that the whims of people who didn't much care affected the lives of so many, and she was upset that she was thinking this in front of Calum, who had written it so frequently. Calum's goatee and sideburns were not salt-and-pepper, but there were flecks of white. She said she had to have a word with Zondi, and left him.

She wound through the room. Everyone in here was rich. She wasn't ashamed, but the vanity of it all was particularly vibrant today. Working in the hospital was miserable at times, but at least it had got her outside the bubble, and she had been helping people, and she missed that desperately. In fact, walking through this room, instead of feeling that she was at the very centre of the bubble, she felt as if everyone else was in separate little bubbles, and she was squeezing between them, but they were expanding into each other, and pressing into her and suffocating her. She almost hyperventilated as she slipped through them towards Adam, Leo and Nicky, who acknowledged her with weak smiles. Zondi had disappeared somewhere.

The brown crowd, away to the left, was bouncing gently in its seats, hope springing eternal. Had she made any of their lives one bit better? Who was she trying to fool? And how many people had she really helped as a doctor? All those patients would have been seen by someone else, somebody who would have been just as good, but here, in this world, how many other people cared the way she cared? Who else was so desperate to make their club a better place? And anyway, she was kidding herself to think the hospital had got her outside the bubble. She had only ever really spoken to her fellow doctors, and a few nurses. You couldn't be friends with the patients. Wouldn't it be more self-indulgent to go back to the life she had originally chosen for herself, which gratified her self-image, than it was to take up this unasked-for burden and to discharge her duty to the best of her ability? The suite emptied on to the terrace for the final act.

Dave emerged after his players. Something had changed for him, and something was finished at last. 'Fingers crossed,' said Strabis, coming from behind. 'I really think we can do it,' he said. 'Don't you?' She couldn't avoid sitting next to him, his leg soft against hers.

Zondi appeared on her other side. He put his hand on her knee. She said that none of this was his fault, and he shook his head. 'I know,' he said. 'I am being vain. To feel responsible is to make myself too important. But I am sad.'

Milagroso gave away a penalty with five minutes to go. Hearts scored it, held on for the draw and Kilburn were relegated.

Aisling sat stock still for an eerie, unreal minute, feeling her panic coalesce into something stronger. Dave walked to the centre circle, and stopped, looking at the sky. Aisling stood, brushed past Strabis, ignored the greedy hands grasping to soothe her, and headed to the pitch.

STRABIS KINSALE'S YEAR

It was the first Saturday in March and everything was progressing perfectly, but Strabis was confused. He was piloting his helicopter south after the Socialists had lost a lunchtime game in Newcastle. The image of Aisling, harried and afraid, twisting her hair as she looked across at him, was stuck in his mind. Aisling was exactly where Strabis wanted her, but the persistence of this mental picture raised complex issues.

He started the season with such a clear plan. While Dave Guinevere took care of the football, Strabis slowly increased his pressure on the Rosslare Group. He was similarly masterful in his use of sibling rivalry. He had waited a long time for this moment of vulnerability. It had come, he'd exploited it with his usual finesse and the Group was yielding itself with pathetic abandon. And yet, he was disappointed. Aisling didn't even understand what was happening. Strabis was not usually concerned with show – he had no weaknesses – but the Rosslare Group deserved to be a culmination.

Strabis feared, at the age of forty-four, that he was losing his hunger for business. This was acceptable. A man must be prepared to adapt. He tipped the nose of the helicopter forward. The M11 cut satisfyingly through the brown patchwork of fields. He reached Harlow and yawed west towards the cottage. Esther sat silently alongside in stockings and heels, her hands soft-cupped in her lap. The first time they flew, Strabis told her that he didn't like chatter. He wondered, not for the first time, whether he might keep her around. Strabis had always been a lone hunter, and when people spoke about creating something to be passed on to the next generation, they used to seem foolish to him. He built up Quo Vadis? for the benefit of his living self. And yet. Was it conceivable that a child would give him a new object? He did not value Esther for herself, but she bore the seed of Manus and any son of Strabis must come from good stock.

As he drove home, he pretended not to notice Esther's rising excitement. It was better when he made her wait. When they got to the house and she pressed herself eagerly into him, he told her to fix some toast and a whisky. She barely hesitated. Strabis smiled at the flush that rose up the back of her neck, at the awkward rise and sway of her hips. Some women walked naturally in heels – Aisling, for instance – but Strabis preferred the ones who had to battle the constraint. Or so he had always thought. This evening, Esther's clumsiness irritated him. That night, too hot, he lay awake. He had no one he could confide in, nor would he have wanted that, but his internal dialogue ran along these lines:

—*If you are ready for the next phase of your life, must it contain a challenge?*

—*Certainly it must, for I am a predator.*

—*If that is so, what challenges present themselves? Is fatherhood enough?*

—*I do not think so, though I am prepared to believe that is part of it.*

—*Esther's genes are Manus's genes.*

—*Yes, but so are Aisling's, and Aisling is more able than Esther. She is the more logical choice, on that front, for a predator.*

—*Is it simply the challenge of winning Aisling over?*

—*No. She is already weak and it will not be difficult. It is more the matter of saving her from herself.*

—*Why do you care about that?*

—*That is the question.*

Strabis needed to confirm his suspicions before he would allow himself to proceed. The next morning, without preamble, he told Esther that some time next week he would bring Aisling to the cottage, to 'scope out the lie of the land'. Esther was terrified, which he found surprisingly delicious.

He arranged to meet Aisling at seven o'clock two evenings later. At five thirty, to clear his mind, Strabis swam. His riverside penthouse had a glass gantry jutting out from the living room. On this, also made of glass but one-way, sat his lap pool, a twenty-five-metre trench, open to the air and filled with heated, filtered rainwater. Strabis stood naked on the start-block, hands on his hips, looking north. If anyone could see him, lean and broad-shouldered, sharply defined, relaxed and confident, they would have to be impressed. Standing astride the city like this, he would appear younger than his years, dominating the sky and the urban sprawl, like a hero in a comic book. He wondered if anyone did see him. They would have to use binoculars and be lucky – he stood for a short while only – and he did not grudge them the view. From below was a different story, of course, hence the one-way glass. Without it, people would be able to *watch* him, rather than merely *see*. The wind was fresh, pricking his skin into goosebumps. The low, pallid sun picked out every dirty corner of the city. The various greens, much too late, were still doubtful over whether to commit to the new year. Strabis noticed such things. He knew the blossoming would come, but the manner entranced him as much as the fact. He donned his goggles so he could watch the pedestrians and the oblivious Thames. He dived, and swam powerfully for an hour. He showered carefully but without soap.

He arrived at Aisling's at twenty to eight, wondering whether her annoyance would show. She opened the door demurely, scared and trying too hard. She was like Esther in some ways, not that either sister would admit it. He guided her towards the car, and with the tiniest of jolts, he realised that he felt protective. Strabis prided himself on his self-knowledge: the sisters were alike in their vulnerability, but his reaction to Aisling was not simply to predate.

'Where are we going?' she asked.

'Somewhere private,' he replied.

'I trust I'm not going to be ravished?'

'Hush.' Strabis flicked his Porsche through the north-London traffic, powerful and precise. He turned on to the motorway, and howled the engine. The air was thin and light, insubstantial even. Aisling was objectively more beautiful than Esther, and cleverer and more adept. She would make a better consort.

'You wanted to talk?' she said.

'Over food.' After twenty minutes, he left the A1, steered through a maze of hedge-deep lanes and pulled into the gravel drive of the cottage. 'I told you we'd be private,' he said. 'Don't be scared.' He fetched the freezer bag from the tiny boot and unlocked the front door while she remained in the car, testing him. He didn't look back. Eventually, she let herself out and followed him inside.

'What's this all about?'

'I am trying to win your trust,' he grinned. 'I might just not be the person you think I am.' He took the filleting knife out of the block and stroked it a couple of times against the whetstone. While she watched, he performed his dance, slicing the tuna, salmon and eel, heating the sake, wrapping the prawn in rice, folding the seaweed and preparing the dishes of wasabi and soy. The process didn't take him ten minutes. Sushi was a little training and a lot of getting hold of the best fish, and Strabis's buyer was the first man at the market this morning.

'Who heated the house? And the rice? Do you have someone to run around your houses getting them ready?'

'Yes.'

'Does Esther know I'm here?'

'No.' Strabis arranged the plates, and sat down at the broad oak table. Aisling was still standing. 'I don't think I've ever been so charmed,' she said.

'This is not about being charming,' Strabis said. 'I'm not going to seduce you, whatever you want. Come on, the fish'll get cold.' She got the joke, which impressed him.

'So, Strabis Kinsale. What *is* this about, then?'

'You may not believe —'

'Oh my god! This salmon is amazing!'

'It's nothing to do with me. I have a good buyer. That's all there is with fish.' Aisling looked surprised. She wanted to praise his modesty, but she was afraid to show weakness. 'I am going to tell you something I have not told anyone else,' he said.

'Don't tell me, tell Esther.'

'I'm not sure she would understand.' He stopped. Aisling had to swim to the hook.

'I've never gone for eel before, but this is unbelievable.'

'Like I said before, it's all about the buyer.'

'I'm not a goldfish.' Spiky, but it was camouflage. 'Okay then,' she continued. 'I could pretend I'm not interested and listen to more stupid fucking hints, but I can't be bothered. What is it?'

'I don't expect you to believe me at once, Aisling, but I've changed.'

'My sister has wrought some magical transformation, and you want my blessing? Go for your life, mate.' Aisling's voice betrayed her, high and girlish with nerves. The lights were set low, and their orange softened her hair into honey. She must hope her stillness looked like strength, but she was frozen in submission, lips apart, head cocked and looking up with wide eyes too made up. He honoured her pride.

'It isn't your sister. I'm forty-four, Aisling, twenty years older than you look, and I have realised that the things I have spent my life striving for will not sustain me much longer.' The best lies were based on truth.

'You're giving up on the Rosslare Group?' she said.

He laughed, and replied, 'No. Well, maybe, in a way. I will have the Group, but that's not what I want to talk to you about.'

'What then?'

'You will find this hard to believe, but I love the Socialists.'

'Why should I find it hard to believe?'

It was a good answer. Strabis said, 'I admire what you are doing. I want to help.'

'You have no idea what I've gone through to get this far. In the end, you'll give up.' Her voice hurdled as she spoke.

'From the perspective of the Rosslare Group —'

'I don't give a shit about the Rosslare Group! No, I mean, fuck, I didn't mean that.' She gulped at her admission. 'The Group is not up for discussion.'

'We both know I could exploit your situation, but if I were to do so, I would risk damaging KSC beyond repair, and I will not do that because I'm a fan.' And this was the moment, looking at Aisling, that Strabis realised that these were no longer mere tactics. All those hours watching Kilburn, waiting to pounce, had wormed their way into him. The low light played off the silver bracelet around Aisling's thin wrist. How could he have feared the loss of his previous purpose? One chapter ends and another begins. Soon, Aisling at his side, he'd rescue the club from the mess it had become. He didn't blame Aisling for the mess, because she had been dragged into something far over her head. But saving KSC was for later – the Rosslare Group chapter had to finish first. Tonight was still about playing on Aisling's gullibility, about him evaluating her at close hand. She pushed her hair back behind her left ear, exposing the side of her face and neck, and a little green earring, and the silver chain of her necklace, which her hand adjusted as it dropped, opening the neck of her shirt very slightly and exposing the topmost lace of her bra. 'You are not used to strong men,' he said.

Aisling controlled her reaction well, but not well enough. She ate the rest of her fish, and took another sip of sake. She poured some more, and also some for him. He could not drink this cup and still drive. Eventually she said, 'What do you mean?'

'Let me talk to you as a friend, because, whatever you believe, I could be your friend. You still feel something powerful for Guinevere, and the reason you can't sack him is that he is a man you cannot master. I do not think this has ever happened to you before.'

'Not every man wants me, Strabis, you'll be shocked to learn.' She played with the wasabi. 'There's nothing happening between me and Dave, if that's what you think. It was one night years ago. We're just friends.'

The plump pads above her cheekbones were set rigid. She must hate Strabis putting the truth into words. 'Listen to me when I tell you this: you will never win a strong man – a man who is worthy of you – by resisting him. There must be a moment when he knows you are in his hands. It's not a modern thing to say, but you have to surrender, and not through a symbol, not by surrendering your football club to his pathetic whim. You must surrender your self, face to his face, completely.'

'That's not how I am.'

'It's how you want to be. And if you do not do it, you will never have Dave Guinevere.'

Aisling cupped her sake in both hands, shoulders small, eyes huge. Strabis had never said these things to a woman before. 'Is this what you brought me here to say?' she said. 'To give me sex tips.'

He regretted, understood and forgave her crudeness. 'I have more money than I will ever need,' he said. 'Very recently, on a day like any other day, I realised that I do not have everything I want.'

'Give it a break, Strabis.' She was hanging on every word.

'My price for KSC will be the Rosslare Group. You know that. But when that day comes, the club will need more than money to get it back on its feet.'

'Why?'

'Trust me, Ash. This is something I understand. You're here so I can tell you that when it happens, because I'm a fan, I'll find you the people you need to run Kilburn.'

'That's it? That's all this is about?'

'I think you know what this is about. I want you to know that I will take the Rosslare Group from you, but that you can trust me. That's all.' Strabis had seldom felt so alive. Every phrase he delivered was perfect for its purpose. He could drink the sake and stay here tonight, which Aisling obviously wanted, but their relationship must not begin with her getting her way. 'This is an important time in my life,' he said, and he looked at her shyly, which was something he had practised especially for this moment. 'The club has taken a wrong turning. The thought of rescuing it makes me feel good.'

'Strabis,' she said, and touched her fingers lightly to the back of his hand. 'I'm ...'

'I've said what I needed to say,' he went on, pushing his cup to one side. 'I hope you will think carefully, and accept my offer when the time comes. Now, I shall take you home.' Aisling tried to let out her sigh silently, but it came in jerks. He let her open her own door again, and when they were back in East Kilburn, and she leaned across to kiss him, he took the side of her head in his hand and touched his cheek to hers once. Before he knew what she was doing, she reached her right hand into his crotch and squeezed. He jerked away from her, but he could not stop her knowing. Coldly, he said, 'No, Aisling. Go now.' She giggled, out of nervousness and embarrassment, and left.

He drove straight home, torn between happiness that his plan had worked perfectly, and annoyance at Aisling's lack of self-control, which was something he would have to train her out of. Later, when the annoyance died away, Strabis thought again about Aisling's hand, and felt the residue of an unusual thrill, which, after due consideration, he decided was the thrill of something unpredicted. He liked surprises now? After all this time, the changes were like a flood.

He drove to Esther's to end their relationship, but when he saw her nervous face, he decided he deserved some reward for resisting Aisling. He told Esther in the morning.

March fluttered fitfully on. London's greens finally grew deeper and the air brightened. Esther behaved with reasonable restraint, except for once, when she saw Strabis talking with Will Beauchamp.

Strabis wished that he did not have to damage KSC, which would soon be his, but his hands were tied. He could do nothing to stop Dave Guinevere without implicating himself. And, anyway, he needed to show Aisling that she couldn't resist him in any field. Then he could demonstrate his magnanimity from a position of strength. In so doing, he would demonstrate that Strabis, not Dave, was the man who could give her what she wanted. He would bring the Socialists back from the dead when all her hope had gone.

Every time Strabis saw Aisling, he drank her in. Her attention never wavered from him, either. It was exquisite torture, which was what Esther had called her love for him, but this was on a higher level than Esther could possibly experience. After the FA Cup semi-final, when Dave played his senior players and they threw away KSC's last chance to save the season, Aisling looked so desperate that Strabis felt he was wrenching apart. He took her hand and said, 'There is always next year.'

'Is there?' she replied, and his heart soared. This was how it felt to feel certain.

Strabis acted on his certainty, in ways beyond the reach of ordinary men. He asked Will Beauchamp whom he would choose to manage Kilburn next season if practicality were no object, and then Strabis spent two days on his phone and in his plane. He sent Aisling a bunch of chrysanthemums with a note which said simply, *Thursday morning. Keep it free for an Adventure. Eight sharp, warm clothes. Sx.*

Thursday was crystalline, as he had checked it would be. Strabis drew up outside Aisling's house at 7.59. He knocked on the door, and she answered immediately. She looked uncertain, excited and beautiful. He bent to kiss her mouth – there was no point in resisting today – and she was startled, which Strabis found peculiar until he remembered that Aisling didn't know what was about to happen.

He opened the car door to reward her for being ready on time. It was cool, but he had the roof down. Although it wasn't the fastest route, he drove her towards the cottage, as a red herring. 'What's this all about, Mr Kinsale?' she said. 'I'm not that kind of girl.' He grinned. Let her think this was all about being dragged to his lair, which was probably something that Aisling, who was used to over-intellectualising idiots like that barrister she used to go out with, would find primitive and thrilling. She would soon learn that he was rather more sophisticated than that. He whipped past the cottage. She gave him a look and he raised his eyebrow in return. They were two people on a single wavelength. A few minutes later, he wheeled into Porter's Park. 'Huh?' she said. 'I don't play golf.'

'Who said this was about golf?'

'Ooh, we are coy today, Mr Kinsale.' He liked her calling him Mr Kinsale. He opened her door and took her hand as he helped her out of the car. Her fingers were supple and warm through thin leather gloves. Her make-up was perfect, which showed that she was getting stronger and more confident with him, even though she must still be nervous.

'Now —' he began, but she interrupted him.

'Before the excitement begins, I have to powder my nose. I imagine the thrill of learning why you've brought me here shall be such that I might not be able to pee in five minutes.' Strabis gestured her inside with an ironic bow. He recognised the games women played to give themselves an illusion of control, and he stood broad-shouldered, face into the sun, nostrils flaring in the chilly air, letting the cold trickle slowly down his throat. This was a day of high yellow quality, to be savoured like fine aquavit, not drunk in numbing gulps like cheap vodka.

Aisling emerged. 'So?' she said behind him. He pretended to be lost in the moment, cheeks hard, monarch of all he surveyed. 'Strabis?' He turned and in a catlike movement he took her hand in his, swung her to his side, and led her round the clubhouse to the little open patch of land the club let him use from time to time in gratitude for his (largely) anonymous financial support. When Aisling saw the balloon, she gave a little gasp and looked at him as if she didn't believe it. His people had kept it under-inflated and tethered low, so it was hidden behind the clubhouse and stand of trees, but at the sight of Strabis, they leaped into action. His arm was now round Aisling's shoulder, hers around his waist. Her head touched the top of his chest, and she watched the balloon fill and strain. 'Wow, Mr K!' she said.

The balloon was orange, its only adornment a white question mark, visible but understated. He nodded to the crew, checked everything was ready, lifted Aisling into the basket as if she were a child, vaulted in himself, and cast off. Everything went with fluid perfection. Aisling looked over the edge, straight down, as they ascended – first-timers always did that – and then towards London, clear and enormous in the near distance. 'It's amazing,' she said. 'I thought it would be quieter.'

'In a minute,' said Strabis. 'We'll take her higher and then I'll turn the gas off. I'll do the champagne, you open the hamper.' Peeling away the foil and twisting the wire, Strabis watched Aisling giddy as she saw the treats. The salmon was caught yesterday, in Ireland, on his estate.

'You're spoiling me, Strabis,' she said.

'This is nothing, Lady R.' They clinked glasses, the crystal ringing high and true, and leaned their elbows on the basket's edge, looking south. Strabis let the moment linger and hang and draw out.

'Do you have a telescope or something?'

'I have binoculars, they're better. You can see Kilburn Park quite easily. And St Brendan's.'

'This is amazing,' she repeated. She spent some time looking at the stadium, and then she walked around the flame, trying not to show her eagerness. 'Why am I here? Is this all some big trap and I'm the helpless fly?' She thought she was joking, and half of her was.

'I love you,' Strabis said. She didn't expect such directness, and she was wrong-footed.

'I bet you say that to all the girls,' she said.

'I've never said it to anyone. I've been waiting for you.' She looked away. He thought she flushed, but up here, in the wind, with the champagne, it was hard to be sure. He'd said what he meant to say, and he expected her to be surprised and not to respond instantly, so everything was going to plan, but he hadn't realised how vulnerable he would feel in these brittle moments between revealing himself and everything being resolved. He hadn't meant to move on until she admitted her love also, but she was standing there, beautiful with confusion, stray hairs flicking past her ear, and the sight dragged his hand to his pocket. 'Aisling Rosslare,' he said, 'I've done everything I planned to do with my life before I met you; I thought that I was above needing a woman to complete me, or children. All that changed when I met you, and —'

'You met me years ago, Strabis.'

She shouldn't interrupt. 'I didn't meet you, because I was lost in myself. I was blind, but now I see. You are the one for me, and if you do not say yes, I swear I will wait for you for ever. I know, absolutely, that there can never be another woman for me.' He was on his knees now, and he held out the ring. He could have afforded something more expensive, but this was about style not money, and the sapphires and diamonds were exquisite against the soft platinum. Aisling didn't wear huge rocks, and to have given her something flashy would have shown he hadn't noticed. She took off her gloves. She was lit from within, but still in shock as she reached for the ring. As she took it, she folded his hand in hers and pulled him to his feet, but she didn't say anything. She looked at the slender band, and half motioned to try it on. Then she turned, pouting with wonder.

'This is unbelievable,' she said. 'It's unbelievably sudden. How can you be sure?'

'I'm always sure,' said Strabis.

'We've never even kissed.' He pulled her into his arms, and she resisted at first, responded guardedly and broke away. She was still nervous. It was as much as he could do to release her, but that was the thing to do. 'Wow!' she said. 'But . . . I'm sorry, I can't get my head round this. What about Esther?'

'That was over weeks ago. She never meant anything to me. You know that.'

'I thought that. But —'

'Esther will be upset, but there's nothing you and I can do. What's between us is too strong – you must feel that – Esther has to deal with it as well as she can.'

'I suppose,' she looked down at the ring again, trembling. Strabis was shaking too. Every detail, every long, agonising second was imprinting itself on his soul. The play of sun and shade on Aisling's right boot as it pointed its toe in to its mate, secretly signalling her submission; the way she leaned her hip against the wicker for strength; the cornflower of her eyes shaming the sky: these were the things Strabis would describe when they retold the story together. 'Oh my God, Strabis,' she said. 'I need a few moments.' She looked at him, girlish and afraid. He forced himself to remember his own reputation. Maybe she *did* think he behaved like this with the others? No. She couldn't think that. 'It's so sudden,' she said again.

'It isn't for me. I've known for weeks.'

'How can you be sure? How can I know you're sure?'

'I got you a present.'

'A present?'

'It's not here. I mean, it's more of a surprise than a present. To show how I feel. You'll understand when I explain. It's to do with the Socialists.'

'Huh?'

'I love the club, Aisling. I told you I loved it, and I really do. I want to help you, and the club will need money, lots of it, and when we're together, I won't be mean. And more than that, I'll be here to protect you. You don't understand how deceitful some people can be. I'll protect you from people who try to take advantage of your innocence.'

'That's very generous.'

'That's not my present. I'm just telling you that our marriage will be a partnership in every sense. What's mine will be yours.' A few months ago, Strabis would have seen talk like this as some kind of madness, but right now, high above Hertfordshire, where the similarly reserved Darcy wooed and won Lizzie Bennet, Strabis would have gladly given anything for Aisling to say yes. Like a child accepting the world is round, he finally understood and believed in the power of love. The implications of this, written in the pink glisten of Aisling's parted mouth, stopped him for a moment. She still couldn't believe she was his!

'What's the present?' she asked, her breath catching.

'We both know Dave Guinevere has to go,' Strabis said. 'There's no reason to be embarrassed. You've been loyal to him, but he hasn't repaid you, and I see it in your face at every game. He looks at you and you turn away. He's lost his faith, Aisling. You tried to give it back to him, but he's too far gone. What you and he shared was an illusion, and you understand it now, however hard it is to admit.'

'That's not much of a present.'

Strabis had spoken in the wrong order, carried away. He said, 'Frikkie Cloete has agreed to replace him.'

'Frikkie Cloete? That's unbelievable!' Cloete, the most successful coach in European club history, who had won medals with Ajax, Roma and Rojo Madrid, was preparing the Dutch national team for the next European Championships. He had categorically retired from club football in order to do so. To persuade him to change his mind had taken a personal visit, a vast pay rise and the promise of a fortune to spend on new players. It was, by any standards, a kingly gift – a romantic gesture to balance against the ring's subtle stones. 'This is all so unbelievable, Strabis. It's like a dream.'

'You're not dreaming,' said Strabis. 'This is your reality now.'

'I need time.'

'You have all the time in the world,' he said, but Strabis had no more arrows to fire. She stood at the edge of the basket, looking north, and he thought how easy it would be to take her by the ankles and flip her over the edge. He approached her from behind and put his arms around her shoulders, linking his hands below her breasts. He kissed the top of her head, smelling her. He turned her around. 'I love you, Aisling Rosslare,' he said. 'I love you. I love you completely.' He understood from the joy in her eyes as he said it that there was nothing so potent as a strong man yielding, and that this, not Frikkie Cloete or diamonds, was the greatest gift he could give her. Every action of his past had shown the world that Strabis Kinsale was a man of steel, or titanium even, who could not be brought low unless he chose. Now, in the arms of his one true love, he chose.

'I'm sure now,' she said.

'I love you completely.'

'I'd say you love me *madly*.'

'Okay. *Madly*.' He bent to kiss her but she pushed him away, looked down at the ring cradled in her right hand, and tossed it high over her shoulder. He gasped at the speck flashing in the sun as it arced from the basket and started to fall, and he looked back at Aisling. 'You didn't like it? You can choose anything, I don't mind.' Her eyebrows drew together incredulously. There was something he was missing. 'What?' he asked.

'You really don't get it?'

'Get what? I promise I don't mind about the ring.' But the numb first moments were already wearing off. He was like the surfer feeling for the leg that's been bitten off by the shark.

'How stupid do you think I am, Strabis?' She still didn't believe he was serious! How was this possible after all he'd done?

'What do I have to do to convince you?' he asked. 'Just tell me.'

'I'm convinced, don't worry, but how stupid would I have to be to marry a dick like you? You're nothing compared to Dave.' The sun cut across her face, throwing her right side into shadow. She was taunting him, and Strabis wasn't prepared to be laughed at. He grabbed her. She slapped him, and stood back, eyes blazing, daring him to do it again. Maybe, even, she wanted him to do it. Strabis fought desperately against his anger. He'd faced setbacks before, and he overcame them because he didn't let his emotions interfere. Aisling hadn't mentioned Dave by chance. He turned to the far side of the basket and looked west, feeling the cane strands slip and slide beneath his grip.

Aisling still loved Guinevere, after all this time. It must be the child they never had. Strabis wanted to hold and protect her, to explain that she could let Guinevere go, because he was here to protect her. But he didn't do these things. A master falconer must realise that sometimes, when a new bird is particularly valiant, she can only learn by flying free.

In trying to provoke him, Aisling was crying for help. She was crying out to be mastered. Strabis had been mistaken in displaying vulnerability. She loved Guinevere, who was intent on destroying her, because Guinevere showed her no mercy or weakness. Looking at Aisling in this passionless light, Strabis could see that she must yearn for him to over-power her defences, right here, right now, but that he must resist. It would be fierce and urgent, and Strabis wanted Aisling as no man could ever have wanted a woman, but she would possibly see it as a triumph and she might even claim afterwards that he had forced her. The solu-tion was clear. Guinevere could play the powerbroker, but Strabis had the power. He could break Aisling utterly, take away her company, her club, her everything. That was his original plan, and he cursed himself for deviating from it. She must learn who was the greater man, then she would abase herself and they would have this conversation again.

He drove her home, the perfect, distant gentleman. They didn't speak. He parked outside her house. 'Let battle commence,' he said. She laughed.

'You're handsome when you're being strict, I'll give you that, but you're still a dick,' she said. Strabis wanted to embrace her and tell her it would be all right in the end.

In the box before the game with Putney Bridge, only two matches left in the season, Strabis stood carefully in Aisling's eyeline. Esther simpered towards him, pretending to be casual. It wouldn't do any harm to remind Aisling that he had other options. Esther clutched his arm, giggling. He stroked her cheek and whispered in her ear. Her knee jutted between his as she flashed her neck up at him. After a couple of minutes, he told her to get him a mineral water. He patted her shoulder as she went. That should do the trick. Then he advanced on his peregrine.

'What the fuck are you doing?' Aisling said. 'Where's Esther gone?'

'I've told you, your sister means nothing to me. Less than nothing.'

'I know, you fuckwit. That's my point.'

'That's not fair. I only do it —'

'You're doing it because you're a manipulative dick. Why can't you learn that there's a right way and there's a wrong way? This is bullshit. You're going to have to do better than this.'

'I will,' he said. He could feel sweat pooling in the hollow of his spine. 'I will, my love.' He turned towards the terrace to catch his breath, and as if by fate, he saw Will watching him. How could he have been

464

so stupid? What had been going through his mind? Aisling was perfectly within her rights to be angry.

But, as he thought about it, he realised there was more to Aisling's anger than simple righteousness, because when had she ever protected her sister before? Aisling was jealous, just as he intended. It had been an unnecessary risk, though, and now Aisling feared that he might be manipulative. He had to prove he wasn't a manipulator.

This is what Strabis was thinking about while he sat through the first half, during which Kilburn, neutered by Dave Guinevere's manipulative tactics, huffed and puffed to no avail. Periodically, Strabis sensed that Will Beauchamp was watching him. Beauchamp was another manipulator. Strabis felt cold at the thought that Beauchamp might tell Aisling that Strabis was involved in Dave's manipulation of results.

At half-time, Beauchamp tried to corner Strabis, but Strabis avoided him with ease and grace. Through the main window, he looked at the pitch, where groundsmen were repairing divots and sprinkling them with fairy dust to make everything the way it was before it was torn. When he won the Rosslare Group from Aisling, he'd do so using simple strength, to show her that his mastery didn't depend on manipulation.

Suddenly Will was at his shoulder. 'I presume you saw what Guinevere did,' he probed. 'Leaving out Drayly and making Cole play right back? Not picking Nuñez?'

'It's sordid,' said Strabis.

'So it is. Still, it suits your purposes.'

'What's that supposed to mean?'

'You know what I mean,' Will said. Strabis didn't reply. 'Remember, as soon as you want the players brought to heel, give me the nod and I can sort them out.'

'I don't need you,' said Strabis, calmly. 'What Guinevere is doing to Aisling is disgraceful, and you're trying to manipulate it to your own advantage. I'm telling you now that when we go down, I'm keeping hold of Kilburn, and I'll make it great again, and it will be me that did it. None of you bastards – not Guinevere, not any of these players, and not you – will have a place at the table, and there's nothing you can do about it. You're a manipulator, and that's not the kind of person I work with.' That put Will Beauchamp firmly in his place, thought Strabis. These people would find out that Strabis Kinsale was a winner who always did the right thing, with honour.

What Guinevere was doing was useful for the moment, but it had been Guinevere's idea.

After the game, he approached Aisling. 'I'm sorry,' he said. 'I'll talk to Esther and explain the situation again. And as for the rest, we are opponents in business, but you can trust me. You can always trust me.' As she opened her mouth to thank him, Dave Guinevere arrived, as tall as Strabis, but not imposing. Guinevere's good, unpolished shoes were flecked with pale mud, as were his trouser bottoms. His fawn coat was presentable from a distance, but the creases of the lapel, and the edges by the button, showed patches worn bare. The drizzle had soaked dark into the shoulders and Guinevere's hair, which looked like pale wire touched with rust when it was dry, sopped across his creased high brow. His shoulders were broader than they first appeared.

Strabis, who understood the dilemma his presence caused Aisling, withdrew to the bathroom, buoyant in the unaccustomed warmth of his generosity. He could get used to doing the right thing. The toilets here at Putney were art deco, unflashy and squared, with sharp-angled handles and lamps everywhere. They were better than the more prosaic facilities at Kilburn, which was an inconsequential thought, up to a point, but Strabis was gong to revamp KSC root and branch. He would make it the best club in the world in every conceivable field, even in the fields where only Strabis was measuring. He stood side-on to the mirror, and turned quickly towards it, not losing any height, and flashing his happiest grin, the one which appeared to open him up completely, and made them think they were the only one who could ever have seen it. Strabis was disquieted that the grin looked exactly the same when he didn't mean it.

He opened the door, and turned the corner into Dave Guinevere. Strabis bounced away, because he'd been off balance. Without thinking, he blurted, 'Your days are numbered, Guinevere.' Guinevere stared levelly at him, and Strabis needed to explain. 'Don't worry, I won't tell anybody, but I'm not letting you hurt her any more.'

'You'll keep,' said Guinevere. He twisted his shoulders and pushed round Strabis out into the corridor.

Back in the box, Strabis saw that Will Beauchamp was talking with Aisling and Adam, and the chill returned, so strong that it would almost have been panic in a lesser man. He hurried to join them. Will spitefully told them about Dave, but he didn't mention Strabis's role.

*

Strabis swam, thinking. He had provoked Will Beauchamp, and Will had shown his mettle by responding. Strabis could respect that, especially since Beauchamp had also shown his common sense by leaving Strabis out of it. The pair might still be able to do business in the future. Now Will was running the Socialists for the season's last week, and the club might survive. This would be irritating, because saving a relegated KSC would be the best thing Strabis could give Aisling, but Strabis would not stoop to manipulating Will into losing. He was done with manipulation.

All the same, he was intrigued that Aisling's little friend Leo had asked to meet him privately. Strabis had been inclined to refuse, but Leo said it was crucial. There was an intercom at the western end of the pool, and when Leo buzzed, Strabis let him in and told him to make himself comfortable in the big room.

Five minutes later, Strabis emerged from the pool. He reckoned Leo was not an athlete, and would be easily intimidated by physical prowess, so he didn't cover himself. Leo looked horrified. Strabis said he'd be back in five, and he changed into jeans and a tight T-shirt. When he emerged, Leo hadn't moved. 'Drink?' he asked.

'I'm fine, thanks.' Leo looked around. 'Great place.'

'It suits me for now, but it's just a bachelor pad. So, to what do I owe the pleasure? I presume you're here to warn me off Aisling.'

'No. It's not . . . Adam has told me what you're doing to get hold of the Rosslare Group.'

'With all due respect, Adam Greswell is not privy to my plans in that —'

'It's not rocket science, is it?'

'If so, then —'

'It won't work,' said Leo. Strabis was looking out of the window, waiting. 'Aisling's not like Esther.'

'You don't need to tell me that,' said Strabis.

'Do you love her?'

'I'm not discussing this with you.'

'You won't win Aisling by crushing her, and you won't crush her. She'll destroy herself before she lets anyone else do it.' Leo looked uncomfortable to be betraying such secrets, but Strabis was listening. 'She knows what you're trying to do, so she won't let you do it. She'll cling to the club, even with no money, and she won't give up the Rosslare Group under duress. She's serious about her duty.'

'She's strong, and I admire that, but she'll yield.'

'You have no idea. Even if – and it's an if – she gave up the Rosslare Group in return for the club, she would hate you for it, for ever.'

'What are you telling me?'

Leo bowed his head and said, 'Whatever you think, I want what's best for Aisling. We both know she's obsessed with KSC, and she's never really cared about the Rosslare Group. If you ever want any kind of partnership with her, you've got to show you know what she cares about. You've got to give her something she wants, not a fucking diamond.'

'I offered her my*self*,' said Strabis, 'not a fucking diamond.'

'If you take away her pride, she will never forgive you.'

'What are you suggesting?' The reporter shrugged uselessly. The solution was obvious to Strabis. It was something he'd already considered. The moment Aisling knew she was beaten and she would have to give up the Rosslare Group – whether that was on Saturday when KSC went down and the Rosslare Group was not liquid enough to pay Kilburn's debts, or some time in the near future when one of his other plans for the Group paid off – he would give her the club. It was the perfect gift, because he would only give it to her the moment she couldn't afford to pay for it. Then, Aisling would be tethered to him, but it would look to the world as if she still flew fierce and free. Strabis stood tall, chin and chest subtly out, and looked serenely across London. 'I know what to give her, Leo.'

'Are you sure? Don't buy her a car or something, the only thing you've got she wants is —'

'I know, Leo. The Socialists.'

It was early in the second half of the game against Hearts, and the Socialists were leading 1–0. Strabis was disappointed, because he wanted to make his gift today, but it looked as if he would have to wait and achieve his goals via the Rosslare Group instead. He probably shouldn't have sat next to Aisling, but he couldn't resist. Still, no matter, because he divined from the press in her limber knee that she didn't mind, whatever the rest of her body language.

When Will Beauchamp lost control, left the box and went down to the pitch, Strabis suspected that Dave had somehow found a way to circumvent Aisling's restrictions. Aisling stopped following the ball with her head. While Beauchamp gestured to the fourth official on the touchline, she was staring at Dave Guinevere. Aisling's hope and trust had been misplaced in this travesty of a man, this shadow of someone who once was something. He looked at Beauchamp and Guinevere, and he saw two manipulators, each as bad as the other. But, secretly, he hoped that Guinevere's plan would succeed. He reached into his pocket, feeling the envelope.

Hearts scored their penalty, hung on to draw, and Kilburn were relegated.

Strabis felt Aisling collect herself, refusing to cry. He had never loved her more. She bravely faced the sympathic fools and their windy condolence. Only Strabis could give her what she wanted, and vice versa. He followed her through the room. She seemed unable to listen properly, replying by rote, everything in slow motion, letting the pity splash off her. Zondi, Adam, Leo and Nicky stood together by the door. It was understandable that she should run to them for comfort, but no, she barely acknowledged them on her way out. She needed to be alone, poor girl. He must find and comfort her. 'Where's she gone?' he demanded.

'I think she is going to the pitch, sir,' said Zondi. 'I think she is going to comfort Dave.'

'I have to find her. Now.' He stared hard at Leo, and said, 'I have something to give her.'

'Really?' said Leo.

'Really,' said Strabis. He handed the envelope to Adam saying, 'Read it if you don't trust me, but do it while we're walking.' Zondi led them all through the corridors, past the old chairmen, past pictures of Manus and Esther, but not Aisling. He would change that too. Everything was going to change around here. Zondi didn't try to engage him in conversation, and nor did any of the others. The little African probably didn't like or trust him, but soon he would realise that Strabis and Aisling were made for each other, and that KSC would be one of the main beneficiaries.

He walked between the dressing rooms. Some Socialists were stumbling heavily into the one on the right; the one on the left was filled with singing. How hard would it be to strengthen Kilburn at Hearts' specific expense? It might be costly, but he wasn't doing this to make money, that was the whole point: he was doing it for Aisling and for the Socialists, because he was a lover and a fan.

He strode out of the tunnel, and Zondi peeled away towards his fellow has-beens, who looked as if they already knew they were packing their bags. Strabis would keep the youngsters, however pissed off they were about staying at Kilburn. They would learn they couldn't fuck with him, but he would also hint at the rewards that awaited. Carrot and stick. That wasn't important now because, forty yards away, Aisling was about to join Dave. She reached for Dave's forearm and Dave let her. Strabis picked up his pace. Then she put her other hand on him and Dave shook them both off angrily. Strabis couldn't hear what they were saying yet, they were speaking quietly even though it was obvious they were arguing. Strabis's shirt stuck to his back but his throat was dry. Strabis caught Dave's eye over Aisling's shoulder, but Dave ignored him. 'It's over, Aisling,' Dave said. 'You know it is.'

'What the fuck's that supposed to mean? You can't leave it like this.' Dave stared at the empty brown stand. 'You can't leave me like this! Not after what you've done!' Aisling's voice cracked as she spoke.

'It's over,' Dave repeated. 'I warned you from the start.'

'You can't do this to me, David.' Her shoulders slumped, and her face screwed up, desperately trying to hold back the tears.

It was unbearable, and Strabis said, 'Aisling!'

She spun into Strabis's open gaze. She was shocked, and looked at Adam next to him, who nodded urgently, but Aisling still didn't realise that Strabis was here to save her. 'I can't bear your gloating, Strabis,' she said. 'Later, but not now.'

'I'm not here to gloat.'

'Fuck off you're not. But I'm going to save this club, whatever you two fuckers think. My father left it to me. He trusted me, and I won't let him down.'

'You can't do it on your own,' Strabis said gently.

'Give it a break, Strabis. I've resisted you once.' But her voice wavered.

'You can't even sack Dave without me.'

'What? You'd stop me getting rid of him? You're all as bad as he is. I don't care. Fuck you all. Fuck you —'

'I didn't say I'd stand in your way. All I said was that you need me. You need a friend, Aisling. And you've got to see, you need money if you want to get Kilburn back up into this league. You need a lot of money.'

'I'm not stupid. Do you think I haven't thought about this? I'll have to sell the Rosslare Group, and I'll try to sell it to someone who isn't you, but you might still get hold of it and that's a risk I have to take, but —'

'Aisling!' said Dave. 'No! That's not why . . . Walk away from KSC. You've got to walk away.'

'No she doesn't,' said Strabis. 'You don't know what's best for this girl, but I do. You don't understand anything about her. She needs Kilburn.' Dave took a step towards Aisling, then a few steps away. Neither of them was looking at Strabis but he was the focus of their attention. Leo, Adam and Nicky were listening, and Esther and Will, who had followed them downstairs.

'I won't go,' said Dave to Aisling. 'It'll cost you a fortune to sack me.'

He was being petulant, but before Strabis could intercede, Aisling said, 'Strabis won't let me sack you anyway, apparently.'

'I never said —' Strabis began.

'What do you want, Strabis? Do you want me to beg? Do you want me on my knees? Do you want me to promise you the Rosslare Group? Do you think I haven't seen all this coming?'

'I'm sure you did, but I'm not an oncoming train, Ash. I'm the light at the end of the tunnel.'

'Fuck off,' said Dave. 'You're saying that in front of your audience, but you're loving this.' Aisling nodded mechanically.

She still couldn't believe he was capable of doing the right thing. Strabis said nothing. At the centre of a rapt circle, he turned slowly and said to Adam, 'Show her, Adam. Tell her it's for real.' Adam passed the heavy woven sheet to Aisling. 'I'll never ask you to beg,' he said, 'unlike some people. I want a partnership of equals, based on mutual trust. That's why I'm giving you my club.'

She took the paper and read. She looked at Adam and asked, 'Is this . . . Is it?'

'Yes,' said Adam. 'No strings. It's a very generous gift.' Strabis was developing new respect for Adam, who should possibly be allowed to retain his job, if that's what he wanted. 'All you have to do is sign the paper.'

'I'll sign first,' said Strabis.

'Why?' said Aisling.

'Because I love you,' said Strabis, finishing with a flourish. He handed her the pen.

DAVE GUINEVERE'S YEAR

Keats Grove
18/6/05

Dear David,

Okey-doke: Leo's going to arrive in Nzasa in a couple of weeks. I don't suppose it's necessary because Punty being pregnant is all the excuse you'd need to bail out of Tanga, but this way Leo gets his story as well. Birds and stones. Nicky and Leo still think we're crazy, by the way, and that Strabis will see through us. Adam, the dear little pet, thinks we won't be able to keep it up. I can if you can. I can't see another way, since S is being such an arsehole.

Zondi agrees with you about not telling Louie. Louie's such a good guy, but he'd never be able to stay quiet, and once Monica knows, etc. I hope they forgive us.

Are you sure about bringing over Nzasa Boy? I know that over the top's the plan, but isn't he a bit obvious? Zondi's already got plenty of colour with Rod Norman and Milagroso Nuñez, and there's the equal-wages stuff too – we don't want to overplay it, do we? Or make some poor kid feel stupid?

I sound like a schoolteacher. You know what you're doing. I trust you, I'm just nervous. I can't believe. . .

*

Dave was putting Leo up in Nzasa while the latter researched his story on aid corruption. Leo was frothy company but he had a still, calm core. Dave could see how Leo would be able to cope with the Nicky that Aisling took such pleasure in describing.

Dave had no telly, so all there was to do in the evening was talk and read. Naturally, they talked about Aisling. 'You love her, don't you?' said Leo.

'Yes,' said Dave. Leo sat back. The house was floored in red earth tiles and sprinkled with small lights. Frustrated moths buzzed and battered at the enclosing mesh, the waves built, broke, rushed and broke again, and the distant forest screeched. Leo said that it probably wasn't any louder than London, but he was used to the city's white noise. They discussed quiet. Maybe it was silent in the desert, or the Arctic. The well-worn, tall-backed chair, faded loose cushions on a lashed wooden frame, was incredibly comfortable. You could get a lot of reading done here, or thinking, if you kept it together. Dave said, 'Nicky doesn't approve, does she?'

'She's worried. It's understandable.'

Dave asked, eventually, 'Is Aisling okay?

'Meaning?'

'I get letters from the others. Sally, once in a while. She says Aisling's never got over the abortion.'

'Jesus, Dave.'

'I don't think that's true, I think it's Sal being Sal, but you can see why I ask? When I get back, people are going to bring it up, so I have to be sure. As sure as I can be, anyway.'

'How would I know the answer anyway?'

'I know. I really don't think it is that.'

'I don't either, and nor does Nicky. It isn't that.'

'I'm going to look like such an arsehole.' In Nicky's opinion, relayed by Leo on her firm instructions, this ridiculous plan was a pretext on both Dave and Aisling's part. Its purpose was to get them back in the same country, at which point they would fall into each other's arms and come up with a more sensible way of dealing with the problem of Kilburn United, which was only a football club.

By mid-February, the Socialists' fans finally Chinese-whispered themselves into some vague comprehension of the club's finances, and at some indefinable moment 'relegation' changed from being something no one took seriously into being an imminent apocalypse, a shearing blade that would cut Kilburn's future away from its glorious past. Socialist fans were a pampered elite, fat on victory, unwilling to contemplate the possibility that their club could become a 'former giant', scuffling eternally around the outer darkness. But 'former giants' were there for all to see, object lessons in hubris and confusion. South Newcastle still attracted forty thousand a week, but could never get out of the First Division. And look at Arsenal as they grunted and strained their way through the lower leagues in front of Highbury's desolate, crumbling stands. Time's scythe plays no favourites, and South Newcastle and Arsenal had both been Ozymandias. The only ray of light was the fifth-round FA Cup tie against perennial Premiership mediocrities Torquay. Again, the youngsters sparkled while the likes of Vlocker and Drayly fumed on the bench. The fans bayed for Guinevere to play the kids in the Premiership, but he said, 'We're a squad. We put out the best team for each game. I hope the players will inspire each other. I'm picking teams to produce the right future for this football club.' Every newspaper in the country took up the fans' cause, laying into Kilburn's underperforming stars. Cole, Drayly and the others were stung, finding this disrespectful, and they pulled themselves together to win the next two matches. Aisling stood by Guinevere, criticising short-termist reporters and fans, and saying that the FA Cup victories showed that the manager knew what he was doing.

The next match was against Spencer. The Socialists drew it, and remained in the drop zone. That evening, Dave sat at home, cup of tea on the arm of his chair, and read. He was living in a modest house, walled with books. It had no memories for him, which he relished. It bewildered him that people his age were still going clubbing, or even to pubs. Dave found it hard to be around anyone else. Possibly that would change when this charade was done with, but maybe he had descended into premature misanthropy and that was that. He checked his watch again. At ten o'clock, he fetched the batphone from his bedside table and called Aisling. 'Hiya,' she said.

'Hi. Well?'

'Well enough.'

The batphone didn't make up for not being able to see her properly, but it was fun, in its way. Pay as you go, only ever calling one number. It's not as if anybody would spy on their records, but little rituals are intimate. 'What is it?' asked Dave.

'It's started,' she said.

'Strabis?'

'Yup.' Dave knew this was coming. 'David?'

'I'm fine. What did you do?'

'He was staring, so I played with my hair, bit my lip, looked scared, you know. I hate this.'

'Did it work?'

'I don't know.' Silence. 'Yes, probably. He'll think I'm keen but I don't realise it.' They dropped the subject and talked about nothing for half an hour. Years in letters, and now on the phone. They were getting closer, and he was sure in every way he could measure.

A few weeks later, Strabis took Aisling out for a mysterious evening. Dave didn't go to bed. It was nearly midnight when she called. 'I thought you weren't going to call,' said Dave.

'No you didn't.'

'What was he like?'

'Charming.'

'What did you do?'

'I feel soiled, if that helps.' It did, obviously. 'He took me to a cottage near Radlett and made me sushi.'

'Are you sure he's not acting too?'

'I checked.'

'How?'

'Trust me, David.'

'You seducing him was more bearable in theory,' Dave said. 'What did he say about KSC?' Aisling said the plan held, as far as it went, but she felt like a bitch. 'We can pity Strabis afterwards, if he doesn't win, which he might. We've got to accept that. He's really good at this.'

'How does phone sex even work?'

'No, Asho.'

'I say what I'm doing, and you do it with your hands? Or imagine it while you, you know. It has to be one of those two, right?'

'I don't know.'

'Can you make it more lifelike if you use toys? Or does that get fiddly?'

'You probably have to go hands free.'

'I've got a headset.'

'I hate this too, but I want to wait until it's real.'

'I don't see why? It's not as if you don't —'

'I'm not saying I don't fantasise about you. And I don't fantasise about anyone else, if that's any help.'

'You're so romantic.'

She called again after the balloon, and then they were as sure as they could be that it would work, but Aisling felt terrible. 'He loves me,' she said.

'You're a trophy for him, Asho. Another game.' Aisling didn't dignify this with a response. 'Look what he did to Esther. Being in love does not stop him being an arsehole. This has always been the plan.'

'I know, but it's cruel. It's an abuse of trust.'

'What do you think we've been doing all year?'

'Has this all been a mistake?'

'I don't know.' Dave really didn't. He said, 'Remember how I felt at the start of the season?'

'I understand it better now.'

A few days later, the day Mr Brown had her puppies, they spoke again. 'I know a bit about biology,' she said, 'and it is my considered opinion that Mr Brown had an orgy. They look nothing like each other.'

'Zondi's been so funny about Mr Brown getting fat.'

'I know.' Aisling didn't phone to talk about Zondi or the puppies. 'I *am* okay with what we're doing,' she said. 'Strabis will get over it. Greatest good for the greatest number, etc.'

'It's shit, I know.'

'I fucking hope we're right, Davey. Everything changes. I change all the time.'

'You're looking at the bus photo, aren't you?'

'Yes.'

'Fetch your camera.' They kept talking while Aisling did so, and Dave got his, and Dave poured himself some champagne. They took pictures of themselves. Dave said he'd send his over tomorrow. Aisling agreed to stick it next to hers on the back of the 189 picture as a reminder of who they were tonight.

Aisling rang Dave much earlier than usual after the Putney Bridge game, but he was showering and didn't hear. By the time he tried to phone her back, she'd gone to a birthday party. He texted that she should ring when she got home. When she did so, she was drunk.

'Sorry, Davey, I know it's late.'

'Good party?'

'No. Yes. I'm looking forward to going to parties with you. Now, this is a fucking urgent nightmare, Davey. Will Beauchamp has worked out what we're doing, or what you're doing anyway, 'cos you're the transparent one and I'm the ninja.'

'What's he going to do about it?'

'Ooh, let me check. Am I a soothsayer? Hmmm . . .'

'Aisling.'

'You're so strict. I don't know. He wants to get his hands on the moolah he thinks Strabis is bringing to the club, so he doesn't want to burn any boats. Or bridges. I don't know which.'

'It doesn't make any difference.'

'No no no. He told me with Adam and Strabis there. If I don't do anything, Will and Strabis will work out that I know what you've been doing. They could use that and fair play to the fuckers. Will even offered to take over training this week. What are we going to do? Are you going to have to talk to Milagroso?' There was a short silence. 'Dave?'

'I don't know. Probably.'

'Hey Davey, it's okay. Milagroso will do it, won't he? You said he would.'

'I should have spoken to him before.'

'He'll do it. You could pluck the birds from the trees with your honey tongue.'

'Your humour's a real high-wire act sometimes, isn't it?'

'And half of it you don't even get.'

'Let me think about it. I'll call you tomorrow morning.'

'Afternoon.'

'Okay.'

Dave called her back the next day at one. 'How are you feeling?' he asked.

'Shit. Sorry if I was ...'

'You were charming.'

'Thank you.' Dave should have known there would be a final twist, and that it would come to this. He should have spoken to Milagroso at the outset but he had wanted to do everything himself, to bear full responsibility. Aisling said, 'Have you used your morning wisely? Are you a man with a plan?'

'Yes. You have to speak to Will. Agree to let him do it and say that I'll be kept out of the changing room, and that there will be no substitutions under any circumstances short of injury.'

'But —'

'You have to do something or they'll realise you've known what's been happening. This is a scenario I can work with. If I can get Milagroso on board, then this way no one can take him off if he's getting obvious. If I can't get Milagroso on board, we've got all week to come up with something else. Anyway, this is only half of what we have to do. How's Leo? Does he think he can fool Strabis?'

'He's shitting bricks.'

'I can't see why this frightens him any more than tricking cabinet ministers in Nzasa.'

'He's scared of fucking it up for me. Nicky will kill him.'

'Meeting her is never going to live up to the hype.'

'It's so close, Davey.'

And so, because nothing would be improved by putting it off, Dave hauled his bike out of the small tin shed he'd built inside his gate, tucked his trousers into his socks and assessed the lowering sky. He didn't need his lights, but he turned them on anyway and he pedalled out and up the hill alongside Queen's Park. He pulled up at a red signal, and the taxi driver to his left did a double take and wound down his window. Dave braced himself, but the driver said, 'Good luck, Mr Guinevere. Good luck Saturday. You deserve some good luck, mate.' Dave thanked him and rode off before the man realised how touched Dave was, and how near his last reserves.

It started to drizzle. Dave pedalled automatically through the traffic, the day dulling everything and the drizzle bringing a whirr of droplets up into the mudguard. It was horrible, but sometimes you couldn't wait half an hour for the rain to stop, even on days like today when the bright grey was already edging out the dark, because you'd already mapped out your path, and that was your path.

Milagroso refused even to speak to Dave, and Dave couldn't blame him. Later that evening, Dave cycled to Primrose Hill, entered by the secret gate, and climbed. He was deliberately early, because although he chose to live in a house without memories, that didn't mean he had no memory, or that he wasn't prepared to swim in it from time to time. It was fine so long as you didn't drown. The paths were almost dry now, and he loped softly to the brow of the hill looking at the sea of pricking lights, moving and still, yellow, white and red. The bench was twenty feet behind him, where he'd sat with Sally a million years ago, younger and stupider than he could properly comprehend, though even then he wasn't as young and stupid as Punty. He arched his back, breathing in, and looked at the sky. There were stars, but barely. He missed them since Africa. The city made up for it, was just as beautiful. Light was light, after all, or that's what he tried to tell himself.

Lower down the hill to Dave's right, Zondi and Mr Brown trundled into view. Mr Brown was off her lead, but the pair moved naturally at each other's pace. Dave looked forward to receiving his puppy. When he selected the skinny little runt, and before he could say he planned to call him Bingo, Zondi said happily that Dave had made the right choice, and his puppy's name was Jock. Jock was always the first off the teat when he heard a noise and the first to reach towards a new hand, even if his siblings were big enough to beat him away. Zondi walked with the small strides which had taken him through or over whatever had ever been in his path. Dave envied him this measured cadence, which was not indifference to the obstacles. Zondi was not derailed by the discovery of his great one love, or by its loss, or by this now with Adam, which was an equal love in many ways, but must be gentler, surely? Dave believed that Zondi had a talent for feeling and acknowledging love, but still he must ache sometimes.

'Hello,' said Zondi.

'Hello.' The three of them stood, looking south. A breeze picked up, and Dave looked down to see it tickle Mr Brown's ears, which it did, but the dog set herself like a statue, refusing to heed it. Zondi was not like a statue, he was just still. Dave smiled. Zondi could read your mind sometimes, it felt like. Zondi took off his gloves – it was too warm for gloves, really – and opened a bag of biltong. He offered it to Dave, who refused. Then he gave a stick to Mr Brown, who chewed methodically, savouring every swallow. Zondi agreed to talk to Milagroso.

At half-time in the game against Hearts, with forty-five minutes to endure until all this was over, Dave sat on an orange plastic chair, listening to Will through the door. It was the speech Dave would have given. Dave hunched forwards, bony elbows digging into the top of his thighs and hands cupping his face, fingers upwards. The tips of each third finger rested at the corner of his eyes, cold in the cleft of skin, hovering above the edge of his eyeballs. He was tired. He stood. Functionaries walked back and forth, and they looked at him. He shrugged his shoulders, embarrassed. How could he still be embarrassed by anything? The tunnel made him feel maudlin, mawkish even. It is too easy to say that some places have that effect, though it's partly true. He could walk through this tunnel many times and feel barely a thing, but tonight, when he was alone and stuck helpless on the knife-edge, or watershed, or whatever it was between the past and whichever of the futures it would be, he couldn't resist. How often had he stood here, on the best days and nights of his life? So recently, some of those days, but another world. How long ago did it seem for Tom and Torquil, Dirk and Carlo? He supposed it wouldn't seem that long to them, except maybe if they thought about how long it was since he'd been their teammate.

He pressed the soles of his feet into his shoes, rolling his weight on to the heels, and then the balls, and then the inner and outer edges, and then he rocked towards his toes. In these shoes, he couldn't even feel the rough granulation of the floor, but as he shifted, the memory of his weight bearing down on to the pressure points of studded boots flowed up from his feet and made him dizzy. The times he had stood here with Achilles and the others, ready to run into the brightness. The last time he stood here with Achilles, and Achilles came over to him, his gaze liquid with concern, put his hand on Dave's shoulder and said, simply, 'Good luck,' and Dave shook the hand from him, and Achilles said, 'Fuck you then, *querido*.' Zondi saw it all.

The door opened and Will emerged. He said to Dave, 'I've won again, mate. I'll always win. We both know it.'

Moments later, the players followed. Dave's certainty, which had held him steady throughout the year, had deserted him. He hadn't spoken to Milagroso at the outset because he'd been digging moats, and now, when Milagroso looked across, Dave averted his eyes. Let the Socialists go wherever they were going. Fuck you then, *querido*.

Milagroso was still there. He was looking past Dave to Zondi, quiet behind him in the shadows. Zondi said, 'Who do you trust?' Milagroso turned and ran out to the sun.

The Socialists drew. Volendam, Derkin, Blackie and Benjamin sat in the warm sun. The club would come back from this, but it wouldn't be their club any more. Their club died today. You can say they were being overwrought, and it's an easy accusation if you don't know what you're talking about, if you've never been there at the end of a team. It's a momentary thing, but in that moment, it's momentous. If you can't see that, then so little for your powers of empathy.

But let's not be simplistic. Not all the Socialists felt it so keenly; not one team was dying, but many teams, as many as there were players to imagine what was lost. Volendam, Derkin, Blackie and

Benjamin sat together, because Kilburn had been their only real team. They did not know what to do next, whether they should stay, or go, or if anyone would even want them now. Volendam was ashamed for the fans; Benjamin was ashamed that he didn't want to play in a lower division; Derkin was ashamed that he had ever sat with Vales and Drayly rather than these, the best friends he would ever have; and Blackie was still in his tracksuit and hadn't been able to do anything, but there was nowhere else he could be. They mourned for all of the teams that had made up their team, even if this last team was not the team they mourned. Ngwere and Simmonds mourned it because it was their first proper club, which gave them their chance, but they were at the start of their careers. Drayly, Cole, Vales and Vlocker would be happy to leave Kilburn, but they were embarrassed at what had happened, each in his measure. Vales, also in his tracksuit still, wondered where he might go next, afraid, secretly, that this had been his last real chance. Vlocker mourned because he had seen during the game that he was not as hungry as Ngwere, and he never would be again, which was not something he had ever thought about before. Nuñez was also a Socialist when he was young, and he was spinning and breathless at what he had done, mourning without knowing what to mourn. Rod Norman and a couple of others mourned because it was sad, but they also knew that some senior players would leave, and this could give them their chance in the first team. It would be exciting too to get Kilburn back up to the Premiership, which they would surely do, because the club was too big to stay down. Louie Cohen sat in the goal, his mourning subsumed in anger at Dave Guinevere, not trusting himself to move just yet. All his teams over the years, all his friends, betrayed by one man's vanity.

Dave Guinevere shook the hand of his opposing manager, and walked slowly on to the pitch. He patted his players on the back, for the cameras, and walked to the centre circle, where he stood, head back, staring at the sun. Then Aisling came, and then Strabis, and the others. Strabis signed his piece of paper, and handed it over.

'Jesus,' said Will Beauchamp as Aisling signed. 'This seems genuinely romantic, even though the Socialists are still fucked up the arse, and Ash can't use Rosslare money to help them escape unless she wants Strabis to get hold of the Group, and so this piece of paper doesn't really change anything. Or is it just me that's noticed?'

Strabis turned equably. 'That's not going to be a problem. I'm still a fan. Aisling knows she can depend on me. All she has to do is say one little word.'

'Don't you find this unbelievable?' said Dave.

'I'm the world's best actor,' said Strabis.

'Second best,' said Aisling.

...Things looked desperate for the relegated Socialists. With spiralling debts and a huge wage bill, it seemed as if an immediate investment was the only way to stave off disaster. Many observers expected Lady Rosslare to raise the necessary money by selling the legendary Rosslare Group, but she refused to do so and the Group found itself under enormous pressure from the predatory Strabis Kinsale. Under these circumstances, Lady Rosslare felt unable to weaken the Group by borrowing against its assets.

Kilburn sold off many high-profile stars, but the club's obvious desperation forced it to accept less than the market rate in many cases. KSC was left with significant debts and no way of paying its wages.

But then, in an astonishing development, fully in keeping with the club's legendary tradition and ethos, a number of the remaining players, including the veterans Benjamin, Derkin, Volendam, Blackie and Nuñez, alongside a talented crop of youngsters including the soon-to-be-legendary Jon Ngwere, announced that they would play on for peppercorn salaries until KSC righted itself financially.

Dave Guinevere married Lady Rosslare, and with the full backing of the club's remaining players, he took a more hands-on approach, and the club rediscovered its legendary *esprit de corps*. KSC became the first team from outside the top league to lift the FA Cup in more than a quarter of a century, which brought much-needed prize money and access to European football, and they won immediate promotion back to the Premiership.

KSC's legendary approach won worldwide acclaim. The club's usual critics claimed it was smug and elitist, but its success was achieved without the huge injections of money that sustained many of its rivals, and in particular Spencer, which was purchased by Strabis Kinsale and his wife, Esther, the sister of Lady Rosslare. The competition between Kilburn and Spencer was as bitter and intense as any in Premiership history, fuelled as it was by personal as well as sporting passions, and came to an end only when Mrs Kinsale sensationally murdered her husband after finding him in bed with the star of one of the most popular television soap operas of the day.

After a glittering decade under Guinevere and his successor, the legendary Spaniard Milagroso Nuñez, the Socialists declined into another period of mid-table obscurity before . . .

POSTCARD TO CALUM HORTON, DATED 5/8/06

Hi Calum,
It wasn't a tragedy or a comedy. Can you see what it was yet? We're having a great honeymoon.
Love and kisses,
Aisling and Dave

ACKNOWLEDGEMENTS

I do have a friend called Sally Stares. She says it's okay that I have used her name for a character much less cool than she is. The analysis of sports photography, which probably made you think I was both clever and wise, was lifted from David Winner's *Brilliant Orange*. Zahed Amanullah from altmuslim.com very kindly discussed current trends in Islam; his opinons are not shared by any character in the book. The 'great man' I mention in the World Cup chapter is J. B. Priestley, and he wrote about fans swapping judgements like lords of the earth in *The Good Companions*. Stephen Brown read an early version of the book's opening. What he said seemed helpful at the time.

Thank you to my agent, Louise Greenberg; to my editors, Dan Franklin and Alex Bowler; to the rest of the team at Jonathan Cape; to Spencer HC, Jesters CC and The Mighty Fin; to my friends, even those who don't live in Kilburn; and to my family, far and near. I wish my father could have read this.